Catherine Fox was educated at Durh
She is the author of five adult novels.
of Passion, *Love for the Lost, Acts and Omissions* and *Unseen Things Above*; a Young Adult fantasy novel, *Wolf Tide*; and a memoir, *Fight the Good Fight: From vicar's wife to killing machine*, which relates her quest to achieve a black belt in judo. She lives in Liverpool, where her husband is dean of the cathedral.

# LOVE *for the* LOST

## CATHERINE FOX

Marylebone House

First published in Great Britain in 2000
by Penguin Books

This edition published in 2015

Marylebone House
36 Causton Street
London SW1P 4ST
www.marylebonehousebooks.co.uk

Copyright © Catherine Fox 2000, 2015

All rights reserved. No part of this book may be reproduced or transmitted in
any form or by any means, electronic or mechanical, including photocopying,
recording, or by any information storage and retrieval system, without
permission in writing from the publisher.

Marylebone House does not necessarily endorse the individual views
contained in its publications.

Scripture quotations are from the Revised Standard Version of the Bible,
copyright © 1946, 1952 and 1971 by the Division of Christian Education
of the National Council of the Churches of Christ in the USA.
Used by permission. All rights reserved.

Extracts from *The Alternative Service Book 1980* are copyright © The
Archbishops' Council 1980 and are reproduced by permission.
Extracts from The Book of Common Prayer, the rights in which are vested
in the Crown, are reproduced by permission of the Crown's Patentee,
Cambridge University Press.

*British Library Cataloguing-in-Publication Data*
A catalogue record for this book is available from the British Library

ISBN 978–1–910674–03–1
eBook ISBN 978–1–910674–04–8

Typeset by Graphicraft Limited, Hong Kong
First printed in Great Britain by Ashford Colour Press
Subsequently digitally printed in Great Britain

eBook by Graphicraft Limited, Hong Kong

Produced on paper from sustainable forests

For Manda,
lost and found,
and in memory of Michael Vasey,
Michael Hough and Catherine Hooper.
*Fides nostra victoria.*

# CHAPTER 1

When she was ten years old Isobel Knox was put in charge of lost property. If she found some stray item lying about the classroom it was her job to find the owner. One day she came across a pencil-sharpener on the cloakroom floor.

'Mr Woodford, can I ask the class whose this is?'

The teacher eased himself back in his chair. 'Go on,' he invited her.

After a suspicious moment Isobel waved the sharpener and called out in her clear voice: 'Whose is this?'

'You mean,' interrupted the teacher, '"To whom does this belong?"'

Isobel turned and stared at him as though unable to believe she had heard correctly. He was waiting for her to repeat it, but she simply couldn't.

'I was never taught to say that.'

'Don't get uppity when I'm correcting you!' roared the teacher suddenly.

Isobel's mouth fell open. What? What had she done now? It was true! Her mother had been an English teacher. She would have *told* Isobel if you were meant to say 'To whom does this belong?'

But Mr Woodford was still bellowing, his big face getting redder and redder. 'You think you own this class! Queen Isobel! You have to be right all the time, don't you? Well, nobody's right all the time, madam! Not even Isobel Knox.'

'I know,' said Isobel. Some of the other children were sniggering.

'And you don't know everything!'

'I *know* I don't,' agreed Isobel in desperation. She was gripping the pencil-sharpener so tightly it was digging into her palm. Her own face was burning as hotly as the teacher's. But she could not bring herself to say those stupid words. 'To whom!'

'Does this pencil-sharpener belong to anyone here?' she tried.

On the way home from school she let herself cry at last. She sat on the stile in the middle of the barley fields and wept at the injustice of it all. Mr Woodford had not accepted her compromise phrasing. He had raged all the louder. She had given up trying to explain. Instead all her efforts went into not crying. If you lifted your chin and stared fiercely up at the ceiling the tears had to drain back into your tear ducts. It was a scientific fact. But he thought she was trying to be insolent and had moved her to a desk on her own away from Tatiana.

'Well done!' Tatiana had whispered, when hometime finally came and they were getting their anoraks. 'You were looking at him as if you really hated him.'

'I do.'

'Oh, he's just a great fat sack of wobblified jellified blubber.' She gave Isobel's arm a squeeze. 'Mr Fatty Jellybelly Blubberbum. I'm *glad* he couldn't make you cry.'

Tatiana was her only true friend. She was moving away at the end of term. Mr Woodford knew this. Isobel hated him.

'We won't let him spoil our last few weeks,' Tatiana had promised. 'We won't give him the satisfaction.' They'd cantered across the playground to a new version of the William Tell overture: Blubberbum, blubberbum, blubberbum-bum-bum!

But Tatiana would make lots of new friends in Yorkshire.

And it wasn't as if Isobel had done anything wrong, even!

One summer afternoon, twenty-three years after the pencil-sharpener incident, Isobel left her vestry and strode through the churchyard. It was too hot for striding, but she needed to get on. She passed the narrow space against the north wall of the church that the sun never reached, where Agnes the anchorite was enclosed in 1329. Isobel had researched thoroughly and discovered that at some point Agnes had left her cell and 'wandered again in the world, torn to pieces by the Tempter'. Happily, she had repented, and the Bishop, in his mercy, had commanded that she be thrust back into her enclosure and guarded there.

Charming view of God's grace, thought Isobel. She had no time for medieval piety with its visions of dripping blood and so forth.

Thank heaven women could play a full role in church life now-adays. They could take their place at the altar at last, and not be immured in the church wall in homage to some warped idea of femininity. She strode on, a tall, slim figure, slightly androgynous-looking in her mannish trousers and black clerical shirt.

The afternoon was heavy with the scent of lime blossom. The trees rose up in a green wall along the opposite side of the road, raining nectar on the streets and pavements all around. The air throbbed with myriad insect voices in busy rapture among the blossom. Now and then a bee staggered drunk up into the blue. Down below, Asleby-on-Tees lay strung out, long and narrow, between the railway and the meandering river. Beyond it were fields, factories in their fuggy haze, and, low and blue on the horizon, the Cleveland hills.

The anchorite's cell was an excellent symbol of the Church's attitude towards women, Isobel decided as she marched home. Brick them up where they can't get into mischief. But the walls were down now. Isobel was one of the first women who had passed unhindered through theological college into the ministry. She had not endured the heartache of waiting years and seeing wave after wave of her male colleagues enter the priesthood without her. She reminded herself how fortunate she was. Not many people were able to spend their time doing the thing they most enjoyed. Isobel was one of the lucky few. The ordained ministry provided her with everything she needed. There were those who looked at her and thought it a shame that such a good-looking girl should still be single, but she was reconciled. If she was honest, she had never been particularly interested in sex, although a great deal of her twenties had been devoted to the futile search for Mr Right. It was clear now that God had been calling her to celibacy all along.

Isobel raised her hand to lift the hair from the back of her neck. She stopped short and smiled. The heavy coils had gone, of course. Just before her priesting a week earlier she had had all her hair cut off. Thirty-three was a bit old for flowing blonde locks. Everyone had been horrified, as though it were a violation of nature, but she had found it a wonderfully liberating experience. In some curious way it was bound up in her priesting, which had been as momen-tous as a wedding for her. No bride walking down the aisle could have been filled with purer joy. Let them call it sublimation if they would. Sublime was the word for it – to be the right person in the right job at the right time.

She came to a stop outside her house and took out her car keys. Yes, she was fortunate. There were still plenty of things she must work at, however. The longer one went on in the Christian life the more aware one became of one's failings. Isobel knew she had an impatient, dismissive streak in her nature. Her daily life was full of sources of irritation. She saw herself as a vigilant gardener, rooting out any seedlings of annoyance the minute they sprouted. Some days she was on top of the job, but on others weeds ripped through the soil until she was a bristling thicket of giant hogweed. But, God willing, these intruders would be finally kept at bay by the hardy perennials of self-control and generosity.

Isobel looked at the gouge on the smart red paint of her car where she had scraped it on the garage door. A great deal of weeding in the spiritual garden had been needed here. So unfair! She was a good driver. On this occasion, however, she had not only misjudged the angle, but a voice in her head had said fatalistically, 'Oh, well, the damage is done now,' so instead of stopping and reversing she had continued and scratched the full length of the wing. I'll have to sort it out before it gets rusty, she reminded herself. The can of red paint accused her from the passenger's seat.

She got into the broiling car and set off for the supermarket. Shopping was a weekly irritation. Isobel was not a domestic creature, although her obsessive tidiness led everyone to assume she was. But one had to eat. Besides, a friend from theological college was stopping off on his way up to Scotland. Edward was the sort of man who grew restive if not fed and watered at frequent intervals.

Isobel took her usual short-cut along the deserted road, which crossed a patch of industrial wasteground. The landscape shimmered in the haze. Bindweed scrambled untidily over bushes and fences. The acres of dry grass were broken up by clumps of ragwort and rosebay willowherb. Their yellow and pink clashed, and Isobel wondered peevishly why God had ordained that they should grow next to one another. She wound down the window, only to let in hot gusts of Teesside air, thick with the sweet, sickly, chemical smell

4

that hung over the area. Doing goodness knew what damage to everyone's respiratory systems. She leant forward and unstuck her shirt from her back.

The car rounded a bend. There ahead of her was a source of irritation so large it bordered on outrage. Every time she passed it angered her. Some imbecile had sprayed a message on the disused railway bridge: STAMP OUT AIDS. KILL A PUFF TODAY.

Suddenly Isobel braked. The can of paint shot forward and landed on the floor. She retrieved it, got out of the car and climbed up the grassy bank. Rattle rattle rattle, went the bead angrily, as she shook the can. She pulled off the cap and, reaching up, sprayed a neat line through the word 'puff' and wrote 'poof' above it.

She experienced a moment of towering satisfaction. Then a police car drove past. It stopped. Reversed. Stopped again. A young officer got out. He was tall, red-haired, and there was a faint swagger in his walk. Isobel's face blazed. Instinct urged her to toss away the can or pull out her clerical collar, but it was too late. He stopped at the bottom of the bank and beckoned sternly. She was forced to slither down to where he was standing. He put out his hand, for all the world like a physics master confiscating a *Jackie* magazine. She surrendered the can. Criminal damage, she thought. Magistrates Court. Community Service. Sweat formed on her face. She felt it starting to trickle down her back and between her breasts.

He was waiting for her to meet his eye. Isobel was tall and seldom looked up to any man, but today she had no choice. She saw that he was not only taller but considerably younger than she was. Is something amusing you, Officer? She bit it back. He tilted the can gently backwards and forwards. She heard the bead sliding up and down. Now then, now then, it seemed to say. He looked up at the graffiti. 'Why did you not cross the whole thing out?' he asked at last.

'I – I –' stuttered Isobel, looking back at the wall aghast. Why hadn't she?

The policeman was turning and walking away, taking the can with him. She opened her mouth to call him back and justify herself, but he got into his car and drove off.

5

Isobel sat down abruptly on the scorched grass. She felt like a child again. All through her school career teachers had tried to take her down a peg or two and she'd never been able to work out why. Was this it? She was the sort of person who would correct the spelling on an offensive slogan without challenging the offence itself. People were dying of Aids. Homosexuals were being vilified and witch-hunted. What was a spelling error to this? She was guilty of straining out a gnat and swallowing a camel, as our Lord had said. She had ignored the weightier matters of justice and mercy. In short, she was a Pharisaical hypocrite. By crossing out the whole thing she would have been allying herself with the outcast as any minister of the Gospel should. Even that smirking policeman had seen that. No, she reproved herself. I mustn't take it out on him. I'm the one in the wrong here.

Isobel sat for a long time on the bank praying. The blond grass waved slightly in the breeze. The sky was rippling with larksong above the occasional clash and grind from the nearby iron foundry. In the end she sighed and got up, dusting off the seat of her smart black trousers. This wasn't getting the shopping done. She got back into the stifling car and drove to the supermarket.

He'd be here soon. She looked around her house and felt thwarted. It was clean and tidy, but it wasn't home exactly, and it was never going to be. There was so much about it one would never have chosen. The carpets, for instance, while serviceable, were patterned. And all those acres of woodchipped walls. Better than a frenzy of florals, she kept reminding herself. It was only for three years, in any case. Yet there were still times – now, for instance, when she was viewing the place afresh in anticipation of a visitor – when she was galled by the gulf between her vision of 'home' and the space she actually inhabited. Admittedly, Edward never noticed interiors unless something like a low door frame impinged directly on his consciousness.

In her mind's eye she lived in a calm environment of bleached wood, gleaming chrome and expensive neutral fabrics; but this house did not belong to her and it seemed pointless to waste too much money on improving things. It was worth hanging on till she was in a position to buy a little bolt-hole of her own. This wouldn't be for a few years, since she didn't know which part of the country she'd be in next. In the meantime she saved her money, doing without those little treats others indulged in routinely on the grounds that she would one day have the best treat of all: a nice house and money to spend on it. She had good taste, but fretted that someone looking round her dining room wouldn't discern this. The room contained one or two lovely pieces in a wasteland of busy brown lozenged Axminster.

She laid the table with her white bone-china dinner service. She'd never be able to afford such good quality now on a curate's stipend. Indeed, it had made quite a hole in her librarian's salary, but there was no point buying cheap rubbish. Provided one was careful it was an investment. She'd had it four years and there wasn't a single chip or crack anywhere.

'Isobel!' boomed Edward, getting out of his car. 'Your hair!'

'Edward!' responded Isobel. She kissed him crossly on the cheek. 'What's wrong with my hair?'

'Your crowning glory!' he mourned. 'What possessed you? It looks awful!'

'Honestly, Edward, you can be so rude.' She snatched the bunch of roses he was holding out. 'Come in.'

He followed her into her house. 'Gosh, sorry, Iz. It's just a shock.'

'A drink?' she asked threateningly.

'You could always say it was brain surgery, I suppose,' he said, as she poured him some wine.

'I like it.' She spaced the words out. 'Behave, or I won't feed you.'

'You're a hard woman, Isobel.'

They settled into their usual routine of mild bickering as she prepared some salad. He had that boisterous public-school masculinity that expanded to fill the space available. She felt crowded by his big voice and bellowing laugh, although she was fond of him in an exasperated way.

Over dinner he began lamenting the number of teenage girls who turned up at his house with spiritual dilemmas for him to resolve.

'I need a wife to protect me,' he said. 'I know, Iz – if we're both still single when we're forty, let's get married.'

'No. Let's not, Edward,' she replied firmly. 'More wine?'

'Better not. Shooting up to Bishopside for the night. Thought I'd better pat my godson on the head and all that.'

'Give Annie and Will my love,' said Isobel.

'Certainly shall,' agreed Edward heartily.

There was a silence. Perhaps they were both remembering how Annie had left theological college pregnant, unmarried, disgraced. When the small quiet ceremony belatedly took place and the happy couple were waved off into wedded bliss, Edward and Isobel had gone for a drink. He had blurted out something like, Well, what could one do, when the girls one fancied skedaddled with one's oldest friends? It had been a case of mutual chagrin, as it happened, for Isobel had been nursing quite a serious interest in Will. She hadn't mentioned this to Edward, of course. No point.

They turned to the subject of holidays. Isobel admitted that she had no plans; she had not been able to see beyond her priesting. Edward had been invited by friends to share a *gîte* in Normandy and wondered whether he might drag Isobel along too.

'Well,' began Isobel cautiously. She felt that this invitation followed a little too swiftly on the heels of a proposal of marriage, albeit a jesting one. If there were any hopes burgeoning in Edward's bosom they needed squashing.

'Oh, go on, Iz,' urged Edward, construing her uncharacteristic hesitation as a good sign. 'The Andersons are super people. Bound to be fun. Loads of cheap plonk, local cider. Masses of culture,' he added, veering in a new direction as her frown deepened. 'Norman architecture and whatnot. Come on. Give it a whirl.'

'Do they have any children?'

'Oh, a few,' he said. 'Three or four.'

'Four?'

'Or is it five, actually? But what's a couple of sprogs here or there? Not our problem.'

'Hmm,' said Isobel. 'I'm not going as an unpaid au pair, you know.'

'I'm sure they wouldn't dream! Cordelia's terribly competent.'

'Hmm.'

He continued to badger her and in the end she agreed to think it over.

'Well,' said Edward, some time later, 'better make tracks.'

She went with him to his car.

He ruffled her cropped hair. 'Actually, I think it's rather sexy in a dykey kind of way.'

'Well, I might be a dyke, for all you know, Edward,' she responded, in an effort to jolt him.

'Nonsense. You're a damned attractive woman, Isobel.'

Honestly! she thought, as he drove off. Edward was the kind of man who thought there was no such thing as a lesbian, just a woman who hadn't done one-to-one Bible study with him. She raised a hand and waved pointedly at the house across the street where she knew Kath Bollom, the cleanest housewife on Teesside, would be positioned behind her net curtain. Isobel had offended Kath in week one by dispensing with her services as cleaner. All her predecessors had employed her. But for goodness' sake! I'm quite capable of tidying up after myself. Privately she regarded paid help as a sign of feebleness, and had been glad to learn that the vicar did his own housework, too.

She went through to her kitchen and stood on the back step with a glass of wine, looking out at the summer night. It was the evening she usually phoned her parents, but she couldn't face it, for some reason. Why was she feeling so rattled? Was it Edward's company? That half-acknowledged tug of attraction, despite his utter unsuitability?

Bats were flickering and darting across the rooftops where the last swallows had been hunting an hour before. Isobel could hear the occasional cry of a peacock in the park. 'Peacocks!' visitors would cry. 'You're so lucky!' Huh. Sometimes in the mating season the wretched things came and roosted on her roof and spent the night honking and yowling and keeping her awake. She would see them the next morning, strutting up there against the sky, their gaudy tails trailing across the slates.

A spicy wave rose from the honeysuckle that grew along her fence. At some stage she was going to have to prune it back. Long tendrils swung and bowed across the narrow path beside the garage, and she had to swipe them aside every time she wanted to use the back gate. But gardening took time. The previous curate's wife had kept the garden immaculate, and the neighbours – Kath, in particular – were not backward in making comparisons between Jackie Davenport and Isobel. Just because I'm a woman I'm expected to keep everything perfect! snorted Isobel to herself. She was compared unfavourably with Andy Davenport as well – because she was a woman. But as Harry, the vicar, wisely pointed out, curates always come into favour retrospectively. Andy had been nowhere near as popular when he was actually in the parish.

Isobel smiled. Dear Harry. She was lucky to have a boss she could respect. Not all curates were so fortunate. He treated her as a colleague, not as a pretty woman. Plenty of male clergy were incapable of professional behaviour, felt obliged to compliment her on her appearance or, worse, pat and squeeze her. Harry was never guilty of such offences. He wasn't even bothered by the fact that she was a full inch taller than him.

Yes, her life was good. God was gracious. She was just beginning to feel content when she remembered the policeman. A sense of her own meanness swept over her again. She shut the door on the perfumed night and went up to bed.

# CHAPTER 2

*Isobel is helpful and has a keen sense of responsibility. She is always eager to advise other pupils and contribute to class discussion. She is diligent and her work is neat and of a high standard. Her sense of superiority is mellowing and I am sure she will continue to do well when she begins grammar school in September. Mrs J. M. Peck.*

Isobel's mother and father let her read this end-of-year report because that was the liberal *Guardian*-reading sort of parents they were. Isobel was pleased with it, although she was puzzled by the part about her mellowing sense of superiority.

The year had not been easy. She had missed Tatiana terribly. They wrote to each other every week, but that was small compensation. The other children had always tended to admire rather than like Isobel, and half the time they scarcely did that. She had joined, by default, the group of big, grown-up eleven-year-old girls. It was a sort of loose affiliation of early bra-wearers. They stopped playing elaborate imaginative games and took to loitering in the toilets in sullen groups with their arms folded, talking about boyfriends and pop music. Isobel hated them. She hated bras, she hated boys. She knew nothing about pop music because her family didn't have a telly. But what could she do? She was one of them. Her body had betrayed her. She had the biggest bust in the school. Her surname, which had been lying dormant all her life, burgeoned malevolently. Isobel Knockers. She shot up in height, but her bosoms gleefully kept pace. By the time she was fourteen she would be six feet tall with a bust out of a *Carry On* film. At eleven she was already five foot eight and bursting out of the broderie-anglaise teen bras her mother had bought her. The boys would chant at her from a safe distance:

> *Sunshine girl I'm looking down your bra,*
> *I see two mountains, I wonder what they are.*
> *If you'll invite me, I'll squeeze them tightly.*
> *Not bloody likely! my sunshine girl.*

It was not until she'd had corrective surgery at the age of twenty-two that Isobel knew what it was for a man to look her in the eye when he addressed her.

It was going to be another scorching day. Isobel woke intending to be in a better mood. Perhaps yesterday's irritation had had a simple physical cause – she had been too hot. Today she laid aside her black and put on some pale linen trousers and a light blue silk clerical shirt. She'd had it made specially, because she couldn't abide those ridiculous puffed-sleeved clerical blouses the outfitters deemed appropriate for women clergy. As though we were vicarettes, for heaven's sake! scoffed Isobel. Besides, the ready-made ones were all poly-cotton. It was worth paying a bit extra to get natural fibres. She went downstairs for a quick bite of breakfast, then took her little cafetière and a coffee cup through to her study for a time of private prayer and Bible study.

Before she began praying she couldn't resist looking once more at the white envelope that lay with her Bible and *Alternative Service Book*. 'Diocese of Durham,' said the black type. 'Letter of Orders. PRIEST. The Rev. I. M. KNOX, B.A.' Isobel pulled out a sheet of paper. 'Know all men by these presents . . .' began the Bishop, in Gothic script. She rubbed her thumb over the embossed seal. '. . . Did admit and ordain Our Beloved in Christ Isobel Mary Knox (of whose sufficient learning and godly conversation We were assured) into the Holy Order of Priest.' She folded it up and slid it back into the envelope, feeling a little too like a bride gloating over her marriage certificate.

But surely it was all right to rejoice? She thought back to the previous Sunday and her first celebration of communion. As an Evangelical one didn't make a song and dance about one's first mass, but the occasion had been special all the same. She had approached it with reverence and humility, deeply aware of the privilege of saying the words that Christ Himself had uttered on the night in which He was betrayed. The office of deacon was theoretically an important one, but the way things had developed historically it was difficult to view a deacon as anything but a priest manqué. Thank goodness women were no longer confined to such roles.

Some of the words of the ordination service came back to her: 'You are to search for his children in the wilderness of this world's temptations and to guide them through its confusions, so that they may be saved through Christ for ever.'

She prayed for grace to carry out this commission. 'To seek for Christ's sheep that are dispersed abroad', as the old Prayer Book put it. Like a loving shepherd. But then an unhappy thought sprang to mind – she was more of a sheepdog, snapping at the heels of the flock and steering it relentlessly into the fold. The sheep didn't really like her. She wasn't one of them. This is not a helpful analogy of ministry, she told herself firmly. She turned to a hymn for inspiration:

> Lord, speak to me, that I may speak
> In living echoes of thy tone;
> As thou hast sought, so let me seek
> Thy erring children lost and lone.

She was humming the tune when she emerged half an hour later. She paused in front of the hall mirror to slip in her clerical collar (Isobel would not have them called dog-collars), apply some of her discreet lipstick and set off to church for morning prayer.

A swift glance across the street reassured her that Kath Bollom was not poised to pounce. Isobel had learnt that it was quicker to take the back route than get caught up in the toils of one of Kath's monologues. The pavement was sticky with lime nectar. She passed the same people she usually did: Doris in her nylon overall and tabard coming back from her office cleaning job, the doctor's wife finishing her morning jog, and Stan out walking his Jack Russell. Stan gave her a raffish grin, which revealed his three remaining teeth, and cackled out some obscure sentence, to which Isobel gave a smile and vague assent. She never understood a word he was saying. At times she was haunted by the thought that he was playing a trick on her and spoke perfectly coherently to everyone else. The local accent seldom presented her with problems any more, apart from giving her the constant urge to correct its bad grammar. It was, roughly speaking, a cross between Yorkshire and Geordie, and she could follow all but the oldest and drunkest of her parishioners.

13

The church was dim and cool after the bright morning outside. The big door echoed as she shut it. She walked up the aisle and saw that Harry was already sitting in his stall in the chancel. He looked up and smiled as she sat in her own stall opposite him. He, too, was in summer clothes, and exuding his normal aura of faint helplessness. This was utterly misleading, but very useful in parish life. It ensured that the women were ready to do anything for him and the men saw him as no threat. He was in his early forties and single.

The church clock chimed eight. Harry waited another moment or two to see whether they would be joined by any parishioners. As usual, they were not. Isobel secretly preferred it this way. She found the psalm and Bible readings for that morning. Gladys Porter had been in already. Buckets of flowers were standing by the pulpit, lilies, carnations, freesias, ready for tomorrow's wedding. Their scent was already filling the chancel.

' "Blessed be the Lord, who day by day bears us as his burden," ' began Harry, picking a sentence from the psalm to start the service. ' "God is our salvation." ' He left a pause. Outside, the morning traffic into Stockton and Middlesbrough was building up. It sounded distant and muffled. Here in the church they might have been becalmed in eternity. ' "O Lord, open our lips." '

' "And our mouths shall proclaim your praise," ' responded Isobel.

That morning they used the Easter anthems. 'Christ our Passover has been sacrificed for us, so let us keep the feast.' Isobel was surprised by a sudden pang of feeling. Most of the time her faith was more a matter of intellectual assent than emotional response. Perhaps the familiar words, with their grand theme of salvation, had touched a chord in her soul.

After the service was over Harry allowed a few more moments of silence before crossing to Isobel.

'We seem to have had another break-in,' he murmured.

'Oh, no! Serious?'

'Not really.'

She followed him to the vestry. Books and papers were strewn across the floor as if a small, impatient tornado had flung them about. Harry and Isobel stood gazing at the chaos.

'This is the third time,' said Isobel at last. 'Have you called the police?'

'No.' Harry rumpled his dark hair absently. 'Is it worth it, do you think? There's no sign of forced entry this time, either. Half the parish has got a vestry key. The police must be getting sick of us.'

Isobel remembered the red-haired policeman. 'You're right,' she said. 'Has anything been taken?'

'Actually, I forgot to check.' Nothing had on the other occasions. Isobel opened and shut a few drawers. The communion wine and silverware were always locked in the safe. There wasn't much else worth stealing, apart from the photocopier, and that was still there.

'No!' exclaimed Harry in horror. Isobel whirled round. 'They've trashed the cupboard!'

'Don't be silly,' said Isobel. 'You know it's always like that.'

They both looked in at the shelves full of bursting carrier-bags and tubs of crayons. There were piles of crumbling *Hymns Ancient and Modern* dedicated to the memory of someone long forgotten, and a bunch of dusty teasels. One of the Magi from the crib set knelt in homage to a biscuit tin, waiting for his broken hand to be glued back on.

Harry sighed. 'I suppose it needs tidying out ...'

'I suppose it does,' agreed Isobel, immune by now to the helpless-Harry act.

They smiled at each other and something darted between them that might have been attraction, had Harry not been gay. Or, at any rate, one assumed he was, although nothing had been said and Isobel wouldn't dream of asking. One had no problems with homosexuality these days. Provided those concerned were celibate, of course. She was standing close enough to catch a whiff of his aftershave. Eventually she'd find the right moment to ask what it was called. It had always intrigued her, for she liked to think of herself as something of an amateur *nez*. A smell once learnt was never forgotten and she could identify a great many scents, to the amazement of their wearers.

She shut the cupboard doors on the mess and they began picking up the scattered papers. It was an order of service for the next Churches Together evening.

'Who do you think can be doing it?' she asked.

'Maybe it's Agnes.'

'No,' said Isobel, who considered herself an expert on the anchorite. 'Agnes is reputed to run wailing through the churchyard.'

'Well, I give up, then.' He shrugged and stacked the sheets together. 'Unless it's someone harbouring a grudge against ecumenical services,' he suggested. 'Me, for instance.'

'Oh, don't be silly.'

He turned away to hide a smile. She suspected he derived an obscure pleasure from provoking her to say this all the time. He was a man of serious principles held frivolously. She feared she might be the reverse and that he was prodding her gently to help her see this.

When the tidying was done they left the church and walked through the graveyard towards the main road. An expensive car pulled out of a driveway and glided away.

Harry watched it go balefully. 'That's *my* house!' he muttered.

'What are you on about?'

'I only joined the Church for the eight-bedroomed Georgian rectory,' he complained. 'And what do I get? Some ticky-tacky parsonage dwarfed by the shadow of the old vicarage! Look at it. They probably knocked down the outdoor privy to make room for it. Give me back my glebelands!' he shouted.

'It was only rectors who had glebelands, not vicars,' she corrected him. 'And, anyway, who wants to live in a draughty old ruin without the money to maintain it?'

'Me,' he replied simply.

There was no point arguing with him when he was in this kind of mood. They parted company. She couldn't resist calling after him, 'I think it's a very nice house!'

He caught the implied reproof and smote his breast, grinning, before disappearing into his drive.

It was true, the house was wonderful; but she had to admit this was only because Harry had a flair for interior design. Without his genius it would have remained little more than a box. He was rumoured to have a four-poster bed, but no parishioner had ever been upstairs in the vicarage. She could see why he hankered after

16

a house with more character, but having survived her teenage years in her parents' 'dream house', dubbed 'The Old Wrecktory' by her brothers, Isobel was grateful for her creature comforts.

She found herself thinking about Harry later in the morning as she went out visiting. Perhaps it was time she learnt to tease him back; but it was an art she'd never really mastered. She couldn't strike Harry's playful note and her jests sounded clodhopping in her ears. Her Youth Group complained that she'd had a sense-of-humour bypass. It wasn't that she didn't get jokes: she just didn't find them particularly funny. All too often she was the last to laugh and the first to stop; a little left out, a little on the edge of any group. She knew people found her standoffish and that her presence made everything twice as funny for everyone else. Fresh gales of laughter would burst out when she left a room, making her wonder if she hadn't got the joke after all. As a teenager she had found this desperately hurtful, but by now had made peace with herself. She was what she was. If people couldn't accept her, well, that was their problem.

And anyway, she thought as she turned down the lane that led to the Goodwills' farm, what was inherently amusing about breaking wind? Perhaps her two older brothers had wrung the last ounce of humour from the common fart when she was growing up. Deliberate farting was banned when the Youth Group met in her house on Sunday nights, which had precipitated the latest craze of burping and speaking simultaneously, the challenge being to say 'The Most Reverend and Right Honourable the Lord Archbishop of Canterbury' in a single protracted belch. Well, it had been mildly amusing the first hundred times, but Isobel had now banned this game as well. They weren't bad kids, really. They came from nice homes. The rough ones – except one wasn't supposed to say rough – came from the council estate on the outskirts of Asleby, and showed up at the open youth club not the Bible study. While not having the remotest insight into the mind of the modern teenager, she managed a reasonable rapport with both sets and knew how to roar like a sergeant major and exact instant obedience if that rapport broke down.

She opened the gate and entered the farmyard. The goose that acted as guard dog saw her, lowered its head and charged, hissing. Isobel continued walking calmly to the door. It was not her custom to be intimidated by anyone or thing. She thrust the bird aside with her foot and rang the doorbell. The goose, an equally determined creature, clamped itself to her trouser leg and clung there grimly until Walter Goodwill opened the door and beat it off.

'Well, you're here,' he observed, as though he had not himself summoned her. 'You'd better come in.'

She followed him into the best room. Old Walter was a wedge-driver, a species well known to the clergy. His only apparent religious concern was to sow seeds of strife between vicar and curate and divide the parish into warring factions. He had fallen out with Harry six years earlier. The issue had been a ludicrously large marble plaque commemorating his departed wife in language so florid it would have startled the poor woman. Harry had been unable – regrettably – to get a faculty to allow it to be erected in the church. 'The Archdeacon,' he had murmured, with a helpless gesture. 'Archdeacon be buggered,' old Walter had shouted. 'I know who's behind this, and I'll not come to that church again while you're vicar!' He'd been as good as his word. Harry told Isobel privately that he saw this as one of the triumphs of his ministry. 'If the Church is the body of Christ, then Walter Goodwill is the appendix,' he'd observed. 'No known function except to grumble and make life hell for the rest of us.'

The visit began with Walter's customary airing of old grievances, starting with Harry's iniquitous treatment of the Freemasons. Drummed them out of the congregation, he had. The church would never prosper now. Lost some of its best members. Isobel tried to let it wash over her, although it was a great trial to her to sit mute while Harry was slandered. She knew that he had touched on the matter only once in a sermon, which scarcely constituted a drumming out. And the church had prospered. It had doubled in size since then. However, she knew better than to attempt to reason. The grumble must run its course. Afterwards she would declare her loyalty to the vicar, as she always did, and Walter would say, Aye, aye, she was a good lass. He understood. She had to side with the vicar. When this exchange was out of the way he would give her a rundown on his health – he was a diabetic – and then they would get to the real business.

Today it turned out that his granddaughter wanted her bairn baptized in Asleby church.

'You're a great-grandfather! Congratulations.'

He grunted.

'However,' she continued, 'I'm afraid that as the family lives in Herefordshire, it won't be possible to have the ceremony here.'

'Eh? Why not? All the Goodwills are baptized in Asleby church,' countered Walter. 'Always have been.'

'Only if they live in the parish,' said Isobel firmly. 'That's the policy.'

This wasn't strictly true, but she wasn't going to waste casuistry on Walter. For a second she thought he was going to explode and bar her from his house along with the vicar, but then he seemed to reflect on her usefulness as a pawn.

'Well, I'll not ask whose idea *that* is. Parish policy? I'll give him parish policy!'

'I'm sorry,' said Isobel, 'but there it is.'

'Aye, well. I don't blame you, pet – Father.' He coughed, never quite certain of the right way to address her. 'You do your best. You do your best.' There was a ruminative pause. Foolishly Isobel didn't seize the moment and escape. 'He never could keep a curate, mind. They never stay. That first curate of his. Canny lad. Johnny, they called him. Should never have let him go.'

Walter maundered on in praise of her predecessors, affecting to believe that Harry had driven off curate after curate.

'You'll be next, mark my words,' he mourned.

'Well, that's life,' said Isobel brightly. 'Shall I say a prayer before I go?'

'Aye, aye. If you must,' he muttered.

He pressed a cold, heavy carrier-bag into her hands as she left. She crossed the yard, wrenched her trouser leg out of the goose's beak and shut the gate. The bag contained a joint of lamb. Walter believed that in being generous to her he was somehow slighting Harry. Isobel tutted. She was always being punished or rewarded

19

on the grounds of not being someone else. She hadn't been in the parish a month before learning she would always be a disappointment to everyone for not being Johnny Whitaker.

Hah! thought Isobel. She had met this paragon on a couple of occasions – the first had been when he took Annie and Will's wedding – and quite frankly couldn't see what all the fuss was about. It was as though the Rev. J. Whitaker was yet another joke she didn't find particularly funny. She had a basic mistrust of handsome men, and his type of dark, flashy good looks had never appealed to her anyway. Everyone raved about his preaching and pastoral work, but in her book he was a little too free in his manner for a clergyman. And chief among his crimes – yes, she knew it was petty of her – he had deliberately got her run out at a diocesan cricket match the previous summer. She could still see him fooling around at the crease, scarcely bothering to stub his fag out, either blocking or slogging the ball to boundary, too lazy to snatch those easy singles – the game was slipping away! And when she'd raised the matter with him he'd run her out and Durham had lost by three wickets!

'Psst, Isobel,' Harry's voice whispered. 'It's only a game.' She flushed at the memory.

Yes. All right. She slowed her furious striding. Johnny Whitaker was no concern of hers. He worked at the opposite end of the diocese and their paths seldom crossed. She'd been far too busy this summer for cricket. She was not going to let the inappropriately named Walter Goodwill ruin her morning. After murmuring a quick prayer for both men – always a good way of channelling her irritation – she continued home at a calmer pace.

She got back in and was about to check the answerphone for messages when the doorbell rang. It was a down-and-out, one of her regular callers. He no longer bothered to spin her a tale about lost Giros and train fares to visit grannies dying in Scotland, just asked for sandwiches. She closed the door and left him on the step while she made him some. He was luckier than usual today, for her fridge was still well stocked after Edward's visit. She handed over the carrier-bag and went back to her answerphone.

The first message was from Natalie, the churchwarden's wife, calling from work to invite Isobel for lunch on Sunday. There was another from the Co-op funeral service and one from a curate in Hartlepool, wondering if her Youth Group would be up for a five-a-side football tournament against his. Finally there was a brief message from her mother saying sorry she'd been out last night – if Isobel had called, that was – she'd be at the local history society tonight, but would ring tomorrow. It was all in the interests of scrupulous fairness. Mrs Knox rang her sons each week so that she could chat to her beloved grandchildren, and she was keen that Isobel should in no way feel overlooked in the family, just because she was single and childless. This was never articulated, but Isobel knew all the same.

After she'd dealt with the calls she sat at her desk to compose her thoughts and look in her diary to see how the rest of the day was shaping up. PCC standing committee tonight at the vicarage. She plucked the agenda from its place in her in-tray and glanced through it. Her eye immediately singled out the item that would take up the most time: the proposal to buy new hymn books. There was a lot of other business to get through as well, but at least this meant that the PCC meeting the following week wouldn't be as tortuous. Personally, if she were Harry, she'd chair these a little more tightly, but he believed that letting everyone have their say saved time and tempers in the long run. Perhaps he was right. She hoped that when she was a vicar she'd be as able to steer a fractious group of people through contentious decisions smoothly.

Today was the Ministers Fraternal lunch. Isobel didn't believe in skipping these interdenominational commitments, tempting though it sometimes was. She'd have the chance to chat to Jenny, the Methodist minister, who was about her age and something of an ally. If they were both less busy their relationship would probably blossom into friendship. As it was, they were forever calling to one another in passing that they must get together some time. Father McGee would be there as well. Isobel had a soft spot for him. He was an old rogue and would doubtless continue to pull her leg about her stealing impressionable Catholic boys away from the true faith. From anyone else this banter would have been offensive, but she was helpless in the face of his outrageous blarney.

'Will you just look at her?' he lamented. 'What am I supposed to do? Buy a blond wig and hear confession in a miniskirt?'

And Harry, listening in, said, 'Gerry, are you flirting with my curate again?'

'He's fierce! He's threatened to break all my fingers if I so much as look at you. Mother of God, see what ecumenism has come to now we have women priests!'

Isobel caught herself smiling at the memory. The afternoon would be taken up with a funeral. Asleby was a small parish and they were not inundated with occasional offices. When funerals came along, Harry shunted them in her direction as she needed the practice. On this occasion it would be straightforward: an elderly woman who had died peacefully in her bed after a long, full life. Her family had come up with some nice anecdotes, which was always helpful. There wasn't much any minister could do with 'He was a miserable old sod and I'm glad he's gone.' Harry kept a list of useful euphemisms pinned up on his noticeboard. 'Not all his relationships were easy ones'; 'She was a woman of strong opinions.'

Isobel opened her prayer book to remind herself of the old form of service, which the family had requested. It wouldn't do to stumble over the words. 'I am the resurrection and the life, saith the Lord: he that believeth in me, though he were dead, yet shall he live.' Isobel felt again that strange pang she had experienced in church at morning prayer. A hunger, almost; or an empty space. Something she had lost but couldn't put a name to.

The feeling slipped away again and with a shake of her head she continued her preparation.

It was early evening. Isobel had just given a pint of her A-positive blood and was lying on a camp bed in the village hall chafing because she wanted to get on with things. For clergy as busy as Isobel, no fragment of time was too small to use profitably. She could have squeezed in one more visit, or at least made a couple of phone calls in the time wasted on recovery. If only she'd thought to bring along a Bible commentary, she could have got cracking on next Sunday's sermon.

The beds were in a row, feet pointing towards the stage where, once a year, execrable performances were put on by the amateur dramatic society. She gazed up at the rafters. From the ceiling were hanging long electric heaters of the kind only ever seen in church and village halls. They had had them in the Wesleyan chapel schoolroom where Isobel had attended Girls' Brigade as a child. Mr and Mrs Knox thought the organization silly, but put up no real opposition as they believed in letting children make up their own minds about religion. They had stuck to this principle even when Isobel had announced at the age of twenty-three that she was hoping to go into the Church. 'Well, if that's what you really want, then we're very happy for you, dear,' they had said, now it had become clear that this was not, after all, a phase that would pass if they sensibly kept quiet. Isobel stared at the heaters. Tatiana and I used to throw beanbags up and try to get them to land on the top, she remembered suddenly.

Isobel seldom thought about the past. She viewed nostalgia as a mild form of dabbling in the occult – you never knew what you might unleash. But for once she made no effort to check the memories as they bubbled up. Their intensity astonished her. She could hear the screeching of little girls during team games, feel the weight of the beanbag in her palm and the grainy crumbling surface of the rubber quoits. She even saw the stage, the table covered in a bobble-edged chenille cloth, dark red, the colour of sumach flowers. There were the table trestles which they used to sit astride and ride like imaginary ponies. She heard the sound of Captain's whistle. 'Marker, fall *in*! Tallest on the right, shortest on the left, in single ranks *size*!' Isobel loved the drill, the discipline, the marching and flags. Girls' Brigaders were smart, not like the Guides and Brownies with their shambolic efforts at church parade. 'Seek, serve and follow Christ!' That was the GB motto. But what was that smell? Scorched beanbag from the overhead heaters. Isobel grinned. Perhaps we weren't such paragons. What had happened to Tatiana? They had lost touch twenty years ago.

She looked at her watch. Another couple of minutes. It was so silly. Isobel never fainted. But it was as well to abide by the rules. She glanced to her left and saw a man's head a yard away on the neighbouring pillow. She looked back at the ceiling at once, disconcerted by an intimate sight in a public setting. But then she felt impelled to check the other side, too. Without turning she could tell that the bed was occupied by a young lad. He must be tall, for his feet hung off the end. His trainers were jiggling in time to his Walkman. She heard the tssh tssh tssh of the music. It was probably someone she knew from the youth club. She looked. Their eyes met. The stranger winked. Isobel gave him a quelling stare and resumed her study of the overhead heaters. The impudent –

Oh, no! It was that policeman. Her cheeks burned. She got up and left the hall without the regulation cup of tea. Was he following? Her pulse was cantering, but there were no footsteps behind her. Idiot, she told herself, as she walked to her car. She'd have to collar him and have the whole thing out. Thank him for not arresting her. If she didn't take a firm stand he was clearly going to get cheeky. She started the engine and reversed with her customary assertiveness straight into a concrete post.

The noise was immense. Isobel leant back and shut her eyes, unable to believe what she had just done. After a moment she made herself get out and inspect the damage. Well, it could have been worse. She glanced round. Nobody had seen. She got back in and drove off.

As she turned on to the main road, she caught a glimpse of the policeman in her rear-view mirror. He seemed to be laughing.

## CHAPTER 3

It was pretty clear to Isobel that boys had a nicer life. She only had to look at her brothers. They could wear trousers the whole time. Nobody told *them* off if they played out in their plimsolls when you were only allowed to wear them for PE because otherwise they wore out and they were expensive, you know. They just said they were playing football, so they were let off. Boys were allowed out on their own, but girls always had to say where they were going, and who with, and when they'd be back.

Isobel would have laughed if she'd heard about Freud and penis envy. Laughed. She despised willies. At school the boys had urinals in a wooden shack. The girls used to squint through the gaps in the planks and giggle.

> *My friend Billy had a ten-foot willy.*
> *He showed it to the girl next door.*
> *She thought it was a snake, so she hit it with a rake,*
> *And now it's only six foot four.*

Isobel and Tatiana developed a method of weeing undetected on the school field. It was risky and had to be referred to in code at all times: 'Picking celandines'. What you had to do was kneel down, arrange your skirt round you, slide a hand under your bum, tug your knicker-crotch to one side and wee with a distant expression on your face. Boys couldn't do this. They were pathetic.

Even when she was grown up Isobel secretly maintained her low opinion of male genitalia. Penis envy? She'd never wanted one. Unless, perhaps, it were handed her on a plate and she got to choose the donor. After an hour with her colleagues at a Deanery Chapter meeting she could usually come up with a few candidates.

*

After the Sunday-morning service Isobel went to the Tylers' for lunch. They were a generous young couple and she was glad that she'd been invited on her own and not with any of the half-dozen other young single women in the congregation. Isobel knew it was reprehensible of her, but she did hate being lumped together with the spinsters. They were what Edward referred to as 'dear sisters' – worthy but dull. She liked to think that the Tylers regarded her as a friend, rather than a Christian duty.

She and Harry were fortunate in their churchwardens. Drew Tyler was cheery, hardworking and competent, and his legal expertise had proved invaluable on more than one occasion. 'And it's nice to have someone who can help shift the font without falling and breaking a hip,' Harry had remarked. His previous church had been full of old ladies.

Isobel beat away the tasselled cushions and bolsters and sank into the sofa with a post-sermon sigh. Her hosts were both in the kitchen. The smell of ham cooked with cloves had greeted them when they had entered the house. If Isobel had been at home she'd have been finishing off the odds and ends left over from entertaining Edward. She couldn't abide waste and never started a new loaf before the old one was finished. This meant she seldom ate fresh bread, which was a pity when she stopped to think about it because there was nothing quite like bread still warm from the bakery, but that was all part of being grown-up, she supposed.

The Tylers' house was a shrine to high Victoriana. Their devotion to it reminded Isobel of her parents and the Wrecktory. Natalie (Isobel still couldn't bring herself to say Nat, as she'd been invited to) and Drew were both solicitors so had money to lavish on their projects. They spent all their free time skip-diving or haunting auction rooms and reclamation yards to track down authentic radiators, then lovingly restore and install them. Occasionally Isobel went with them and yearned for the day when she had her bolt-hole. The Tylers were also unable to resist any car-boot sale in a fifty-mile radius of Asleby, which caused Isobel a certain dilemma. She'd been a keen supporter of the 'Keep Sunday Special' campaign, and couldn't help but disapprove of her friends' Sabbath-breaking hobby. But at least they got a move on with their home improvements. Her parents had been content to live for years without plaster on the walls.

'Here you are,' said Drew, coming in and handing Isobel a glass. 'One very small dry sherry. Nat's just doing the carrots. Can we talk shop for a minute?'

They discussed the battle over pews, which had been rumbling since Christmas. All that was proposed was the removal of the two back rows, for goodness' sake. Isobel had no patience with the objectors. Didn't they realise that, given the age of the building, pews were a relative innovation? The way some of them went on – people on the electoral roll who seldom came to church, she'd noticed – you'd think the things had been there since St Columba sailed the ocean blue. And now someone had got up a Save Our Pews petition. Walter Goodwill's work, no doubt.

'Well, the decision's all gone through the proper channels,' said Drew. 'Once we've got the faculty they can't stop us.'

'Nobody told us about faculties at theological college,' complained Isobel.

Drew laughed. 'Well, don't go making any changes before you get one. Although we do all the time for small things. You can seek retrospective permission. You just have to hope the Archdeacon doesn't notice the tell-tale smell of fresh paint when he comes round for the quinquennial inspection. "What d'you mean, Archdeacon? That kitchen's always been there!"'

'Nobody mentioned quinquennials, either,' said Isobel.

At this point Natalie called them for lunch.

'Promise you won't let Harry sell the pews without telling us,' she begged, after Isobel had said grace. 'We want a couple for the breakfast room. Pitch pine always strips nicely. We'd have to get them cut down, of course.'

Isobel didn't point out that this was hardly authentic Victorian. She liked Nat and Drew even when they called her Iz. As she glanced round the room and noticed a beautiful spindle-backed Victorian high-chair standing in the corner, she wondered. Of course, Isobel would be delighted for them, but she knew from experience that parenthood was a greater divide than marriage, even.

*

Harry and Isobel stood shaking hands with people at the back of church after evensong.

27

'What's all this I hear about a leg of lamb?' asked Harry, as the flow of parishioners dwindled.

'What's all this I hear about a bottle of champagne?' retorted Isobel. Harry had been given it the previous day after the wedding reception. Isobel had pointedly not been invited. The Westcott family had recently left the church over women's ordination and now attended the spiky high St Mark's in the neighbouring parish. Not that this had prevented them wanting Asleby church with its charming lych-gate for the wedding photos, though.

Harry grinned. 'Why don't we get together for dinner and drink a toast to the wedge-drivers?'

They tried to find a free evening, and in the end settled on Thursday.

'But that's your day off,' Isobel pointed out.

'Isobel!' protested Harry. 'I don't count you as work.' There it was again, that flash of something that might have been attraction. It was disrupted by the appearance of Joan, bearing down on them in a cloud of Rive Gauche and Harvey's Bristol Cream. She was a widow in her fifties, who was not an alcoholic. As she frequently explained, she was simply unfortunate in suffering from an acute allergy to alcohol, and it was this that slurred her speech, caused her to stumble in the street, and to persecute Harry with long rambling phone calls she later denied having made.

'Oh, Vicar! Whatever must you think?' Joan clutched Harry's arm and her watery eyes bulged earnestly. A peppermint clattered against her teeth. 'When you saw me coming out of Oddbins the other day, I had *not* just been buying two bottles of sherry.'

Isobel abandoned him. 'What else hadn't you been buying?' she heard him inquire, as she made her way to the vestry to disrobe.

When she got back to her house the Youth Group was already crowded in her porch smoking and cackling. She'd learnt not to hand over her keys after the service so that they could let themselves in before she got back. Although, to be fair, she couldn't prove that they were responsible for that missing bottle of communion wine. She unlocked the door and they bundled into her study.

'Fitz and Welshy, get off your backsides and go and make the tea and coffee,' said Isobel. 'The girls do it every week.'

'But the girls are so good at it!' protested Fitz. She glimpsed a cunning eye peeping through his fringe. He was a doctor's son and knew exactly how to wind her up.

'Just do it.'

'*Jawohl, mein Kommandant!*' They goose-stepped out to the kitchen.

Isobel had to stand over them for fifteen minutes to ensure they didn't just fool about with the teabags. Was it worth it? she wondered. The girls could be counted on to do the job properly, but there was a principle at stake here. To be honest, she found adolescent boys mildly repellent, with their bum-fluff and pimples, their noxious smells and grating voices that still leapt up an octave every so often like badly played saxophones. She marshalled them back through with the mugs.

'Where are the biscuits?' demanded someone.

'I forgot to buy any,' said Isobel. A chorus of moans went up. 'Tough, I'm afraid.'

'Oh, Go-od, Craig, you're disgusting, man,' said Gemma, fanning the air. 'Can we open the window, Isobel? Craig's farted.'

'I never!'

Eventually, with the window open, and the group approximately silent, Isobel began. 'Tonight we're thinking about forgiveness.' She asked them to look up several relevant Bible passages. 'When God forgives us, He forgets our sins,' explained Isobel, with a preacherly gesture.

'Isobel, can I ask you a question?' broke in Fitz. 'If we cut your hands off, would you still be able to speak?'

'Thank you, Fitz. It's as if God takes our sins and drops them into the deepest sea,' Isobel persisted. 'And then He puts up a sign, which says –'

' "No fishing",' they all droned.

Hmm. I must have used that illustration before, thought Isobel. 'Exactly. "No fishing". God doesn't want us to be weighed down by past sins that He's already dealt with. As the Bible says, "If the Son shall set you free, you shall be free indeed." '

She gave them an exercise. They each had to think of the worst thing they had ever done, the sin of which they were the most ashamed, then write it down.

'I know what Welshy's is,' remarked Gemma.

'Simmer down! Simmer down!' called Fitz, in a warbling falsetto to pre-empt Isobel.

She handed round slips of paper and the felt-pen tin. 'And no looking at what other people are writing.'

After some initial snorting and nudging they settled down. Isobel joined in the exercise before Fitz could make an issue of it. She scribbled a brief sentence about the spray-paint incident. There were worse things in her past, but she wasn't in the business of dredging them up – this, surely, was the whole point of the exercise they were engaged in.

A train rumbled past at the end of the allotments. In the silence that followed Isobel heard a wood-pigeon call and the peacocks miaow in the park. She looked round the group at the bowed heads and wondered what unconfessed guilt tormented these young people. She longed to reach out and assure them of God's acceptance, to set them free as she had been set free. But as she was thinking this a memory rose unbidden from the depths and broke surface. It bobbed there, repellent in her mind's eye as a bloated corpse. Her face went hot. I'm forgiven, she reminded herself. That's all dealt with. The memory slid back under the surface. Isobel smoothed her hair. The wood-pigeon called again.

'Finished, everyone?' she asked brightly. 'Right. Fold up your paper and put it in the grate.' They obeyed. Isobel struck a match and they all watched as their sins went up in flames.

' "If we confess our sins," ' read Isobel into the silence, ' "He is faithful and just and will forgive our sins and cleanse us from all unrighteousness." '

After they had all gone Isobel made herself some proper coffee, not the cheap instant she kept for parishioners. She sat down with a long groan. It was over for another week. One day she'd have a curate of her own, if she was lucky, and he or she could do the wretched youth work. It was all good practice, of course. She hoped tonight's session had gone well.

As she began to relax her mind crowded with things she must do. Most of them were easily deferred to the following day or week, but then their place was taken by more intractable problems. The setting up of an Inquirers' Group was one of her cherished schemes. She'd led them with some success as a theological-college student and was keen to repeat the exercise in Asleby. All she needed was some Inquirers. A year had gone past without her really acquiring any. Harry seemed to generate them all the time. What was his secret? she wondered. She'd quizzed him about his strategy for evangelism when she'd come on interview, and he'd confessed he didn't really have one. 'If you preach the Gospel and love the people,' he'd said vaguely, 'then the church will generally grow.' At the time she'd been unimpressed. The thought humbled her now.

And then there was the unresolved tension with her older brother, Alistair. They had fallen out in the New Year. Perhaps, as a Christian minister, she ought to make the first move. Outrage bubbled up. Why had he expected *her* to drop everything and race down to look after his children while his wife was in hospital? Why couldn't *he* take time off work? Why couldn't he *pay* some-one to nanny them? Didn't her work count as work, or something? And to have him fling her profession in her face like that! 'Well, if *that's* your Christian compassion, you can stuff it, Isobel!' He'd slammed the receiver down and they hadn't spoken since. Goodness only knows what he'd said to their parents. Mr and Mrs Knox were keeping well out of it. Mr Knox probably took Alistair's part. He had no very high opinion of faith unbacked by works. Mrs Knox, on the other hand, got cross at the idea of women being exploited simply because they were women. She'd have swooped to granny the children, of course, but she'd been in New Zealand when the crisis struck.

Isobel's conscience taunted her in Alistair's words. She couldn't understand why she hadn't simply said, in *Christian compassion*, 'I'm really sorry, but I simply can't come. I've got three funerals next week and the vicar's on holiday.' Which would have been the truth. Even Alistair would have understood that. Instead she'd gone off at the deep end about him assuming she was endlessly available ... The incident had obviously hit a raw nerve. Memories, probably.

Memories. Yes. She had a sudden flashback to her eleven-year-old self, coming back from school to a dark, cold house. Dad away working in Saudi Arabia for a year. Mum in bed with a headache. In bed all day. Ice on the insides of the windows. 'Darling, can you bear to get the dinner? I've got this rotten headache ...' Opening the cans of beans. Boiling potatoes on the cranky old electric oven in the gutted kitchen. Later they'd have an Aga. Old pine dressers. Butcher's blocks. You name it. When Dad got back. Isobel huddled against the cooker in her school coat.

'Not beans again,' her brothers would groan.

'Get it yourself, then!' she'd scream at them, as they stuffed their fat faces.

'I'm not bloody well doing the cooking,' they replied.

When she complained to Mum, Mum only said, 'Darling, could you bear to? I know they're useless. It's only for a bit.'

Mum would make it up to her. Treats, outings, just Mum and Isobel. She promised. If only Isobel could bear it. Please? I don't know how I'd cope without you, darling.

Till Dad gets home. We'll just have to bear it till Dad gets home.

When Dad got home the treats were somehow forgotten. Mrs Knox was too busy stripping the woodwork and discovering hidden fireplaces.

Isobel shook herself, picked up the phone and rang her brother.

The following morning her study still reeked faintly of teenagers. At least she'd made contact with Alistair. He'd accepted her apology with good grace, but complacently, as his due. He took her point about the year in the Old Wrecktory when Dad had been away. He supposed neither he nor Chris had pulled their weight, now he cast his mind back. 'For Christ's sake – sorry – but, honestly, it was all so long ago. Stop brooding, Iz. You sound like Mum.' This was the best weapon in her brothers' arsenal, and they both used it shamelessly.

Isobel tried to remember a single occasion when Alistair had been in the wrong. He was like their father. He might say, 'OK, I take your point,' but there was never any *mea culpa* about it. A thing was either true, untrue or one reserved judgement about it until further evidence came to light. Emotions didn't really enter into it. Of course, they were *there,* but after noting one's feelings, there was no need to be governed by them. Being scared was never a good reason for not doing something. No point feeling guilty over something you could do nothing about. If you ate less and exercised more you'd lose weight. This was the kind of maxim that had shaped their childhood. Bursting into tears and being feeble might be understandable, but in the end it got you nowhere. That's what Mum was like. She swept out the grate. The ashes of cancelled sin crumbled to nothing under her brush.

On the morning of her day off Isobel woke with a heavy heart. If she didn't organize something in advance then she ended up mooching about the house, trying to resist the temptation to do a spot of work. Harry's policy was to get right out of the parish, which was all very well if one had friends nearby who were not at work. She occasionally had lunch in Middlesbrough with Natalie, but there wasn't really anyone she could spend the whole day with. Sometimes she popped in on an old theological-college friend who lived on Tyneside, but she hesitated to invite herself round yet again. Annie always seemed genuinely pleased of company – perhaps all young mothers were? – but Isobel was never able to shake off an irrational suspicion that Annie didn't really like her. Then there was the added complication of her husband Will. Naturally, she no longer entertained any sense of being attracted to him, but his presence disconcerted her. He was such a strange mixture. Caustic, yet unpredictably compassionate. He had risked his life rescuing two children from a burning building two years earlier, but would never talk about it. She knew from Annie that he still suffered chronic back pain from the injury he'd sustained in the process. No wonder the man was irascible. One understood that, but Isobel tried to time her visits for when he'd be out at work. She was also hampered by the knowledge that his younger

33

brother was Sebastian Penn, the film star. There was always an outside chance of running into him, and Isobel cringed at the thought of appearing to be a groupie, much though one admired his talent.

She got up and, over breakfast, leafed through her collection of pamphlets and brochures to find some worthwhile way of filling the day. If all else failed, she could get out on to the moors with her binoculars and do a spot of bird-watching. There was always a chance of seeing something unusual and phoning her father to tell him about it. She was the only one of his offspring who remotely shared his obsession. But she didn't really fancy a day by herself. Companionship was one of those luxuries that married couples took for granted. It would be nice if Annie occasionally *invited* Isobel. But she was probably too tied up with looking after Teddy – a delightful but somewhat demanding child.

Then there was Thelma. She'd been Isobel's friend at library college and now worked in Ripon. Isobel knew Thelma wouldn't be working this afternoon and might like to spend a couple of hours at the Bowes museum or something. She braced herself and rang.

In the car Isobel listened to a tape from a sermon series. It was thought-provoking stuff, but didn't quite banish her residual irritation with her friend, who had agreed to meet up with the air of one grudgingly granting a favour: 'It's really rather short notice, Isobel.'

'Push off, then, you old trout,' muttered Isobel retrospectively. Still, one couldn't just dump old friends.

It wasn't till she was on the way home after a less than relaxing afternoon that it occurred to Isobel that she could have spent the day more profitably getting the back of the car sorted out.

It was Thursday evening. Isobel wondered whether she ought to dress for dinner with Harry. Given that he had assured her that it was his day off and she was not 'work', would her appearance on his doorstep in a clerical shirt be a failure to return the compliment? It was not her day off, though, and she doubted she'd have a moment to pop home and change after the visits she still had to do. She called in on Doug, the treasurer, to give him her expenses for the last month. He always wrote her a cheque there and then without querying the amount. She suspected that she claimed rather less than her predecessor, although Doug never said so.

After this she popped in to see Sue from the music group, who had just had her first baby, a much longed-for child who had been conceived after bouts of grim medical intervention that Isobel had helped her endure. She'd gone with her to various clinics when Mike was unable to take time off work and had prayed for her and supported her through it all. The baby was called Hannah Isobel, and Isobel looked forward to the pleasure of baptizing her in a few months' time. She made no secret of the fact that she adored babies. However, it was nice to have the chance to coo without hordes of cheeky parishioners saying, 'It suits you!' The visit was well timed. The baby wouldn't settle and Sue was at her wits' end. Isobel scooped up little Hannah and took her to the kitchen while she made Sue a cup of tea one-handed. Madam screamed throughout the whole procedure, but Isobel had been an auntie for many years and was not fazed.

'I'm sorry,' wept Sue. 'I've changed her, I've fed her ...'

'Don't worry,' replied Isobel, jiggling the small bundle proficiently. 'You drink that while we take a turn in the garden.'

The fresh air or the sunshine seemed to calm the child, and in a couple of minutes she fell asleep, exhausted, in Isobel's arms.

'She was just tired, that's all,' pronounced Isobel, tactfully concealing her sense of triumph. 'Shall I pop her in her cradle?'

'Please. I don't know how you did it.'

'Why don't you get some sleep, too?'

'Perhaps I'd better. Mum's coming up tomorrow to help out.'

Isobel let herself out quietly. She'd call in again in a day or two.

She got back in her car and drove to Jan's. Jan was the other churchwarden and would be able to countersign Isobel's expenses cheque. When she had first arrived in the parish, people had warned her that Jan was something of a dragon. Isobel's response to dragons was to confront them fearlessly and without delay. Her strategy had been rewarded. Here, apparently, was a dragon with no taste for insipid damsels. She liked 'em feisty. Still, there was always a momentary bracing of oneself before ringing Jan's doorbell. Today there was no answer, so Isobel went round the back where she found Jan wielding some weedkiller.

'I thought you were organic,' said Isobel.

'Hah! No one's organic when it comes to ground elder.' Jan was stalking about like Clint Eastwood, blowing the weeds away one by one. 'Do you feel lucky, punk? Go ahead. Make my day.'

'I don't know why you watch that violent rubbish,' said Isobel.

'Because I'm in my dotage. I've renounced any pretensions to refinement.'

Isobel doubted Jan had ever had any. She was a JP, a former headteacher who had taken early retirement from a tough comprehensive. In a funny way she was the best friend Isobel had in the parish. Certainly hers was the only house where Isobel called without a pastoral pretext. A lot of people assumed, in their tiresome, clichéd way, that a retired headmistress living alone must be a lesbian. No doubt this gave rise to speculation about her relationship with the curate. It was all idle gossip. Isobel happened to know that Jan had been married and that her only son had been killed in a car crash at the age of seventeen. The marriage had not survived this tragedy.

'I need your signature on a cheque,' said Isobel.

'All in good time.' Jan waved her away. 'I hear you backed into a bollard. Are you in love?'

'Don't be ridiculous. A lapse of concentration. I'd been giving blood.'

'And you're having dinner *à deux* with Harry tonight.' Jan put down her gun and pulled out a sharp knife. 'I'm just repeating what I hear.'

'Well, don't. I come here to escape all that.'

'Oh dear, Derek,' said Jan, to the Siamese cat, 'she's gone all huffy. I know, let's make amends and get her some artichokes.'

Isobel followed Jan to the vegetable patch. Derek butted his head against Isobel's legs and she bent down to stroke him. He turned his blank blue stare on her.

'He's fascinated by your haircut,' Jan said, as she went to work with her knife among the prickly globes. 'I've explained it's the sincerest form of flattery, but he's convinced you're taking the piss.'

'I wouldn't start on the subject of hairdressing if I were you,' remarked Isobel.

'Cheeky bugger.' Jan's grey hair looked as though she cut it by stealth on a moonless night with her garden shears. Isobel couldn't understand it. Jan would have been a striking woman if she'd made the least effort with her appearance. Even so, people looked at her twice in the street, as though thinking she must have been some-one famous in her youth.

'There.' Jan straightened up with a grunt.

Isobel followed her back to the kitchen and watched as the artichokes were wrapped bouquet-wise in yesterday's *Guardian*. 'I haven't a clue what you're supposed to do with them,' she admitted.

'You hand them to Harry with a helpless simper, that's what you do with them,' said Jan. 'Oh, I've got a good one for you. You'll enjoy this.' Isobel's heart sank. She never did when people said that. 'You know the back road into Stockton? There's a piece of graffiti on the bridge. You must have seen it: "Stamp out Aids, kill a puff." '

'Yes,' said Isobel. She bent over Derek again to hide her face.

'Well, someone's been along and corrected the spelling of "puff"!' crowed Jan.

'It might have been more appropriate to cross the whole thing out.'

'Oh, bollocks! Bollocks! I despair of you.' Jan thumped the artichokes on to the table. 'Isobel, just tell me who it was who sewed your bottom up and I'll go round and sort them out. Can't you see? It's a sort of camp meta-comment on the whole issue of homophobia. Aha! A ladylike smirk. What's so funny?'

'I did it.'

'You never!'

Isobel told her the whole story. Jan guffawed and poured a couple of gins that would have stunned a bo'sun. These days, they dispensed with the I-really-shouldn't-oh-all-right-then ritual. Jan put her feet on the table and tilted her chair back. 'Well, here's looking at you, kid.'

They drank. The kitchen was a complete mess, as usual. Most of the surfaces were obscured under piles of crockery, paper, books and detritus of various projects dating back several months. This room had been the setting for Isobel's one experience of getting completely plastered. It had happened swiftly and accidentally. Jan had invited her for dinner in her first week in Asleby. Having been warned by Harry to expect a gourmet evening, Isobel had skipped lunch. Jan had served champagne cocktails before the meal and these, combined with hunger and the antibiotics Isobel happened to be taking, had acted like a cosh. For ten minutes Isobel feared she wasn't going to make it to the dinner table. She'd sat stroking Derek mechanically while the kitchen heaved and listed around her. Fortunately Jan was a great raconteur so Isobel was not called upon to make conversation, merely to nod vertiginously in agreement as often as she dared.

'Don't even think about it, Del-boy,' said Jan to the cat, who was sizing up the leap on to the workbench. She'd trained him out of clambering over the draining-board and licking the dirty dishes by means of a high-powered water pistol. Derek wandered off prissily, pretending he'd never heard.

'I'm convinced he was a drag queen in a former incarnation,' said Jan.

Isobel wondered how long it would be before she started joshing her about being in love with the policeman. But Jan sat there with a wise twinkle in her eye and said nothing.

In the end it was the gin that did the talking. 'Of course, I'm grateful he didn't arrest me, or anything.'

'Mmm-hmm.'

'What d'you mean, "mmm-hmm"? Look, he's a babe in arms. I have boys like him in my Youth Group.' Isobel smoothed her hair. 'I'm grateful, that's all.'

'Mmm-hmm.'

Isobel clamped her lips shut at this provocation.

'Just think,' said Jan, with a chuckle. 'If he'd nicked you, you might've ended up in front of me in all my magisterial splendour. I'd've had you scrubbing subway walls all over Teesside, my friend.'

'I don't know why I tell you anything,' flounced Isobel. She stood up. The gin hit her.

'Steady as she goes!' called Jan.

'Oh, shut up.'

They went to the door.

'Better leave the car here. Our first curate got done for drunk-driving, you know. It was Christmas and Harry over-consecrated at Midnight Mass. The curate downed a whole chalice of *vino sacro* after the service, silly sod. Got pulled over on the way home. "Been celebrating, have we, sir?" "No, no! I was only deaconing!" Or so the story goes.' Jan laughed at the memory.

'I suppose that was Johnny Whitaker,' said Isobel repressively.

'Yep. Making sheep's eyes at me across the court. Still banned him from driving for a year, mind you. Strict but fair, the eternal headmistress – that's me.' She observed Isobel's expression. 'What's wrong? Don't fancy the smouldering type, eh?'

'Don't be ridiculous. It's not –'

'You could have fried an egg on his naked chest,' pronounced Jan.

'What a revolting thought,' said Isobel, stumbling on the door-step then regaining her poise.

'It is, rather,' Jan agreed. 'Chest hair matted in the yolk – not very appealing. Oh, stop looking so bloody prim. I've got a lot of time for Johnny. He was the one who wooed me back into the fold, you know.'

'I'm sure he's a good pastor,' Isobel managed.

'Ooh, very good. Ve-e-ery, very good.' Jan patted her on the arm. 'Well, goodbye, dear one. Goose Harry for me.'

Dreadful old woman, thought Isobel. While she could believe in many things most sensible people deemed incredible – the Virgin Birth, the Resurrection – she still had problems with the idea of Jan as a headmistress. She gave a little snort of mirth at the thought of Johnny Whitaker's culinary appeal. Frying tonight! Ahem. Nothing wrong with her sense of humour that a large gin wouldn't put right.

It was a beautiful evening. Isobel breathed deeply. She could smell freshly cut grass from the golf course as she walked. Her shadow passed in and out of the longer shadows of houses and trees all down the road until she reached the church. For once she turned a blind eye to the boys up in the ancient yew. Normally she called out that the tree was over a thousand years old, and would they please respect that by coming down immediately. She passed underneath and heard some sshing overhead. Huge beams propped up the lower branches and the two diverging trunks were held together by a massive chain. 'Climb me,' murmured the tree. 'Hide in my depths.' Isobel never had, although she'd been a great tree-climber as a child.

She let herself into the vestry and put the artichokes on the table. Just enough time to run off the handouts for tomorrow's confirmation class. The photocopier twittered to itself as it warmed up. Outside the children's voices, which had fallen silent at her approach, began calling again. There was the thump, thump of a football being kicked against the wall. She gazed around. The room took on a gin-sodden intensity. How she loved it all, the people, the funny old place, the clutter, her whole life, really. Bleep, bleep, went the photocopier to tell her it was ready. She turned, but as she turned something moved.

She whipped round again. Everything was still: the papers on the table, the water glass. Her breathing rasped in the silence. She tried to reconstruct what she'd seen. The tail-end of a movement. A dancing patch of sunlight on the wall? Or what? Someone at the window? Slowly she turned back to the copier and pressed a button. One by one the copies slid out. Her eyes followed the gleam of light passing backwards and forwards under the screen. There was something behind her. She could sense it by the hair on the back of her neck. The machine finished. Silence. Something was there and it was creeping closer, like in that childhood game, Grandmother's footsteps.

She whirled round. The room froze. She waited for some tell-tale movement. Nothing. She held her breath to see if she could catch the sound of someone else's breathing.

In the end she switched off the machine, gathered up the sheets and the heavy bouquet and left. It was not till she was in the open air that she noticed how her heart was racing. She chided herself. It wasn't like her to let her imagination play tricks. Perhaps she'd been more troubled by those silly break-ins than she'd realized. She had a good look round outside to satisfy herself that no one was lurking. Single women were always vulnerable. It was sensible to be watchful. She beat about in the shrubbery.

Watchful, yes, but she was damned if she was going to invent assailants behind every bush. Feeling suddenly foolish, she straightened up and strode towards the vicarage. No point saying anything to Harry. He'd smell the gin on her breath and, in the nicest possible way, not take her fears seriously. She went down his drive and rang the doorbell.

## CHAPTER 4

Before she met Tatiana, playtime had been unbearable for Isobel. Sometimes she tagged on to a group, but nobody really wanted her. In class it didn't matter so much if you hadn't got a best friend. You could just do your work. And, in any case, you couldn't choose who you sat with. The teacher decided, and that was that. Isobel shared a desk with Simon Allington. He had freckles and red hair and rubbed out mistakes with his finger, not a proper rubber, so his work was always a mess. He was OK.

But playtime was horrible. Elaine and Susan had been her friends in Mrs Saddler's class, but when Isobel moved up they wouldn't let her play with them any more. You could get a game going by walking up and down with your arms stretched out, chanting, and other children could come and link up with you, arms across your shoulders, till there were enough of you for a game. 'All in for chain-on! All in for chain-on!' That's what the boys yelled. The girls had a different chant: 'Who wants to play mothers and fathers? No boys!' One playtime Isobel had wandered up and down alone with her arms out till they ached. She never tried it again, just played by herself.

Then one day when she was eight years old there was a new girl in her class, Tatiana George. She was brilliant. She showed them how to break the unbreakable chubby crayons. She taught them a rude tongue-twister: 'One smart fellow, he felt smart.' Best of all, she was Russian. She'd been born in Russia. Tatiana was a Russian name. Her little sister was called Perpetua. Nobody else in the school had names like that. One by one the other girls revealed that they'd been born in foreign countries, too. Even Sandra Parker was from Texas. For two weeks everyone wanted to be Tatiana's best friend, until it came out that she'd been born in Hemel Hempstead and her popularity nosedived. The girls realized she was a liar and a show-off. She was bossy. She was posh. She used long words. So what if she could count to a hundred in German? She wore *boys' shoes.*

So at last, Isobel (the only other girl in the class whose mother insisted on Clark's lace-ups) found a friend. That very first lunch-time together they played under the portable classroom, creeping on their bellies in the dry earth and hearing the teacher's footsteps overhead. They were late back to class.

'Where have you been?'

'To the toilet,' said Tatiana.

Isobel felt a rush of shock. Lying never occurred to her as a possible option.

From that day her life was full of magic. Tatiana was psychic. She could pick up thought-waves even through walls. The first time she went to Isobel's for tea they sat in different rooms and one of them would draw a shape (square, circle or triangle) then 'send' it to the other. The receiver would draw the shape that came to mind, then the sender would call out what she'd drawn. Try as she might, Isobel couldn't pick up Tatiana's messages, but when they did it the other way round, Tatiana would usually get it right. 'Amazing!' she kept calling. 'That's what I've drawn, too!' Even Isobel's dad was impressed. After he'd compared their two sheets of shapes, he had to admit that, statistically, there was more to it than random chance. He was also struck by Tatiana's ability to bend spoons like Uri Geller. He gave her a six-inch nail to bend, but as it turned out Tatiana and Isobel were rather busy playing so Tatiana didn't get round to bending the nail that day, although Isobel did remind her several times.

Harry came to the door wearing a plastic apron printed with a curvaceous female outline in black lacy underwear.

'Oh, *honestly,* Harry!'

'Sorry. The Youth Group gave it me last Christmas.' He looked at her thoughtfully for a moment before inviting her in.

She handed him the prickly bouquet and followed him through to the kitchen where the smell of garlic and roasting lamb greeted her. The champagne was already on ice. Two tall glasses stood beside it. There was also a bottle of claret breathing. Isobel regretted the gin. She sat down, removed her clerical collar and undid a symbolic button or two.

'I'm off duty now,' she explained, laying the collar on the table.

'Good. I've just done salad,' said Harry. 'I thought it was too hot for a full roast dinner. I hope that's OK?' It was a courteous ritual of his, being diffident in the kitchen if there was a woman present. He was an infinitely better cook than Isobel and they both knew it. She watched with interest as he trimmed the artichokes and stuck them in a bowl of cold, salty water. He caught her expression.

'Vital precaution,' he explained. 'Unless you're partial to blanched earwig, of course. That's the price you pay for organic veg.'

'Harry, you'd make someone a lovely wife.' It sounded like a cheap gibe at his sexuality and she cursed her want of tact.

'No!' He clutched his hands over the black lacy bosoms. 'You're embarrassing me!'

'Don't be silly.'

'Seriously – am I overdoing the muscle definition? Too long at the gym?'

Isobel gave an exasperated sigh. 'Shall I open the champagne, Harry?' she asked, already peeling off the foil and untwisting the wire.

'Please.' Pop went the cork. Isobel poured, and they sat opposite one another at his kitchen table.

'To us,' he said, raising his glass.

Isobel's heart gave a skip. 'To us. Against the wedge-drivers,' she clarified.

'Of course,' agreed Harry. 'Against the wedge-drivers.'

He rested his head on his hand. He was pleasant-looking, without being particularly handsome. His dark eyes were gazing at her in the 'poor Harry' way that had women queuing up to polish brass and fill tea-urns for him. Champagne, candlelight – all at once she felt self-conscious and pretended to study his walls. They were frescoed with cherubs and a spoof version of the ceiling of the Sistine Chapel with God leaning down to light Adam's cigarette. Isobel found it disrespectful, not to mention rather over the top for a vicarage, but Harry was fond of his muriels, as he called them.

44

They had been painted years before by Johnny Whitaker's wife. If Isobel was honest, that was her main reason for disliking them. Mara Whitaker was a cold, supercilious and spectacularly rude woman and, anyway, Isobel had no time for clergy wives who never went to church. And without wishing to be judgemental, the woman's past wouldn't bear close scrutiny, either. One almost felt sorry for Johnny.

When she looked back Harry was still watching her. They both made as if to speak, to ask the other what they were thinking, perhaps; but in the end they said nothing. Harry got to his feet and melted some butter.

'Do you really work out?' she asked.

'Doesn't it show?'

'Hmm.' She eyed his back view. 'Well, you look in good shape, I suppose.'

' "Cute buns", you mean?'

'Certainly not!'

He gave her a wiggle and plunged the artichokes into a pan of boiling water.

'Harry Preece! Behave.' What had come over him, all of a sudden? She'd witnessed this kind of flirtatiousness in gay men before, without ever being on the receiving end. Women were a sort of dry run for them, she imagined, but it was a little disconcerting all the same. Parishioners often invited the two of them out together, a convenient brace of clergy for the dinner table. Or two birds with one stone, more likely. She was used to that. Eating with him alone seemed to be upsetting some complex balance.

'It's my day off,' he explained.

'Is that what it is?' said Isobel, annoyed to be read so easily. Well, just so long as it didn't get in the way of their professional relationship.

He drained the artichokes and took off his apron. They said grace and began to eat.

'Isobel, I had a terrible, terrible experience yesterday.'

'Yes?' Butter dripped down her chin. She dabbed at it primly with her napkin. Really, there was no polite way of eating artichokes, fiddly, exasperating things that they were.

45

'A woman collared me in the street and told me she kept hearing funny noises in her house, and would I go along and circumcise it for her.'

'Oh, no!' Isobel was all too familiar with Harry's battles against *fous rires*. 'How did you manage to keep a straight face?'

'I didn't. I tried coughing to disguise my laughter. Unfortunately it came out like a sort of hoarse bellow. So I said, "Sorry. Hay fever." I *know* it was a lie,' he said, seeing her frown, 'but what could I do?'

'Did you go to the house?'

'Yes – prayer book and breadknife in hand.'

She raised an eyebrow.

'I pronounced a quick blessing and she seemed satisfied. I was just leaving when she said, "You know, that's the first time I've met someone religious without feeling – without feeling –"' Here Harry was forced to break off. Isobel waited while he wept into his artichokes.

'Without feeling?' she prompted.

'"Without feeling they were just out to pervert me,"' he whimpered.

Isobel gave way to a smile. 'And I suppose you had another attack of hay fever.'

He nodded and wiped his eyes. 'Isobel, I'm so glad you're my curate. You're a good influence on me.'

'Thank you.' Sometimes it was a lonely business being so good for everyone. They ate for a while in silence. The strange incident in the vestry came back to her. 'What would you do if you came across a genuine . . .' she hesitated, '. . . well, ghost, or what-have-you?'

'The same, probably. Prayer of blessing. Or if I was out of my depth there are official diocesan ghostbusters, aren't there?' He cleared the plates away and got the lamb out of the oven. 'Or I'd ask my friend Chris.'

'Is he an exorcist?'

'Not really. A Franciscan – with a sneaky habit of eavesdropping on other people's thoughts.'

'Oh!' said Isobel, trying to sound polite. 'Psychic, you mean?'

'Do you, by any chance, lump monasticism together with crystal healing and tarot cards?' he inquired.

'Of course I don't! Why?'

'Something in your tone. Anyway, Chris: I suppose I'd describe him as a sort of spiritual bloodhound. You've met him, come to think of it.'

'I thought his name was Gabriel.'

'It is, these days. He was Chris at theological college. Or Christ.'

Isobel looked at him reprovingly. The champagne had joined forces with the gin. Her efforts to appear sober made her seem sterner than ever.

'To distinguish him from the other Chris,' explained Harry. 'There was Chris T. and Chris H. We called them Christ and Krishna.' Seeing she was not mollified he added swiftly, 'Shall I carve? Or would that be paternalistic of me?'

'Harry, I can never tell if you're deliberately trying to wind me up.'

'I think you can safely assume I am.' He smiled at her. 'Can I ask you something? Were you head girl at school?'

'Oh, shut up and carve.'

He gave a mock salute, recoiling theatrically when he nearly stabbed himself in the temple. The first slice fell away from the carving-knife. 'Oh, yes. Look at this! Mmm – wah!' He kissed his fingertips. 'Walter Goodwill, may the Lord bless you and keep you.' He handed Isobel a plate. 'See if you can get him to give you shoulder next time. I always think it's nicer.'

After the meal Harry lit some more candles before slumping on the tatty old sofa he kept in his kitchen. Isobel sat beside him with an amaretto biscuit and a cup of coffee while he lit a cigar. She strongly disapproved of smoking, but she could hardly begrudge Harry the occasional post-prandial Havana. She glanced and it struck her that there was even something rather sexy about it. This observation alarmed her into refusing a glass of Cognac. She gazed round the kitchen once more, seeking a safe topic of conversation.

'I must say, Harry, your love of candles and wine is rather high church for an Evangelical.'

'Ah, I'm a closet spike, you see.'

'No, you're not.'

'No, I'm not,' he agreed. 'What am I? I'm an Evangelical by intellectual persuasion. I'm afraid *temperamentally* I'm probably in the smoking-handbag brigade.'

'Incense and icons?'

'You name it.'

*That's for poofs!* Isobel suppressed this mental interjection. 'Pictures of the Pope? Prayers to the Virgin?'

'Not quite that bad.'

'I'm relieved to hear it.'

He smiled at her again and they fell silent once more. She began to relax into the squashy cushions. A waft of Harry's exquisite aftershave reached her nostrils.

'What *is* that aftershave you wear?' she asked.

'I'm not telling you.'

'Why not?' she demanded, surprised.

'In case you find out how much it costs and get stern with me.'

'Buying good-quality products is never extravagant,' pronounced Isobel. 'I've just never found a scent I like enough to invest in. All those ghastly things they puff at you in department stores. Who wants to smell like everyone else?' She stopped, wondered if she was sounding insufferable.

Harry was looking amused. 'So what does it smell like, this unique, elusive scent you're waiting for?'

She noted with approval that he hadn't said 'perfume'. 'Floral. Not cloying. Perhaps a touch of spice.'

'Carnation?'

She looked at him sharply. So he'd identified her Roger et Gallet talc.

'To pluck an idea at random from the stratosphere,' he elaborated.

The conversation was beginning to feel too intimate again. Isobel sipped her coffee, seeking a way to turn the subject.

'You seemed a little *distrait* when you came in tonight,' he said at length. 'Is something troubling you?'

The biscuit she was gripping exploded into crumbs. 'Whoops!' She picked at the scattered fragments on her trousers. 'Oh, it was nothing. I just . . . thought I saw something in the vestry.

48

Probably the result of the, er, gin I had at Jan's.' Her laugh came out too loud.

'You saw something?' he repeated. 'What sort of thing?'

'Something sort of . . . moved. I just caught it out of the corner of my eye. Someone at the window, maybe. There were kids playing in the churchyard. I had a bit of a look round outside, but I couldn't see anything.' He was frowning, so she went on, 'I must be jumpy after those break-ins, I suppose.'

'Is this why you were asking about exorcism? You think it's –'

'Oh!' She laughed again. 'I don't believe in all *that*! I just wondered what the correct procedure would be, if, you know . . .'

But he seemed intent on taking it seriously. 'Tell me if it happens again, Isobel.'

'You're not worried about me, are you? Harry, I can look after myself!'

'Yes. But I'm always here if you need me.'

She stiffened. 'I do find that mildly patronizing, if I may say so. You wouldn't treat a male colleague like this.'

'Yes, I would.'

'Forgive me, but I don't think so.'

He put his coffee down. 'Isobel, your welfare is my concern.'

'Now, listen –'

'Stop bloody arguing!' Her mouth dropped open. Harry seldom swore. 'This is not a gender issue! I'm the vicar, you're the curate. It's my *job* to look after you.'

She flushed. He'd never pulled rank with her before. After a sharp tussle with herself she managed to apologize.

'Good girl,' he said.

She bit her lip. 'Will you *stop* baiting me, Harry.'

'But I love it when the real Isobel escapes.'

'It's not the real me!' she cried. 'You're deliberately trying to make me lose my temper and it's not funny!'

'Ah, I'm sorry,' he said, seeing he had gone too far. 'I'll stop.'

'It's just . . .' Her voice wavered. She took a firm grip: 'It's just that I've never been particularly good at being teased. Which is why everyone finds it irresistible, I suppose.'

'I'm sorry,' he repeated. 'Truly.'

The exchange had soured the atmosphere and before long Isobel consulted her watch and declared a little awkwardly that it was time she left.

He insisted on walking her home.

'Don't be silly, Harry. I walk about in the dark all the time.'

'Bear with me,' he said. 'It's my age. It's my upbringing. I can't *not* see a young lady home. My mother would rise up and haunt me.'

She tutted. 'Oh, all right.'

It was getting dark. They passed through the clouds of perfume from the night-scented stocks that grew along Harry's garden path. As they approached the main road the air was heavy with lime blossom again. Over everything was another smell, the faint mingled odours of the chemical works, the oil refinery and of British Steel that would for ever afterwards conjure up Teesside for Isobel. It was never fully dark in Asleby. The sky always glowed orange. Tonight, however, there were one or two faint stars and a full moon hanging over the rooftops.

'You're taking the service at Chestnut Lodge tomorrow?' asked Harry.

'Yes.'

'Doing a communion in an old people's home is the acid test of churchmanship, you know.'

'How do you mean?'

'A real spike has to consume what's left in the chalice after sixteen old ladies have drooled and slobbered bits of wafer into it. I just thank God I'm an Evangelical and tip it down the sink.'

'Harry, you're revolting.'

He laughed. 'Let me know how you get on.'

They were at Isobel's door.

'Well, thank you for a lovely evening, Harry.'

'You're welcome.' He kissed her cheek, something else he seldom did. Another whiff of the nameless aftershave.

She flushed. 'It was nice being ... Just being with you, without ...'

'And also with you,' he responded, with full liturgical gravity.

'Oh, go away, Harry.' She was smiling as she let herself in.

The moment the door closed she knew something was wrong. Her heart began to pound. She switched on her study light. Books lay strewn across the floor. She was out in the street in an instant, calling Harry back.

He came running. 'What's wrong?'

'Someone . . . They've −' She was trembling too much to speak.

He went past her into the study and saw the mess. 'Wait here. I'll check the rest of the house.'

She stood quaking, listening as he went from room to room, then up the stairs. What if someone was lurking and attacked him? But he was coming back down. All my things! Pictures thrown on the floor, letters and papers tipped out of her filing cabinet.

'Nothing. I'll call the police,' he said. 'Why don't you see if anything's missing?'

She started turning this way and that, reaching, stopping, not knowing what she was doing. Harry's voice was speaking calmly on the phone. A break-in. Come along, Knox, she told herself. That's all it is. A minor break-in. You're all right. She began to get a grip on herself. Credit cards? Still there. CD player? Yes. What else? Cash still in her desk drawer? Yes.

Harry rang off. 'They're sending someone. Anything gone?'

'I don't think so.'

'Did you leave any windows open?'

'Possibly, I'm afraid.'

'Does anyone have your house keys, do you think?'

'Well . . .' They looked at one another, knowing there might be any number of spare copies floating around. A previous curate could have lent them and forgotten, even.

'We'll have to get the locks changed.'

'Oh, I'm sure it'll be fine,' she said, regretting her earlier panic. 'Nothing's gone, after all.'

'Tomorrow I'll ring the locksmith first thing.'

'Harry, I'm perfectly capable of −'

'For my peace of mind, if not yours,' he said.

Seeing he was about to pull rank again, she acquiesced. 'I wonder if it's the same person who keeps getting into the vestry?' she said. Then she remembered her experience there before dinner. 'Oh!'

Harry was looking at her.

'But that's ridiculous!' Her eyes sped over the chaos again. 'It's probably just a prank. The Youth Group, or something.'

He was about to say something, but then they both heard the car pull up outside.

'That was quick,' said Harry. He went to the door. 'Thank you for coming so promptly,' she heard him say. 'In here, Officer.'

Isobel turned. It was the red-haired policeman.

## CHAPTER 5

She gave him a tight smile and, finding herself unable to meet his eye, bent to pick up some papers. Then it occurred to her she oughtn't to disturb anything so she straightened up again hurriedly.

'Was it you that rang, sir?' the policeman asked Harry. He looked round, taking stock. 'And it's your house, Miss?' His tone was scrupulously professional, as though he'd never caught her, spray can in hand, half-way up an embankment. 'You came in and found it like this?'

'Yes.'

'The door hadn't been forced? What about the windows?'

'I don't think so.'

'Mind if I take a look round?'

They followed him from room to room. His radio gabbled spasmodically.

'Did you leave this open?' he asked, pointing to the kitchen window.

'It was hot,' said Isobel.

The policeman shook his head in a particularly annoying they-never-learn way.

'Anything missing?' he asked at length, when they were back in the study.

'I don't think so.'

'Uh-huh.' He stood for some time frowning and looking round again. Perhaps they were taught this gambit at police school, thought Isobel – if you're stumped, try to look thoughtful.

He turned to Harry. 'Aren't you the local priest?'

'We're both priests,' cut in Isobel.

'Right,' said the officer uncertainly.

'I'm the vicar,' explained Harry. 'Ms Knox is the curate.'

'Oh. I'm a Catholic, me,' the policeman responded, as though this shed light on the situation. His accent grated on her. He lapsed back into inscrutable silence again, apart from a bit of tutting under his breath. Oh, for heaven's sake! thought Isobel. No wonder crime figures are soaring. His next question was a little more incisive, however.

'You've had a couple of break-ins doon the church, am I right?' They nodded. 'Same sort of thing, like? No forced entry, nowt missing?' They nodded again. 'Uh-huh. Any theories?'

There was a taut pause.

'Forgive me,' said Isobel, 'but isn't that your job, Officer?'

He looked at her steadily. 'Well, aye, but it'd be helpful to hear what you think, Miss Knox.'

'Ms.'

He didn't repeat it. Harry was obliged to step into the breach. 'I'm afraid we may have been a little careless about keys. There are rather a lot of spare sets, you see.'

'Ah,' he said. 'Spare sets to this house too, you mean?'

'We can't rule it out, I'm afraid,' said Harry.

'D'you not think it might be an idea to change the locks?' he suggested neutrally.

'I'll get on to it,' Harry replied.

'So you've no idea who's behind it?'

There was another tricky pause.

'No,' said Isobel.

'Not really,' agreed Harry.

Well, they hadn't, had they?

This time the uh-huh was tinged with cynicism. 'Well, I'll just take a statement off yous.'

*Yous!*

'Certainly,' said Harry.

They all sat and the policeman bent over his pad. Isobel saw the tip of his tongue emerge as he began to write. 'And if you think of anything later, you could mebbes give us a ring.' He looked up at Isobel and held her gaze. 'I'm not stupid, Miss Knox.'

'I never suggested you were!' He returned to his writing. She turned to Harry to appeal to him. He raised an eyebrow. The implied reproof stung her. She made a rapid review of her behaviour. Perhaps she had been a little caustic, but . . . The policeman was still writing laboriously, pausing to ask the occasional question. By the time he had finished and handed her the statement to read she was writhing inwardly. She scanned it, biro in hand. Her sense of guilt held her back from correcting a couple of glaring misspellings, although the temptation was acute. Harry spotted her dilemma and bolted out to the kitchen to indulge his mirth.

Isobel signed and handed back the statement. 'I'm afraid I've been rude. I'm sorry.'

'Nee worries,' he said. 'You're upset.'

She looked at the mess. All her books. 'I suppose I am.'

''Course you are.'

This was a shade too avuncular from a lad of twenty, but she checked herself. 'One other thing. Um, thank you for the other day. For not arresting me, I mean.'

He flashed her a collusive grin. 'I've still got your paint. Will I bring it roond?'

*Shall.* She gritted her teeth. 'Yes, if you wouldn't mind.'

'Tomorrow night?' He lowered his voice. Harry was coming back. 'About eight?'

Oh, no! Surely . . . Something in his tone . . . 'Yes. OK,' she said hurriedly.

Harry entered and shot her an inquisitive look. She stooped to snatch up some papers from the floor.

'Well, I think that's me done,' said the policeman, resuming his professional tone and getting to his feet.

Isobel and Harry thanked him.

'That's OK. I'd get those locks seen to,' he advised.

'We will,' promised Harry.

'And if anything else occurs to you . . .' He allowed a pause. Isobel and Harry said nothing. 'These things can escalate. First it's crimes against property, next it's crimes against the person – kna what I mean? I'm not trying to scare you. Think about it.'

'Thank you. We will,' said Isobel.

They saw him to the door.

'Was it *just* the Geordie accent?' asked Harry as the police car drove off. 'Or had he done something else to annoy you?'

She ducked the question. 'Was it a Geordie accent?'

55

'How long have you *been* here, Isobel? You must be able to tell Teesside from Tyneside.'

'Oh, they all sound the same to me.' *The working classes.* Clang! 'I mean ... That came out all wrong. I'm afraid I'm still a bit upset.'

He touched her arm. 'Shall I give you a hand sorting things out?'

'Thanks, but I'll do it tomorrow.'

'Will you be all right on your own? I'm sure you could stay with Jan, if ...'

'I'll be fine.'

'You've got a phone by your bed?'

'Yes. And I'll shut all the windows and put the chain on the door. Harry, I'm fine.' His face was a picture of male solicitude thrashing helplessly under the weight of political correctness. She could have hugged him.

'This is getting serious, Isobel. We'll have to talk about it, you know.'

'I know. He thought we were hiding something.'

'He's not stupid, is he?'

'No.'

He regarded her for what felt like an age. 'Neither am I.'

'Of course you're not, Harry,' she said, not wishing to understand him.

After he'd gone she wanted to call him back and ask him to stay, but one couldn't insist on feminist principles one minute then ask for special treatment the next. She'd already been more feeble than she liked – letting him take over, search the house, call the police. Humbling to know that in moments of stress all the old stereotypes reared their heads. Well, she would make herself a cup of tea, then tackle the clearing up. Despite what she'd said, she knew she wouldn't be able to sleep until her books were back on their shelves in the proper order.

There was a phone message she hadn't noticed earlier. It was Mum, wanting a chat; she'd just been on the phone to Alistair. So she knew about the Apology, then, and wanted to angle for more details. Isobel wouldn't oblige, as that would mean talking about that ghastly year when Dad had been in Saudi Arabia. There

56

was nothing Mrs Knox liked more than rummaging through memory's dustbin for clues to one's hang-ups. There was nothing Isobel liked less.

All through school Isobel prided herself on her scrupulous honesty. She had been brought up to believe lying was always wrong, and not only wrong but stupid. One lie would inevitably lead to another and trip you up. However difficult, owning up was always the best course of action. These were the rules of the Knox household. Isobel adhered to them bravely in the classroom where denying things and blaming others were commonplace. In the end her truthfulness was recognized by all. Once, in the top class, during a desk-to-desk search for Teresa Flynn's new jumbo rubber, Mrs Peck halted at Isobel's desk.

'I'm not going to open Isobel's desk, as I *know* she would *never* steal.'

Her zeal prompted Isobel to own up occasionally on behalf of others. One lunchtime she saw Stewart Ogg tittering over a magazine, which he thrust back into his desk when the bell rang. Isobel burned. She could tell what sort of magazine it was. In the end she burst out, 'Mr Woodford, do I have your permission to get something out of Stewart Ogg's desk?'

Permission was granted. Mr Woodford glanced at the magazine then tore it into tiny bits and dropped them in the bin. The whole class overheard the lecture as the pieces fluttered down. There was nothing shameful or dirty about the human body (shred, rip), but there were ways (rip, shred) of photographing it that were degrading and belittling. Isobel glowed with fierce pleasure.

When she opened her recorder box later that afternoon, there on the mouthpiece lay one perfect glossy breast staring up at her like an eye. Stewart Ogg was smirking. She screwed up the fragment in fury and flicked it away.

It was many hours before Isobel managed to fall asleep. Each tiny sound jolted her back into tense wakefulness. The tapping of honey-suckle tendrils on her kitchen window sounded like malevolent fingers groping for an unfastened catch. Had she shut them all properly? Yes. And double, triple checked them. But couldn't sash windows be opened with knives? The scrape of honeysuckle fronds became the noise of a blade sliding between wooden window frames. I'll get locks fitted, she promised herself. At last she slid into a light sleep.

Just before dawn she had a peculiarly vivid dream. She was walking along a woodland path with Alex. There was bracken on both sides, then in amongst it she could see some tall white toadstools. They were standing there erect and shameless. The stench was disgusting. Isobel pretended not to notice, but Alex saw and laughed.

'Look, *phallus impudicus*,' he said.

'It's common stinkhorn,' she snapped, turning away.

She woke. It was light. What a singularly unpleasant dream, she thought. Then the memory of the break-in rushed back. No wonder she was unsettled. But here she was. She'd survived the first night. Things could only get better now. Her clock said six-fifteen.

She rolled on to her back and stared at the leaf shadows dancing on the ceiling. The dream's miasma still clung about her. For her own sake she had long since eradicated Alex from her thoughts. Why had her mind chosen this moment to disgorge him? Isobel was dismissive of the benefits of dream analysis, mostly because her mother in recent years had become so obsessed with it. Five minutes of Mrs Knox on this subject was generally enough to make Isobel long wildly for a world in which it was possible to mislay one's keys without simultaneously betraying some deep-seated sexual ambivalence. Her father, a Yorkshireman at heart, despite his Cambridge veneer, had no time for this kind of rubbish. Perhaps Jung was her mother's subversive method of chipping away at his granite-like scientific pragmatism. Isobel agreed with neither parent but had seen enough of life to acknowledge that the subconscious was an opponent to be reckoned with. There was an insistency to this particular dream. What could it mean? Well, in the first place there was some rather crass masculine imagery, which she imagined might reveal her feelings about men in general. But woodland paths? Bracken? What were they supposed to represent? And Alex? Was she meant to treat him as some kind of symbol?

She drew a deep breath. No, this was the heart of it – not the symbolism, but the man himself, reappearing without permission and flaunting his power over her even in her dreams. Well, we'll see about *that*, she thought. She may have been in love with him all those years, but she'd got him now, trapped in the past like a hornet in amber. She could take him out and look at him, then put him away again. Why not do this at once? In a calm, controlled way she would produce her memories of Alex and look them over. He had no power over her these days other than what she accorded him.

She remembered clearly the first time they'd met. He was one of the panel interviewing her for the job of college librarian. His presence had lent a surreal atmosphere to the occasion. Even while she was talking sensibly about computerization she couldn't stop herself wondering, Why is this man dressed like the hero of a Georgette Heyer novel?

He turned out to be a religious philosopher who had just been made Fellow Librarian. Oxford was unknown territory to her, but it was not long before she discovered from her opposite numbers in other colleges how unusual it was for a Fellow Librarian ever to grace the library with his presence, let alone show active concern for its well-being. Her new post soon turned out to be one of responsibility but no real power. She was excluded from the decision-making bodies. Alex's influence on her behalf in the Senior Common Room was vital. His interest was unashamedly self-interest, however. He was empire-building. It was no secret that he intended to create a centre of excellence for his field of study in order to attract graduate students. His obsession with getting the college library swiftly on the university computer system was a strategic part of this plan. There was considerable resistance to this. Some of the dons were still of the opinion that the typewriter was a dangerous innovation. Her co-operation was crucial. They needed each other.

It was his influence that secured her the post in the first place. She only found that out later and the discovery was a relief, for it made sense of her vague perception that people were treating her with caution or hostility. By then she knew his reputation. His mild manner to her personally and, irrationally, the fact that he was so musical made her slow at first to believe what she heard. She watched him and gradually saw behind those dandyish clothes, the black curls tied back with silk ribbon, a man driven by his own demonic potency. He was never happy except when doing three things simultaneously and executing them perfectly. He was, as everyone had warned her, rapaciously ambitious, hard-drinking, foul-mouthed and promiscuous. To this he added Oxford's two most execrable sins: casual erudition on other people's subjects and prolificacy. Many of his publications were concerned with the interface of theology and science. He was forever collaborating with biologists on altruism, with neurologists on the physiology of religious experience. If there was a cutting edge anywhere, he had to be at it. Isobel had even catalogued articles on film studies with his name on the title page.

'Have I *read* it? I don't have time to read books, for Christ's sake,' he would say, as if this were a point of academic honour. Yet he always knew what was in them. Perhaps, a colleague once sneered, he X-rayed new volumes by passing them under the searing light of his intellect.

Other people were either tools or obstacles to him. He used or trampled them as the need arose. He had little time for friendship. The only person known to get the better of him was his younger brother, an English don in another college. Isobel knew Andrew slightly and loathed him. He was manipulative and sadistic, as languid as his brother was mercurial, and his flagrant homosexuality repelled her. And yet he lived with what he called his 'whore' (the equally unsavoury Mrs Whitaker in her pre-married state), so one never quite knew what was going on. Everything was a game to him. At least Alex took life seriously. He appeared to be universally unpleasant on principle, while Andrew was cruel at whim. The rivalry between them was legendary. Together they were like a couple of unpinned Catherine wheels – wild, brilliant, destructive. They were banned from half the bars and restaurants in town. Once she saw them physically fighting. The viciousness of it sickened and appalled her. They were like six-year-olds, lost to all reason. She called the porters, who had to drag them apart still spitting blood and screaming abuse.

'Why do you do this?' she asked Alex afterwards. 'It's so *shaming*.'

'Because he breathes my air,' was the reply.

The ferocity of their mutual hatred was equalled only by the loyalty with which each would defend the other if he were attacked by a third party.

Outside, the dustmen were making their way along the back alley. I've forgotten to put the bin out, she thought. But she continued to lie, staring at the ceiling. She had a sudden crisp image of her old office. The sunlight lay in a broad stripe across her desk. It was afternoon. She was pretending to herself that she wasn't listening out for Alex's rapid footsteps. At this time of day he would sometimes appear and pause, brain idling, fingers busy on her desk-edge at some phantom piano, and indulge in a little university gossip. Sometimes she had difficulty catching what he said. He was softly spoken and his speech patterns rapid, staccato to the point of stuttering, as if mere words mired down his thoughts. And then he'd be gone, sometimes in mid-sentence even, to rattle off another article, or demolish someone's life's work in a couple of caustic sentences.

He never noticed that she loved him. Like many clever, self-obsessed men, he was capable of colossal emotional obtuseness. She'd have had to slash her wrists in front of him before he'd think to ask if she was feeling all right. Andrew, however, observed her feelings. He would corner her at drinks parties, slide an arm round her and favour her with details of Alex's sexual adventures. She listened with feigned indifference as he murmured in her ear. As far as she knew he never told his brother, either because he preferred to maintain his emotional hold over her, or simply because he relished knowing something Alex didn't. Neither motive endeared him to her.

Yes, compared with Andrew, Alex was a straightforward pleasure. Everyone wondered how she put up with him, of course.

'I'm not afraid of Dr Jacks,' she would tell them. And it was true. They'd only crossed swords once.

Isobel stirred unhappily under her covers, remembering. It was over six years ago, and it still distressed her. She would have dismissed it from her mind, except that that felt uncomfortably like cowardice. For heaven's sake! What was all that to her now?

It was the end of the summer term. Isobel had been working late trying to balance her books before a meeting of the library committee the following day. The library was dark and deserted. She was just leaving when she thought she heard someone crying. Over finals she had ministered to several overwrought students. Perhaps this was someone weeping about poor exam results. She sighed and dutifully followed the sound, ready to put on her kettle and make soothing noises. On this occasion, however, she located the sobbing student in a remote corner on top of a desk and underneath the Fellow Librarian. Her eyes locked with his at the moment of his orgasm. She turned on her heel and walked away. His laughter followed her.

All that night she was in anguish, wringing her hands and pacing up and down. If she made a fuss he would hound her out of her job. It was that simple. He'd done it to her predecessor. She cursed herself for not having joined a union years ago. There was nothing she could do. Yet his behaviour was totally unacceptable — she couldn't let it pass. Even setting aside her own embarrassment, surely it counted as gross professional misconduct. Especially if the girl was one of his own students. Isobel had half recognized her. On the other hand, perhaps it was none of her business. Except she was the college librarian. Naturally, she'd have known how to react if she'd caught a couple of undergraduates at it. She tried in vain to sort it out. Why had he chosen the library? His rooms were just across the quad. Had he wanted her to catch him? Was he trying to get rid of her for some reason?

Then in the small hours another thought struck her like an icicle driven through the heart: had she turned her back on another woman being raped? No. Not Alex. He would never ... surely. He wouldn't! Should she contact the women's officer? Oh, God, tell me what to do! Who could she confide in? There were many who would seize upon the incident as a means of bringing about Alex's downfall. Was she protecting him if she did nothing? Allowing her feelings to cloud her judgement? She even thought fleetingly of ringing her father, who could be counted on to give impartial advice. Strange that this belief should linger on so stubbornly, the childhood tenet that Dad would know what to do. By dawn she was decided.

He was waiting in her office that morning with no apology, just a blunt question: 'Will you be making a formal complaint?'

She raised her chin. 'Not if you assure me you had her consent.'

'*What?*' he exploded. 'Y-y-you fucking – you think I'm a f-fucking fool? Of course I had her consent!'

'I'm sorry,' she said, her face flaming. Nobody spoke to her like this! 'I had to ask.'

'No, you fucking didn't, you stupid bitch. My private life is just that – private.'

'Then I suggest you *conduct* it in private!' she cried.

For a second it all hung in the balance. Then he raised his hands in surrender. He had a sweet smile when he chose to use it. 'OK, OK, OK. I'm sorry. What can I say? I got caught short. It won't happen again.'

That's all it means to him, she thought. A matter of relieving himself. He yawned and stretched, relaxed now he'd dealt with her, as relaxed as he was capable of being. How can I possibly be in love with this vile man?

'You disapprove?'

'Actually, I do, Alex.'

'Why?'

'Oh, promiscuity.' She wrinkled her nose. 'So tacky.'

'Tacky! God, do you think so?' He looked aghast, as though she'd accused him of wearing polyester.

She began leafing through the morning's post and had the slight consolation of hearing him mutter, '*Tacky*', to himself, trying the word on for size, assessing its semantic range.

'Tacky. Tacky-tacky-tacky. I have just been called *tacky* by a woman who doesn't recognize a cry of sexual ecstasy when she hears it.' He left the room. She listened as his footsteps faded away. The library door closed. She sat for a long time with her eyes closed, defiled by the whole experience and her inability to deal with it properly.

The dust lorry roared away. She shook herself mentally. It was all behind her now. And yet, what did it say about her, that for the best part of five years she had been in love with a man for whom rape was neither wicked nor cruel, just foolish – and nowhere near as criminal as tackiness?

It was nearly time to get up. She yawned. Then her phone rang. So early! A pulse of adrenaline went through her. It must be something serious. She donned her best pastoral manner, but it was only Harry.

'Were you asleep?' he asked. 'I just wanted to check you were all right. Don't shout at me.'

'I'm fine.' She laughed in relief. 'I'm still in bed, actually.'

'So am I.' There was a pause. It seemed faintly unsuitable, somehow. 'You managed to sleep?'

'Eventually, thank you.'

'I bet you tidied up last night.'

She admitted it.

'I knew it!' He laughed. 'No rest till everything's shipshape and Dewey decimal-fashion.'

'It's not Dewey decimal,' she said testily.

They chatted inconsequentially for a bit, then rang off. Isobel snuggled up with a smile.

But Alex was not so easily dismissed. He stalked her at the edges of her mind, and just before she left the house for morning prayer she couldn't resist reaching for her dictionary to look up stinkhorn: '*n*. any of various basidiomycetous saprophitic fungi of the genus *Phallus*, such as *P. impudicus*, having an offensive odour'. She smiled. I didn't know I knew that. But even while she was marvelling at her unconscious mycological expertise, another part of her was thinking, So he was right, then.

But, of course, he would have been.

## CHAPTER 6

Isobel was a fiercely competitive child. Perhaps she was born that way, but one thing was certain: having two older brothers honed her instincts to perfection. Labouring under the twin handicaps of age and gender, she spent her life running to keep up with them. They taunted her over their shoulders, eternally two steps ahead. Nothing in this world matched the sweet savour of victory over them. She seldom tasted it, but it was like a potent drug and she craved it with her whole being. No triumph was too petty for her, and no one had a keener sense of justice. Especially when it came to something like dividing up a bag of jelly babies.

'That's not fair! You've both got six and I've only got five!'

'Ah, diddums.'

'Mum! Mum! They've got more than me! *Mum!* MUM!' It always took half a dozen shouts to penetrate Mrs Knox's bunker, by which time the sweets had been scoffed.

'Yes, dear?' (looking up from her novel).

'They had more than me!'

'Well, I expect you can have the most next time. You remind me.'

But, of course, Mum never remembered. Did I say that, dear? Oh, well. Next time. I promise. But promises made by people reading books were worthless. Mum was like a benign figurehead, reading reading reading, while the missiles screamed about her and Isobel was ground under the heel of fraternal fascism.

No wonder she grew up hungry to win. Not for *her* this rubbish about it not mattering whether you won or lost but how you played the game. The words, 'Oh, well, at least I did my best,' were never on her lips. Nor did the knowledge that she'd played badly ever mar the pleasure of winning. If she'd beaten the opposition without really trying, it showed how *even more* brilliant she was than them! Netball, one-potato, noughts-and-crosses, hopscotch – she had to win, or it wasn't fair.

'Boys, boys,' her mother would sometimes plead. 'Couldn't you let Isobel win now and then?'

'Don't be silly,' her father would interject. 'The child's got to learn.'

Perhaps if he'd given some quarter she might have done. 'She'll never learn if people make it easy for her,' he would say, as he raked in the rent for his three hotels on Mayfair. All she learnt from this experience was to bash the board over and charge out in tears, vowing never to play Monopoly again.

She brought the same competitive attitude to her schoolwork, which stood her in good stead when she got to grammar school and was in a class of thirty girls all white-faced with determination to be top, and weeping silently but inconsolably if they only got 73 per cent in biology, when all their other marks were in the eighties.

All this made Isobel a bracing companion. There were even flare-ups between her and Tatiana. These could usually be forestalled by a curious ritual of staking claim to different kinds of superiority before a game commenced. The first, for example, to utter the words, 'Well, I can run twice as fast as ever you can say or think!' was thereby established as fastest. The other just had to swallow her gall. It wasn't nice, but at least it was fair.

Unfortunately, it wasn't always possible to predict what kind of superhuman attributes Tatiana's games would require. One breaktime they were playing on a bare patch of earth where a pile of builders' sand had stood. That afternoon, under Tatiana's supervision, it had become a terrifying sucking vortex that could pull the unwary twirling down into the centre of the earth where the fire trolls lived. An imaginary baby sister had tumbled in and was clinging to a crevice.

'A rope!' screamed Isobel. 'Throw her a rope!'

'We haven't got a rope!' shrieked Tatiana. 'Who's got the longest hair? Look, I have. I'll let that down instead.'

Isobel turned and walked off, brimming with rage.

By hometime they were friends again, having thrashed out some kind of compromise deal to apply to all games in perpetuity, in which *both* of them had hair of exactly the same length: the longest ever in the whole world or in history.

Isobel never grew out of this extreme competitiveness. By the time she was an adult she had realized how unseemly it was, and although she was still a monumentally bad loser, she had learnt to hide it. If there was anything worse than losing, it was the thought of everyone knowing you cared. She taught herself to laugh and shrug, and whenever she was not confident of her ability to appear careless, she didn't compete in the first place. If the truth were told, this was why she hadn't found time to play cricket for the diocese that summer. She had let herself down badly over that running-out incident, and she was not keen to lay herself open afresh to Harry's reminder that it was only a game.

Isobel took one look at the debris floating about in the chalice after the communion at the old people's home and acknowledged Harry was right. She thanked God she was an Evangelical and tipped the contents down the sink. She was a bit funny about shared bodily fluids. Lengthy kissing always struck her as unhygienic, and she heartlessly broke up any snog-a-thons she encountered at the youth club.

She packed her cassock and communion paraphernalia into her case and set off for the church. There was a voice muttering tetchily in her mind as she walked. Harry had insisted that she talk to Brother Gabriel about the break-ins. Isobel regretted having set that particular hare running. She had no doubt that it would all turn out to be a series of pranks by some disaffected youth she'd told off at some time or other. It was only loyalty to Harry that was making her go through with it. Poor old Harry. He must be quite worried. A man had been at the crack of dawn to change the locks on Isobel's door. And Harry had said enough to make Gabriel drop whatever it was that Franciscans did and agree to come that very day.

He wasn't waiting at the church. But, to be fair, she was a little early. She'd walked too fast and was now sweating. The air inside the church was cool on her cheeks. She flapped the back of her shirt. The minutes ticked by. He was hitching down from the Friary in Northumberland, so who knew when he'd get here? Why didn't he catch a train, for goodness' sake? Vows of poverty were all very well in their way. She was starting to chafe at the thought of the time she would waste waiting for him when she heard the church door creaking open. Huh. Here he was, diddling her out of her anticipated anger. He paused and was momentarily framed by the sunlit doorway, then he came down the aisle towards her. His was a slight figure, but the dark robes lent him a dramatic appearance.

'Isobel.' They shook hands.

'Did you have a straightforward journey?' she asked.

'Not bad. There are usually enough lapsed Catholics driving past to mean I'm never waiting long.'

'Good.' There was a silence. Isobel wasn't sure how to proceed. Show him the scene of the crime, perhaps?

Without warning he asked, 'Mind if I strip off?'

She raised an eyebrow. 'It depends how far.'

He laughed and tunnelled his way out of his brown habit. Underneath he was wearing a T-shirt and shorts and looked small and insignificant, with his damp red hair and sandals, like an Englishman abroad. At least he wasn't wearing socks.

'I'll show you the vestry,' she said.

He followed her and stood for a while, looking round with much the same expression as the policeman had worn the previous night.

'Tell me what happened,' he said. She explained. 'Hmm,' he said, frowning thoughtfully. Spiritual sleuthing didn't seem far removed from the earthly kind. Isobel suppressed a snort. 'And did you sense some kind of presence?'

'No. Wait, yes.'

'Something evil?'

'No. Just . . . How odd. It felt like a child. Like a child wanting to be noticed.'

He waited.

'That's all,' she said.

He still waited.

'I'm sorry,' she said. 'I can't think of anything else.'

When he continued to remain silent, she started to get cross. Two can play at that, she thought, folding her arms. But by then he seemed to have moved on. He was frowning again.

'Poltergeist activity is normally associated with the presence of troubled adolescents,' he remarked.

'So you think that's what it is?' she asked.

He shrugged. 'Could be.'

'Well,' she gave a little laugh, 'plenty of troubled adolescents round here.'

'If I were to describe someone, could you say if you recognize her?'

*Her.* Oh, it would be, of course. 'I'll try.'

'OK. Tall. Slim.'

'Could be several people.'

'Blonde hair. Very long.'

'Hmm. Two blondes, both with shoulder-length hair.'

He was biting his lip in concentration. Perhaps the crystal ball was in need of a quick polish. 'Definitely long hair.'

'Nobody I know.' She heard the satisfaction in her voice and added, 'I'm afraid.'

'Funny,' he said. 'Tall, thin, but with, er, huge knockers.'

Isobel felt her cheeks burn. 'I find that extremely offensive.'

He ducked his head. 'Large breasts,' he amended. 'Long blonde hair.'

'Well, apart from the fact that you seem to be describing *me* as a teenager,' she burst out angrily.

His eyes skimmed over her chest. 'But −'

'I had corrective surgery, if you must know.' Well, *that* seemed to have caught him on the hop! She glared as he took a few agitated steps around the vestry, biting his lip and plucking at his shorts, as though his hands were seeking for his friarly rope to fiddle with.

'Look, I'm sorry −' he began.

'Well, I'm not! Forgive me, but you have *no* idea what it was like, all those years! Being treated like a dumb blonde. Every man I passed in the street thought he had the right to gawp or grope or make some comment. Honestly! People are so judgemental! If I'd been born with sticking-out ears and had them pinned back nobody would think anything of it.'

'Isobel −'

But she wasn't listening. Her mind made another furious leap ahead. 'I suppose you think that's what all this is about!' Her hand swept around the room. 'I'm meant to be in *denial*, I suppose. I mutilate the body God gave me, and hey presto! we have poltergeist activity. Well, quite frankly, I find that ridiculous. As far as I'm concerned, it's probably just some silly lad from the Youth Group having a joke.'

He waited. She was breathing hard. 'Did I say any of that?' he asked at length.

In the silence that followed she kicked herself for defending what hadn't been attacked. She'd been protesting too much. Now he'd think there was something in it.

'I'm sorry if I sounded rude,' she said. 'I'm a bit tense. I didn't sleep well last night.' But this was verging on the kind of helpless-female act she despised and she clamped her mouth shut.

Gabriel was staring sadly down at his sandals. His feet looked vulnerable, thin knobbly toes and little tufts of gingery hair. She softened towards him. Pick on someone your own size, Isobel. That was the problem. She could make mincemeat of most men she knew.

'Well,' he said, gathering his thoughts, 'let's have a look round.'

Isobel was on surer ground here and fell into her church-guide patter. They paused by the anchorite's cell. Gabriel flipped through the little pamphlet about Agnes that Isobel had researched and had printed.

'Why did she leave her cell?' he asked.

'Nobody knows,' replied Isobel. 'I should think it drove her mad being cooped up.'

'That's a twentieth-century view,' he said. 'The cell means freedom. Freedom from domesticity and the dangers of childbirth. Freedom to devote your whole being to God.'

'You don't have to be bricked up to do that. Cutting yourself off from the world can't be healthy. I mean . . .' She floundered, remembering she was talking to a monk.

He smiled. 'I think she encountered the whole of heaven and earth in here. Maybe hell too. This is where the cosmic battles are fought, here, where there's nowhere to hide. Just you and your Maker. Maybe that's why she ran away.'

'It's a thought.' And a good one. A pity she hadn't heard his opinion before the pamphlet had gone to press. 'Most people assume she found a man.'

He made a scornful noise. 'Anyway, she came back. That's what matters, isn't it?'

'Hah! The Bishop had her locked up again and guarded.'

'Well, she's at peace now,' asserted Gabriel.

His certainty affronted her. *She* was the Agnes expert. 'Oh, really? People see her charging about the graveyard, you know.'

'Place memory,' he replied. 'Different phenomenon.'

'How do you mean?'

'Well,' he paused in the face of such evident hostility, 'the theory goes a bit like this. Events from history seem to be stored in a specific location and replay themselves, rather like a patchy video recording. Sometimes it's ancient crises triggered by traumas in the present. A bereavement in a house that turns out to be built on a plague pit, or something. Harmless,' he smiled, 'but completely terrifying.'

She stared at him with her father's bullish Yorkshire scepticism. This was precisely the kind of mumbo-jumbo her mother had started to find so compelling.

'Anyway,' he said, looking round him again, 'what we have *here* is different.'

'Look,' she began aggressively, 'is there something I ought to know? Do you honestly think all this has got something to do with me?'

'It looks like it. Taking last night into account.'

Suddenly she felt contaminated, as if he were accusing her of harbouring lice or cockroaches. 'I totally disagree.'

'Isobel, I think there are things you've lost and never grieved over.'

'I assure you there are not.' What was she supposed to do, for heaven's sake – have a memorial service for her missing mammaries? She'd be more likely to dance on their grave. 'Oh, this *denial* nonsense! It's non-falsifiable. If you're suppressing things then by definition you can't know you're doing it.'

'Unless you read the signs.'

'Much better just to knuckle down and get on with life, don't you think?' She smiled politely but firmly, like someone trying to shut the door on a persistent salesman.

'Is it your birthday today?' he asked unexpectedly.

'No.' This time she didn't bother to keep the satisfaction out of her voice.

'Whose birthday is it?' he wondered out loud. 'Someone significant.'

Isobel shrugged. 'Well, thank you for coming.'

He took the hint and picked up his habit with a slightly downcast air. She saw him to the church door.

'Are you having lunch with Harry?' she inquired, feeling cordial now she was getting rid of him.

'Yes.' She saw him open his lips to utter one last mystic gem, then think better of it. 'Well, I'm here if you decide you need me.'

Need you! 'Goodbye.' *And take a running jump!* she told his retreating back.

He wheeled round as if he'd heard her.

For a second she felt like a motorist who has fatally misjudged a corner, but then he smiled and turned away, dwindling once more into an insignificant little man in shorts and rather naff sandals as he made his way down the path.

Isobel returned to the church, sank into a pew and attempted to laugh. I dare say my expression was unmistakable. You wouldn't need to be a mind-reader to tell what I was thinking. But his description of her seventeen-year-old self had been unnerving, to say the least. Especially that dreadful word 'knockers'. Clearly not part of his normal vocabulary. Why had he used it?

She cursed herself for flying off the handle at him like that. It was just that the decision to have surgery had been so fraught. For years her parents had urged her to accept herself as she was, to love the body nature had given her.

'You're not *that* big, for God's sake!' Mrs Knox had stoutly maintained. 'A lot of women pay good money for implants to get a bust like that.'

'Well, I hate them,' Isobel had cried. 'You can get them reduced on the NHS. I've read about it.'

'If when you're grown-up you decide you want an operation, then that's up to you,' her father had said. 'But I think you'll feel differently when you're older. All girls go through a self-conscious phase. It's normal. If it's not about their breasts, it's about their nose, or something else. Don't be hasty.' Her fellow Christians at university had been equally censorious when she'd confided in them. There had been a time when she'd feared her new faith was condemning her to a self-acceptance she'd resisted for years. Perhaps her reaction today revealed that her conscience was still not entirely easy on the subject. Well, what's done is done, she shrugged.

Over the years she had marshalled her arguments – the ones she'd just spat at Gabriel – and saved up her money obsessively. Her parents had visited her at the private clinic after the operation and brought flowers. 'It's your decision,' they had said. 'You know your own mind.'

Oh, but she was so much happier than she'd been a decade ago! Surely they could see that? Ludicrous to think that this was something she'd lost and never grieved for. But there might be other things, of course. Such as? There was an answering hollowness in her, as though she'd knocked on the sliding panel that disguised a hidden room. What have I lost? She sat for some time waiting humbly, but when nothing presented itself, her characteristic impatience surged up again and she strode out of the church. She headed for home, telling herself she had enough to do without grubbing around in her subconscious for guilty secrets.

And, anyway, who was to say that denial wasn't a preferable state? If she was happy as she was, why muddy the water? She'd met plenty of people who paid good money to be locked in years of therapy-induced misery. Let's hear it for denial, she thought.

She turned the corner to her road and felt her heart bump. What if her books had been scattered again? She felt a sudden passionate wish that she didn't live alone, that there would always be someone waiting at home to welcome her back. This was silly and feeble. At least she had a nice house to go to, she chided herself, wrestling with the key in her door. Whatever's wrong with the stupid thing? Why wouldn't it turn? Then she remembered. The lock had been changed. She peered into her study and could actually see the new keys on her desk where she'd left them. She rattled the window in frustration, but it was firmly shut, as the policeman had advised. Damn and *blast*! I'll have to get the spare set from Harry. She stomped off towards the vicarage. Gabriel would be there and would no doubt construe her forgetfulness as further evidence of her parlous spiritual state. Well, so be it. What was he? A quack who'd made a couple of lucky guesses. Whose birthday was it, indeed. That one had been wide of the mark. 'Someone significant'! This was how horoscopes worked – vague statements that the reader clothed with meaning.

Then her hand flew to her throat. No! She composed herself again almost at once, glancing round to see if anyone had seen. The street was empty. It was 18 July. Alex was forty today.

## CHAPTER 7

Isobel had always known where babies came from. Her mother had never fobbed her off with storks and gooseberry bushes. The man put his penis into a special hole between the lady's legs (the vagina) and passed a little seed (sperm) into her, which met up with a tiny egg (ovum). The two grew into a baby, which was born nine months later. What was the big fuss about? Admittedly, parts of it were a little implausible. The willy, for instance, didn't strike Isobel as a likely candidate for posting into a small hole, but she supposed you could kind of tuck and squash it in, a bit like the way you squished Play-doh back into its tub, or something.

The smutty sniggering at primary school baffled Isobel. It was a while before the penny dropped that the IT in question was the same penis–vagina–seed–egg–baby process her mother had described. There was clearly more to it, or everyone wouldn't go on about it the whole time, would they? Candour was encouraged in the Knox household, but Isobel suddenly experienced squirms of awkwardness on the subject. Anyway, her brothers might overhear if she asked a question and mock her.

Tatiana was a useful informant, though inclined to gloat over Isobel's ignorance. She, too, had been spun the seed–egg line by her mother. Mrs George seemed to have been more lavish with the details, though, for Tatiana was able to supply the interesting fact that a man's seeds were lined up on the underside of his willy just beneath the skin and could be felt as little separate bumps, a bit like peas in an unripe pod. Three bumps meant three children, two bumps two children, and so on. Tatiana's dad had four bumps, but the fourth was broken, so her parents weren't going to do IT again, in case the baby was born handicapped, and Isobel had better not say anything to anyone or Tatiana would kill her.

There were two other things Isobel burned to know. Asking Tatiana was the last resort, but in the end (when the dictionary failed to offer any clues), she was prepared to risk being crowed over: 'You're such a baby! Everyone knows *that*!' She sidled up to asking what a rubber johnny was. She'd already worked out from the context that it was something dirty and unpleasant to do with not having babies (possibly related to abortion) and that 'used' (*used?!*) ones could sometimes be spotted in the gutter. Her angling went as follows: 'I know what they're *for*, but I'm not *quite* sure what they look like ...' Tatiana's eyes popped wide in astonishment. 'I mean, what shape are they?'

'Well, they wouldn't exactly be *triangular*, would they?'

So Isobel cast her eyes down again for illumination, scanning the gutters and ruling out anything with three sides.

The other big one was masturbation. The dictionary was scarcely more helpful here: *Self-abuse.* Isobel racked her brains, then looked up *abuse. Mistreat, make bad use of.* But how could you mistreat yourself? Beat yourself? Injure yourself somehow? That couldn't be right. Isobel could remember seeing once at Girls' Brigade camp in Margate a message sprayed up in massive letters on the sea wall: 'Masturbation helps relaxation.' She'd hoped and prayed that some-one would spot it and ask Captain what it meant, but no one had. Isobel was forced to carry on building sandcastles with those words searing down at her.

Masturbation helps relaxation. How? How? How? Oh, it was impossible to puzzle out. The dictionary was part of an adult plot to keep her in darkness and misery.

Well, so what? She didn't care. She didn't *want* to know, anyway. And she didn't want to grow up, either, *ever*. She didn't want to grow breasts and have periods (menstruation) even if they were so wonderful and meant that you were now a WOMAN. Because who wanted to be a woman? Women ran in this stupid way as if their knees were tied together. They never played games or climbed trees. All they did was sit around and talk to each other, and speak in French and say things like 'you-know-what', or 'ahem!', so that you wouldn't understand – as if you'd ever want to. And if you needed something they said, 'In a minute, dear,' and when you waited a minute and asked again, they'd snap, 'I said *in a minute*! Darling, nobody likes a whiny little girl. Why don't you go and play?'

That's what Mum always said. And if she wasn't talking to her stupid friends about ahem ahem, she was always reading. You'd say something quite reasonable like, 'Mum, can I have another sausage? Mum? Mum! MU-U-UM!' You'd have to repeat it twenty times while she ignored you, then all of a sudden, without warning, she'd explode.

'WHAT? All *right*! You don't have to go on and on, for God's sake!' Slap goes the sausage on the plate and back goes Mum to her book, muttering, 'Honestly!'

Nope. Isobel certainly had no intention of becoming a woman, thank you very much!

Isobel collected her spare keys from Harry. It was obvious from his face that he and Gabriel had been discussing her. Well, of course he had. What did she expect? But she was so offended by the thought that she had to take a brisk walk by the river to sort herself out.

Asleby was fortunate in its park. It had once been the gardens of the local manor. The house had been made over to the public and was now a museum. The grounds, consisting of fields and woodlands stretching along a length of the Tees, belonged these days to the local people, who walked their dogs and children there, played football, or practised their tee-shots. Improvements and developments of various kinds were always under way, and the locals always had a great deal to say about the projects. Opinion was divided about the vast aviary that had been erected over one of the oak trees. It was full of blurs of exotic colour and shrieks and squawks from dozens of parakeets and lovebirds. They had stripped the tree of all its foliage and it now stood drab and skeletal in its wire dome as the birds flashed back and forth. She walked a little further and watched the peafowl in another pen. A cock was displaying, arching his glorious fanned tail over some peahens. He rattled his feathers ferociously at them while they ignored him and got on with the business of eating. He postured and circled them. If only you knew how ridiculous you look from behind, my friend, thought Isobel, as she surveyed his urgent quivering quills and dowdy rump.

Then she turned and marched away from him towards the river, kicking at the molehills in the field as she went. Her brother Christopher had once found a tiny blue glass bottle this way in the soft earth. Isobel had been kicking molehills over ever since, without finding anything.

She reached the bank. It was low tide and the river edge stank. She peered down and saw the prints of birds' feet in the drying mud. The sky was grey and the wind blew in hot, impatient gusts, flipping the leaves on the willows and exposing their silvery backs. On the opposite bank sheep grazed in a field. The landscape stretched away past the factories to the distant hills and the unmistakable hooked-claw outline of Roseberry Topping. Ridiculous name, thought Isobel, who felt the old Norse name of Odinsberg should be revived. 'Roseberry Topping' sounded like something cheap and nasty you poured over your pudding.

She sighed crossly, already impatient to go. Her sermon wasn't as far on as she would have liked. Perhaps this was one of the things she'd lost – the ability simply to stand and enjoy the landscape.

> What is this life if, full of care,
> We have no time to stand and stare?

Isobel had learnt the whole of this poem at the age of nine for a school Harvest Festival.

> No time to stand beneath the boughs
> And stare as long as sheep or cows.

Would one want to, come to think of it? There was something particularly imbecilic about the stare of a sheep. But as a child she had loved the words. Well, Gabriel, I suppose I've lost my childhood, she thought, although this was a bland observation, for which adult hadn't? And was that a bad thing? She had met a twit on post-ordination training (revoltingly referred to as 'potty training' by some) who had wittered on about finding his 'inner child'. A swift glance round the room had convinced Isobel that most of the men present would have been better occupied in attempting to discover their inner adult. And yet there were our Lord's words about becoming like little children, of course.

> *What is this life if, full of care,*
> *We have no time to stand and swear?*

That had been Tatiana's amendment. In fact, hadn't they once gone up to the top of the Ivinghoe Beacon and stood and shouted out all the swear words they knew? Then Tatiana had honed the list into rapturous chant: BUGGER-bugger-BELLY-bum-TIT-sod-ARSE! They'd galumphed and stomped around to its glorious rhythm until someone had walked past and heard them. They had spent the next few days in terror of the hiker contacting their school to report them. The chant survived in abbreviated form, *B*-B-*B*-B-T-S-*A*!, which was satisfying in a different way, because no one knew what they were on about.

Well, Tatiana was something else she'd lost. Lost touch, that's what they'd done. Isobel feared this had been her fault. It was sad, really, that she'd never found another relationship to match that one, which had lasted two brief years when they were only kids. Of course, she had Victoria and Annabel from grammar-school days. The three of them had gone on holiday to France only a couple of summers ago. She had plenty of friends from college days and she was good at keeping up with them all – better than some of them deserved, the lazy so-and-sos! A week didn't go by without her phoning one or remembering another's birthday. But somehow an element of duty had crept into these friendships. If she stopped making an effort, would they survive? Would Thelma bother to get in touch? Would Victoria and Annabel do more than scribble a note in a Christmas card? Perhaps she was idealizing her love for Tatiana. Yet their relationship had been special – obsessive, intense, full of smut and hilarity, secrets, dens, codes and magic, and then it had ended. The letters had dwindled away. *Why did I let that happen?* she asked herself. *If it meant so much, why did I let it slip away?* And was this what made her so vigilant about her friends today, the fear of losing them?

But perhaps the truth was that these young schoolgirl friendships always ended: The exclusiveness would be interrupted at some stage by other friendships, by boyfriends and eventually, possibly, by marriage. Maybe little girls were testing out on one another the idea that there might be someone who could be their all-in-all? Well, if that was true, then the experiment had been a failure in Isobel's case. She hadn't had a proper relationship with a man in her adult life. That was to say – Well, anyway, she wasn't married. Which was just as well, given her apparent penchant for unsuitable men. Bastards – she believed that was the technical term. There was Alex, a world-class bastard with brass knobs on, on whom she had wasted five years of her life. More recently there had been Will, probably only a small-time bastard in comparison – she'd devoted months to pursuing him. Not that he would have noticed, being too busy seducing and impregnating her fellow ordinand. It had made some kind of sense when she discovered the two men were cousins, as if there was a recurring pattern in her life. A pity she couldn't fall for someone nice for once. Oh, it was a relief to be out of all that!

This mental exclamation made Isobel frown. She disliked any suggestion that celibacy was a kind of escape or consolation prize. Her single state allowed her to devote herself to serving God and others in a way that was not open to those with family ties. Christ was her all-in-all, and how could that be second-best? Sexuality wasn't really a problem. She was quite good, these days, at channelling her energies. It was just that silly dream and Gabriel's prying questions that were throwing her off-course. She would do as the Scriptures commanded: she would lay aside every weight and run with perseverance the race that was set before her, looking to Jesus, the pioneer and perfecter of her faith. She was proud to be celibate, proud to be a priest.

Her heart felt lighter now. She began to wander along the riverbank. A black water bird flew by – cormorant? Yes, too far inland for a shag. Her gaze followed its path until it landed on an old stump to dry its feathers. Alex's birthday. She shook her head, wondering how Gabriel had hit upon that. Well, she had no theological reason to rule out the possibility that telepathy existed. She wondered what her father would make of it. He doggedly believed that there was always a rational explanation for things, even if we were as yet unable to grasp it. No doubt he'd dismiss claims of telepathy as 99 per cent bogus, and the other 1 per cent – maybe it was some primitive function of the brainstem or whatever, akin to birds migrating or salmon returning to the river where they'd been spawned.

It was ironic that it should have been his rational approach to life that led her to accept the claims of Christianity. At university she had been taken by a friend to a Christian Union meeting where she heard the Gospel presented with a clarity that challenged her inherited agnosticism. She went away and thought and read until it seemed to her that, logically, this must be the truth. If it was the truth then she must devote herself to it. The question 'What's in it for me?' would have struck her as scurrilous. Explaining her new faith to her father was one of the hardest things she'd ever done. She didn't flinch from this duty, and he respected that. But she knew he didn't relish the sight of his child embracing the religion he had rejected. Time would demonstrate the distance between her beliefs and Grandpa's narrow-minded chapel Christianity. Mr Knox never opposed her, but carrying on in the face of his unspoken disapproval was one of the great costs of discipleship. She'd been grateful to Alex for a throwaway remark to the effect that Christianity had its own internal logic once you got into its thought system.

Alex's birthday. She shook her head again. And how did Dr Jacks like being forty? she wondered, with a smirk. The last time she'd seen him he'd promised to kill himself on his fortieth birthday.

'If you haven't already done so,' Isobel had remarked. It was her last night in Oxford. They were in his rooms after a formal dinner. He was disgustingly drunk, fast losing his mysterious charm.

'I don't know why you do it,' she said crossly, as he embarked on another bottle of champagne.

'B-b-bec-bec –' He struck the side of his head angrily, as if trying to dislodge the jammed word. 'Because I'm bored. I'm so fucking *bored*. Bored of this city. Bored of this boring provincial fucking backwater of a fucking planet.'

She couldn't tell if she was meant to laugh at this self-dramatizing hubris.

'Th-th-there's, there's not enough here for me.'

'You need God, then, don't you?'

'You think I don't *know* that?' he spat out. 'There's nothing else, nothing else big enough to fill this raging emptiness, nothing to satisfy my lusts.'

'Yes, yes, I dare say,' she said dampeningly. 'You'll get over it.'

He wasn't listening. 'But there's no God,' he raged. 'You hear me? There's no God! The roof's off the house. We're all orphans. W-w-w-why are you going into the Church, for Christ's sake? You're three hundred years too late.'

'That's your opinion.'

'You'll never make a good priest. You've got the soul of a librarian. I mean, fuck, I'd make a better priest than you and look at me. I'll prove it to you. Watch this. Watch. Watch me.' He crossed the room unsteadily, unhooked a portrait of Calvin from the wall and laid it flat on the desk. 'Time for the John Calvin fun hour.'

'What are you doing?' Then she heard the tiny clatter of a razor blade on glass and saw the white powder.

'This isn't clever, Alex,' she said in alarm.

He laughed, chopping away, making lines. 'Shocked?'

'No. Disappointed. I would have thought –'

He cut her off. 'What about this?' He picked up a philosophical journal, fumbled through and began to read her a section. She strove to grasp the elliptical prose. The scene was taking on a bizarre, nightmarish feel.

'I'm really not interested, Alex.'

'Shocked?' he asked again. She hesitated. 'Well, you should be. The guy's a wanker. Epistemologically th-th-this thing sucks. Yes? Yet trees have died for it. So let's put the bugger to better use.' With that he picked up the razor blade and sliced out a page.

'No!' cried Isobel involuntarily.

He laughed. 'The soul of a librarian.' She winced as he sliced out page after page then selected one and rolled it up.

'I'm not staying to watch this.'

'Yes, you are.'

She stalked to the door, but it was locked. She stood with her hand on the knob, suddenly afraid. Surely one wasn't supposed to mix drink and drugs. Supposing he wanted sex? What if he turned violent? Her mind began racing. Best to seem unconcerned. She glanced back and saw him running his finger round his gums.

'If you've *quite* finished,' she said, in a headmistressy voice, 'perhaps you'd kindly unlock this door.'

He only laughed at her, a mad demonic cackle, as he stripped off his tail coat and bow-tie.

'Alex, I – I really must go now. It's late,' she quavered. He was unbuttoning his shirt and tugging the ribbon from his hair till the curls sprang out wildly. 'Alex, I want to go.'

She rattled the door handle in vain. He watched her with a wide-eyed lunatic stare, then threw back his head and laughed like a madman once more before crossing to his piano. Isobel was no Chopin buff, but it was the fastest she'd ever heard that nocturne played.

In the end he let her go, terrified but untouched. Thank God, thank God, she kept whimpering to herself, as they crossed the quad and stood in the porter's lodge. She was trembling.

'Evening, Dr Jacks,' said the porter, unfazed by the spectacle of a drugged and barefooted theologian with his shirt flapping open.

This is it, she thought. Five years, over.

'Well, goodbye, Alex.' She pecked him affectionately on the cheek. That was how she'd planned it. But before she could stop him, he seized her face in his hands and kissed her like a lover, parting her lips and sucking her tongue slickly into his mouth like some gourmand with an oyster. At the time it left her cold, not to say squeamish, but afterwards the memory made her guts churn with lust.

He released her. 'Go in peace to love and serve the Lord.' She bit back the response angrily. He raised a hand and sketched a sardonic cross.

She climbed into the taxi. When she glanced through the window he was already walking away. She watched in case he looked back, but she knew he would have let her fall from his mind by now. The taxi gathered speed and she slumped back, shutting her eyes. She could still taste the bitter coffee tang of his mouth.

In the distance on the opposite bank the cormorant furled then spread its wings again under the dull sun.

One kiss. Not much to keep you warm on a winter night, was it? She wanted to laugh, but instead she thought, I'm unhappy. I'm so unhappy. What I need is company. Now was impractical, obviously. It was a working day. But tonight I'll go round and see Jan, she promised herself. Or Natalie and Drew. And, dammit, she might as well ring Edward and take up his invitation. In another couple of weeks she could be on holiday in France ...

She turned and retraced her steps back up the field.

# CHAPTER 8

'I ent go' none.' 'I never done nuffink.' ''E go' i' off of 'is nan.' If the teacher heard you talking like this you got told off. There was nothing like a glottal stop or a double negative for bringing Mrs Peck down on you like a ton of bricks. You were supposed to say, 'I *H*aven'T goT any,' and 'I didn'T do anyTHing,' and '*H*is grandma gave iT to *H*im.' This was easy for Isobel, whose mother had brought her up to speak properly. There was nothing wrong with accents as such, went Mrs Knox's theory, but it was important that children should learn proper grammar and pronunciation, or they'd find themselves incapable of speaking and writing correctly when they needed to.

Isobel never learnt to be bilingual like her brothers who, the moment they were out of parental earshot, dropped their Ts and Hs with the worst of them. The other children mocked Isobel for talking posh, so Isobel made a virtue of it. If she was posh, *they* were common. So what if she was different? It was because she was better, so ha ha ha. In school assembly her vowels and consonants carried clearly above the mumbled Ar Farver. Like her unimpeachable honesty, her grammar and pronunciation won her a grudging respect, but few friends.

Yes, by the standards of the scruffy Buckinghamshire village where she grew up, Isobel was indeed posh. Her parents stood out as university-educated professionals. So did Tatiana's. Most of the other fathers were employed, in one way or another, at the local cement works. The factory dominated the countryside, snowing white dust from its five chimneys and keeping the village locked, Narnia-like, in a permanent *faux*-winter – white trees, white roofs, white hedges. Once in a while red dust blew from somewhere in the works and the next time it rained the drops trickled like blood down everyone's windows.

'I grew up in Buckinghamshire,' Isobel would say. It sounded posh. It conjured up leafy Chiltern villages with Jaguars parked round the village pond, not white flinty fields scarred by industry. Isobel's side of the Chilterns had been uncouth for generations. 'Tring, Wing and Ivinghoe, three dirty villages all in a row,' ran the old rhyme. 'If you'd know the reason why, Leighton Buzzard is hard by.' If the wind was in the wrong direction the stench of the Bedfordshire brick factories was foul. The nights of Isobel's childhood were filled with strange groans and clashings from the cement works. No wonder Teesside felt like home.

'I come from the Home Counties,' Isobel told people.

'Oh, lah-di-dah,' mimicked the village children.

When she was eleven the Knoxes moved to a nicer village on the right side of the Chilterns, away from the pollution, to a wonderful, wonderful old house, so much character, doing it up would be such an adventure! Isobel sat in her sleeping-bag huddled by the stove trying to do her homework. She wondered what was so adventurous about freezing to death or having mice behind the panelling and water coming through the bedroom ceiling and never being able to invite anyone home for tea because it was all so embarrassing.

But at least grammar school had been an improvement. There were other daughters of professionals there. She made friends with Victoria and Annabel in the first week and they stayed friends. Phew, someone *else* whose parents didn't have a telly! The three of them stuck together and the dreaded sneer of lah-di-dah didn't seem quite so awful when you weren't the only one.

Durham University came as a shock. Isobel was expecting to fit in somewhere at last, but to her dismay she was confronted by the unsuspected existence of several social strata lying between her and the aristocracy. The streets and corridors echoed to the sound of loud public-school voices. Never before had she encountered people who wore dinner jackets seriously and not because they were doing front-of-house at the local pantomime. She was demoted overnight from posh to second-generation middle-class *grammar-school girl*. The experience brought out her competitive streak. Without ever quite admitting to herself what she was doing, Isobel infiltrated the guernseyed ranks, mingled with them until she began to acquire their clipped tones and taste for Scottish country dancing. By the time she graduated she was wearing Liberty-print Alice bands, and those who didn't know better assumed she'd been to Roedean.

The afternoon dragged. It was the last day of the school term and Isobel's confirmation class was more than usually bovine. She could sense that she was failing to fire their imaginations on the subject of daily personal Bible study. Wiser in retrospect to have given them a week off, but she made the best of it. She almost wished Fitz was there to liven things up. Eventually it was over and they trailed sullenly out. Isobel raised the bottom half of her sash window to let out the smell of bubble gum and adolescent sweat.

She checked who had rung and left a message while she'd had the volume turned down. It was Thelma, miracle of miracles. She'd got tickets to some production of *Uncle Vanya*, which was being mounted in her local village hall, and would Isobel like to come along? Thelma had been helping in an advisory capacity, having recently started Russian evening classes. No, Isobel would *not* like to come along, but Isobel would grit her teeth and accept anyway. She put off returning the call till she could muster a more enthusiastic tone, though. After this was a message from Jenny, the Methodist minister, wondering whether Isobel would like to address the women's meeting and, hey, what about meeting up for a drink sometime? Shame they were both always so busy.

She got into her car and nipped round to see Sue and baby Hannah. It was time to talk baptism dates. Isobel was happily installed on the sofa with the baby lying on her lap gazing up at her while Sue made some tea.

'Feet, feet, wonderful feet!' chanted Isobel, clapping Hannah's booties together. Hannah gurgled. 'How I love my great big *feet!*' Oh, they were so adorable at this age, those dimples. Oh, I'm going to keep you! I'm going to run off with you and keep you!

'You're so good with her,' said Sue, planting the tea at a safe distance on the coffee table.

'I should think I am!' said Isobel to Hannah. 'I should jolly well think I am! I've not been an auntie all these years for nothing, have I?' But they were here to do business. 'So, what dates do you have in mind? Harry's away in August, so what about the first Sunday in September?'

'That's fine. We'd love *you* to do the baptism, actually.'

'Oh! I'd be delighted!'

'After all, she knows you,' said Sue. 'Harry won't mind, will he?'

'I'm sure he won't.' She beamed down at the smiling child. 'Shall we be kind and heat the water in the font for you? Eh? Shall we?'

'Um, there's something else I wanted to talk about,' blurted Sue.

Hearing the serious tone, Isobel reluctantly handed Hannah back in order to be able to concentrate on more adult conversation. It turned out that Mike's job was under threat; and if he was made redundant it was possible that Sue would have to return to work to keep paying the mortgage. Isobel expressed pity, promised to pray about it, and offered one or two sensible pieces of advice about crossing bridges when one came to them.

'I know,' said Sue. 'It's just that things feel so different once you've got a baby.'

Normally Isobel found this one of the most irritating sentiments parents expressed, but today she nodded sympathetically. It was such a shame for them that after years of longing for a child their lives should be burdened by financial worries and job insecurity.

When she got back it was five-thirty, a tricky time of day for a curate. If she decided to do more visiting, half the parish would be in eating tea, according to the local working-class custom. They wouldn't want to be disturbed, but sometimes it was a good way of catching people. The white-collar workers – ICI high-flyers and so forth – would scarcely be driving home yet. Still, one could always find a number of irksome tasks waiting to be done. There was the parachute for the Youth Group games evening that had to be collected from the curate in Middlesbrough. And somebody needed to pick up another roll of newsprint from the *Gazette* for those brainstorming sessions deemed vital to church life. *Brainstorming!* snorted Isobel. And its twin *buzz groups*. They plagued her wherever she went. The words 'I'd like you, now, to turn, if you would, to the person sitting next to you ...' never failed to provoke an upsurge of violent irritation in her. Each time, she suppressed it and turned with a gentle smile to her neighbour to set a good example. Asking whether these activities were effective educative tools felt as disloyal as questioning the authority of Scripture.

Harry knew how she felt, and at meetings and conferences when they were asked to divide up into small groups, he'd catch her eye and give a fey little flounce from the other side of the room. When leading such sessions himself he always said, 'And now I'd like you to split up into small groups – Oh, no! Not small groups! Yes, yes, small groups.'

Oh, Harry. She found herself smiling, as she often did when she thought about him. Perhaps his levity was a good corrective for her – what was the word, exactly? – seriousness? Her prim, disapproving seriousness. *You have the soul of a librarian.* Funny how Alex's words still hurt so many years on. He knew how to wound, that man. However, he was wrong. She *was* a good priest. Harry had said as much. He thanked her for her loyalty and hard work, commenting that vicars were not always so fortunate in their curates. This was as close as he would ever come to confiding that her predecessor, Andy Davenport, had been a bit of a layabout, however diligent his wife had been in her gardening.

An hour later Isobel pulled up outside her house again, having accomplished half a dozen insignificant chores that could equally well have been done by someone else, were it not for the inconvenience of organizing someone else to do them. It was the syndrome that ensured the clergy were always the ones to put the chairs away after meetings. She wrestled the heavy roll of paper out of the boot and staggered with it up her path. Damn. She'd left her window open all the time. Again she experienced a little spurt of fear that mayhem would greet her in the study, but everything was as she'd left it.

She dumped the paper in a corner and sat down at once to her sermon. The answerphone was winking again. She dealt with the messages and paused for a moment to still herself with a quick prayer. It was a sticky evening with the threat of thunder in the air. I'll shower and change before I go round to Jan's, she promised herself. The sermon was being stubborn. 'Oh, come on,' she muttered. 'You must have something worthwhile to say about the fruit of the Spirit. Love, joy, peace,' she murmured. The cursor blinked, impatient as a tapping foot. Then she shoved away her *Alternative Service Book*. The passage was quoted there in the Jerusalem Bible – not her favourite version. She reached for her own Bible and turned to Galatians. 'For the desires of the flesh are against the Spirit, and the desires of the Spirit are against the flesh; for these are opposed to each other, to prevent you from doing what you would.'

Occasionally it worried her that she seldom experienced the flesh/spirit struggle particularly acutely. She ran her eye down the colourful list of fleshly excesses – fornication, impurity, drunkenness, carousing – when did she ever wrestle with these? In her heart of hearts she had little sympathy for those who slipped up in this way. Time and again she was astonished that men (yes, it was usually *men* in the non-generic sense) of the cloth fell into blatant sexual sins. Surely adultery was such an obvious pitfall that they could steer themselves round it. 'Huge deep dangerous hole in road,' the signs all said. 'Please drive carefully.' But did they? They did not. She tried to respond compassionately, but deep down she wondered what was wrong with a bit of old-fashioned self-denial.

There were, however, other sins on the list – jealousy and self-ishness, to name but two – and she decided to focus her sermon here. Was not our Lord himself harsher in his condemnation of hypocrisy than of adultery? She settled down and began to type.

At a quarter to eight she was in the shower arguing with her-self. Part of her was feeling guilty about accepting Jan's invitation and taking the evening off when her sermon wasn't finished. Another part was accusing her of being a workaholic. Work two sessions in a day, take a session off. That's what they'd been taught at theological college. Oh, ha ha. How many clergy did that? She'd only managed it a handful of times in the last year. She wasn't too naughty about working on her day off because she knew Harry would check up on her. Overwork was the one thing he was stern about. In his second curacy he'd made himself ill with stress and had been forced to learn healthier patterns. Isobel knew she'd have to get round to doing the same one day, but at present she was too busy. It was like juggling Crown Derby teacups: once you'd started there was no way of stopping without a breakage of some sort.

The evening was grey and clammy. She dusted herself with her carnation talc and dressed hurriedly, pulling on a new summer dress. Her reflection took her by surprise and she dithered. Was it too girlish? She wasn't convinced of the wisdom of showing her knees. But, dammit, she had good legs. It wasn't as if she was showing her knickers, after all. Compared with what she saw waiting at bus stops on a Saturday evening this was modest. She'd missed out on miniskirts first time round. Even if she hadn't been too much of a tomboy to be cajoled out of her jeans, her mother was funny about fashion. Platform shoes ruined your pelvis. Nobody *needed* knee-length leather boots for winter. You'll thank me when you're forty and you still have nice feet. You're pretty enough without makeup, dear. Anyway, it gives you spots. Look at Karen Armitage.

It struck Isobel afresh that her mother was rather an odd mixture. All those staunch liberal credentials undermined by the most appalling bits of snobbery. Isobel was entirely free to choose her own clothes, but her mother had to admit that hotpants were silly and she was not going to buy Isobel a pair. If Isobel wanted to save up her birthday money, that was up to her, but her mother had to say that it was a bit of a waste. Why not buy a nice book? But Mum, it's not *fair*. Everyone *else* in my class has got them. Well, you don't want to look like everyone else, do you?

Isobel towelled her hair dry and was checking what happened to the back of her skirt if she bent over when the doorbell rang. For one foolish moment she lunged for her dressing-gown as if she'd been caught prancing about in a negligee. She ran downstairs running her fingers through her damp hair.

A tall shape was silhouetted against the glass. Oh, no – the policeman! She smoothed her dress and opened the door.

'Hello,' she said.

Without his uniform he was just a boy. He ran his eyes over her in gratified surprise. 'Hiya.'

He thinks this is for his benefit! Vital to squash him at once. 'Um, look, I'm afraid I'd forgotten all about your coming tonight. Sorry.' His face fell. Feeling heartless she added, in a kind voice, 'I see you've brought my paint.'

'Off out, then, are you?'

'Yes. I'm afraid so.' She held out her hand for the can, but he didn't notice.

'Anyone special?'

She withdrew her hand and said, in her frostiest tones. 'I don't think that's any of your business.'

'Have I met him?'

'Why do you assume it's a man?'

The effect of these words was satisfying. His mouth dropped open. 'Ye never are!'

She inclined her head. Her mother's voice reminded her that deliberately misleading someone was as bad as lying.

'Are you?' he persisted. 'Seriously? You're a lesbian?'

'It's really none of your business.' The advantage was slipping from her. She saw him smile. 'The paint, if you please.'

'Ah-ah.' He held the can out of reach. 'What ya ganna dee wi' it?'

There was a pause while she decoded this. 'I don't actually make a habit of spraying walls!' she snapped, flushing. He looked at her in surprise. 'Oh, you meant the *car.*'

'Why, aye. You cannot just spray ower the scratch, y'kna. You've –' He broke off. 'Now what've I done? Oh, aye. Not talking proper – *ly*,' he added. 'Anyway, you've left it too long. The rust'll just come through. I'll show you.'

To her annoyance she found herself following him up the path. Come along, Knox. Whatever's the matter with you? Assert yourself.

'See here?' He was bending over the scraped wing, tutting at her folly. 'Rust. You'll have to sand it back, prime it, then sand it again – when it's dry, mind – *then* you can spray it.'

Typical cocky working-class male! She caught herself back. Where did these shocking prejudices spring from? She made herself remark politely, 'Well, that sounds like a job for the garage. I've got to get the back done, anyway.'

'Hmm.' He surveyed the bashed-in boot and shook his head.

'It's a question of finding time to do these things.' Her tone was getting defensive.

'Ye're mad, ye. Ye did that ages ago. It's a canny car – you should take care of it.'

Isobel knew this already, and it didn't help to have him articulate it. 'Yes. Thank you.'

'Want us to do the wing for you?'

'No, no. I couldn't possibly.'

'Nee bother. I'll just get my things.'

'No, look . . .' What was his name? He was setting off. 'Listen, I'm sorry I'm just about to go out.'

'Are you driving?'

She was forced to admit she wasn't.

'There you are, then. I can do it while you're out. It'll not take long.' He was off again.

'Well, you must let me pay you,' she called after him.

'Buy us a pint sometime.' He got into his car and drove off.

I'm not quite coping with this, am I? said Isobel to herself.

Jan's house was tidy. A hint of wax polish lingered in the air. It was even possible to sit on the sofa for once without major preliminary excavations.

'What happened here?' cried Isobel. 'Are you feeling all right?'

'Bloody cheek,' said Jan. Gin chugged happily into a glass. 'I bestir myself in the cause of cleanliness once in a while.'

Derek came and twined himself round Isobel's legs.

'Watch him,' cautioned Jan. 'He's got a thing about bare flesh. He'll be following you home. Nice frock, by the way.'

'Thank you. A bit girlish?'

'You're a girl, for God's sake. Let go, once in a while.' She handed Isobel her gin and slumped down on the other end of the sofa with a mighty sigh. 'Have you been seeing your *gendarme*?'

Isobel related what had just taken place. She kept her tone matter-of-fact, but was dismayed to hear the account becoming incoherent. It included about five or six wholly inaccurate uses of the word 'obviously'.

Jan chuckled into her drink. 'It's all right, dear one.' She patted Isobel's knee. 'You don't owe me any explanations.'

Derek leapt into Isobel's lap and nestled down.

'If I die, will you look after him for me?' asked Jan. 'Come to think of it, will you look after me if he dies? You know how we old ladies get about our cats.'

'I don't think Derek likes me enough.'

'Oh, Derek's your average fickle male. He likes anyone with a can-opener.'

The cat stared at Jan in steady disapproval. Mozart's *Requiem* was playing softly. Isobel leant her head back and shut her eyes, letting the music wash over her. A little foretaste of heaven – that was how she always thought of this piece.

'Have you had a beastly day?' asked Jan, after a while. 'Harry told me about the break-in.'

Isobel nodded with her eyes closed.

'Poor old you.'

'How was your day?' asked Isobel.

'Beastly.'

'Well, you shouldn't do housework,' said Isobel. 'You know how it upsets you.'

'Actually, it's an anniversary. Hugo's death. It's always beastly, so I might as well do the annual tidy-up.'

'Oh, no.' Isobel sat up, opening her eyes. 'Jan, I'm sorry.' Hugo was her son.

'Well, well,' said Jan. 'He'd have been thirty-six this year.'

Three years older than me. The adolescent in the photograph grown into a man. With his mother's dramatic dark eyes. We would have met. Maybe tonight, even. His gaze would have skimmed over the room, taking in the gleaming polished surfaces, and he'd have laughed at his mother for tidying up on his account. For a moment the air seemed to throb with the presence of the dead son.

'Don't worry. I finished crying years ago. Here,' she passed Isobel a sheet of paper, 'I dug this out.' It was the order of service for Hugo's funeral.

Isobel began reading it with professional interest. These were the ones every minister dreaded – a seventeen-year-old cut down in a senseless accident.

' "Guide Me, O Thou Great Jehovah" ,' she read, casting Jan a malicious glance.

'Well, he was a keen rugby player.'

' "The Lord's My Shepherd",' smiled Isobel.

'Yes, yes, all right. I wasn't a churchgoer, in those days. I didn't have someone like you to save me from the obvious.'

'What happened to "Abide With Me"?' asked Isobel, turning the page.

'You do take the piss, don't you?'

'An extract from Tennyson's "In Memoriam", read by a friend of Hugo's.' Isobel's eyes scanned the lines:

> *Behold, we know not anything;*
> *I can but trust that good shall fall*
> *At last – far off – at last, to all,*
> *And every winter change to spring.*
>
> *So runs my dream: but what am I?*
> *An infant crying in the night:*
> *An infant crying for the light:*
> *And with no language but a cry.*

'Oh dear,' murmured Isobel. 'That's wonderful.' 'In Memoriam': always on the lookout for useful resources, she made a mental note.

'Not a dry eye in the house,' Jan affirmed. 'He read it perfectly, full of bitter rage. I can still hear his voice now. Beautifully self-controlled, considering how pissed he was.'

Isobel frowned at this. Pie-eyed mourners were a liturgical nightmare. At her second funeral she'd had a widow trying to hurl herself on to the coffin as it was lowered into the grave. The memory still turned her cold, although she'd coped somehow at the time. 'Are you still in touch?'

'Actually, I'm half expecting him tonight.' She looked at her watch, then sighed. 'We used to meet every year, but last year he didn't turn up.'

'You've invited him for today, though?'

'Yes.' She shrugged. 'No reply.'

Selfish pig, thought Isobel, burning inwardly for her friend. Poor old Jan, tidying and polishing, jumping every time a car passed or the phone rang. And he just leaves her to mark the day alone, without a word of explanation or apology. Surely he could have made some polite excuse. Common courtesy demanded that much. Her indignation didn't entirely mask her hurt that she'd been invited as a stop-gap in case he didn't appear again.

'Don't pity me too much, dearest. I've survived worse disappointments. He'll show up one of these years in his own sweet time.'

At that point a car slowed to a stop outside as if ironically following a cue. They waited, Jan with an amused smile on her face, Isobel with her heart pounding, absurdly – why? – as if she were on the brink of something significant that her body anticipated but her mind hadn't grasped. A car door slammed. Footsteps on the path. With a broad grin now Jan went to open the door.

'So! Only a year late. Where have you been?'

There was a laugh. Isobel froze, then a familiar voice drawled, 'Oh, "going to and fro in the earth, and walking up and down on it".'

'Well, come on in, Satan, my dear. Have a drink, meet the curate.'

Isobel got hastily to her feet and tugged at her skirt as he came in. They faced each other. For a second she watched him trying to place her, then he smiled.

'Well, well, well. The blessed Isobel, ever virgin.'

It was Andrew Jacks, Alex's younger brother.

## CHAPTER 9

'You know each other!' exclaimed Jan.

'Andrew.' Isobel opted for a firm handshake to ward off the possibility of being kissed, but bungled it. They stubbed fingers and he leant close anyway, kissing first one cheek then the other, taking his time and making her feel gauche. He smelt like Alex. There was no urbane way of refuting the implied intimacy. His eyes mocked her as she retreated into her gin.

'What's the connection, then?' asked Jan. 'Oxford?'

'Yes,' they both said together. Andrew gestured for Isobel to continue. This was not politeness, she realized as soon as she embarked on an explanation: 'I was librarian in – in – at his brother's college.'

'My brother Alex.' He made it sound like a gentle reproof for failing to utter Alex's name. She said nothing. 'Our paths crossed now and then,' went on Andrew. 'Isobel hated me. A little unfairly, I always felt, but there it is.'

'Well, I expect you were utterly vile to her,' said Jan.

'Me?' He laughed and the two of them hugged. Isobel sat down again and began to stroke Derek, not wishing to intrude on their shared grief.

'I'm glad you came,' said Jan. 'What can I get you?'

'Wine. Red.'

'What! Have you renounced the demon malt?' demanded Jan. 'Well, it just so happens that I've got a nice Pinot Noir. Do you deserve it?'

'If it's the best.'

She rolled her eyes and went to the kitchen.

Isobel continued to stroke Derek, not glancing at Andrew in case he read in her look an attempt to trace a likeness to his brother. He came and sat beside her. At once the cat sprang from her lap to his.

'A little tactless, Derek,' he remarked. His fingers worked their way deftly into the fur round the cat's neck and before long Derek was purring orgasmically. 'You big queen,' crooned Andrew. Isobel sat stiffly while they canoodled.

Jan returned and presented a bottle. Andrew viewed the label superciliously. She poured some into a glass and he twirled it, then tasted. Isobel repressed her irritation at this camp little pantomime.

'Well?' inquired Jan.

'Mmm. Now that,' said Andrew, 'is my kind of wine.'

'Pretentious, you mean?'

He ignored her. 'It goes down exquisitely.'

Jan laughed. Isobel pursed her lips in disapproval, her stock response to what was evidently smut but which she didn't understand. The penny dropped and she tutted.

'Have you been waiting a long time to use that one?' asked Jan.

' "It is extempore, from my mother-wit." '

'Bollocks!' she retorted, pouring him a full glass. Isobel saw with a rush of jealousy how fond Jan was of him. 'Don't tell me you've switched to grape products.'

'It's a bugger,' he sighed, 'but there comes a point when long-term vanity takes precedence over instant gratification.'

'Were you starting to look raddled?' asked Jan. 'You poor lamb.'

'I don't think you've changed at all,' said Isobel, breaking her silence and sounding more hostile than she'd intended. A small hush fell.

'Ah,' he said, 'but you should see the portrait in the attic.'

Isobel took a sip of gin.

'*Dorian Gray*,' he whispered.

'I *know*!' she snapped.

Andrew smirked. She'd forgotten his habit of treating her like an ignoramus. He perceived an insecurity and worked it mercilessly.

'Well,' said Jan, 'I'll go and sling the pasta on and, no, you may not help. You always interfere,' she told Andrew, as she went out to the kitchen again.

Derek purred a rapturous *ostinato* to the *Requiem*.

'Who's this?' asked Andrew, attention caught by the music.

'Mozart,' replied Isobel in surprise.

He looked at her as though she'd cracked a feeble pun, and she realized his inquiry was of a more recondite nature. Who were the singers, perhaps, or the conductor.

'Oh, yes,' he said, apparently answering his own question.

They sat in silence once more. Isobel felt raw. Don't be ridiculous, she chided herself. What does it matter? But the incident had resurrected a host of similar petty humiliations from her Oxford days. She was out of practice at the games clever people played. Andrew was probably going to torment her about Alex. An offhand inquiry would pre-empt him. She tried to compose one. The attack, when it came, was from a different quarter, however:

'So what's the nature of your relationship with Jan?'

'We're friends.'

'Friends? As in *just good friends*?'

'As in close friends.'

'And you always dress up for your close female friends?'

She felt a faint jangle of alarm. 'I *dress up* if I'm going out.'

'Ah. I thought women didn't bother just for each other.' He watched with interest as she flushed again. 'But, then, what would I know?'

Isobel remained silent on the grounds that this could theoretically be construed as Olympian, whereas defensive blurting could not.

'Anyway, that's good, isn't it?' When she didn't respond he brushed her arm softly with the back of his hand. 'Yes? Good that you're "close friends". You're each a little less lonely than you might otherwise have been. What more can we ask of life?'

She moved her arm away. 'How's Alex?'

He yawned. 'Oh, Alex is Alex. Actually, he's forty today.'

'I know,' she said, without thinking.

He laughed. 'Did you light a candle at his shrine?'

'Don't be silly.'

'Isobel, Isobel!' he chided, reaching out a hand to stroke her hair.

She jerked away. 'Do you mind?'

'I like it short. You look like a beautiful wayward boy.'

'Oh, *thanks!*'

'My pleasure.'

He leant back and closed his eyes, humming softly along with the music. Isobel stared rigidly ahead. This was exactly how she'd felt at fifteen – a great galumphing sweating girl, in the wrong clothes, blurting the wrong things, transgressing rules that unfairly had never been explained to her. I'll never be unaffected with Jan again, she thought. He had sullied one of her few uncomplicated pleasures. It was probably just malice, but she wouldn't be able to dismiss the possibility that he knew something she didn't. She despaired at the naivety that made her such easy prey, and the social cowardice that precluded her asking a blunt question and sorting the matter out. She ought to have been asked a year ago. It was too late now.

Jan appeared at the doorway. 'It's ready.'

Andrew tipped the sated Derek on to the floor and got up, offering Isobel his hand. She ignored it.

'I hope he's been behaving himself,' said Jan.

'As ever,' he replied.

'Hmph,' said Jan. 'Come along, then. Sit yourselves down.'

They went through to the dining room. Jan gave Isobel's arm a reassuring squeeze as she passed. Isobel smiled, without quite meeting her eye. They sat.

'Well,' said Jan, 'I think I should call upon the curate to say grace, then I'll bring things in.'

'Oh! Yes, if – Certainly.' Isobel bowed her head and uttered a few conventional words. She looked up expecting to encounter Andrew's sneering atheistical gaze, but he was crossing himself. She averted her eyes swiftly to the vase of sweet peas. A little shiny black beetle, like a jet bead, made its way across a pink petal. She watched as it buried itself deep in a secret crevice. Then Jan placed a bowl of chilled soup in front of her.

They began to eat. Isobel concentrated on her food, inhibited both by Andrew's company and also by her new speculations about Jan. She was rescued before too long by her customary impatience. Oh, for heaven's sake! It's just Jan, my old friend Jan. Nothing's changed. Even if it turned out that Jan was a lesbian – and Isobel was sure she wasn't – she hoped she wasn't vain enough to imagine that every gay woman automatically fancied her. She began to look for an opportunity to join in the conversation, but by now they were talking cosily about the past and she was stuck for the moment in the role of observer. She watched Andrew. Why had he crossed himself? She hoped this wasn't his latest affectation. The screaming high-church queens she'd met in Oxford had always made her flesh crawl. Her pastoral antennae started to quiver. There was something going on beneath that languid façade. He sensed her interest and looked at her questioningly. Jan got up and began collecting the soup bowls.

'How's the lovely Raphael?' she asked.

'The lovely Raphael?' he repeated. 'Oh, dead.'

At first it seemed like a bad joke. Isobel saw the bowls falling from Jan's grasp in slow motion. She had all the time in the world to reach out and catch them, but somehow she had scarcely moved by the time they crashed to the floor.

'No!' cried Jan. 'Andrew!'

He was stooping to pick up the pieces.

'Andrew, that's impossible.' Tears streamed down Jan's cheeks.

'Impossible, but true,' he said lightly. 'Don't touch me!' He recoiled from her outstretched hands, then the glimpse of jagged grief vanished. 'A brush?' he suggested. 'Dustpan?'

Jan stood weeping with her hands pressed to her mouth as if the words conveyed nothing to her. Isobel slipped out and hunted in the kitchen cupboards. So that was it. The hardest thing she'd learnt in her funeral visits was to let the bereaved go at their own pace, to check her impulse to tell them how to grieve. She understood Andrew's brittle flippancy and vowed to be patient, however hard he made it. When she came back with the dustpan and brush Jan was asking, 'When? Oh, Andrew, what happened?'

'Last February. That's why I didn't come last year. I meant to write.' He shrugged.

Isobel swept up the fragments with a clatter. The brush was clotted with soup. She shook it, but it would need washing. She straightened up.

'There,' she said absurdly, as if it were dealt with. Neither of them noticed her.

'Oh, God!' cried Jan. 'It wasn't Aids, was it?'

'We don't *ask* that, darling,' he said nastily. 'We say, "Oh, I'm so *sorry*, was he very old?"'

'Well, was he?' snapped Isobel, forgetting her resolve. She bit her lip. 'Sorry.'

'He was fifty-one.'

Isobel turned to Jan to see if she could infer the answer.

'But it was an inoperable brain tumour, *happily*,' he went on, 'so *that's* OK.'

Isobel went to the kitchen, no longer trusting herself. She wrapped the broken china in old newspaper. Andrew followed her and added the larger pieces.

Jan stood in front of the Aga. 'I've forgotten what I'm doing.'

'Pasta,' prompted Andrew.

'Pasta,' repeated Jan. 'Pasta. That's right.' She stood helplessly, so he took over and drained it. Isobel dumped the paper parcel in the bin and rinsed the brush.

'That's the wonderful thing about grief,' he said, when they were seated again. 'It provides the perfect excuse for inexcusable behaviour.'

'You've never needed an excuse,' said Jan, blowing her nose and sounding more like herself.

'True,' he said. 'But, then, I've spent most of my adult life grieving. Would I have been a nicer person if the Fates hadn't shat upon me? We'll never know.'

'Why didn't you write?' demanded Jan. 'What a way to break it to me.'

'I was aiming for a redistribution of misery along socialist lines,' he said. 'Out of deference to your political views.' He began to eat.

We're going to have to play along, thought Isobel. She picked up her knife and fork and after a moment Jan did the same. In the distance there was a growl of thunder. I didn't leave my computer on, did I? thought Isobel. A colleague at Oxford had once been word-processing during a storm with disastrous results. She tried to remember actually switching it off, but couldn't. These actions were automatic, though, like locking the door. She would have done. But the fear niggled away for the rest of the evening as the storm rumbled closer.

They went back to the sitting room for coffee. 'And how does parish ministry suit you, Isobel?' asked Andrew. Derek was asleep on his lap.

She tensed. 'Very well, thank you.'

'You're happy and fulfilled?'

'Most of the time.'

'And you still believe in God and so forth?'

'I'd hardly remain in the Church if I didn't,' she retorted.

'Your fearsome integrity!' he mocked.

'Stop baiting her,' ordered Jan.

Isobel looked out of the window. It was getting dark. Sheet lightning was licking and flickering across the sky, eerie in the silence.

'So what are you doing with yourself these days?' Jan asked Andrew.

'*Je m'amuse*,' he replied. 'In my donnish way.' He stretched. 'I might run away and join a monastery. You never know.'

'I don't think they take people on the rebound,' said Isobel. Jan looked scandalized. Instantly Isobel was ashamed. 'Sorry. That was an awful –'

'No, no,' he cut in. 'Bitch boldly or not at all.'

A painful silence fell.

'How did someone as nice as Raphael put up with you for so long?' asked Jan, in the end.

'Because he was so nice, of course,' he replied. 'We represented a kind of slim-line two-point Calvinism: irresistible grace and total depravity.'

There was a sudden explosion of thunder and they all jumped. Derek yowled and fled. The window-panes rattled. A moment later the lights went out.

'Jesus! That was close,' said Andrew. 'I feel like a lightning conductor for the wrath of God.'

Jan laughed. 'Why? What have you done now?'

'Impersonated a priest.' They stared at him in the gloom. His face was lit fleetingly by another flash of lightning. Jan got up to find some matches.

'Another tarts and vicars party?' she asked.

'No. I gave the last rites to a dying man, actually.'

A frisson of horror went through Isobel.

Jan's hand paused with the lit match. 'Raphael?'

'Yes.'

She lit the candle and set it down on the table beside him. His beautiful features were illuminated like a painting by de La Tour.

Jan sat. 'Tell us, my love.'

They waited. After a while he began: 'At the end he didn't know who I was any more.' He waved away their murmurs of pity. 'He thought I was the priest and wanted absolution. Just one of those benighted Irish things.' This aside was aimed at Isobel. 'It was too late to fetch someone – he was dying in front of me. What was I supposed to do?'

They waited again, uncertain whether this was rhetorical.

'Well?' he prompted. 'Isobel? You're the professional.' He was mocking her, but she was obliged to treat his inquiry seriously.

'Well, under those circumstances you don't have to be a priest to pray a prayer of blessing,' she asserted. 'In the same way that midwives can baptize infants who are likely to die. The important thing is –'

He interrupted: 'So you don't hold an ontological view of the priesthood?'

'I believe in the priesthood of all believers,' she hedged, ontology being momentarily elusive.

'But I'm not a believer.'

Isobel reminded herself that this was a bereaved man, and said gently, 'If you don't believe, and you were just acting out of compassion, I can't see what's worrying you.'

'Nothing's *worrying* me,' he said. 'I'm just fascinated. Assuming, for the sake of argument, God exists, can a prayer by a hardened atheist invoke His blessing on a dying man?'

'It's God who blesses,' replied Isobel tartly. 'You're nothing. The individual's nothing,' she amended.

'Do you say that kind of thing from the pulpit?' he inquired. ' "*You're nothing.*" Hmm. It has a certain Book-of-Common-Prayer vigour to it, but pastorally it's rather unfortunate.'

In desperation, Isobel prayed. She felt an abrupt stilling of the inner storm. His eyes gleamed at her maliciously in the candlelight. Jan was poised, ready to intervene. Then Isobel experienced one of those moments of heightened awareness that come occasionally to the minister.

'What are you afraid of?' she heard herself ask.

'Afraid?' He laughed. Isobel saw she had somehow struck home. 'Yes. I suppose I am. "I fled Him, down the nights and down the days; / I fled him down the arches of the years",' he quoted.

' "The Hound of Heaven",' said Isobel, getting in before he could tell her. 'What are you talking about?'

'I struck a bargain that night,' he said, 'and I've spent the last year and a half trying to weasel out of it.' There was another crack of thunder. They all jumped again. He gestured as if to say, You see? 'The question is – the question I was, in my annoying way, working round to asking you – how does one know if one has a vocation?'

A yelp of laughter leapt to Isobel's lips. She choked on it. 'Um, I think if it's a *genuine* call, then eventually you'll find it's inescapable.'

'Shit,' he said.

Well, your language will have to improve for a start, thought Isobel.

'Do you really see yourself as a parish priest?' hooted Jan, voicing Isobel's rude scepticism for her.

'Well, there's always college chaplaincy,' he replied. 'I could continue my studies, corrupt the youth in my care and piss away my hospitality allowance unhindered.'

'No ontological change there, then,' said Jan.

'Precisely.'

The banter continued in this vein. Oh, honestly! thought Isobel. But what if God *was* calling him? Her disgust and derision faltered. She was assailed instead by jealousy. Oh, but that's not fair! You can't do that! It was so unjust that people could roll like swine in their own filth all their lives and then repent, while the rest of us have slogged on being good and – She stopped in horror. I sound like the prodigal son's elder brother. *'Rejoice,'* the words of Jesus in the parable urged her. *'This my son was dead, and is alive again; he was lost, and is found.'* Well, she was glad, obviously. It would be simpler if Andrew were to stop fooling around and manifest some more noticeable signs of grace instead. But that was God's business, not hers. She would pray for him and try to be patient.

An hour or so later Isobel had to remind herself of this promise when Andrew insisted on walking her home. She'd been looking forward to a spot of solitude and the chance to reflect. The storm had almost rumbled itself out, but it was still raining.

'That thing looks like a flasher's mac,' said Andrew, indicating the crumpled garment Jan had lent Isobel. He was wearing an ankle-length black raincoat, which Isobel suspected had cost a fortune. He let it flap open casually, thereby defeating the object of wearing it, unless – huh! – the object was *style*. She set off at a brisk pace, but he linked his arm through hers and slowed her down to a leisurely stroll. Her fists bunched in her pockets.

'Relax,' he said.

'I'm –' She abandoned the sentence.

The night was still sultry. Why did everyone say a storm would clear the air? It never did. She could hear the rain pattering all around, and now and then a weightier drop fell from a branch overhead into the undergrowth, slapping a hidden leaf.

She was burningly aware of Andrew's arm through hers. Human touch for Isobel usually came in two forms: a businesslike handshake or an unwelcome pat. Nobody linked arms with her companionably, or held her hand down the length of a road, the way she and Tatiana had held hands on the way home from school. If only we could in our society, she thought. It was a shame there wasn't an acceptable form of public intimacy for friends. It was reserved for the very old, or the very young. She felt a shy tenderness towards Andrew creeping over her. If they spoke it would vanish. I've felt this before, she thought. I know – that time when a baby bird came and landed on my head. She'd known that she couldn't call her mother without frightening the bird away. All she could do was stand, frozen in delight until the moment ended.

'What are you thinking?' he asked.

'I was remembering when I was nine and a bird landed on my head.'

He stopped and stared at her. 'You,' he said, 'are a deeply strange woman.'

They walked on again. A Harry-like fit of laughter seized her. She wrestled with it, but eventually Andrew felt her quivering.

He looked at her again. 'Are you laughing or crying?'

'Laughing,' she wept.

'Thank God. I thought for one terrible moment I was going to have to apologize.'

Isobel snorted sarcastically.

'I keep doing it,' he complained. 'The whole bloody time! It's like some cosmic post-coital remorse. I wake up at three in the morning and think of all the people I've ever wronged.'

'Like counting sheep?' asked Isobel. 'Sorry.'

'That's *so* irritating,' he said. 'Put the knife in, twist it, then repent.'

'What were you saying?' she asked humbly.

'Perhaps I should take out an ad in *The Times* – "Andrew Jacks wishes to apologize to the human race." Oh, *God*. What am I going to do, Isobel?' He clutched her arm close and leant his head briefly on her shoulder. His damp hair brushed her cheek.

'Well,' she began, shocked that he should lay himself open to her like this, 'couldn't you stop running from God? What are you so scared of?'

He sighed. 'At the risk of flogging poor old Thompson to death, I'm scared, "Lest having Him, I must have naught beside."'

'The priesthood's not *that* bad!' she joked.

'But what about the religious life?'

'The religious life?' she repeated. 'In general? Oh, the *Religious Life*! You mean, you want to become a Franciscan, or something?'

'God, no!' he shuddered. 'Benedictine. And I don't *want* to!'

'Goodness!' Isobel felt nonplussed. 'Well, to be honest, I've really no knowledge of Roman Catholic monasticism.'

'There *are* Anglican Benedictines. Christ, you Evangelicals are so parochial.'

Oh, unlike you cosmopolitan Anglo *Car*-tholics, she thought. 'How long have you felt called?'

He muttered something.

'What?'

'I said, since I was twelve,' he snapped.

'Twelve!' Another shaft of envy seared through her.

'What do you think?' he asked.

'It sounds like the real thing, somehow.' She grinned. It was too tempting. 'You know, someone I knew at university was definitely *definitely* not going to be a missionary doctor in Papua New Guinea. Guess what she's doing now?' gurgled Isobel.

'Oh, shut up, you cow!'

She bit her lips. 'Surely it would be a relief to give in?' A thought occurred to her. 'Is celibacy the problem?'

'Ah. My legendary promiscuity. Well, actually – if you ever repeat this to anyone, by the way, you'll die a slow and horrible death, and anyway, I'll flatly deny it and shag fifteen dockers on the spot.'

There was a pause. A car swished slowly past along the road beside them. ' "Well, actually" what?' prompted Isobel.

'Well, actually, actually, *actually*, I've never been *that* promiscuous, really. God, this is embarrassing.'

'Really? Forgive me, but it was quite a convincing act.'

'Thank you. I worked hard on it.'

They walked on for a bit without speaking. Isobel tried to banish her unchristian glee at seeing Andrew squirm for once. She suspected he still hadn't quite got it all off his chest, and tried to compose her features into a pastoral expression ready for his next utterance.

'Look,' he began, 'just between you and me in the confessional, I'm basically a monogamous animal. I'll admit, I've had my share of mindless sex, but *mindless* sex, for Christ's sake? What's the point? After all, the mind's the sexiest thing. Or don't you think so?' he asked, seeing her frown.

'I was wondering what promiscuity was, if it's not having your share of mindless sex.'

He stared loftily. 'Having more than your share, naturally.'

They reached her house. 'Have you talked to anyone else about all this?' she asked.

'No. I chose you, because you have no bearing on my life. In fact, you're nothing. *Sorry,*' he added.

Hah. 'Well, thank you for walking me home, Andrew.'

He put his arms round her and hugged her fiercely. Caught by surprise, she hadn't managed to get her arms positioned properly. They were pinioned between their torsos and her face was squashed into his shoulder.

'Nice coat,' she mumbled.

'It was Raph's. It still smells of him.'

She tried to make a compassionate gesture with her trapped arms. 'I'm so sorry.'

He pressed his cheek against hers, then let her go. 'Pray for me.'

'Of course.'

He sauntered off with a casual wave of the hand. She couldn't tell if it had been rain or tears on his face.

## CHAPTER 10

Isobel was not brought up to believe swearing was wrong. It was a sign of a limited vocabulary, though. An intelligent, imaginative person never needed to resort to obscenity. English was a rich language. There was always another way of expressing yourself. Look at Shakespeare. Parts of the body should be called by their proper names. There was nothing shameful or smutty about sex or going to the lavatory. They were perfectly natural things, and not to be used as swear words; that would be illogical.

It was a little odd, therefore, that when Mrs Knox discovered a limerick in Isobel's Girls' Brigade blazer pocket *in Isobel's handwriting* ('There was an old fellow called Billy/Who had a triangular willy') she should describe it as a 'dirty poem' and admit to being 'very disappointed'. She hoped Isobel understood that it was neither Clever nor Funny.

After that, Tatiana and Isobel were more careful. As often as they dared they peeped at the rude playing-cards in the bureau drawer at Tatiana's house. They'd flip through them under the cover of loud rummaging noises. Their favourite showed a woman with her naked breasts slumped on the guitar she was ostensibly playing. Curved wood mimicked curved flesh. If Mrs George came into the room Tatiana would grab some innocent item and shut the drawer, saying, 'Oh, *there* it is, at last! Come along, Isobel.' The two of them would wander out, Tatiana innocently, Isobel all hot and guilty.

There was nothing like that in Isobel's house, although she discovered a book of paintings that reduced her to the same state of flustered trembling if anyone caught her looking at it. *Le Déjeuner sur l'herbe.* Why was that woman sitting there with nothing on while all the men were still dressed? Had she stripped for them? She pored over the picture, finger in another page, alert to flip to a landscape at the sound of approaching footsteps.

The summer she was eleven, a big, busty eleven, her middle brother Christopher had a French penfriend staying on exchange. Didier's eyebrows met in the middle and he kept cornering Isobel and squeezing her breasts and kissing her with his rubbery tongue. It was awful, awful. Christopher didn't know what to do about him, either. He and Isobel couldn't even look at one another, it was so embarrassing. It was like the times they had to walk the neighbour's ghastly dog, and it kept trying to mount other dogs with its thing kind of coming out from inside itself, all pink and pointing like Didier's horrible tongue. It made Isobel feel sick and dirty. She tried to stay near her mother, but Mum didn't realize and kept saying things like, 'Oh, I'm sure Isobel would like to go with you to the pictures, wouldn't you, Isobel?' She couldn't exactly explain why not.

Then her other brother, Alistair, a big fifteen-year-old, caught Didier slobbering her and thumped him. 'Stay away from my sister, you, or I'll break every bone in your froggy body.' He offered to tell Mum and Dad, but Isobel said, no, thanks, it was OK. Didier slunk away.

Afterwards Isobel couldn't work out why she hadn't bashed him one herself. Well, one thing was certain – if anyone else ever tried it, she'd b– well kick him in the hmm-hmms, even if it *was* terribly dangerous and he might never be able to have children.

That night Isobel dreamt about Tatiana. They'd met up again and were standing in some kind of hut or old chicken coop on a hillside. They could peep out at the world through the knot-holes in the walls. They laughed at how as kids they'd said they would know one another even after years. I'll always be sure it's you, Tatiana would say, because you've got a brown dot in your right eye. And you've got a zig-zaggy vein in your right eye, Isobel would reply. So as adults they peered close into one another's eyes and it was true. They laughed until they cried that it should still be exactly the same after all those years.

She woke with a terrible feeling of loss. The desolation was so profound that she half thought Tatiana, wherever she was, had died in the night. It was absurd, but Isobel could almost believe that the two of them were linked telepathically, as Tatiana would have put it. Then she remembered Andrew and his sorrow – poor man – and decided that this explained her own state of mind.

The weather was disgusting. Isobel opened her study window and it was like a sauna out there. Her shirt was already clinging to her. She was just sitting down to pray when she noticed her computer. I've left it on all night, she thought. The screen was blank. Puzzled, she moved the mouse and pressed a couple of keys. Oh, no – the storm! At once she told herself to stay calm. There'd been a power-cut. She would only have lost the last bit of editing, assuming she'd forgotten to save it. She turned the machine off, then on again. Still blank. She stared, then began tapping keys and jiggling wires in mounting dismay. Nothing. The hard disk had gone.

Isobel closed her eyes. Damn. Damn damn *damn*! She took a deep, shaky breath while she mentally surveyed the problem. Well, the thing was insured. She always backed everything up. True, she'd have to manage without for a few days, which was a nuisance. It wasn't the end of the world, though. There was always Harry's computer in an emergency. It was all right.

But DAMN! She wondered briefly if it was possible that after scanning her extensive vocabulary she might find that SHIT was the only word that would really do in this context. She restrained herself and stamped her foot instead. How could you have been so *stupid*, Knox? She wanted to seize the machine and shake it till it divulged all her files.

This was hardly the mood most conducive to quiet devotions. She flung herself down in her chair and tried none the less, shooting the computer the occasional hate-filled glance. Saturday. She consulted her notebook. Her prayer-life was disciplined. The people she prayed for were divided up into different days of the week. She prayed daily for different streets in the parish and followed the diocesan prayer diary. Her notebook also contained points culled from the news so that she could pray in an informed way about current events. She added Andrew to her list, knowing that otherwise she might forget her promise.

As always she began with praise, but that morning her devotions felt stilted, as though she were proposing a vote of thanks to God at a formal dinner, listing His splendid achievements and attributes and wishing Him every success in his future ventures. She confessed her various shortcomings then ploughed dutifully through her intercessions, doubling back to confession to repent of her feelings on discovering it was Johnny Whitaker's turn in the diocesan prayer diary. At last she turned to her Bible, asking that God would speak to her through the written word.

At present she was working through the New Testament, something she did every couple of years. Today it was Matthew's Gospel, chapter 20, the parable of the workers in the vineyard. She knew the passage well already. It told of the generous grace of God, which was wonderful, of course; but she experienced a spasm of outrage every time she read the story. One might as well be frank about these things. All her instincts about fair play were affronted. Her heart burned on behalf of the poor workers who'd laboured all day in the pounding sun only to see a bunch of slackers given the same wages as them. Yet, from another point of view it was fair, because the first set of workers had agreed to a decent day's wage, and that was what they'd got. It was no business of theirs if the owner of the vineyard chose generously to pay everyone else the same. Thus the first will be last and the last first.

Isobel acknowledged that. It was marvellous. But – shaming to admit this – she knew deep down she was still on the side of the hard workers. 'It's a disgrace,' she could imagine them muttering. 'The disgraceful grace of God' – there was a neat little phrase to weave into a sermon. Yes, it was true. Even after so many years as a disciple of Christ she still had a distinct worldly streak. Witness her jealous response to Andrew last night. A truly Christ-like heart would have rejoiced. This was clearly an area she was going to have to work on. She resolved to strive for a more spontaneously generous spirit.

Isobel shut her Bible feeling invigorated. Sometimes the word of God really was 'sharper than a two-edged sword'. It was necessary to open oneself to the Gospel's demands, however humbling the experience might be – as she was forever reminding her parishioners. In her sermons she stressed repeatedly the need for disciplined personal prayer and Bible study, but the congregation was, in this respect, stony ground. All she succeeded in doing was making them feel guilty.

She slipped in her clerical collar and set off for morning prayer. She hadn't gone more than a few paces when she was hailed by a creaking 'Cooee!' from across the street. Isobel cursed. It was Kath Bollom, already in her nylon pinny doing battle with the bacteria world. She had been lying in wait and now heaved herself down her path in her bursting slippers, panting (angina, only one lung, forty cigarettes a day) and laden like a tanker with gossip. Isobel waited with a smile on her lips and something less cordial in her heart.

'Oh, Isobel! Are you all right?' And she was off, with Isobel hinting at pressing engagements by glancing at her watch and edging away. Kath shuffled along, keeping pace. It was almost impossible to interrupt her as she had that politician's trick of never drawing breath at the end of a sentence. Isobel would have to pray for her to have an attack of wheezing or they would sidle like this all the way to church.

'Ee! We were that worried!' Kath was saying. 'I sent our Charlie over to see if you were all right, with the lights going off like that. He knocked but there was no answer. "Oh, she'll be out visiting," I says, "unless she's in there, hurt, you'd better try again, go on," I says, "go round the back and see if you can see owt, she's got no nets," so he – Oh! do you not know? Your house was struck, last night, *bang*, ee, I almost died, we had the fire brigade out to you, the whole street was out watching, your chimney could have been on fire, you know, I looked out for you coming back, but it was getting late, and then I saw you had a young man with you, "Oh, she'll be all right," I says to Charlie, "she's got a young man with her." *Well*, they couldn't see owt, the fire brigade, but mind, I says to – what do they call him? Tall lad, Mam used to do the quiz at the club, no, it's gone – anyway, I says to him, "I wouldn't care, but there was our Christine's mother-in-law's house at Redcar was struck that time and she had a fire in her loft space, and *that* didn't start till the next morning, smouldered all night, that's what the fire brigade said to her," but he – *Tony!* that's him, aye, Tony – he says, no, they'd had a good look and it was fine, not to worry, but you do, though, don't you? You never know, so if you want our Len to pop up and have a look round he will, he was a plumber before he –' Kath broke off here with a terrifying whooping gasp.

'Thank you,' said Isobel, grasping the moment. 'That's most kind, but I'm sure everything's OK.' She consulted her watch and set off at a sprint, seeing Kath fighting to regain her breath. 'Must dash! Late for morning prayer.'

'See you're getting your car done!' wheezed Kath after her. 'Funny, these things go in threes, you know, seems like a canny lad, policeman, isn't he? From up Newcastle way, they're rough up there, mind, but he seems like a canny lad, friend of yours, is he? . . .'

The monologue faded. Isobel gave her a cheery wave as she escaped round the corner on to the main road. Shut up and do something useful, she thought. Like hoovering the pavement. And now I'm late! She continued at a smart pace.

My house was struck by lightning! Her scalp prickled. Perhaps it was she, not Andrew, who was the lightning conductor for the wrath of God. It was difficult not to take it personally. But, of course, an all-knowing all-seeing God would have spotted that she was a mile up the road at the time. Unless the intended target was her computer. It reminded her of Harry's burst pipe last winter which had ruined several ghastly carpets and nothing else, apart from one copy of the *Alternative Service Book*. What was God trying to say *there*, Harry had wondered. He was inclined to view the incident as God's affirmation of his ministry, since he now had posh carpets courtesy of Ecclesiastical Insurance. No diocesan relocation grant could run to that kind of luxury, so God was obviously telling Harry to stay in Asleby until he retired.

Silly man, thought Isobel indulgently, as she hurried into church. He allowed her time to catch her breath, then they said morning prayer.

'Sorry I was late,' she said afterwards. 'I was caught by Kath.'

'Aha, you were Bollomed,' said Harry. 'Useful swear word, that.'

'I can't escape her. She never draws breath.'

'Here's a tip. Interrupt loudly in agreement then tack your goodbye on to the end. "*Yes!* You're *absolutely* right and now I'm supposed to be at the crem, 'bye!"'

'She says my house was struck by lightning.'

'What!'

'Everything's absolutely fine,' she reassured him. 'Kath called the fire brigade who checked, and −'

'Are you OK?' he interrupted. She almost guffawed when she saw he had his deeply pastoral face on.

'Oh, I'm fine. I was out. So either it wasn't meant for me, or God's a bad shot, ha ha!' But Harry wasn't laughing. 'Oh, honestly, Harry. You're not superstitious, are you?'

'No, of course not. It's − You're worrying me, Isobel. It's your manner.'

'My *manner*? How do you mean?'

'I can't say, exactly. Just a feeling.' He shook his head. 'Do you think you need a holiday? Have you got anything planned?'

She swallowed her sense of insult and told him about Normandy. He brightened. 'Oh, the only annoying thing is,' she went on, remembering, 'I must have left my computer on in the storm −'

'Oh, no! Not the hard disk?'

'Afraid so. Silly of me. I've never left it on before. However. No problem. It's insured. Everything's backed up, so . . .' Even Isobel could hear it now. Her manner: very worrying.

'What?' asked Harry.

'What do you mean, what?'

'You were looking at me.'

'Well, you're looking at me.' Her voice sounded shrill in her ears. He looked tiny and distant, although part of her could see that this was nonsense, everything was normal. His lips were moving. It was like a feverish dream. A second later his words crystallized into sense.

'A couple of bits of business,' he had just said. 'I've had a letter from Bazza-boy.' This was how Barrington Lindop, their archdeacon, was usually known behind his back. 'St Mark's is about to fall vacant and the plan is to join them with us to form a new team ministry. He says that's "the way forward" for Asleby.'

Isobel cast her mind back to the Deanery Synod meeting where they had discussed staffing levels. Two full-time posts had to be lost somehow in the deanery. They had talked about combining various

116

parish jobs with diocesan posts, but nobody had proposed creating a team.

'Oh,' said Isobel eventually. 'Is that a good thing? What will it mean practically?'

'For the diocese? To put it crudely, it's a way of saving on stipends. They can run more church centres with fewer clergy. For you, O good and faithful curate, it may mean more responsibility. How would you feel about running St Mark's daughter church?'

'Well,' said Isobel, flushing with pleasure, 'that would certainly be a challenge.'

'We'll talk more about it later. For *me*,' he continued, 'it would mean *power*!' He flung wide his arms and cried, 'At last! Rector of all I survey from the river Tees to the A66! Ahem. Not that that's important to me, of course.'

Isobel couldn't help smiling.

'One snag, however,' he said. 'We have to go on a "New Teams" Conference in September. Three-line whip, I'm afraid.' He handed her a photocopied sheet. 'Keep the dates free, please.'

'Oh, no,' muttered Isobel. They walked back down the aisle.

'You can be in my buzz group, if you like,' Harry offered. 'Bzz bzz.'

'Oh, shut up.'

He was still buzzing happily as they went out of the church door, but stopped short on the step. Isobel looked. It was Andrew. He was regarding Harry with a quizzical expression.

'Andrew!' exclaimed Isobel. She was about to attempt an introduction when to her surprise Harry stepped forward and shook Andrew earnestly by the hand.

'Andrew Jacks? The famous polymath?'

'Oh, fuck off, Harry,' said Andrew.

They hugged. Isobel averted her gaze, assailed by all manner of speculations about their obvious familiarity.

'I open my paper: Andrew Jacks. I turn on my radio: Andrew Jacks. Get out of my life!' cried Harry. 'What's your goal? World domination?'

'God, no! How vulgar. Just influence, Harry, influence.' He turned to Isobel. 'This bastard married the man I love.'

'To a woman,' explained Harry.

Isobel laughed rather brayingly at this joke. 'So,' she said, but couldn't think of anything to add.

'*Thank you* for bringing early polyphonic church music to a wider audience,' said Harry, gravely.

'One must mediate for the masses.'

'That's Radio 3 for you. Are you staying with Jan?' he asked. 'I missed you last year.'

'Well, here I am.' Andrew shrugged.

Isobel waited tensely, fearing Harry would blunder.

'And while I'm here I'm hoping to fumble your Father Willis,' continued Andrew.

Harry laughed. 'Was this what prompted you to take up the organ – the scope for double entendres?'

'Please. I can wring smut out of a wood block. After all, music consists of banging, blowing or fiddling.'

'The gay person's guide to the orchestra,' observed Harry. 'What about the harp?'

Andrew flared his nostrils. 'Pluck me.'

Harry laughed again, then caught Isobel's expression and was instantly sobered. 'Ahem. Isobel, I'll see you tonight at the house-group leaders' meeting. Do get that holiday booked, won't you?'

'Of course. Goodbye. Goodbye, Andrew,' she called as he disappeared into the church.

He waved. She turned away and set off for home so that she wouldn't see Harry following him in. For goodness' sake! Apart from the smutty banter it was all perfectly innocent. As if to confirm this, some emphatic piece of Bach reached her ears. The sound receded behind her as she walked away. And as if Harry didn't know how to conduct himself! Honestly, homosexuality was so embarrassing. The English language was filled with landmines whenever she strayed on to the subject. Expressions she never normally used would crowd to her lips: 'get to the bottom of it', 'queer the pitch'.

She arrived home and went to her study to make a list. Lists always calmed her when everything seemed to be getting out of hand. Phone Edward re hols. Sort out computer, insurance, etc.

Sermon. Then she remembered her car and slipped out to examine the wing. She ran a fingertip over the primer. The policeman would be back later to finish the job. She would not be able to get rid of him.

The air stood still. The scene was charged with ominous portent. Isobel saw herself fleetingly as a victim of predestination, caught up in its machinations with no free will of her own. It's all going to unfold according to its own logic, she thought, and all my efforts are futile.

Back in her study she made another list – this time of the events that had conspired to make her feel this way. There were the break-ins, especially the one in her own house less than two days ago; Andrew turning up out of the blue; her dream about Alex; Brother Gabriel's spooky insights; the lightning bolt; her dream about Tatiana. When one stopped to think, it was little wonder she was feeling strange! Dear old Harry was right. A holiday was called for. She picked up her phone at once and rang Edward.

## CHAPTER 11

*One more day in school, one more day in sorrow!*
*One more day in that old dump and we'll be gone tomorrow!*
*God made the bees, the bees made the honey,*
*We do all the ruddy work, teachers get the money!*

There was a gang of boys going up the road ahead of them roaring this, although they were a day late really, because yippee! they'd all just broken up that minute.

And Tatiana was coming home for tea. Mrs Knox had met them in the car for once, but they'd decided to walk home across the fields, so Mum had driven off with all the exercise books, the model desert island, the projects on trees, dogs, rabbits, the PE kits and half-finished raffia mats and sports-day certificates, leaving them free free free!

Up the hill they scampered in their plimsolls (by special dispensation only, Isobel needn't think she could live in hers through the holidays). There was the telegraph pole Isobel had once run in to and knocked herself out because she was turning round to shout, 'Ha ha! I'm winning!' Across the road (right, left and right again) and down the narrow lane that led to the stile. A month before the path had been sprinkled with tiny elderflowers, fairy confetti.

Over the stile then away! with the barley shushing on either side like the sea. They could do anything they liked. They were going to run screaming past Fatty Fertilizer's, of course, to see if old Ma Fertilizer would come out and shout at them again, 'Oi! You trying to stop the bloody 'ens laying or summink?'

But first they'd play on the windmill steps and sniff the creosoted wood and listen to the mill creaking and ticking in the sunshine and pretend they were in the Olden Days:

*And the whirring sail goes round*
*And the whirring sail goes round.*

They wouldn't play too long, or the police would be out looking for them, thinking they'd got into a car with a strange man; and anyway, it was chocolate tea cakes for tea, Mum had promised, so they could play Old Yeller, rolling their eyes and letting the chewed-up marshmallow dribble from their lips like a dog with rabies, until Mum looked up from her book and told them to stop being disgusting.

And afterwards they'd play on the shed roof (not really allowed) or on the conveyor belts in the quarry (definitely not allowed) or maybe they'd go and swing on the Tarzan rope on the Man's Land behind the Knoxes' garden (allowed, in the sense of being not yet discovered and banned).

After they'd done all these things (without being caught!) they climbed to the top of the conker tree and turned it into a pirate ship, rocking and shaking the branches until the tiny green conkers hailed down. Avast there, ye landlubbers! Yo ho ho and a bottle of rum! No, wait – rottle of BUM! Hee hee hee! They almost fell out of the tree laughing, they were too weak to hold on properly.

They were going to be friends for ever. It would make no difference that Tatiana was moving house tomorrow. No difference at all.

Isobel returned from France feeling like a new woman. The holiday had been both recreational and re-creational, as she was to tell the congregation in a sermon.

She called round to see Jan and deliver a bottle of Calvados and some pongy cheese. She talked of Coutance Cathedral and the historic port of Granville, but eventually admitted that for the first time in her life she'd allowed most of her holiday to drift unaccountably away in long, semi-sozzled afternoons in the garden that merged into evenings and ended under a sky crowded with stars.

'Well, thank God for that,' said Jan. 'How was the family you went with?'

'Very pleasant,' replied Isobel. Jan waited. 'Well, Rupert, the husband, was a bit irritating at times. Inclined to be bossy. A bit of a know-all. And you can shut up,' she added, seeing Jan's expression.

It had not occurred to her till now that Rupert might have been a male version of herself. She'd only got as far as noticing he was rather like her older brothers. He'd annoyed her on the first day by asking if she ever ran into Johnny Whitaker at all; they'd been at theological college together. Honestly! she thought. Even on *holiday* there's no escaping Johnny blessed Whitaker. Rupert continued to quiz her about the Whitakers over the next couple of days, until his wife ruffled his hair and said, 'Mara's one of his old flames, isn't she, darling?' and he'd denied it, huffily: Nonsense, couldn't one inquire after old friends any more?

'Cordelia was nice,' said Isobel. Jan waited again, but Isobel had nothing to add. Cordelia was nice; there was nothing more one could say. Except that Cordelia had long blonde hair, which caused Isobel a pang of regret.

As she walked home from Jan's later, Isobel looked up at the few faint stars in the orangey Teesside night and sighed. Oh, well. Part of the charm of holidays was their transience. One wouldn't want to laze about for ever.

Her own bed felt strange. She would have to relearn all Asleby's night-time noises after the silence of Normandy. There they'd heard nothing but the song of crickets after dark. Apart from a strange bleeping sound they'd never satisfactorily identified. Isobel thought it was a frog. Edward insisted it was something electronic.

'Sounds like radar,' he said.

'Actually,' said Rupert, 'I think it could be a scops owl.'

'A *what*?' demanded Edward.

'A scops owl.'

'Owls don't bleep.'

'Scops owls do.'

'No. It's some kind of bloody machine.'

'Nonsense. It's a bloody scops owl.'

'Bull.'

'Right. I'm getting a torch. I'll show you.'

Isobel and Cordelia heard them in the distance laughing and crashing in the undergrowth. The torch beam scythed this way and that in the treetops.

'Where is it then, eh? Where's this bloody scops owl?'

122

'Well, you've scared it off, haven't you?'

Isobel, frustrated at not knowing the answer, had made a mental note to ask her father.

'Babies,' murmured Cordelia, to the child she was nursing. 'Men are just big babies, aren't they? Hmm? Baby, baby, baby.' Her breast was pale in the moonlight. The child made tiny clucking sounds as it sucked. 'I hope our horrors aren't pestering you too much?'

'No, no,' Isobel assured her. They were nice children, but after a long day she was grateful the Andersons were strict about bedtimes. She had a wonderful self-indulgent time bouncing the baby – setting aside Edward's tactless remark about it being high time she got one of her own – but had to admit she was less enthusiastic about the older children. They were so loud. There were so many of them. She couldn't imagine ever having Cordelia's vast store of dreamy patience. Fortunately it was Edward that the children pestered. They swarmed over him.

'Edward, Edward! Play cricket with us again!'

'Please!' prompted Cordelia and Rupert in unison.

'Please, Edward.'

'Let's tickle Edward!'

'Let's push Edward in the sea!'

The two little girls squirmed and flirted with him. Surely I wasn't like that at the age of six? thought Isobel.

'Edward, are you going to marry Isobel?'

'I asked her but she said no,' replied Edward.

'Why?'

'Ah, well, Isobel's a real princess, you see, and real princesses have to marry a prince and I'm only a poor parson.'

'Don't be silly. Isobel, why won't you marry him?'

'Darlings, leave Isobel alone,' called Cordelia.

Although both Cordelia and Rupert would have been interested in the answer. Isobel had seen them exchange glances. On the last night of the holiday they wandered off to bed early yawning, leaving Edward and Isobel still lying under the stars with the rest of the wine.

Isobel breathed in the night air. It was tinged with apple and yeast. A late tractor trundled past with a load of hay, then there was silence apart from the crickets and the radar owl. Isobel knew she ought to go in. A fortnight had been long enough for her to start finding Edward's physical presence troublesome again. It was like being back at college, with him wandering down the corridor in nothing but a towel. That afternoon he'd sat sprawled in a garden chair unwittingly allowing her a generous view up the leg of his baggy shorts while she was trying to read her novel. He'd been oblivious, deep in a typescript that Annie had written, snorting with mirth and shaking his head by turns, but stubbornly refusing to let Isobel read it, on the grounds that she'd be shocked. As if she'd be shocked by anything Annie Brown could come up with. The image recurred: Edward's penis lurking in its khaki lair.

His arm was warm against hers. She really had better go in now.

'Isobel . . .'

'Mmm?'

'Mind if I ask you something? As an old and trusted friend.'

'Go ahead.'

'Where am I going wrong?'

Her heart sank. 'How do you mean?'

'Well, you know. On the girl front. The ones I'm keen on are either married or they're not interested.'

'Oh, I'm sure when the right person comes along . . .'

'They seem to *like* me,' he continued, 'you know, Edward's a good solid chap, and all that, but they'd never marry me because, frankly, they just don't fancy me. That's what I think.'

'Unless it's the other way round,' she suggested, taking pity on his fragile male ego. 'Perhaps they fancy you rotten, but would never actually marry you.'

'Really?' He turned this thought round and rejected it. 'No. Shouldn't think so. Super idea, but let's face it, it's the relationship side of things that girls are keen on, not the . . . the . . .'

'Raw animal passion?' supplied Isobel.

'Exactly. Thank you. That's more the man's thing. Girls want romance,' he asserted.

'I think you're forgetting I *am* one.'

'Are one what? Oh, *girl*. Of course you are. And a very lovely one, too.' He patted her thigh.

124

'And therefore I know what I'm saying.'

'What about?'

'About passion!' she snapped.

'You!' he guffawed. 'No, wait!' He caught her arm as she sat up, offended. 'Sorry. Izzy, Izzy, what were you saying? Please?'

'I was trying to reassure you, you ungrateful pig.'

'Sorry. Fire away. I'm listening.'

'Well, all I was *saying*,' she enunciated, sounding primmer than ever in her embarrassment, 'is that while I wouldn't marry you, I do, nevertheless, find you ... attractive.'

'Good Lord! Really? I'd never have guessed.' There was another silence. 'How attractive?'

'I knew you'd ask that!' So much for the fragile male ego.

'Go on.'

'I'm not discussing it.'

'Kiss me, then. Spot of the old raw animal passion. Go on – quick snog. No one's looking.' He brought his mouth to within inches of hers.

'Don't be ridiculous!' She tried to shove him away, but he was too solid.

'Why not?'

'Because it mightn't stop there.'

'My word as an officer and a gentleman.'

'Oh, shut up! I'm going in.'

She scrambled to her feet and headed towards the bright doorway. There was a toad in the hall, tempted in by the cool of the tiles. Isobel bent over it, watching. It squatted there, motionless, its throat pulsing, like an omen of something. Then it limped away into the dark. She went up to bed. A moment later she heard Edward coming in and pulling the door to.

She got undressed but couldn't sleep. In the end she knelt at the open window and breathed in the cidrous night. Meteors fell like apple blossom from the sky. If they'd taken a fractionally different turn in the road back there, if Edward had reached out and held her back as she struggled to her feet, she might be watching those same stars from down in the garden, looking up at them, while he ...

125

Isobel wrestled crossly with her duvet at home. The problem with holidays was that one relaxed one's guard. Edward had apologized the following morning for his unsporting behaviour; and she had told him sweetly that she hoped he'd meet a lovely girl before long who'd agree with every word he said. He replied that this sounded dire: he adored bossy women.

She was still stung by his heartless guffaw, though. Honestly! Just because she was single people assumed she must be some kind of wizened-up asexual virgin. She had appetites the same as the next person. In fact, she could have shown Edward a trick or two that would have shocked him -- pardon the expression – rigid. Not that she'd ever dream of boasting about anything relating to episodes in her life that were all over and done with and forgiven, but really! Edward would do well not to judge so much by appearances.

August passed lazily by. It was always a slack time in parish life. Isobel remembered it from the previous year when she was newly ordained. Back then she'd almost panicked, not knowing how she'd ever fill the time. The memory made her smile.

This year she was kept on her mettle by a group of idle lads who had started turning up at the youth club and causing trouble. One evening a couple had clearly been experimenting with dodgy substances so she threw them out. This had the effect of transferring the trouble to the church-hall grounds where it was impossible for her to keep an eye on it. They lit a fire and she dispatched a couple of other lads to put it out with a fire extinguisher, judging that to call the fire brigade would only up the stakes. Some of the other teenagers were nervous, but Isobel was fairly sure it was a question of gritting her teeth. The problem would die down when the school term began again. At the end of the session she tidied up, ignoring them as they mooned through the windows at her, and locked the hall carefully. The following morning Dick, the verger, discovered one of the windows had been broken and the police had to be called.

Apart from this, time passed quietly. Natalie and Drew were on holiday in Thailand. She drove past a sign for an antiques fair and thought of them. Her mother rang to ask if Isobel had any plans to pop down this summer, but Isobel explained that she had used up most of her leave in France. It would have to wait till Christmas. You could always come and see me, she thought, but didn't say. It would throw her mother into a frenzy of concern – had they been fair? Had they visited their grandchildren more often than their daughter?

The day came for the performance of *Uncle Vanya*. As she drove down, Isobel composed herself for an evening of Thelma's company. How did I let myself be talked into this? she wondered, her annoyance mounting despite her best efforts. Thank goodness Harry would not be there to disgrace himself and infect her with his awful giggling bouts. At Asleby's Amateur Dramatic Society's last performance he'd snorted so audibly at the line, 'Admit it! John's your girlfriend!' she'd vowed never to sit near him again.

So, *Uncle Vanya*. Isobel looked through the photocopied programme for typos. The hall lights were switched off. Isobel would have been the first to admit she was not entirely familiar with the text. It was therefore some time before she realised that the character standing so still in profile stage left was, in fact, the prompt. There was no curtain, so any scene changes took place laboriously in full view as one backdrop was rolled up and replaced by another. The most compelling aspect of the whole drama was the part played by the loose carpet. At some point or other every single character tripped and plunged headlong towards the small table before righting themselves to shocked gasps from the audience.

'Well?' said Thelma challengingly, once it was over.

'A bold choice of play,' was all Isobel could manage. 'Most people would have done *The Importance of –*'

'Oh, but comedy's so *difficult*,' broke in Thelma. 'The timing.'

'Oh, I don't know,' said Isobel, thinking of the loose carpet. 'But thank you for an interesting evening. I must return the compliment and invite you to the next play they do in Asleby.'

*

August also provided time to catch up on filing. Isobel still couldn't believe the amount of bumf that came through her letterbox. In a magnanimous moment she did the readers' and intercessors' rotas for the next couple of months. Harry would bless her for it. He was on holiday in Italy with a friend, gender and status unknown. Isobel hadn't inquired. She missed him. It was a bit strange going to the vicar of St Mark's farewell party alone. Father McGee was there and said, 'While the cat's away . . .' He sat next to her during the bunfight and valedictory speeches, and twinkled and flirted in his incorrigible way. It crossed her mind afterwards that he'd spotted she was feeling a bit left out. Bless him.

Half the congregation was away. The Sunday services felt subdued. Jan was in Gloucestershire on her brother-in-law's canal boat and Isobel felt the lack of good friends nearby. People just round the corner, that's what she needed. There was no one around to do things at short notice. Nobody she could ring on impulse and say, 'Fancy a spin to the coast?'

Still, at least the weather was pleasant. Isobel spent time with the Youth Group, arranging rounders matches in the park against the youth group from Hartlepool, and midnight trips to Redcar beach. Many of the youngsters needed distracting from their forthcoming exam results. Fitz experienced a sudden surge of popularity among his peers on the arrival of the French *assistante* his parents were hosting for a couple of terms. Large groups of spotty lads congregated at the Fitzgeralds' house each evening to play computer games and wait for a glimpse of Véronique as she sashayed from bathroom to bedroom. Isobel overheard them fantasizing about systems of mirrors and spyholes and snickering smuttily in the back of the minibus as she drove them back from ten-pin bowling. Dream on, boys. If Véronique so much as glanced your way you'd be tongue-tied for a fortnight.

Another blessing of the slack period was the time it afforded for swimming and running. Isobel liked to keep in good shape, but she'd noticed that regular exercise was one of the first things to go when one's diary began to fill up. She set off round the park one teatime, aware she'd eaten more than she ought in France.

Running spelt freedom for her. It was like being a child again, before the awful years of the Bosom when she'd had to run – stagger was a better word – with her arms folded across her chest to tether her bouncing breasts. It had been a bitter trial to her.

She'd always been the fastest sprinter in the school, the best at long and high jump. She had a good throwing arm and was acknowledged, even by her brothers, to be a safe pair of hands on the cricket pitch. Puberty was purdah. It imposed an alien womanly decorum on her.

As she ran along the river path she rejoiced. Her arms were free! Her heart soared. She could have turned cartwheels. In fact – she checked all around – she would. There was nobody about. I bet I still can, she thought. *Yes!* Aagh! Slight wrenching down the ribcage, but not bad for thirty-three. She powered up the steep field, overtaking the doctor's wife (ha ha!), and arriving at her gate ecstatic.

She bent over, hands on knees, panting. Yes, I really must do this regularly; book it into the diary as a priority, even. Every aspect of my life will benefit, she told herself. Harry was always down at the gym or the squash club. He assured her the evangelistic possibilities there were endless.

'Good run?' asked a voice.

She straightened up. It was the policeman. She tugged the sweaty T-shirt away from her body self-consciously.

'Yes. Thanks. I've –'

'It's aal reet. Get your breath back.'

She nodded and continued panting, willing her lungs back under control. She'd got a stitch. Her face was burning. It was probably an unbecoming puce with livid white round the mouth and nose. She glanced at him. He was in tracksuit bottoms and football shirt, looking like half the lads in Asleby. He'd be how old – twenty? In his hand was her spray can. She caught the peardrop whiff of paint, and saw he'd been finishing off the scraped wing.

She bent close, still panting. 'That's good. Thanks.' The tricky matter of offering money loomed. 'Look. Need a drink.' She jabbed a finger towards the house.

'Oh, cheers,' he said, mistaking this for an invitation and following her in.

Damn, she thought. They went through to her kitchen. By now her knees were trembling from the exertion of the run and it wasn't a stitch, it was that ill-advised cartwheel. She'd pulled something. Her hands were almost too weak to press the ice cubes out of the tray into her glass of water.

'Here, give us that.' He did it for her.

She drank gratefully. Her breathing was getting somewhere near to normal. 'What can I get you? Coffee? Something cold?'

'Got any Coke?'

She found a large half-empty plastic bottle of cheap cola left over from a Youth Group picnic. It gave an ominously tiny fizz when opened. She poured some, hoping it wasn't too flat.

'I'm afraid I don't know your name,' she said, as she handed him the glass.

'DV.'

'What's that short for?'

'David,' he replied, looking at her a little strangely.

Oh, *Davy*! Wretched accent.

'Only I normally get Shorty,' he went on.

'Aha. Because you're so tall,' she said astutely.

He gave her the same strange look. 'Because it's my name. Davy Short.'

'Oh, I *see*.' She felt an urge to laugh. 'Well, David,' she began, trying to get a grip.

'Davy,' he corrected her.

'Davy. Thank you for sorting my car out. You must let me know how much I owe you.'

'Don't be daft, man.'

He had a kind of guileless enthusiasm, which made it difficult to insist. 'Well, that's very kind of you.'

'Nee bother.'

They fell silent. She was desperate for a shower, but it felt rude to throw him out.

'Is he local, like?' asked Davy, after a while.

'I'm sorry?'

'Is he local?'

'Is who local?'

'Your lad.'

'My *lad*?'

'Aye. Dark. Good-looking. In his twenties. Seen you out with him.'

It dawned on her he must mean Andrew. In his twenties, indeed!
'Oh, *him*.'

'Why, how many have you got?'

'Never you mind.'

'Just sussing out the opposition, like,' he said cheerfully.

She fixed him with her sternest stare. He looked unabashed.
'How old are you?'

'Twenty-two.'

'I'm eleven years older than you,' she told him. 'So I hope you
aren't getting any ridiculous ideas.'

'Just tell us if you're seeing anyone.'

'It's none of your business.'

'I'd like to make it mine.'

She laughed in amazement. 'Look, Davy,' she said kindly, 'let me
explain. I'm not interested in starting a relationship with anyone.
I imagine, as a Roman Catholic, you're familiar with the idea of
celibacy?'

'But you're C of E.'

'It's not a question of denomination,' she explained. 'It's a vocation that can come to anyone, lay or ordained, Protestant or
Catholic, young or old.'

'How can you tell if it's come to you?'

'Well, a sense of inner conviction.'

There was a long pause. He was nodding respectfully.

'And what's so funny about that?' she demanded sharply.

'Nothing.' He took a mouthful of cola, but snorted on it. She
pounded his back rather more firmly than was necessary as he
choked and spluttered with laughter.

'Ee, I'm sorry. Went down the wrong way.' He wiped his eyes
and cleared his throat. 'So. You're celibate, then?' His eyes flicked
over her.

'Stop laughing!'

'I'm not! I respect your views.'

'Then I'd be grateful if you took me seriously,' she snapped.

'I will. Honest, I will.'

'Thank you.' Isobel swirled the water in her glass. The ice rattled.

'So when can I see you again?'

131

Her mouth dropped open. 'You see? You haven't been listening to a word I said!'

'I have! Can we not be friends? You still owe me a pint. You promised us one for doing the car.'

She sighed in exasperation. All she wanted now was for him to go so that she could have a shower. 'All right.'

They settled on the following evening and she eventually got rid of him by promising faithfully to book her car in at the garage and get the back sorted out. She stood under the shower ready to whimper with relief. It was like having a large hound springing about the place.

At Isobel's suggestion they met at a pub outside the parish. With an alcoholic in the congregation it wasn't appropriate for the clergy to drink locally. She was surprised to note that her stomach was fluttering as she entered the pub, as though this were an assignation. He was waiting for her. After a brief skirmish over money – he appeared to have forgotten the point of the outing – she managed to buy him his pint. She was regretting having agreed to come, but five minutes of his company reminded her of the reason for her weakness. There was no dampening his high spirits. He was unsquashable. Her usual arsenal of frosty looks and crushing rejoinders glanced off him harmlessly. She spelt out once more in very explicit terms that there was no possibility of anything more than friendship between them. He nodded cheerfully and said that was fine by him. What could she do but take him at his word?

It was a surprisingly pleasant evening. Davy turned out to be good company. Once she'd relaxed she began to enjoy his sense of humour. It gradually dawned on her that he was more intelligent than she'd assumed. This was a humbling discovery. But, then, she'd turned out to be a much better pool player than he'd supposed (ha ha), so they'd both had to readjust their impression of the other.

'Hear you've had more trouble at the church,' he said, over a second pint.

'Yes. Idle lads invading the youth club. Broken window. Nothing serious. I gave some names to the officer who called.'

He surprised her by rattling off a list of Asleby's troublemakers. 'Same ones that broke into your house?' he asked.

'No.'

'Off the record?'

She hesitated.

'Look, it's not too late. If we catch them now and have a word, it'll prevent more trouble later,' he said. 'They'll get cheeky, Isobel.'

'Off the record,' she felt herself colouring, 'my colleague and I are of the opinion that it might be paranormal activity. We've had an expert in.'

His eyes widened. She watched respect battle with incredulity. 'Well, that's your field, then,' he conceded cautiously. 'But if there's ever anything I can do . . .'

'Well, actually,' she said, 'we're planning to do a session on drugs. I'm sure you'd have a lot of interesting insights into the problem.'

'Legalize the lot,' he said promptly. 'Save us a hell of a lot of trouble.'

She gawped.

'That's just my opinion.'

To her astonishment he was serious. His view was well thought out, but possibly *not* one she felt able to provide a platform for in a church Youth Group meeting.

As they were leaving the pub Isobel thought she caught sight of a couple of parishioners and it unnerved her. She hadn't been doing anything wrong, but nevertheless, she felt uncomfortable, and was reluctant to commit herself to seeing Davy again, despite his importunings.

She puzzled over this new friendship as she lay in bed. Was her anxiety simply over how it would appear to others? This was a genuine concern. As a priest she wasn't simply a free agent, a private individual. Even walking arm in arm with someone was evidently open to misinterpretation. Her behaviour must never become a stumbling block to others. Harry would be able to guide her on this matter. She rolled over and tried to sleep. Her memory seethed with pub noise. She couldn't resist going over the pool game stroke by stroke, savouring Davy's dismay as she wiped the floor with him.

The following day Harry got back from his holiday. Isobel wasn't expecting to see him until Sunday in church, but there he was on her doorstep, looking tanned and relaxed and offering her a bottle of wine and one of some exceptionally good extra-virgin olive oil.

'Harry!' She was astonished at how pleased she was to see him.

He kissed her cheek and came in. She made coffee and he told her about Italy. His friend appeared to be male, which was fine, of course. She brought him up to date on what had been happening, told him about the trouble at the youth club, the fact that Sue wanted her baby baptized in September, that the vicar of St Mark's had now left. They talked about the prospect of team ministry and Harry's meeting with the Archdeacon in early September to discuss the matter.

After he'd gone she remembered about Davy. Well, there was plenty of time to mention that later. It wasn't that important, after all.

## CHAPTER 12

Something warned Isobel to say no, but sitting in the headmistress's office and hearing her integrity and maturity so fulsomely praised, the honour of being head girl had seemed too great to refuse.

'You are a responsible girl in whom the staff and I place the highest confidence, knowing you will not let us down. You set the younger girls a positive example and will give the sixth form the kind of Moral Lead it needs.'

The sixth form did not want a Moral Lead. They wanted to carry on calling their untimetabled lessons 'frees', not 'study periods', and they wanted to spend them in the common room, not in the library. They wanted to talk about sex and leave coffee mugs lying around and put their feet on tables. They did not want to stay behind after school to have their minds broadened by lively topical discussions.

They made Isobel's life a misery. Not that she was subjected to a campaign of bullying. That would imply a degree of commitment and organization deeply unfashionable in the sixth form. But any small mistake on her part – a slopped coffee, a dropped biro, a wrong verb ending – was greeted with a groan of 'Oh, *Isobel*!' She'd never been popular, but until she was head girl she'd managed to keep her head below the parapet. If it hadn't been for Victoria and Annabel, school would have become unbearable. With their constant companionship she was able to bear the sneers of the rest in silence. They interpreted this as snootiness.

'Perhaps you'd like to share the joke with the rest of us, Julie?' snapped Mrs Penge. She was shy and cruelly pale-skinned. Her cheeks were flushed with two scarlet spots. Staffroom politics had decreed that she, being the newest and youngest member, must take the sixth-formers for general studies.

''S all right, thanks,' replied Julie. She was wearing a badge that read, 'If it's flaccid get your hands on it.' She always pronounced flaccid wrong, but Isobel had the wit not to correct her.

On the table in front of them was a model of 'the lady' – prim plastic genitalia with the reproductive organs pinkly visible through the transparent shell. Mrs Penge was dabbing gingerly in the direction of the labia with a diaphragm: 'The lady inserts it into the . . . in *here*, so that it covers the cervix, preventing any sperm *travelling* up and causing pregnancy.' Odd things were happening to her intonation. The tips of her ears were red.

The group were normally loud and coarse on sexual matters. They held themselves in, but the wave of suppressed mirth washed back and forth across the room, receding each time before the teacher's accusing stare, only to swell again behind her back.

'There are many methods of contraception.' Mrs Penge rattled off a list, brandishing coils and condoms with a kind of blinking defiance, like someone trying to master their fear of snakes. 'Well, pass them round and have a look!' she snapped. 'These classes are for your benefit.'

Julie dropped the condom (whoops!) when passing it to Isobel who was forced to bend down and pick it up. She kept her face blank, but they mocked her after the lesson anyway, talking about her as though she wasn't in the room.

'God, her face. She looked completely disgusted.'

'Well, it's probably the first time she'd touched one.'

'One what?' Cackle cackle.

'Oo, you dirty cow!'

Isobel stayed after school for an Oxbridge lesson with the other swotty girls. Dryden did nothing to dispel her slow-burning resentment. What made them so sure she was frigid? They knew nothing of what she was like inside. Nothing of the fierce appetites, the fantasies fuelled, not by *Cosmopolitan* but by Rochester, Donne, Lawrence. *Her nimble tongue, Love's lesser lightning, played/Within my mouth* . . .

'Isobel? What effect does that triplet have?'

'Um . . .'

'Oh, girls, I don't know what's the matter with you today!'

Isobel stood alone at the bus stop oblivious to the traffic's roar. *Licence my roving hands* . . . She hugged her school books close and shuddered. The sound of screeching brakes brought her back with a jolt. A black sports car reversed with a whoosh of tyres to where she was standing. She ignored it. Music pumped away.

'Wanna lift?'

She glanced frostily. He was in his twenties. Dark. Blood rushed to her face. Oh, God, so good-looking, but in a suntan and gold-jewellery way. The car had furry dice and long whippy aerials. She turned away again.

'No, thank you.'

'Head girl, eh?'

She clapped her hand over her badge and glared at him.

He laughed. 'Go on. Be a devil.' He made kissing noises. 'What's your name, then, Head Girl?'

'Here's my bus,' she said in relief.

He drove off.

All night she writhed in her bed at the thought of him. Masturbation helps relaxation. Slaking a fire with petrol. *Your shoulders, your bruised throat!/Your breasts, your nakedness!*

Sex was very wonderful. Isobel mimicked her mother's voice. Mum was not so old-fashioned that she thought you should wait till you were married, but sex was very special and worth waiting for. Isobel shouldn't waste herself on the first silly excitable boy who wanted to get her into bed. She should insist on being treated with respect. Above all she must be *sensible*. Sex was fun, but all too often people ended up getting hurt. Sleeping around was never a good idea. Exactly – VD and the risk of pregnancy. It was important to wait until you felt seriously about someone. Of *course* she told the boys the same thing! But Isobel must face the fact that *society* was more lenient about lads sowing their wild oats. No, it wasn't fair. Was there anything Isobel wanted to know? Well, so long as she knew she could always ask ...

Yeah, sure. Mum – what's it actually *like*? What does it feel like to have a man slide up inside you? What was the moment really like when you crossed from ignorance into knowledge in one slippery thrust – so *this* is it? Would you cry out in surprised recognition? Or disappointment? So *that* was it.

All night she kept going back and doing it differently. She retrieved her snooty 'No, thank you' and got into the car, back to his place, no, out on to the hills, still in the car, or pushed roughly to the springy turf, clothes tugged aside, he'd know what to do, be gentle with me, oh, God! *Come slowly – Eden!*

Never get into a car with a strange man. Insist on being treated with respect. Above all, be sensible.

He was there at hometime the following day, parked arrogantly across the school gates, leaning against the car with his arms folded and a cigarette in his mouth. She felt sick and cold, then someone said, 'Oh-my-*God*!' It was Julie. There was a second's pause in which Isobel's life hung in the balance. Then she walked straight up to him, an odd ringing noise in her ears. He opened the door and she got in. They drove off. Both of them were laughing, but for different reasons. The look on Julie's face was going to last Isobel for the rest of her life.

There was a whiff of autumn in the air. On one of those late August days summer had rolled over and started to drift away. It was still warm and the evenings were golden, but it was the gold of harvest. There was a different note in the rustling of the leaves, a restlessness. It affected Isobel with a sense of mounting anticipation every year, like a mistimed bout of spring fever. She supposed she was still attuned to the academic calendar and that was why her soul clamoured for fresh horizons and new beginnings.

Little Hannah's baptism was the highlight of that September. The quality of genuine thanksgiving for the gift of her life was almost palpable in the church that morning. Isobel had officiated at too many baptisms where the parents had little or no awareness of the divine and for whom the service was at best a folk-religion naming ceremony and at worst a tedious prelude to the booze-up. To be part of an occasion when the promises were fervently meant, and the child herself so much the answer to prayer, was one of the great privileges of ministry.

She carried Hannah proudly down the aisle and round the church after the baptism while the congregation responded, 'We are members together of the body of Christ; we are children of the same heavenly Father; we are inheritors together of the kingdom of God. We welcome you.' Bless you, she thought, looking down into the smiling face. You won't remember a thing about today, but I will, and I'll tell you about it when you're big enough to understand.

Isobel's feverish energy continued as September passed by. She found herself starting to channel it surreptitiously into speculation about the proposed team ministry. Once it was formed, she'd have a congregation of her own to get her teeth into, if that wasn't too unfortunate an image. No formal announcement about the proposal had yet been made in either parish. Apart from Harry there was nobody to share her excitement with. After he'd met the Archdeacon, both PCCs would have a chance to take part in the 'process of consultation'. It'll all take so long! wailed Isobel to herself. She found excuses for driving around what would become her pastoral district and dawdling past the church building. St Margaret's. A female patron saint struck her as a good omen. Her mind buzzed with plans and strategies. She oughtn't, strictly speaking, to be indulging her fantasies at such an early stage, but daydreaming never hurt anyone. It was like having a harmless little romance that no one knew about.

As the weeks went by she continued to see Davy. She had examined her own heart and decided that there was no danger of his inspiring any inconvenient amorous sparks. Articulating this to herself was a relief. It freed her to enjoy his company without forever agonizing about motives or what everyone might think. At some point the wagging parish tongues would inform Harry that his curate was seeing rather a lot of that young policeman. If Harry then chose to raise the matter with her, fair enough. She hesitated to describe the relationship as 'brother and sister'. Her own brothers had never been as kind to her as Davy was. Occasionally when Alistair had a friend over, Chris might end up playing with her, *faute de mieux*. Being the middle child he sometimes had to switch between being one of the big ones and one of the little ones. Alistair could be counted on to defend her. He bashed anyone who picked on his little sister, while reserving the right to bash her himself if the need arose.

But Davy was sweet. It was nice to have someone other than Jan with whom she could feel totally relaxed. She could drive the four miles to his house and flop down on his sofa. He dragged her off ten-pin bowling or out to the pictures. There had never been a surfeit of people in her life who thought to do that kind of thing. Imagine – an outing she hadn't had to arrange herself! Most of the time she enjoyed his company, although his raw energy and enthusiasm made her feel quite old at times.

'Davy, how many times do I have to tell you I am *not interested in football!*'

'You are, you are! You just don't realize it yet. Watch this penalty.'

'I've got to go and –'

'Watch watch watch!' He made her sit in front of his vast state-of-the-art TV. 'It'll not take a minute. There! Ah, that's dead canny, that.'

'Yes, yes. Now –'

'No, you don't understand. Watch. Watch it, man!' She was forced to endure the goal frame by frame. His accent, largely comprehensible to her, these days, would still plunge into stark gibberish for entire sentences at a time when the football was on. 'There! It looks like it's gannin' oot ...' She let it wash over her, then foolishly informed him that she hadn't followed a word he'd said, and was obliged to watch it all over again.

'There you are – you're hooked. Tell you what, I'll take you to St James's Park.'

'Davy, I'M NOT INTERESTED!'

'How will I get a ticket? Oh, aye, next European Cup match. Look! It's time for our favourite programme.'

'I'm *not* watching *A Question of Sport!*'

But it looked as though she was. And as the weeks went by something of his fanaticism infected her. Much to his amusement, her competitive streak was roused and she began to get caught up in the matches they watched together.

' "Come along, kick it, kick it!" ' he mocked. 'It's aal tactics wi' you, isn't it?'

Sports round-ups started to register with her. She noted the football results and could anticipate what kind of mood he'd be in. He claimed his red hair came from the Viking raids and whenever Newcastle scored this theory seemed plausible. His roar was the stuff of race memory; torched villages, ravished virgins and blood lust.

'I read in the paper that a man's testosterone levels are affected by how his team performs,' she told him.

'By, there'll be some serious shaggin' on the Toon the neet. Was that an offer, like?'

'Get off!' She cuffed him away, laughing. Although he was physically demonstrative, he never overstepped the mark. There was only one occasion when his behaviour had rung alarm bells.

They were out walking in Swaledale on Isobel's day off. Without warning a fighter jet shot over the rim of the hill behind her with a sound like an explosion. She flung herself down in terror.

Davy, who had seen it coming, pulled her to her feet again.

'Stop laughing!' she shouted, but her voice was drowned in the noise. He gave her a bear hug. She could still feel him chuckling. The jet roared away and silence closed back across the valley in its wake.

He hugged her closer. 'Ee, I can feel your heart.'

This had gone on quite long enough. As she pulled away she detected a fractional tug of resistance. She looked at him sharply and read a wordless request on his face. She shook her head.

'Sure?' he asked.

'*Quite* sure.'

'OK.' He gave a cheerful shrug.

They walked on. Silly boy! She'd made herself clear from the outset. But what if he'd been quietly hoping all this time? Was he suffering under that bluff exterior and she'd been too obtuse to notice?

'Davy, you're not . . . pining, are you?'

'What, me?' he hooted.

What me! They always deny it, she thought angrily. 'You don't think I'm encouraging you, do you?'

He considered this. 'Nah. If I really thought that, I'd've put clean underpants on.'

'*Thank* you for that little insight into your personal hygiene.'

They continued up the hill. Isobel felt the conversation still needed rounding off.

'So long as we understand one another.'

'Nee worries. I was just checking, like.'

'Well, stop checking.'

'OK. But I'm warnin' ye – if you pin w' doon and rip wor clothes off, I cannot promise to struggle.'

'Is that what you spend your time thinking about?'

'No! Well, aye. Now and then,' he admitted. 'Mebbes every thirty seconds.'

'Honestly, Davy.' She tutted. The issue wasn't as resolved as she would have liked, but she let it go.

It was dusk by the time they were driving home in Davy's car. He was working the late shift in Stockton. From what he'd told her he seemed to be on the receiving end of a lot of constabulary wit on account of his ethnic origins. She'd witnessed one example herself. The two of them were coming out of a pub one evening. A patrol car sidled up.

'Ha'away, Shorty. What d'you call a Geordie in a suit? The defendant.'

'Haddawayanshite,' replied Davy.

Isobel heard laughter from the car as it pulled away again. She turned to him.

'Why do you put up with it?' she asked.

'Oh, it's just a bit fun.' He shrugged. 'I'd rather be working here than Newcastle. I'd be nickin' me schoolmates the whole time.'

'Ah, yes. Crime's bad on Tyneside,' said Isobel, knowledgeably. 'I did placement in Bishopside when I was at theological college.'

'Well, it's the same all over,' he said. 'We'll be kept busy tonight. Unless the weather gets worse. Crime plummets when PC Rain's on duty.'

Sometimes she wondered how he maintained his optimism when he saw so much drunkenness, violence and rank stupidity in the course of his job. He genuinely liked people, while she, if she were being brutally frank, had a tendency to despise the human race. Particularly the male half. She tried not to let this prejudice her treatment of them, of course.

On their way back from Swaledale they passed beside a field of burning stubble. It was like a glimpse of medieval hell, with sparks flying, demon shapes striding in the smoke and a moon turned to blood. A rabbit darted into the road, skittering in the glare of the lights. Davy braked.

'Ha'away, son. Make your mind up.' The rabbit bolted for the verge, then at the last moment doubled back. 'Aw, *man!*' They both felt the bump under the wheels. 'Sorry.'

'It wasn't your fault.'

'I hate it, though.'

'Never mind. Rabbits are a terrible pest.'

'Ee! You cruel woman! You cannot say that. That was some mother's son. He was probably just popping ower the road for to see his mates and now he's dead!' he mourned. 'They'll be looking at their watches and saying, "Well, Hoppy, what's keeping our Skippy? It's not like him to –"'

'Oh, don't be ridiculous.'

'It's called anthropomorphizing. Fancy him knowing a word like that,' he added, correctly interpreting her expression.

Isobel said nothing. They drove the rest of the way in silence. He pulled up outside Isobel's house.

'We're not aal thick, ye kna,' he said, deliberately broadening his accent.

She got out of the car. 'I never said you were. Goodnight.'

The image of the burning field lingered in her mind. As she drifted asleep that night she kept jumping awake again at the thud of the rabbit under the tyre. At last she slept, but it was an uneasy sleep, full of puzzling dreams. At about three she woke with a start, thinking she'd heard her name called. The night was silent. She heard the usual industrial noises in the distance and the swishing of wind through leaves. I imagined it, she decided, but she couldn't shake off the thought that it had been some kind of warning. She lay awake, wondering what was troubling her. She tried various ideas. Sermon? That wretched team ministry conference? Davy? Yes. It was Davy. What had gone wrong that evening, exactly? Why on earth did she behave like such a raging snob? He didn't deserve it. Maybe she'd internalized her mother's double standards: rough accents were fine *per se*, though one would never dream of talking that way oneself. But she feared it went deeper. Was there something dark in herself, some streak of cruelty summoned forth by his artless generosity? I'll phone him tomorrow and apologize. There's nothing I can do now. At last she fell back to sleep.

There was a man making love to her. They were in his car. Her feet were up on the dashboard. It was Alex. She could control this dream, steer it in the direction she wanted. She would make him into Alex. But she was losing her grip, rising back up into consciousness as he thrust away between her thighs. Alex, Alex. But she could see the furry dice dangling behind his head, bobbing away, jiggle jiggle jiggle, the long whippy aerial wagging. It was Gary, and – most frustratingly of all – she was going to wake up before she came.

Yuck, thought Isobel. She hugged her arms across her chest, felt a jolt of shock, then laughed at herself. It was a long time since she'd forgotten how small her breasts were. For the first few months after the operation she had been forever recoiling in surprise from her new contours.

She got up and had a shower, dismissing her nocturnal lust from her mind. It was just one of those things; hormones, probably, ovulation . . . One couldn't prevent temptations occurring. It was all a question of what one did with them. 'You can't stop the vultures flying over, but you can stop them roosting in your tree' – a tag from a sermon she'd heard somewhere. Suppressing sexual urges willy-nilly was asking for trouble, but Isobel was responsibly acknowledging her instincts before God, then turning her mind to higher things.

The phone rang, annoyingly, in the middle of her sermon preparation. Her hand hovered over the receiver. She'd better answer it. If she didn't she'd fret that it had been a crisis of some sort. It turned out to be a woman who'd got herself into 'a bit of a state' and was wanting a visit. She'd tried the vicar, only he was out.

Isobel set off, not with terribly good grace. The address was in what she wasn't supposed to call the 'rougher' end of the parish. She'd visited there before, but had never felt she'd gained an entrance in the community.

She rang the doorbell and a man appeared. He was in his late forties with a moustache and stubble, which he ran his hand over as if belatedly remembering he shouldn't appear unshaven before a minister of religion.

'I'll get the wife.' This was what local men always said when confronted by a dog-collar on the doorstep. 'Come in. Lee!' he bawled. 'Get yer mam!' The TV blared. 'Sit yerself down, pet.'

A teenage lad appeared briefly in the doorway and froze. She wouldn't have recognized him if he hadn't drawn attention to himself with a look of stark terror. Gotcha! One of the trouble-makers from the youth club. He bolted. The front door banged.

'Lee! Little b–. I'll get her meself. Brenda!'

The house smelt of chip pan and cigarette smoke.

'I'm coming, I'm coming!' A big gypsy of a woman entered, gold earrings jangling. Isobel could see she'd been crying. 'Hello, love. Thanks for coming.' She tucked a tissue down the front of her black V-necked T-shirt into the kind of cleavage Isobel had once sported.

'What've you put her in here for?' she demanded of her man. 'Ee, *God*, he's useless. Come along, love. I'll take you through to the front room.' This was standard treatment for the clergy. It had a distancing effect. Vicars were posh professionals, not friends. 'Les, put the kettle on and bring us some coffee,' she ordered.

'Right you are, pet.' He disappeared into the kitchen.

'*If* I can trust him not to spill sugar all over me surfaces,' she grumbled, as they went into the best room.

They sat.

'How can I help you?' asked Isobel. The smell of peach pot-pourri filled her nostrils.

Brenda's face contorted briefly. 'You'll probably think I'm daft.'

'I'm sure I won't.'

'It's just that, look, if there's a bairn dies and it's not christened, will it go to hell?'

'No,' said Isobel.

'It won't?' Brenda brightened.

'No. Was this a baby you knew?'

'Oh, it's not dead. I was just worrying. It's my niece's bairn. They've just discovered he's got a hole in his heart and they've got to operate. She says she won't be getting him christened because she doesn't believe in God and she's not a hypocrite. Well, I can see that, but what about the bairn, that's what I'm thinking?'

'It's all right,' Isobel assured her. I could have dealt with that over the phone, she thought crossly. Now she was committed to staying for coffee. There might be more to come, of course. People often sidled up to the thing they really wanted to talk about.

'I'd got myself into a right state, what with tonight.' Brenda was relaxing now. 'I wasn't sure I could face it. You've got to be in the right mood. It's me Ann Summ —' Here she broke off in horror.

'Yes?' prompted Isobel.

'It's just for a laugh, really. Nobody takes it seriously. It's just a lasses' get-together with a couple of bottles of wine and a few games. It's a laugh,' she repeated.

'A party?'

'You must think I'm terrible.'

'Not at all,' replied Isobel, slightly at a loss. 'We all need to let our hair down now and then.'

Brenda eyed her in surprise. 'Well, like I was saying, I wasn't sure I could face it. Still, thanks for putting me right.'

Isobel sensed they were on the brink of something important, and was just framing a leading question to speed things along when Brenda said, 'I'm sorry it's such a state in here.'

Isobel glanced round. 'It looks fine to me.' After all, artexing and frilly net curtains were only a matter of taste, not indicators of human worth.

The husband crept in with the coffee and was sent away again for biscuits. He brought them, then sidled back out.

'I've been meaning to get it all done out, oh, for years now. New carpet, new paper. The lot. I quite fancy a dildo rail.'

'Dado rail,' corrected Isobel, with a tremor.

'Why, what did I say?'

'Never mind. Carry on.'

'Oh, new curtains with tie-backs. I've seen a lovely peachy fabric I like. Audrey's good with swags and tie-backs, so ...'

Don't think about it! Peachy fabric, peachy fabric. But Isobel was plunging steeply into hysteria while Brenda elaborated her soft-furnishing vision. This must be the house Harry had been called out to circumcise. The realization conjured up a vivid sense of his presence. Isobel clamped the inside of her lower lip in her teeth.

'I don't know,' Brenda was saying. 'I just feel like I need a complete change. A fresh start.'

This was the threshold of a spiritual breakthrough, and Isobel knew she was losing it. The image of a dildo rail assailed her afresh and she exploded with a shameful snort. No wonder Harry had faked hay fever. Isobel was beyond anything so enterprising.

'I'm so sorry.' She giggled.

'Was it something I said?'

Isobel nodded. 'This never happens to me!' she wailed. Stop it! Stop it! She buried her face in her hands. This is awful! Eventually she steadied herself enough to raise her face and say, 'I'm afraid you said . . .' Her voice dropped without warning into a deeply serious tone. 'Um, you said dildo instead of dado, and I . . .' Brenda was staring at her and all at once Isobel couldn't think for the life of her why it had seemed so funny. She cleared her throat. 'I'm sorry.'

'What's one of them, then?'

'Ah! Well,' she assumed her best schoolmarm voice, 'it's an artificial penis.' This last word escaped as a high-pitched squeal.

'You what?'

'Penis,' whimpered Isobel.

Brenda gave a guffaw of dirty laughter. For the next couple of minutes neither could speak. Brenda rocked and slapped her thighs while Isobel gasped, 'Oh dear, I'm sorry,' over and over again. Tears poured down her face. She would never, never stare disapprovingly at Harry again and wonder why he couldn't pull himself together.

'Ee, I wouldn't care,' whooped Brenda, 'only I've got a whole boxful next door!'

'Wha-a-?'

'Thingummies. For me Ann Summers party tonight.' She wiped her eyes. 'Ee!'

So that's what she was looking so shifty about, thought Isobel. The idea steadied her. 'You were saying something about wanting a fresh start?'

Brenda sighed and began fiddling with her gold charm bracelet. 'I dunno. I just feel like there's a hole. Here.' She jabbed at the minimal space between her breasts. The edifice wobbled. 'Like there's something missing from my life.'

Over the next hour Isobel listened as Brenda poured out her life story. How much pain was carried around in those ordinary lives. All those worries and tragedies. Perhaps Isobel had been stupefied by her bout of laughter, but somehow she couldn't muster her usual reassurances. All she could suggest was that Brenda and a group of friends might like to meet with her or Harry to discuss the Christian faith. Brenda agreed to think it over.

'Vicar's a nice lad,' she said. 'Gets terrible hay fever, though. He was round here once, coughing, eyes streaming. Had to put me cyclamen out in the yard.'

'Mmm,' managed Isobel.

'How does he cope with the flowers in church, I'm wondering?'

She left feeling she had failed. It was, without doubt, the most disastrous pastoral visit she'd made in her time in Asleby. All those openings for explaining the Gospel – wasted! And that appalling fit of hysterics. It welled up again at the memory. She doubted Brenda would join an Inquirers' Group. In her experience a 'yes' to that kind of invitation meant 'maybe'; 'maybe' meant 'no'.

As she walked along castigating herself a bike whizzed past, wheeled round and skidded to a halt in front of her. It was Lee.

'Did you grass me up?'

She stared at him and let him sweat a little. 'Maybe I did. Maybe I didn't.'

'Ha'away, did you?'

Amazing how these swaggering lads were still terrified of their mothers. She relented. 'Actually, I didn't, Lee. But trust me, one more whiff of trouble from you and your mates and I'll be straight round to your mam.'

He muttered something, which she was not naive enough to construe as thanks, then he whizzed away again. She saw him in

148

the distance jumping the bike showily up the kerb, possibly for her benefit, but more likely out of *joie de vivre* at his unexpected reprieve.

Isobel returned to her sermon, feeling as though she'd been through a mangle.

That evening Davy called round on his way to work. It felt odd to see him in his uniform. Before she could apologize he brandished something triumphantly in her face. Tickets to see Newcastle play in October. His face fell when she opened her diary and saw that it was the night of the confirmation.

'Ah, well,' he shrugged, 'another time.'

'I'm sorry. And I'm sorry about last night as well. I don't mean to be such a pig.'

'Careful with that word.'

'Oh!' She laughed. 'Well, snob, then. I don't know why I'm like it.'

'It's OK. Forget it.'

'Thanks.' On impulse she reached up and kissed him on the cheek. It was intended purely as a friendly gesture, but he blushed scarlet. His embarrassment infected her and for a moment they were locked in awkward silence.

'Well,' she said, 'I think I may have solved the problem at the youth club.'

'Really?'

She told him about her encounter with Lee.

'Well done,' he said. 'Lee's a canny lad, mind. They're not real villains. Not in Asleby.'

'Some of them are relatively disadvantaged,' she remarked defensively, as if he'd implied she had a cushy job.

He guffawed. 'You should see some of the lads we see. "Relatively disadvantaged"!'

'Well, what term do you use?'

'We call 'em scum, mostly,' he admitted cheerfully. 'Or arseholes.'

Isobel pursed her lips.

'Funnily enough,' he remarked, 'I grew up in a relatively disadvantaged area myself. And look at me now.'

149

Isobel did not respond. They were back in the territory they'd strayed into last night. She sensed that any discussion they might have on the causes of crime was unlikely to be particularly profitable.

After he'd gone she had a quick cup of coffee before setting off for housegroup. It was the first meeting after the summer break and they were starting a series of Bible studies on Genesis. Isobel was not leading them, but she still felt a sense of responsibility for the way the evening went. If it had been up to her she'd have cut the prayer time at the end a little shorter. But perhaps she was the only one whose thoughts were straying. Her mind went back to the encounter with Davy in her hallway and she felt a retrospective throb of excitement. She squashed it at once with a prayer.

## CHAPTER 13

If there was one boy Isobel really hated it was Neil Forbes. He was always coming up behind her, pulling her hair, then running off and hiding in the boys' toilets where she couldn't get him.

'Forbesy fancies Knockers! Forbesy fancies Knockers!' the other boys used to chant.

Every playtime for weeks and weeks and weeks he jabbed her in the back or pulled her hair and ran off. Suddenly she'd had enough. She ran after him, breasts bobbing and rage boiling up and up with every step. She could hardly see she was so mad; and when he bolted into the boys' she crashed in after him.

'Isobel's in the boys'!' shrieked the girls.

It stank in there.

He stood scared but defiant by the urinals. They were both panting. She was blocking his way to the door.

'I'm telling. You're not allowed in here.'

Wham!

*Never* kick a boy between the legs! cried her mother's voice.

Isobel walked out, leaving him curled up and keening on the floor.

'Well done, Isobel!' said the girls, as they crowded round her. For a few minutes she was popular. 'He really asked for it.'

But Isobel felt sick inside.

Isobel was waiting for Harry and trying to achieve the right frame of mind for the conference on new team ministry. She'd let herself down rather that morning by complaining at some length about having to go. In the end Harry had said, 'Well, in my experience the amount you get out of these things is usually about equal to what you put in.'

It was a mild enough comment, but Isobel always felt Harry's criticisms acutely. He was one of the few men she truly admired and respected. His approval was a matter of real importance to her.

Where had he got to? She looked out of her study window and to her annoyance saw a dog fouling her garden path. And the owner was just standing there watching! Isobel rapped sharply on the window. The dog scampered away and the man sauntered off after it.

Well, really! She stomped out to clear up the mess before it got tracked into the house. The episode hardly enhanced her mood.

Harry arrived in his car and they headed north to the Friary where the conference was to take place. Isobel drew a deep breath. At least they would be in beautiful surroundings, even if she would have to endure the presence of her fellow clergy at close quarters for two and a half days. Not to mention Brother Gabriel lurking presciently about in the corridors. But the setting, yes, that was lovely. Harry was strangely subdued.

'Are you OK?' she asked.

'Yes, thanks.' He hesitated. 'Hmm. I'd better tell you. It's bound to crop up while we're away.'

'What is?' she said in alarm.

'Bad news, I'm afraid. St Mark's PCC met last night and they've just passed resolutions A, B and C.'

'What? But they can't!'

'Well, they're required by canon law to debate the issue of women priests and flying bishops the first time there's an interregnum.'

'I know that! But they can't have *passed* them! They can't!'

'They have. I'm really sorry, Isobel.'

She blinked rapidly. But my church, everything I was hoping for! They don't want me. No, hold on, hold on. It wasn't personal. St Mark's was a more Catholic parish. It was simply a doctrinal thing. They opposed women's ordination. It's not personal, she repeated to herself.

She swallowed. 'But what will happen to the new team? You can't have half the parish under alternative episcopal oversight and half not.'

'Exactly,' he said grimly. 'They want their "own priest". The minute they got wind of the team idea they set about looking for a way to bugger things up.'

For once Isobel didn't rebuke him.

'However,' he went on, 'it's a problem for the senior staff to sort out, not us. And they will no doubt tackle it with their customary bold, proactive strategy called "Oh dear. Hmm, let's wait and see what happens, shall we?" Basically, Isobel, we'd better resign ourselves to the fact that there'll be no progress during your time in Asleby.'

They drove on in silence. Isobel found the very existence of these resolutions offensive. Far too much energy and money had gone into placating the opponents of women's priesting. As far as she was concerned a vote was a vote. If they didn't like the result they could lump it. 'Bye-bye, and don't forget to send us a postcard of the Vatican.' But to set up a system which guaranteed the continued existence of a sub-church that refused to accept what was now legal and binding! How can they *still* be so bigoted! What were they trying to say? That she was deluded in her belief that God had called her? That women weren't fit to set foot in the chancel? In the abstract this was bad enough; but now, just a mile down the road, was a church that had resolved never to have a woman vicar, never to allow a woman to preside at communion and to have no truck with any bishop who ordained women.

'It feels like a slap in the face,' she said.

'I'm sure it does. Can I just . . .' He hesitated again. 'Speaking with my patronizing male-establishment-figure hat on, can I encourage you *not* to take this as a personal affront? It's an anti-Asleby move, not an anti-Isobel one. It's sheer bloody-mindedness.'

'I realize that,' she said stiffly.

'The problem we'll both have to deal with is how to channel our anger appropriately.'

'Oh, I'm not angry.'

'Well, I'm bloody furious.'

There was a pause. Isobel had no wish to appear inadequate. 'Of course, it's jolly annoying. Frustrating. For both of us. For you in particular.'

Harry made no reply. He was not a man to parade his emotions and Isobel seldom enjoyed any real insight into what he was feeling.

For a moment he was a stranger, steely and silent, not her dear old Harry, subject to fits of giggles during hymns. The difference unnerved her.

'I *will* be angry if I find I've been dragged to this conference under false pretences,' she joked, but this sally barely won a smile. She was left to her own thoughts for the rest of the journey.

So she must relinquish the idea of St Margaret's. Well, serve her right for letting her imagination run riot. Impatience was her besetting sin. Perhaps God was trying to teach her something through this unfortunate episode. Harry was right, as usual. She must *not* take it personally. There were too many women who undermined their own cause by appearing bitter. Isobel had always tried to see the gender issue as a straightforward matter of equality, not as a personal crusade. But it still felt like such a stinging blow.

They arrived at the Friary. Enthusiasm, generosity of spirit, recited Isobel, while Harry parked. They got out. Anyway, beautiful surroundings. She took a deep breath, turned round, and her good intentions promptly imploded.

Johnny Whitaker.

She saw her 'Oh, no!' mirrored on his face.

'Johnny!' exclaimed Harry in delight. 'What are you doing here?'

'Same as you,' he replied. 'Team Ministry – the Way Forward for Bishopside.' His guffaw rang out. 'How's it hanging, Harry?'

The two of them hugged. Isobel waited while Harry was subjected to the hair-rumpling and general mauling about that constituted a greeting from his former curate. He emerged a little breathless, but restored to his cheerful self by that old Whitaker magic. Huh, thought Isobel.

'And how's Isobel?' asked Johnny, extending a formal hand.

She shook it with a tight-lipped 'Fine, thanks.'

At least it was an improvement on last time, when he'd given her a squeeze round the waist. Her protest had met with the 'explanation' that he'd given up smoking and had to find something to do with his hands. She noted that the cigarettes were back in evidence today, and felt vindicated in her low opinion of his moral fibre.

They gathered immediately for afternoon tea in the common room, which left Isobel no chance to slip off and deal with her ill-temper. A swift glance around confirmed her worst fears. It was going to be purgatory. There was Gabriel. She gave him a nod. He and some of the other brothers were circulating and making people welcome. She spotted some high churchmen (the Betty Black Blouses, as Harry called them) gathered in one corner. She could just about cope with them, despite their stance on women in the Church. At least they took their faith seriously. What she couldn't stomach was the little bunch of lah-di-dah liberals who'd trained at Lightfoot House, Cambridge, with their affected louche-ness and young-fogey leather elbow patches. She'd encountered them on post-ordination training. They recoiled fastidiously from any expression of personal piety, as though they thought that believing in God and mentioning it publicly were solecisms of embarrassing magnitude. For them Evangelicalism was the spiritual equivalent of drinking Babycham, and they treated Isobel with a patronizing pity that implied she'd been lobotomized.

Harry was still in conversation with Johnny. Isobel scanned the crowd for someone to talk to and felt a rush of her old misery. *I never fit in anywhere. I want to go home.* Still, better make the best of it. She recognized a woman curate from Sunderland and strode across to chat to her.

The first session was pretty grisly. The people leading the con-ference invited everyone to reflect on the concerns, worries and hopes they had brought with them; then to draw on a piece of paper 'something to carry those concerns in'.

Isobel cudgelled her pedestrian imagination and sketched a briefcase. They were then asked to 'share' what they had drawn and why. There were no right or wrong answers. All responses were equally valid. She was relieved to see that most people had chosen suitcases or rucksacks, so at least she wasn't the dullest, most prosaic person in the room. Harry's biro had got slightly carried away and his treasure chest came complete with desert island, sea, sharks and pirate ship. Isobel had known him doodle similar scenes in Deanery Synod. Johnny Whitaker had drawn a six-ton truck, on the grounds that nothing else was big enough. Isobel repressed her instinctive reaction that he was cheating. It was not, after all, a competition.

She tried to soothe away her bitterness in evensong. After a moment she acknowledged she was a little hurt that Harry should abandon her company in favour of Johnny's. Which was very silly of her. The two men were close friends and seldom saw each other. And be honest, Isobel, she told herself, you're ignoring Harry's advice and letting your anger about St Mark's PCC spill over into other areas. Johnny Whitaker was not without his faults, but he had not passed those hurtful resolutions. Nor would he, despite his occasional unreconstructed chauvinism. The service was an opportunity for her to focus on God.

Unfortunately the opportunity was spoiled. The Old Testament lesson was from the Song of Songs and the arcane words of the lover to his beloved reduced first Johnny and Harry, and then by degrees the rest of the back two rows, to fits of terrible mirth. Isobel, having forgotten her own bout at Brenda's, wished they'd control themselves. Even Gabriel in his stall at the front was struggling.

They went straight from chapel to dinner. Ahead of her in the corridor Isobel could hear Johnny quoting, ' "Your breasts are like twin fawns of gazelle." I just don't get it, me. I mean, I've looked at gazelles. I've looked at . . . What's wrong, Harry?'

'Stop it,' pleaded Harry. 'It hurts.'

Isobel pursed her lips and went and sat with the woman she'd spoken to earlier. Penelope was a bit of a misery-guts, to be honest, and even more prone than Isobel to retort 'or *she*' to any sexist faux pas made by her companions. During the meal Isobel tried to concentrate on her table's conversation, but all the time she was hankering to know what was being said on the other side of the room and why they were all guffawing.

After the evening session a group of them set off down to the village for a drink. A general invitation was flung out, but Isobel hardly felt included in it. And, anyway, she'd much rather go for a walk than sit in a smoky pub.

It was another beautiful golden evening. She made a conscious effort to leave her disappointment over St Margaret's behind her and let the countryside do its restorative work. She wandered round the back of the house to the field, which led steeply down to the wooded riverbank. High above in the treetops the rooks were cawing their goodnights. In the past she'd seen red squirrels here. Underfoot were the discarded pine cones they'd chewed, but no sign of the squirrels themselves. She had a vision of them watching, then joining hands and dancing in a circle after she'd passed. That's the sort of thing Tatiana and I used to pretend, she thought. The woods of her childhood were always populated with half-believed-in elves and fauns. When she'd played with Tatiana they'd been watched over by a thousand bright eyes; eyes that winked away when you whirled round on them. Nowadays the only eyes Isobel imagined belonged to the would-be rapist lurking in the undergrowth.

Bother. Why had she let herself think that? It was so unfair. Men didn't have to worry like this. How often did they calculate the risks of a solitary country walk, or look down an unlit street and wonder whether, if it came to it, they could sprint in their new shoes? Isobel was not prone to frightening herself unnecessarily. She knew the dangers were negligible and that statistically she was far more likely to be assaulted by a man she knew. But she resented not being able to walk carelessly on a beautiful night.

It was getting dark. She headed back. The lights of the Friary shone through the trees. Something moved in the bushes. Isobel froze. A fox emerged not four yards ahead of her. She watched it trot calmly across the lawn in the twilight and melt away again into the shadows, untroubled by her presence.

She went into the house, blinking in the brightness. Gabriel was coming along the corridor towards her.

'Nice walk?'

'Yes, thank you,' she replied. The Friary was silent. 'I've just seen a fox. Really close up.'

He nodded. 'They've got a bit cheeky. We have a "no shooting and hunting" policy in the grounds.'

Isobel recalled a mawkish image of St Francis surrounded by wildlife and smiled politely. 'Well, I'm sure your patron would approve of –' She broke off in surprise as Gabriel aimed an imaginary gun.

157

'Bang! Goodbye, Brother Fox.' He smiled at her shocked expression. 'I grew up on a farm.'

She stared after him as he walked off. Well, no reason to be surprised that Gabriel had a past. Franciscans hardly sprang fully formed from the mind of God, did they? She really was going to have to address her anti-monastic prejudices at some stage.

Her room was comfortable and warm. After a time of prayer, in which she hoped her hurts and disappointments were fully laid to rest, she went to bed. She was drifting to sleep when the silence was broken by voices in the night. It was the revellers returning. Johnny Whitaker's laugh rose above the rest. Isobel rolled over with an angry flounce.

The next day her temper was even more frayed. She'd been kept awake half the night by the snores of the person in the next room. It hardly felt Christian to bang on the flimsy wall and shout, 'For goodness' sake, shut up!' She had to endure some Lightfootian drollery from the liberals over breakfast as she toiled through her bowl of penitential Franciscan muesli.

She wisely judged that her best course of action was to avoid Johnny Whitaker as much as possible. This wasn't easy. The people leading the conference reserved the right to allocate people to groups for inscrutable reasons of their own, and short of saying, 'I'm not going with him!' there was nothing Isobel could do about it. Even if she avoided him in the dreaded buzz groups he would be there in the plenary session, subverting any serious discussion with his constant joke-cracking. And Harry, under his influence, wasn't any better.

Quite frankly, it was all a bit much. Isobel gave way to her irritation on a couple of occasions and crossed swords with Johnny. However, it wasn't as if she was unjustified. He persisted in affecting a rough Geordie accent, although they all knew he was perfectly capable of speaking properly when he chose. It was this Jack-the-lad-I'm-working-class-me business that finally got to her. He was *not* working class. She said as much. He may have come from a working-class background, but these days he was a graduate in a middle-class profession living in a large, detached house.

'Aye, but I'm on a working-class income,' he'd replied, to general laughter. He'd continued holding forth about the Church being too middle class, as though she'd never opened her mouth. It had been exactly the same when she, backed up by Penelope, had picked him up on his blatantly non-inclusive language.

The day was spent in various exercises designed to help them understand group dynamics and models of leadership. One of them was so futile that she'd almost walked out. I bet they wouldn't think *that* response was equally valid! 'Arrange yourselves in order,' they'd been told. What kind of order? Any kind. The group had to decide.

'Ha'away, quick. Alphabetical,' said Johnny. 'Then we can gan doon the pub before lunch.'

For a moment Isobel was almost in sympathy with him.

The day ground on. Everyone else was enduring it with good humour. Some even thought the sessions helpful. Isobel tried to look alert and interested so that the leaders wouldn't say, 'I wonder why you find this so *threatening*?' Despite her efforts she knew her face must be a picture. At dinnertime Harry made a point of coming to sit with her. He lifted the lid of the serving dish in front of him. 'Aha. I see the vegetables are having a plenary session.'

Isobel glanced at the steaming mixture and tried to smile.

'Is everything all right?' he asked quietly.

'I just find the whole thing so pointless,' she muttered.

'Is there any *particular* reason you're taking it out on Johnny?'

Me! Isobel swelled at the injustice of it. What about him? 'I hope I'm not taking it out on anybody,' she managed.

'Oh, come off it. What's wrong, Isobel?'

'Nothing! And if you don't mind my saying so, you're always taking his part!' she hissed.

He raised an eyebrow at this and turned to talk to the person on his other side, leaving her to lament her childish outburst.

Later on she was relieved to see he'd overlooked it. He invited her out to the pub and she accepted. Fortunately Johnny wasn't walking down with them. He was trying to phone The Wife, as he called her.

It was a pleasant enough pub. The Lightfeet were already there, of course, under clouds of self-consciously worldly cigarette smoke. Their keenness to get to the pub was matched only by their eagerness to escape parish duties by coming away on a conference, thought Isobel. Harry bought her a drink and they found a quiet smoke-free corner. It was a relief to have him to herself again.

Before long they were joined by some clergy from Sunderland. Penelope sat down wearily and said she'd have sparkling apple juice, *if* they had any, otherwise mineral water. Honestly, thought Isobel. For people like Penelope the glass was not only half-empty but liable to be knocked over at any moment. Harry was chatting politely to her, leaving Isobel to make conversation with the man on her right. Talk turned to funerals and they all began to exchange horror stories. Harry related how, when he was a curate, he'd been sitting in a staff meeting in the vicarage when both he and the vicar had seen a hearse go past.

'"Yours or mine?" said the vicar. "Mine!" I sprinted down to the church and just made it,' said Harry.

They all laughed. Isobel saw Johnny come in. He bought himself a pint then joined them.

'Did you get through?' she heard Harry murmur.

'Nah.' Johnny got out his cigarettes.

Isobel leant forward and said – politely, she thought – 'Do you mind?'

He glanced around. 'I don't see any no-smoking signs.'

'All the same, I'd much rather you didn't. We sat here because –'

He lit the cigarette and blew the smoke up to the ceiling. She flushed angrily as his eyes challenged her.

'What's your problem, pet? Run out of balls to break in Asleby?'

Isobel gasped.

'Hey!' objected Harry. To Isobel's chagrin he was complaining more about the slur on his manhood than the insult to her.

The rest of the group looked acutely uncomfortable.

'That's a bit out of order, John,' said one. The others murmured in agreement.

'She's been pissing on me from a great moral height aal fuckin' dee,' said Johnny. 'And I've had enough.'

'There's *no* call for that!' snapped Isobel.

'And there's you wanting to be tret like one of the lads,' he sneered. 'You cannot have it both ways, sweetheart.'

'Actually,' put in Harry, 'some of us lads don't much care for your language either.'

'Thank you, Harry,' said Isobel. She turned to Johnny. 'You see?' Perhaps gloating like this was unwise; but she was completely unprepared for the reaction it provoked.

'Fuck off!' he exploded. 'Just fuck off, Isobel, man. I've had it with you.' He stubbed out his cigarette and picked up his pint. 'I'm away.'

He left a stunned silence in his wake. Isobel's hand trembled as she picked up her drink. Harry tutted softly.

'Well,' said Penelope, 'that's a bit excessive. Are you all right, Isobel?'

She nodded. She was shaken, but deep down a nasty part of her was gleeful. She'd felt the same as a child when her brothers copped it.

It was a while before the conversation returned to normal.

When they left, an hour or so later, Johnny reappeared and crossed over to Isobel, looking penitent. He indicated that he wanted to speak privately, but Isobel stood her ground. He'd insulted her publicly enough.

He drew close. 'Look, I'm really sorry about that,' he said.

She inclined her head.

'I've always had a temper on me.'

'Then perhaps it's time you learnt to control it,' said Isobel.

Whereupon he stormed out again. She turned to Harry for vindication.

'That,' he said, 'was not generous, Isobel.'

'But it's true! He –'

'I don't want to hear.'

Isobel seethed with self-justification as they walked back to the Friary. All she'd said was . . . It was so unfair! She'd only asked him not to smoke! She hated being at odds with Harry, but she was *not* going to apologize for something that wasn't her fault. Johnny *should* learn to control his temper. He was an ordained minister,

161

for goodness' sake! Her eyes began to smart. Harry was not talking to her. To have him rebuke her like that in the hearing of others! She remembered his question over dinner. Was it possible that she was venting her spleen on Johnny after all? Deliberately goading him? Her hateful glee at his outburst came back to her. By the time they reached the house she was in some anguish.

She caught Harry's arm. 'Look, I'll go and apologize to him.'

'Good,' he said curtly.

She bit her lip and hurried up to Johnny's room. He wasn't there. Now what was she going to do? He could be anywhere. If she wasn't careful she was going to end up in tears, and Isobel never cried. Oh, this whole stupid business! She'd better go and sit in the chapel and compose herself.

She hurried down and opened the door. It was dark in there, just the red sanctuary light and the softly illuminated crucifix above the altar. There was incense in the air. She closed the door and knelt, waiting while her eyes grew accustomed to the dimness.

I don't understand myself, she thought. What is it about this man that means I can scarcely bear to be in the same room as him? She could find no answer. What would I do if a parishioner came to me with this problem? First, she would point out that it is our duty to love, not like, our fellow human beings. You can still act in a generous way, she would suggest, even if – But this was hopeless. She'd wrestled and prayed with every fibre of her being, yet her feelings towards Johnny were still ungovernable. What other insight might she offer this imaginary parishioner? Well, she might gently point out that what often annoys us in others is often our own faults. But this wouldn't do for Johnny. His faults were the opposite of hers. His irreverent wit, his overly free manner, his uncontrolled temper. Unless this was the point: what she resented in him was what she *repressed* in herself. Aha! Now she was getting somewhere.

What was he? He was warm and spontaneous. He was affectionate and physical. All the things I'm not and perhaps would like to be? But here Isobel felt she was grinding to a halt again. The other thing she would ask her counsellee was: Does he remind you of someone?

No sooner had she asked this than the answer burst in upon Isobel. She slapped both hands down on the pew in rage. No! Not *Gary*. She scrambled to her feet, then forced herself to kneel again. That is so pathetic, she thought in despair. And yet it was true. Gary the working-class lad. Dark, flashy, even the earring was right! Oh, spare me. She punched her fist into her palm. I'm such a fool.

Memories surged back – feet on dashboard, jiggling dice – she beat them off. It had all been dealt with. God had forgiven her. Surely if the grace of God meant anything it meant that she was free from the 'power of cancelled sin', as the hymn-writer put it.

But it was a relief to know. Yes, it was obvious now. Johnny evoked memories from a period in her past of which she was profoundly ashamed. Small wonder his presence ruffled her. Now that she realized this, she could commit it to God in prayer, and she'd be able to relate properly to Johnny. Good. She made as if to get to her feet once more, but detected a restraining impulse. Wait, there's more, it seemed to say.

More? She waited. What was it? An odd feeling crept over her – the answer was obvious, right under her nose. At any moment she would spot it. She frowned. It was no good. She'd have to come at it obliquely. When had she first been aware of her hostility to Johnny? Instantly, at first sight when he'd taken Annie and Will's wedding. Then, in her first week in Asleby, everyone had been praising him. She'd encountered his name at every house she visited. Professional jealousy, too?

Of course, the *obvious* explanation was that she was attracted to him. This was not the case, though. She'd put that idea to herself on numerous occasions and drawn a blank. He simply wasn't her type. Except, possibly, on a rather crass physical level. Like Gary. She made herself look at this squarely. It was humiliating, but the truth was that Gary had unleashed the 'raw animal passion' that Edward had so ridiculed. So. One must concede it possible that she felt the same about Johnny. At a crass physical level. Very well.

She could feel her face burning. Why was she making such a song and dance about it? Surely there was no shame attached to being attracted to an attractive man – and Johnny was attractive, one might as well be frank about that. She would be less than human if she didn't feel that way. Was it not possible to give thanks for those feelings? They were God-given, were they not? It was wrong to deny them. It was all a question of what one did with them. She might also give thanks for Johnny himself, for his attractiveness, his many good qualities –

She faltered here. If she went further down this path she would end up acknowledging that it might not be only her animal passions that Johnny would satisfy. Unlike Gary, he was intelligent and educated. He was also a Christian minister. He might, in fact, be the embodiment of all that she looked for in a partner.

Which would leave her in the intolerable position of suffering unrequited love for a married man.

Isobel sat for a long time in silence. She gazed at the figure of Christ on the cross. His anguish had been public. He had borne it with dignity.

Unrequited love. It was such a small, private cross to bear. She'd been through it all before, hadn't she, with Alex? I'm an ordinary mortal. Why should I escape just because I'm ordained? Give me grace to bear it with dignity.

## CHAPTER 14

What have you done? What have you done? Isobel asked herself, as the black sports car snarled up the long hill out of the town.

'You're going too fast!' she cried.

'You ent seen nuffink yet, darling.'

The ten minutes home were the most terrifying Isobel had ever experienced. Gary drove like a rally driver, taking bends on the wrong side of the road, laughing at her closed eyes and white knuckles. They entered her quiet village at seventy miles an hour and pulled up on the Old Wrecktory drive in a scrunch of gravel.

'Thank you,' said Isobel weakly, for she had been brought up well.

He switched off the engine. A magpie gave a harsh churring cry from the rooftop, then there was silence.

'Well? Aren't you going to ask me in, then?' he inquired.

'Um . . .'

'For coffee,' he prompted, seeing she didn't know how to play this game.

'Oh! Yes. All right.' It would have seemed rude to refuse.

They got out of the car. She found her keys and opened the door. Her fingers were trembling.

'Nice place,' he said, looking about the hallway at the tiled floor and polished banisters. 'Worth a bit, them.'

They went to the kitchen. She made them each a mug of coffee. He admired the built-in dresser, then prowled about downstairs as if casing the joint. She trailed after him until they ended up in the kitchen again. Now what would happen? Why on earth had she let him in? He came and stood closer, leaning against the dresser and watching her. Oh, God! she thought in panic.

'What's up?' he asked.

'My – my mum,' she blurted. 'She'll be back soon. Any minute.'

'So?' He came a little closer.

'I think I can hear her car,' she cried.

He grinned. 'Well, I'll stop and say 'ello, then.' But seeing her fear he relented. 'All right, darling. I'll love you and leave you.' He put the mug down on the draining-board, waggled his fingers at her and walked out. Remembering her manners she went with him to the door.

'Same time tomorrow?' he asked.

'I – I don't know. No.'

'Wotcher scared of?'

'Your driving!' she flashed,

He laughed. 'And?'

'Nothing,' she said defensively.

'"Nuffing," she says.' He took her chin in his hand. She smelt his smoker's breath as his mouth approached hers – He's going to –

'How old are you?'

'Sixteen.'

'Sweet sixteen and never been kissed. Soon put that right.'

Love's lesser lightning. On and on ...

In the end, when she was quivering from head to foot, he stopped. 'What about another little drive, eh? Find ourselves a nice quiet spot ...'

'All right,' she whispered.


It was a long night for Isobel. How was she to frame her apology to Johnny? Admitting her true feelings was neither desirable nor helpful. It would be like handing him an unexploded bomb. Yet she felt a simple 'sorry' for her ungraciousness didn't do justice to the enormity of what had taken place. The problem had kept her from sleeping; but at least the worry helped staunch the flow of memories about Gary. She drifted off at last only to be visited by a lurid dream of being tied to the main mast and ravished by a buccaneer in thigh boots. Honestly, why did one's subconscious operate in such bodice-ripping clichés?

Morning brought the creeping dread that everyone on the conference had witnessed her behaving like a thirteen-year-old with a crush and now pitied or derided her in their hearts. Well, she must simply make the best of it.

She was up before breakfast walking in the grounds. After a while she sat on a bench and took a deep breath. The wind was rushing in the leaves. It was a bright morning. She stared across the wet lawn and could see one dewdrop picked out by the sun's rays. It blazed, and as she slowly turned her head she saw it melt through all the colours of the spectrum. In the distance the wind was buffeting the trees on the wooded hill. The larches gleamed against the sombreness of the other pines. A crowd of woodpigeons whirled up into the sky as though a gust had tossed them; then the first handful of autumn leaves swirled up in echo, high, higher, twinkling in the sunlight.

It will pass, Isobel told herself. As surely as the seasons turn and the tide ebbs. I survived Alex, for goodness' sake. I can manage this. God would not permit her to be tempted beyond what she could endure. The Bible assured her of that. And, in any case, after today she wouldn't see Johnny again for months. No, wait – he was coming to Asleby's Harvest Supper. But at least they weren't colleagues. Now that *would* be a disaster. Imagine if she fell for Harry! Yes, she could perceive the gracious hand of God in this. Perhaps she needed the experience. She was a little too inclined to think of herself as set apart from her fellow mortals. The Lord had permitted even St Paul his thorn in the flesh. God's strength was made perfect in weakness – there was a good text to hang on to.

She looked at her watch. It was nearly breakfast time. She stood up and began to walk towards the house. As she turned the corner by the yew hedge there was Johnny two yards from her.

They both stopped. Isobel flushed crimson.

'Hello,' she said.

'Hiya.'

He was about to light a cigarette. She thought he was hesitating so she flapped a hand. 'Go ahead. Please.'

The look on his face plainly said he didn't need her permission. He blew away a cloud of smoke.

'I tried to find you last night,' she hurried on. 'To say sorry. It was ungenerous of me.' Now he could do it back to her – throw the apology in her face. 'So, um, sorry.'

But he smiled. 'That's OK.'

'I've been feeling awful.'

'Forget it. It was six and two threes. You caught me at a bad moment. You weren't to know.'

'Well, thanks.' There was an awkward pause. Isobel reached out a hand to the hedge and began fingering the leaves. 'I know I've been aggressive. It's not your fault,' she said, her incorrigible honesty overruling all common sense. 'It's just that, well, it's occurred to me that what's *in fact* going on is that you remind me of someone who I − Someone from my past who −' She peered at the pinkish waxy berries. 'And so ...'

Johnny laughed. 'Who was that, then? The gamekeeper?'

'Just someone I knew,' she said stiffly, twiddling a berry until it fell off. He'd guessed. 'Someone *else* very annoying,' she added, hoping this sounded more like her usual self. She met his eye.

He wiped the grin off his face. After a moment she resumed her study of the hedge. A new topic of conversation was urgently needed.

'It's yew,' she offered.

After a moment he replied, 'Aye. I'm sorry.'

There was another pause. Then Isobel blushed deeply. 'No, no! *Yew*, not *you*.' He thought she meant − 'Ha ha! As in yew *tree*.' She snapped a sprig off and flourished it at him.

'Oh, *right*.' He coloured and took the twig from her. Now it was his turn to be seized by botanical curiosity. He frowned at the leaves, evidently struggling between amusement and cursing himself.

'There's one in our churchyard,' she observed desperately.

'Aye, so there is. I remember.'

'It's very ancient.'

'Great view from the top, mind.'

'But you aren't supposed to climb it!' she protested.

'Who says?'

'Well, it's not allowed. You might damage it. It's ancient,' she repeated. 'You have to respect that.'

'Don't be daft, man. Kids have been climbing it for centuries.'

'All the same,' said Isobel.

'You're a real one for rules, aren't you?'

'I should hope we all are!'

'Not just for the sake of it, no.'

They began to walk towards the house. She didn't care for this criticism, and it revived her hostility towards him.

'May I ask you something?' she said. 'That cricket match last summer. Did you get me out on purpose?'

'Why, aye.'

'I knew it!' she cried triumphantly.

'Well, you called me a fat oaf.'

'I did not!'

' "Run, you fat oaf!" '

Isobel considered this. She supposed it was just about possible. 'Well, you should have been exerting yourself.'

'It was my call.'

'You lost us the match!' she squeaked.

'Isobel,' he said, 'it was worth it.' They crunched along the quiet path. 'And I'm not fat,' he added, slapping his midriff. 'That's pure muscle, that.'

Harry was in the hallway. She saw his eyes take in the apparent reconciliation.

'She's calling us fat,' complained Johnny. 'Can you credit it?'

Harry peered thoughtfully. 'Well, perhaps you are softening up.'

'I'm bloody not! Don't you start. I can get this at home.'

They went in for breakfast together, laughing.

The conference was over. Most people had already gone. Harry, keen for one last fix of Franciscan liturgy, had begged to stay for evening prayer. Isobel had agreed readily enough, although it wasn't entirely her cup of tea. Johnny was with them as they sat in the chapel waiting for the service to begin. But that wasn't a problem. Isobel was relieved to discover how relaxed she felt in his company now they'd cleared the air. He was a good man. Attractive, obviously, but mercifully *not* a problem.

She was concerned for him, though; and she was fairly sure Harry shared her worries. 'I've nowt to get back for,' Johnny had said, when asked whether he was leaving. Isobel had opened her mouth to remark that his wife wouldn't thank him for saying that, but a sudden suspicion made her hold her tongue.

After a pause Harry suggested equably, 'Well, why not join us for evening prayer?'

Isobel had always considered it unfortunate that Johnny's wife didn't support him in his ministry. Perhaps this was taking its toll on their marriage? She recalled the incident in the pub – he'd been trying to phone home and hadn't got through. Supposing he'd parted from his wife on bad terms as he set out for the conference and –

But here Isobel was forced to break off. The service was beginning. The office was unfamiliar and Isobel was unable to relax into it. She'd never quite grasped the point of four services a day, or whatever it was. Still, it was her duty and her joy at all times and in all places, etc.

The Old Testament reading drew close and she felt Harry stiffen beside her, as if in recollection of what the Song of Songs had reduced him and Johnny to a couple of evenings before. A precarious solemnity settled over their pew as Gabriel rose to read. Isobel suppressed a surge of irritation. Yes, yes, it was part of the canon of Scripture, but one really had to consider the appropriateness of reading what was essentially erotic verse in the context of public worship. The effect was worsened by the fact that poor old Gabriel was having to read the woman's part. Isobel felt for him, willing Harry and Johnny to keep a grip on themselves.

> *'O that you were like a brother to me,*
> *that nursed at my mother's breast!*
> *If I met you outside, I would kiss you,*
> *and none would despise me.'*

Then, without warning, a different meaning swept through the text like a dangerous undertow. Isobel ducked her head in confusion and tried to banish the thought; but the words had became subversive, charged with homoerotic longing:

> *'I would give you spiced wine to drink,*
> *the juice of my pomegranates.*
> *O that his left hand were under my head,*
> *and that his right hand embraced me!'*

Neither Johnny nor Harry seemed inclined to laugh. It was as though a shadow had crossed the chapel, a presentiment of grief to come.

> 'Love is strong as death,
>     jealousy is cruel as the grave.
> Its flashes are flashes of fire,
>     a most vehement flame.
> Many waters cannot quench love,
>     neither can floods drown it.
> If a man offered for love
>     all the wealth of his house,
>     it would be utterly scorned.'

Gabriel sat down again. A deep silence fell. Isobel felt a little shaken. Outside the wind was still stirring the branches. *The wind blows where it wills*, she thought, *and you hear the sound of it, but you do not know whence it comes or whither it goes.*

Later, as they were stowing their bags in the car, Gabriel joined them to say goodbye. It occurred to Isobel that he'd never once sought her out for a serious conversation, which was odd in the light of their encounter in Asleby. She couldn't decide whether she was offended or relieved.

'Well, goodbye, Johnny,' Harry was saying, as he emerged from a prolonged bear hug. 'Phone me. I mean it. Any time.'

'Ha'away, I'm fine, man. Everything's fine,' replied Johnny, confirming Isobel's conviction that it wasn't.

'Goodbye, Johnny,' she said, in a relaxed way, in case Gabriel's vatic gaze was turned in her direction.

''Bye, sweetheart. Be kind to Harry,' Johnny admonished her, kissing her cheek. 'He's littler than you.'

'Oi!' said Harry.

Johnny laughed. 'She'll have you for breakfast.'

'She's very welcome to try.'

There was a pause.

'And on that happy note . . .' Harry opened the car door for Isobel. They drove off.

Isobel itched to discuss Johnny. She scrutinized her motives. Surely it was Christian compassion? One ought to be prayerfully concerned if one's fellow clergy were going through the mill. To be over-cautious would be to exaggerate her feelings towards him; feelings which were, after all, pretty unexceptionable.

Harry cleared his throat. 'Ah, sorry about that back there. I forgot myself for a second.'

'Hmm?'

'I find it hard not to get drawn into his banter sometimes.'

'Oh, that's fine,' she assured him.

'Thanks.'

Isobel tried in vain to reconstruct the scene to discover what he was apologizing for. Anyway, the subject of Johnny was fortuitously now broached.

'Is . . . everything all right between him and his wife?' Isobel felt a blush threatening. 'Only I wondered . . .'

'Um,' said Harry. 'Let's just say that their relationship has always been a bit volatile.'

'Right.' His tone wasn't confiding, but Isobel couldn't resist pressing on. 'Perhaps it's unfortunate she doesn't support his ministry?'

'You don't know that, Isobel,' said Harry, a little sharply.

'Well, she doesn't go to church.'

'That doesn't follow.'

Isobel said no more. She'd noticed before that Mrs Prickly Whitaker was capable of arousing intense loyalty in the male bosom. It was as unaccountable as it was annoying. But, still, she wished both her and Johnny well.

'You seem to have managed something of a rapport with Johnny,' said Harry. 'I appreciate your making the effort.'

'Oh, that's all right.'

'Can I be really nosy?' he inquired. 'Why do you dislike him so much?'

'Oh, I don't, I don't.' This felt like lying. She hesitated. 'Not really. It's just that, when I stopped to think about it, I eventually worked out that he sort of reminds me of someone.' She was blushing painfully. 'I was probably blaming him, subconsciously, for . . . oh, various things. Once I'd spotted what was going on, it was fine, of course. So . . .'

Harry glanced at her, registered her embarrassment, then kept his eyes tactfully on the road ahead. 'Good. So long as you're not languishing from unrequited passion, or anything.'

'Don't be ridiculous!' she trilled.

'It happens,' he said.

'Not if one's sensible.'

'Ah, yes. But now and then one meets someone it's impossible to be sensible about.'

'Then one must exercise a spot of self-discipline.'

'Indeed one must,' agreed Harry. 'Tell me about that nice police officer.'

She jumped. 'Davy? What about him?'

'Well, you tell me.'

'He's just a friend.'

Harry raised an eyebrow.

'I'm quite capable of being sensible about *him*, thank you very much. He's a boy!'

'Well,' said Harry, 'if you say so.'

'I certainly do say so. For goodness' sake, Harry. Give me some credit.'

'I do. Maybe it's just me, but I sometimes feel there's, I don't know, a huge iceberg blundering about when I'm talking to you.'

'Iceberg? What are you on about?'

'I'm worried you're kidding yourself. About, you know, er, *sex*. There – I've said it. Am I blushing?'

'Don't be silly!' snapped Isobel, who was. 'Of course I'm not kidding myself. That I'm aware of,' she added scrupulously.

'Exactly. That's what worries me – the fact that you might not be aware of it.'

'Well, if I'm not *aware* of it, what am I supposed to do?' she demanded, in exasperation.

'Be *aware* you aren't aware,' he suggested. 'Or might not be.'

She snorted. 'That sorts *that* out.'

'Just a little vicarly hint, you know. Feel free to ignore it if it's not relevant.'

'I will.' I bet this is Gabriel's doing. Planting ideas in Harry's head. She spent the rest of the journey brimming with resentment.

173

She couldn't believe Gary had driven her out to a quiet spot just to talk. But they sat on the hillside and she told him about school. Maybe he was just listening to lull her into a false sense of security before pouncing. She told him about her A levels, about Julie and the other girls who were horrible to her, but before long she wavered into silence.

'So, what do you do, then?' she demanded jerkily.

'Me? Oh, this and that. I'm a car dealer. I sell cars to the rich and gullible. Cigarette?'

'I don't smoke.'

'Sensible. Bad 'abit.' He lit up. 'What you doing Friday?'

'I'm at school.'

'In the evening,' he said patiently.

'Oh! Nothing.'

'Fancy a drink?'

'I'm not old enough.'

'You look eighteen. Who's to know? Be a devil.'

'But it's against the law.'

He laughed. 'Know what I think? Somewhere inside this goody-goody head girl there's a bad girl begging to be let out.' Without warning he bent and laid his ear against her breast. She froze, heart bumping madly. 'Listen,' he said. ' "Let me out, let me out!" ' He raised his head. She looked into his dark eyes.

'I'm a virgin,' she blurted.

'Um, I think I'd kind of worked that out,' he said. 'Are you saving yourself, then?'

She blushed. 'You think I'm old-fashioned!'

'Yeah. No. I'm jealous. You've still got it to look forward to.'

'I'm not trying to save myself,' she admitted. 'It's just . . . the situation has never arisen.' She gazed off over the hills.

'Would you like it to?'

She hesitated.

'Shall I stick around just in case?' he asked.

On Friday she was a devil. After one too many illegal drinks he drove her to a deserted lane and the situation arose.

## CHAPTER 15

Everything looked strange to Isobel when she got home. The rooms had the museum-like quality of a house left unlived-in. She was punch-drunk from lack of sleep, but after a moment or two everything receded back into familiarity. She flicked on some lights, filled the kettle, sorted through her post. Bit by bit the place woke up.

There was a letter from her mother. Isobel's heart sank. Mrs Knox only resorted to the written word for things too delicate to broach over the phone. What bombshell was being dropped on her today? She perused the letter and learnt that her parents were planning to spend Christmas in Turkey (appropriately enough! joked Mum), and therefore the traditional Knox family gathering would not be taking place at their house this year. Her mother hoped Isobel wouldn't mind. She'd suspected for ages that her children only came out of loyalty and, anyway, it wasn't really fair on the parents of her daughters-in-law – shouldn't they have a turn? She wasn't trying to say she didn't enjoy doing the family Christmas – oh dear, this was getting a bit tangled! – but she couldn't help thinking it might be nice for her children to establish their own family traditions. She hated the idea that everyone felt they *had* to come, so here was an opportunity to break the pattern in case that's what everyone wanted but was too afraid of offending her to suggest. Was that all right? Of course, next year they could all come again. *If* that's what everyone wanted.

Isobel went and made a pot of Lapsang. *A chance to establish their own family traditions.* That was all very well for her brothers, who were married and had families. But what about Isobel? She knew her mother would have agonized over this, and not raised the subject in case that seemed patronizing and singlist. Her parents never commented on Isobel's unmarried state or asked about boyfriends. So long as she was happy and fulfilled, that was what

175

mattered. She was grateful for their tact, except that it occasionally made her want to scream. If only she couldn't see the footprints of her mother's tiptoeing so clearly. She guessed, for instance, that a hint would have been dropped to both brothers – Just a thought, might they not like to invite Isobel for Christmas? Isobel went through to check her answer-machine and yes! Alistair and Chris, one after the other, just ringing for a chat (they never did) and, oh, by the way, if she didn't have any plans for Christmas, what about joining them?

Hah! She was just walking out when a third message began.

'Hiya, Isobel. It's me.'

Johnny! She whirled round.

'Are you there? No? It's Davy.'

She slumped over the desk and laughed at her foolishness. Davy's voice chuntered on. That's why his accent always grated on me, she thought. I suppose now I'll start to find it *endearing*. She erased all three messages and went back to the kitchen. Her hands were still trembling as she poured the tea.

She took her cup and stood on her back doorstep, looking out across the gardens towards the row of limes that bordered the park. They were turning now. Apples hung heavy on Mrs Porter's tree. Before long she'd bring a carrier-bag of windfalls round to Isobel, who would sneak them to Harry because she never knew what to do with five pounds of half-rotten apples. Harry would make them into apple grog for the Harvest Supper.

What was it about the sight of ripening apples on a tree that was so piercingly reminiscent of childhood? There had been an apple tree in the garden of the house where she'd grown up that produced huge sweet-tasting red and yellow cookers. We had a swing hanging from its branches, she remembered. We weren't supposed to play on it at this time of year, except we did, bringing apples bombing down into the grass accidentally on purpose, polishing off the cement dust on our jumpers, then scoffing them out of sight in the shed. She could picture herself climbing the tree in the early morning to pick apples for the school harvest festival. Snatches of a song echoed in her memory:

*Farmer, farmer, sow your seed,*
*Up the field and down.*

For all she knew primary-school children were still singing it. The tune played on, but she couldn't resurrect any more of the words. As she sipped her smoky tea she caught herself wondering whether Johnny had leant on this same door frame when he'd lived here a decade before. For a second she could feel him standing where she was, looking out across the same back gardens, smoking the inevitable cigarette. Funny that it had never really struck her before that she was living in his old house.

Still, she had things to be getting on with. She washed her cup and went to her study.

The days shortened. The air was full of mulchy decay and bonfires. A spider built a vast web across the study window and sat in the middle of it, waiting. Sometimes Isobel looked up from her desk and watched long desperate dramas in silhouette against the early-evening sky, before the spider finally inched the victim up to her lair at the corner of the frame. Leaves fell and left ghostly imprints of themselves on the wet pavements. Fungi bulged from rotting trees in the park, filling the woods with their dank mushroomy smell. The skeletal cartwheels of giant hogweed were hung with dew. Isobel began counting the weeks till Advent. Soon the run-up to Christmas would be upon her and she'd be insanely busy, despite Harry's gentle reminders.

For the next couple of weeks, though, there would still be a little slack in her life, a little leisure. She was vigilant and strict with herself, but she began to fear her mind was under-occupied. Part of it seemed to have peeled off and begun a parallel existence. She could sense it speculating: I wonder if Johnny visited this shop? Or observing: he must have walked along this road most mornings. Isobel gave such thoughts short shrift. She ridiculed them for the weak, pathetic things they were, but was powerless to suppress them completely. They lurked there unarticulated, accumulating, until gradually she found herself inhabiting a world charged with the presence of a man she never let herself think about.

Each street in the parish had known his footfall. The church had echoed to his voice. The stall she knelt in, the chalice she raised, the peg she hung her cassock on, all had felt his touch. Her friends had once been his. Whenever she visited Natalie and Drew there was a chance his name would crop up. He had helped them strip and sand their wooden floors and had once narrowly prevented them from knocking down a load-bearing wall in their refurbishing zeal. They remembered his time in Asleby fondly and she knew how easy it would be to set them off on a series of Johnny Whitaker anecdotes. She sat and gazed at their waxed kitchen floor and resisted the temptation. Ironic how irritated she'd been by their partiality only months before.

There was no respite when she went home. That board on the landing had creaked under his weight. This doorknob had known his grip. His hand had run down the stair rail that hers was lingering on now.

Enough. *Enough!*

'Run with perseverance the race which is set before you,' she reminded herself, 'looking to Jesus, the author and finisher of our faith.' She'd get over it. It was simply a question of cultivating the right mental habits. Of 'exercising a spot of self-discipline'. She winced as she remembered how arrogantly she'd said that to Harry a few weeks back. It was not proving quite as simple as she'd anticipated. However, the thing would starve away if she didn't nourish it with idle fantasies. It was unlucky that Johnny was due to come to the Harvest Supper next Sunday, but there it was. Keep contact to the minimum. Don't indulge in any foolish thoughts. Everything would be fine.

It was Thursday evening. Isobel returned home from an unsatisfactory visit to a couple who wanted their baby christened. She'd gone through the vows with them to check that they understood what they were taking on. The wife had admitted frankly that she didn't believe any of it, but she was more than happy to say it anyway. Isobel told her plainly that this presented them with problems, since neither she nor Harry would feel comfortable to conduct the service under those circumstances. She suggested they take more time to think things over, and ask themselves why they wanted a service of Christian initiation if they didn't believe in God. She invited them to come along to Sunday worship for a few weeks to find out more, and despite some blustering from the husband, she would not agree to set a date. 'But we've got the club booked for after, and everything.' Isobel said she was sorry about that, but stuck politely to her guns. The episode left a nasty taste in her mouth. She would have phoned Harry, but it was his day off. It would have to wait till after morning prayer tomorrow.

After spending half an hour praying over the encounter Isobel braced herself for a bout of filing. She wasn't preaching on Sunday for once. It was family worship in the morning and Harry was taking the children's address, thank goodness. Isobel hated doing it, although the practice was valuable, of course. How come Harry was so good at it, when he had no children of his own? 'Maybe it's because I'm incredibly immature,' was his suggestion. 'I'm right on their wavelength.' And Johnny was preaching in the evening. Isobel fixed her emotions with a beady stare. They just about passed muster. Anyhow, what was the worst that could happen? She'd get tongue-tied and make a bit of an idiot of herself. The experience would probably be good for her.

She glanced at a vestment catalogue then binned it because it only showed men modelling the cassocks and vestments. Deanery Synod minutes. Payslip from the Church Commissioners. Christian Aid. Ember list from Coverdale Hall. She leafed through to find out how her fellow curates were getting on. Her own entry spelt Asleby wrong and her photo now looked completely out of date. Yes, she'd been absolutely right to get her hair cut, so there, Edward. She filed her most recent bank statements. Financially everything looked pretty healthy, although the holiday in France had cost a little more than she'd anticipated. She had sensibly siphoned off a certain amount each month into a separate account so that buying Christmas presents didn't become a burden. Really, it was just a question of getting organized. There was no need to get into debt. It was hardly as if Christmas came without warning. Isobel always knew to within a pound how much money was in her current account. There was no excuse for inefficiency in personal finances as far as she was concerned. She'd never been overdrawn except once, when she'd accidentally deposited a cheque in the wrong account.

The evening dragged on. She was half listening for the roar of a macho engine. Davy had appeared on her doorstep a few evenings before to show off his new motorbike, bursting with pride like a five-year-old with his first Action Man. If she'd bothered to concentrate she would now know every amazing feature the beast possessed, how much it cost, the rival merits of other bikes not in the end bought, the projected repayment scheme and how long, on average, he spent each day making love to it.

Isobel was hardened to this kind of talk. Her brothers were both motorbike freaks. Gelded by family life they now drove Renault Espaces, but an incautious sentence could set them off on a maudlin tour round every nut and bolt of their first Suzukis. She was smug to see them thus humbled, since they had never, *ever* let her ride their bikes or even deigned to take her out on the back of them. Other girls were a different matter. She occasionally overheard them discussing the bird-pulling power of their machines. 'Oh, boys, can't you take Isobel out now and then?' pleaded Mrs Knox.

'I wouldn't be seen *dead* with them!' Isobel would cry pre-emptively. Inside, however, she burned each time those machines roared off, leaving her behind to do her French homework.

Davy possessed a more generous spirit and so at last, after all those years, Isobel fulfilled her ambition. Dressed in a set of his old leathers she clung round his waist and they set off. He pulled up almost at once and removed his helmet.

'You've got to relax, or you'll have us both off,' he told her. 'Just relax and lean when I do, like we're one person.' He grinned. 'This is no time for feminism, sweetheart.'

She glared at him, but did as she was told. Her initial terror gave way to exhilaration. Yes! Yes! Before long, riding pillion wasn't enough for her.

'Can I have a go?' she called. 'On my own, I mean?'

He stopped the bike and pulled off his helmet again. She saw he was laughing.

'What's so funny? I want a go.'

'You! You cannot handle a bike this size!'

Indignation leapt up. 'Why not, may I ask?'

'You're a lass. No offence, like. You're just not strong enough.'

'I bet I am!'

He laughed again and dismounted. 'OK. If you can wheel it over there and back, I'll let you ride it.'

But as it turned out the stupid thing was too heavy and practically fell on top of her. Davy had to grab it before she was flattened.

'See what I mean?' he said. 'Aw, don't get mad. You just want something a bit smaller, pet.'

DON'T CALL ME PET!

'Tell you what. If you want, I could ask our Simon. He's still got his old Yamaha . . .'

She blocked his voice out and hated him all the way home.

Which was why she'd been betrayed into possibly the most puerile piece of behaviour that she'd been guilty of for years. They were back at his house for coffee.

'I'm a lot stronger than I look,' she announced.

'You are?'

She seized hold of him and attempted the one judo throw she could remember from childhood lessons. He toppled to the floor, pulling her down with him.

'Hey, not bad.'

'See?' she said triumphantly.

'Aye, but you took us by surprise.'

'Get out of this, then.' She managed to get a scarf-hold on him, one arm round his neck, pinning him down ribcage to ribcage. 'Go on.'

He struggled. 'Bloody hell.'

'Told you!'

Suddenly the impropriety of rolling around on the floor with him struck her. She let go and scrambled to her feet.

'No, wait!' he protested. 'You didn't give us a fair chance! Ha 'away!'

'Get up!' she hissed.

'I could've got away, y'kna,' he taunted. 'Honest. I wasn't really trying.'

'It won't work, Davy.'

'Oh, well. Worth a try.' He got up, grinning, and went to make the coffee.

I can't believe you did that! What were you *thinking* of? she harangued herself.

He was still grinning when he came back and handed her a mug. They sat down in front of the television.

'Look, could you just forget I did that?' she began awkwardly. 'I'm sorry. It's just that my brothers never let me have a go on their bikes.'

He was all solicitude, eyes flicking only occasionally towards the set as he promised to take her out any time, borrow a suitable bike for her, teach her himself – 'Pass the ball, you selfish git!' – sorry, get her L-plates –

'All right, all right. Thank you, Davy.'

'I mean it.'

She smiled and shook her head in despair. Ridiculous boy. 'Just a ride now and then will be fine.'

'OK.' His attention was now given fully to the game. 'Funny, that.'

'What?' She resigned herself to some complex analysis of the play.

'Same every time a good-looking blonde pins w' doon. Wor strength just deserts w'.'

Isobel had deciphered enough of this to realize he deserved a clip round the ear.

Smiling at the memory, she looked at her watch. A spin out to the moors would just be nice. At that point the phone rang.

Still smiling, she answered it and heard his voice.

'Hello, you,' she said.

'Hello, *me*?' he repeated.

'Yes. I was just thinking about you.'

'You were?' He sounded surprised. 'What were you thinking?'

'Never you mind.'

He laughed. 'Like that, eh? Was I good, then, was I?'

There was a pause, then Isobel caught up. Preposterous! 'Actually, you were useless.'

'Don't lie. You were whimpering.'

Isobel's jaw dropped. 'Out of sheer *boredom*!' she countered.

He chuckled again. 'I've not heard it called that before. Multiple boredom, like?'

Astounded at finding herself outdone, she switched to schoolmarm tactics. 'I think this has gone *quite* far enough.'

'You started it, flower.'

Isobel resorted to frosty silence.

'Ee, you've made me forget why I was ringing. Oh, aye – what time's your evening service again?'

'Why?' she asked in surprise. 'Are you thinking of coming?'

'Well, funnily enough I thought I might look in – seeing as I'm preaching and all that.'

*Johnny*! Aagh! 'Six-six-thirty,' she bleated.

'What?'

'Six. Thirty.'

'Six-thirty?'

'Yes.' What have I said? What have I done? Her mind fumbled back, trying to remember.

'Are you OK, Isobel?'

'I'm fine!'

'Good. I'll aim to be there by six.'

'Lovely!' she trilled. 'We're all looking forward to it.'

They hung up and Isobel sat stunned in horror. What on earth was she going to do? She could hardly ring him back now and explain. That's what Harry must have meant by being drawn into Johnny's banter. The best she could hope was that he'd forget all about it.

Later, when the phone rang again and it really was Davy, Isobel was quite shirty with him.

Her mother was right. Once you'd acquired a taste for it, sex was wonderful. Isobel being (above all) Sensible, made a trip to the doctor's and went on the pill. Red-faced, she informed her mother of this. 'That's very sensible of you, dear,' said Mrs Knox. She'd met Gary. So had Mr Knox. They realized at once he was a phase that Isobel would grow out of if they wisely said nothing. Sensing this, Isobel kept them apart. Her parents didn't understand. She loved him despite . . . oh, you know, him being so different.

If only he wouldn't buy her presents, though. Gold charm bracelets. Red satin undies. Padded greetings cards in their own boxes. She hid them in a box at the bottom of her wardrobe under her hockey-boots, sick with guilt at the amount he spent on her.

A more mercenary woman might have steered his largesse into more acceptable channels, but she was helpless. Her upbringing impelled her towards gratitude, but at the same time demanded honesty.

'Gary, you mustn't keep buying me things!' she burst out.

'But I want to,' he said. 'You're special.'

In his book you didn't just take a nice girl for granted. She wasn't some cheap slag he'd picked up at a disco, he said. She was a cheap slag he'd picked up at a bus stop – no, no, seriously. She was different. She was a good influence on him. Kept him out of trouble.

'Just so long as it doesn't interfere with your school work,' Mrs Knox said.

'It's the summer *holidays*, Mother,' snapped Isobel.

'Well, next term is Oxbridge, don't forget.'

'Oh, *honestly*, Mother. I know what I'm doing.'

But then one day in October – oops! – she failed to prepare for an English lesson. The teacher was incredulous. This had never happened before! She trusted Isobel had a satisfactory explanation.

'I was doing something else at the weekend,' said Isobel coolly.

For a second she thought the teacher was going to say, 'What, pray?' And she would have said, 'Having sex.' But after a disapproving pause the lesson simply continued with someone else guiding the class through Keats as a narrative poet.

She told Gary for a laugh – for some reason he loved hearing about her school – but to her surprise he turned strict. Right. From now on, no sex till you've done your homework. Many years later Isobel occasionally stumbled upon pockets of knowledge that had been learnt in that period. They had a sharpness, a visceral intensity not normally associated with Chartism.

God, she thought, wading through her French translation so she could be with him. I'm a whore, a complete whore. I simply can't do without it. When he went away on his mysterious business trips she grew desperate, like the girl in Christina Rossetti's poem who had eaten the goblin fruit and was wasting away, craving for more, more, for the taste of its flesh crushed against teeth and palate and the goblin juices running down.

## CHAPTER 16

That night Isobel dreamed about Tatiana again. They were on holiday in the Lake District and Tatiana was taking Isobel to a secret cave she had discovered.

'I keep dreaming about you,' said Isobel, 'that we meet up again. Then I wake up and it's only a dream.'

'Well, this isn't a dream,' said Tatiana.

'Oh, I know,' agreed Isobel. 'It's much too realistic.'

'Um, Isobel,' said Harry, on Saturday after morning prayer, 'we seem to have a problem. Did you refuse to do a baptism this week?'

'Of course not!' she exclaimed indignantly. 'I fobbed them off because they said they didn't believe a word of the service, but –'

'I'm afraid they've been to the press with their story.' He handed her a copy of the local paper. 'Curate Turns Christening Couple Away.'

'What?' she cried. 'That's a complete fabrication! Who wrote this? They never even checked with me – "unavailable for comment"! That's a complete lie!'

Harry sighed. 'They rang me saying they were doing a piece on naming ceremonies and did we have a policy of refusing to baptize non-churchgoers. I said not, but that it was our duty to make sure people understood the vows.'

'They printed that,' she said, reading on.

'The journalist said he'd phoned you, but you were out.'

But Isobel was engrossed in the paper. 'No!' she burst out.

*Jenny Willis, minister of Asleby Methodist church, has stepped in to help the disappointed couple. The service will go ahead as planned later this month in her church. 'Jesus taught us to let the children come to him,' explained Miss Willis. 'We aren't in the business of turning folk away.'*

The words felt like a knifeblade slid into the heart. How could Jenny be so disloyal? Isobel raised her eyes and looked at Harry in disbelief. 'Treat it as a learning experience,' he said. 'Er . . . perhaps if you'd told me about that couple I'd've been a bit more clued up when the journalist rang. Another time, maybe.'

'I meant to,' she said miserably. She'd go down in local history as the curate who turned babies away.

'I don't suppose Jenny had any idea what was going on,' Harry reassured her. 'Someone on that rag's got it in for us.'

'I'm jolly well going to complain!'

'Probably not worth it.' He sighed.

'But everyone will think –'

'I'll back you up. By the way, if journalists ring, never give an off-the-cuff response. Ask what it's about, then tell them it's not convenient and you'll ring back. That'll give you time to prepare.'

'They taught us that at theological college.'

'Good.' Seeing how dejected she looked he laid a hand on her arm. 'Don't worry. You've done nothing wrong.'

She took a deep breath. 'I think the father was cross because he'd already booked the club for the party afterwards. He was probably worried about losing his deposit.'

Harry rolled his eyes. 'That's us – a little lower than the caterers. Why bring religion into it? Why not just dunk the baby in a pint pot and have done?'

Isobel got home to find a distraught message from Jenny who had just seen the local paper. Isobel rang and discovered Harry was right. The couple hadn't mentioned their encounter with Isobel and the reporter had said he was simply doing a piece on baptism. Jenny assured Isobel that she would never disagree with her publicly like that and Isobel hung up feeling at least partially reassured. She tried to shake off the incident and pray forgivingly for the journalist, but the headline was seared into her memory.

*

Isobel spent the rest of the morning calling on parishioners who hadn't attended church recently, and encouraging them to come to the harvest services. 'Oh, yes, we're coming to the evening,' most of them said. 'Because it's Johnny.' Eventually she found this as irritating as she'd always done.

186

Just before lunch she popped down to church to see how the ladies were getting on with the decorations. The air smelt of harvest festivals: that mixture of fruit and vegetables, chrysanthemums, and mingled with them, the smell of bread from the large plaited harvest loaf.

'So!' called Jan's voice. 'You'd withhold the grace of God from an infant, would you?'

'Certainly not!' retorted Isobel. 'I was stitched up.'

'Poor old you.' Jan appeared from behind a vast spray of leaves. 'Come and admire! Be ravished! Be astounded!'

It was indeed a spectacular display. Some of the other women glanced sourly at the work of art Jan had just finished, perhaps feeling that floral arrangements ought to consist of flowers and not include such things as prize leeks, dried hogweed, branches of apple trees complete with fruit, or rhubarb gone dramatically to seed.

'There. What do you think? I always feel like I'm in a Barbara Pym novel when I'm doing this,' said Jan. 'Except we don't go in for petty squabbles over who gets to do the lectern. Do we, ladies?'

There were some tight smiles at this. Isobel could never tell if Jan was aware of the resentment her high-handedness caused. Harry's policy was to let them get on with it. He never listened to anyone who tried to bend his ear over this kind of thing. He would throw up his hands in mock alarm and cry, 'Oh, I couldn't *possibly* interfere!' Isobel knew she would never master his knack of doing resolutely as he chose without giving offence.

'This is by way of a shrine to the great marrow god,' said Jan, pointing to the mound heaped at the foot of the pulpit against a sheaf of wheat and barley. 'We get so many of the buggers, I thought we'd make them into a focal point.'

'I don't approve of corn dollies,' remarked Isobel, flicking one with a fingernail. 'They're pagan fertility symbols.'

'That's what I said,' called Mrs Porter, from behind a pillar.

'But it's the Holy Family!' cried Jan. 'Joseph, Mary and, look, there's the Christ-child!'

Isobel pursed her lips.

'It's an ironic post-modern harvest for late-twentieth-century urban Britain,' Jan explained. 'Come for lunch.'

Isobel followed her out of the church, knowing that in doing so she was nailing her colours to the mast. The ladies would mutter that it was favouritism, but Isobel felt she could just about rise above that. Even clergy must be permitted one or two friends.

'Smoked salmon,' announced Jan, as she started the car.

Isobel decided that a little hint was in order. 'You might not realize, Jan,' she began, 'that some of the other ladies are a bit upset at the way you've taken over.'

'But that's terrible,' said Jan calmly.

'You might at least be subtle.'

Jan chuckled. 'I only interfere on compassionate grounds, to save them from themselves. Admit it – they've got about as much vision and taste as an Argos catalogue.'

Isobel said nothing. She had from time to time bought things (practical household things), from Argos, and she knew that Jan knew this.

'I'm afraid they're locked in a BFC mentality,' went on Jan. 'Beige fitted carpets. And everything else fitted as well. From kitchens to wardrobes. Fitted, fitted, fitted. They even have those sock things you put your used carrier-bags in.'

'They're jolly useful!' said Isobel, nettled at last out of her haughty silence.

'Yes, but they look like severed limbs. Like bits of Guy Fawkes that no one got round to burning.'

'You're absurd. What's so wonderful about having a million empty carrier-bags bursting out of your cupboards?'

'Ah, it's the principle of the thing,' said Jan, parking the car. 'Free spirit, creativity.'

'Otherwise known as mess.'

'And God forbid that there should be any mess in Isobel's life!'

They went into the house. Its state was fully in keeping with Jan's philosophy. Isobel was forced to step over three piles – newspaper, tins, bottles – and half a lawnmower on her way to the kitchen.

'Gin?' asked Jan. 'No, I know, why don't we open a really nice bottle of white Macon or something?'

'Not in the middle of the day, thank you.'

'You and your little rules.'

'I'm *working*,' said Isobel. '*You're a one for rules, aren't you?*' Johnny's voice murmured in her memory. She smoothed her hair. Jan put the smoked salmon on a plate and hacked some uneven doorsteps of bread.

'That's the problem with straight loaves,' quipped Isobel. 'You're always left with an awkward wedge-shaped bit at the end.'

'Ho ho, very droll. Pass me that lemon.'

Isobel's little attempts at humour were usually put down in this manner. Jan opened a bottle of wine. Isobel stood firm and accepted a glass of elderflower *pressé* instead.

'That's a gross insult to a noble fish,' complained Jan. 'I don't know why I bother with you.'

'I can hardly go round visiting reeking of booze.' Isobel took a mouthful of salmon. 'Oh. *Oh*. This is *wonderful*.'

'I told you. It's from Teesdale. One of my little men brought it this morning.'

Jan had more little men in her life than Snow White. They fixed her guttering, brought her honey from their hives, serviced her car and, if there was anything they could not handle personally, they knew of other little men who could.

'Well, I think we're just about done down at church,' said Jan, after a while. 'I might make a vast wreath thingy decorated with tins of tomato soup and lavish swags of red crêpe paper.'

'It'll look like Christmas in Tesco's.'

'True. But we've got to do something with all those bloody tins. I know – we can line 'em up round the edge of the pulpit and count how many are still there after Johnny's finished preaching.' She shook her head nostalgically. 'Ah, he was always a great gesturer, was Johnny.'

'Hmm,' said Isobel, concentrating on her salmon.

'Now, now,' remonstrated Jan. 'He's a lovely, lovely man, and if you had any sense of team spirit you'd join in the communal vamping.'

'He might bring his lovely, lovely wife,' Isobel pointed out.

'Hmmph! I doubt it.'

'What's she like?' asked Isobel, bending over her salmon once more.

'Fey, moody and irritating.'

'Oh, surely . . .' Isobel was conscious of a small glow at hearing Mara abused.

'Sorry. Never liked the woman,' admitted Jan. 'She used to visit Johnny here when he was curate. Strung that poor boy along sadistically for years before she deigned to marry him. The *misery* he went through! "Didn't want to be a vicar's wife," ' mimicked Jan. 'For God's sake! He was training for the ministry when she met him. It was hardly a bolt from the blue. You can't play pick 'n' mix with people. You take the lot or not at all.'

'Harry's rather fond of her, I think,' ventured Isobel.

'I know. And so, one speculates, is Johnny. *Chacun à son goût.* They always struck me as an unlikely couple, I must say. Even her most devoted admirer would have to admit she lacks a certain *embonpoint.*'

'Sorry?'

'Oh, come on, Ms Prim. Wouldn't you have Johnny marked down as the archetypal tit man?'

Isobel spluttered into her elderflower. 'That's outrageous!'

Later, when she left, Isobel felt sullied by this conversation. She wished she'd cut it off a little more swiftly. For all that she didn't care for Mrs Whitaker, it simply wouldn't do to encourage others – even tacitly – to run her down. 'Be as careful of the reputation of others as you would be of your own' was one of Isobel's maxims. No, the whole episode had been extremely unhelpful. She even had to repress the temptation of comparing her own contours with those of Johnny's wife. Oh, get a life, Isobel! she adjured herself, in the words her Youth Group so often employed. Well, she had a life; a rich, fulfilling one. In a few weeks this blip would probably seem amusing; and in the meantime she had a job to do.

By the end of the day Isobel was feeling a little happier with herself. Among the chivvying harvest visits she had made was one to Brenda. Isobel had been feeling guilty about her ever since that first disastrous visit and the dado rail. To her surprise Brenda had been waiting for her to call again, because she was keen to get up a discussion group. Isobel vaguely remembered suggesting it.

'There's about a dozen of us,' Brenda had announced. Isobel was astounded. 'We can meet on a night – unless it's Wednesday, because that's quiz night, and Friday's no good for Sally – or we can meet on a Wednesday afternoon, or . . .'

Eventually Tuesday night was selected. Isobel invited them to use her house, and had gone home feeling that perhaps she had done something right, after all, on that first occasion. Here, at last, was her Inquirers' Group. It was humbling when one was used by God unwittingly. She could think of a dozen instances of people thanking her for something helpful she'd said in a sermon which she knew she'd never uttered.

Isobel and Harry were in their robes in the vestry. It was twenty-five past six. Harry glanced once more at the clock. 'Hmm. This is cutting it a bit fine, even for Johnny.'

Isobel peeped out of the door and saw that the church was full. She shut it again. The sound of the organ continued, muffled.

'He can't have forgotten,' she said, a little consciously. 'I was speaking to him on the phone only the other day.'

They stood waiting. The clock ticked.

'Well,' began Harry, 'if the worst comes to the worst I could –' he broke off as a car door slammed. They both listened as footsteps hurtled through the churchyard towards the vestry. Johnny burst in, an armful of robes flapping.

'Sorry, sorry, sorry! Got delayed. How much time have I got?' He flung the robes down on the table and grabbed his cassock. Isobel tutted inwardly.

'Have you been in a fight, John?' asked Harry.

Johnny froze, then crossed rapidly to the mirror. 'Shit. Oh, well. Can't be helped.' He seized his robes.

Isobel stared appalled at the angry red mark beside his eye. 'What happened? Were you attacked?'

He laughed. 'You could put it like that.' He dived into his cassock.

'Do you want some ice?' asked Harry.

'Nah. I'll be fine.'

191

'Have you reported it to the police?' asked Isobel. Out of the corner of her eye she caught an abrupt gesture from Harry. 'What?' He shook his head at her.

'Police aren't interested,' Johnny replied, busy with his buttons.

'Well, they should be!' exclaimed Isobel. There was another desperate signal from Harry.

Johnny intercepted it. 'Something bothering you, Harry?' he asked. Immediately the atmosphere felt dangerous.

Harry raised his hands in apology.

What's going on? Isobel wanted to cry. Johnny reached for his surplice, shook it, then suddenly flung it aside.

'I've forgotten my fucking scarf!'

Isobel's gasped. The air vibrated with rage.

'Calm down,' came Harry's voice. 'I can lend you one.' He laid a hand on Johnny's arm.

For a second Isobel feared he was going to punch him, then Johnny drooped. 'Yeah. Sorry, I'll be OK in a second.'

They waited. Johnny was breathing deeply. Outside the organ struck up another tune. Isobel went to the cupboard and found a black preaching scarf. Her hands were trembling as she passed it to Johnny.

He roused himself and laughed. 'All I did was ask if it was PMT.'

His wife! Isobel took a pace backwards in shock.

'Normally I remember to duck,' he said. 'I mustn't've been concentrating.'

How can he crack jokes at a time like this? She glanced at the clock. It was after half past six. What on earth were they going to do? He couldn't preach in this state. She was hardly fit to face the congregation herself. Thank God for Harry's rock-like calm.

'OK now?' Harry asked.

Johnny nodded. 'Just about.'

'You're all right to preach?'

'Why, aye.'

You're mad to let him! thought Isobel. She tried to catch Harry's eye, but he was looking at Johnny, as if trying to gauge how volatile his mood was. Johnny met his gaze.

In the end Harry nodded, apparently satisfied. 'Right. I'll go in now with Isobel and start the service. You can have a few minutes to, um, collect your thoughts.'

'I don't need – oh, right you are.'

Isobel pretended not to have seen Harry's swiftly mimed cigarette.

They paused for a short prayer before going in. Isobel's pulse was still jittery, but as Harry's quiet voice prayed, a kind of calm descended. She was able to go out into the packed church. The congregation was oblivious, of course. Harry made a mild announcement to the effect that Johnny had been delayed, but would be with them shortly. But what if he can't face it at the last minute? worried Isobel. Or, worse, what if he breaks down in the middle of the sermon? If only Harry had simply sent him home. She drew some strength from Harry's relaxed manner, and in the event, his trust was not misplaced.

When Johnny appeared he seemed so very composed that Isobel was almost indignant. How could he stand there like that? Didn't it verge on the hypocritical? It certainly showed an alarming ability to compartmentalize. Isobel laced her hands so tightly together they ached afterwards and prayed, as she always did, that God would speak to her through the sermon.

It was not what she would have classed as a sermon. A little bit too much knockabout comedy and not enough exegesis, to her mind. It was very amusing, of course. Harry was reduced to weeping in his stall. Isobel sensed her own laughter was edged with hysteria. At one point she let out a helpless honking sound after everyone else had stopped laughing, which set them all off again. She was just beginning to think, This is all very well, but where's your message? when the tone changed. He was still using the same off-the-cuff conversational manner, wandering about at the front, but he was talking now about the grace of God. She'd never heard him talk seriously about his faith before, and it struck her with something like shock: he really believes this! Of course he does, she rebuked herself. It worried her to think her own view of God's grace appeared niggardly in comparison.

He finished and went to his stall. Harry had his eyes closed. Isobel watched his lips move in what she knew must be a prayer of gratitude. She stood to announce the next hymn.

After the service Harry was cornered by Joan the merry widow. Isobel caught wafts of drunken conversation as she and Johnny returned to the vestry to disrobe.

'Well,' began Isobel.

'Bloody hell,' interrupted Johnny. 'That was *death*.' Off came the surplice, out came the cigarettes. He shot into the churchyard and lit up.

Isobel followed nervously. 'You preached very well.'

'By God's grace.'

She felt again that jolt of surprise that he really meant it. He looked so disreputable standing there smoking in his cassock.

'Just the Harvest Supper, now,' said Isobel. 'Are you staying?'

'Aye. Harry and me are doing a skit.'

'Good.' She longed to ask if he was all right, but wasn't sure how this would be received.

He inhaled deeply. The cigarette end glowed in the twilight. Then he looked at Isobel and seemed belatedly to focus on her. He frowned. 'What got into you the other night? On the phone, I mean.'

'Oh! Ha ha!' She laughed. '*That*. Um, I mistook you for someone else.' With a bit of luck the dusk was hiding her blush.

'And there was me thinking my luck was in.'

Isobel squawked, 'I *beg* your pardon?'

'Who did you think it was?'

'I – None of your business!'

He was grinning. 'How many rough Geordies have you got in your life, then, eh?'

Finding no suitable reply, Isobel stalked back to the vestry. His laughter followed her.

'Well, I think that went off all right,' said Jan. 'Congratulations, you three.'

'Yes, well done,' echoed Natalie.

They were all back at the vicarage where Harry just happened to have a particularly nice 1975 burgundy all ready and waiting.

'You big ponce,' said Johnny, ruffling Harry's hair.

'I keep cheap beer for people like you,' replied Harry. 'Isobel – wine? Or a banana, perhaps?'

'Very funny.' Isobel had fallen victim to her own competitiveness during the entertainments. The clergy blindfold banana-eating race had been rigged by Fitz. She had removed her scarf triumphantly to thunderous applause after bolting three bananas – only to discover she'd been the only one competing. Very amusing indeed. Her limited sense of humour failed her altogether when it came to practical jokes.

The wine was enough to mollify her. They sat laughing and chatting in Harry's kitchen. Johnny admired again the murals his wife had painted all those years before.

'How is Mara?' asked Drew.

Help! thought Isobel.

But Johnny answered casually enough. 'Mara? She's her normal sunshiny self.'

Jan hooted. 'Tell me, what does she think of your going back into parish ministry? I thought the deal was you did industrial chaplaincy, so she wouldn't have to be a vicar's wife.'

Johnny hesitated. 'Fair question.'

'Why have you ratted? Tell me to bugger off, if you like,' offered Jan.

'Bugger off.' He laughed. 'Same as ever, aren't you? Straight for the jugular.' He turned to Isobel. 'You know what she did to me when I was a curate? Banned me from driving! I begged, I pleaded –'

'Tough. You were way over the limit,' cut in Jan. 'Come on, why have you gone back to parish ministry?'

He rolled his eyes. 'You never give up, do you? OK, I guess I thought the writing's on the wall for sector ministry. There are fewer and fewer chaplaincy posts all the time. Half the time the diocese want you to take on a church as well, split post. Oh, great, so I get to do two jobs! You may as well just settle for straight parish work.' He shrugged. 'It's what I'm best at.'

And you deserve a wife who can accept that, thought Isobel.

'Hmm,' said Jan. 'All right. I'll let you off.'

'What happened to your eye?' asked Natalie, who was sitting closest to him.

'It's the wife. She beats me up.'

They all laughed.

'Seriously, though,' said Natalie.

'I was bending over and caught myself on the corner of the car boot. How's the house coming on, like? Knocked any more walls down?'

Isobel felt another spurt of anger on his behalf that he should have to resort to this kind of deception.

Natalie and Drew smiled at one another. 'Will you tell them?' asked Drew.

'No, you.'

She's pregnant, Isobel realized in a flash.

'Well, we've been doing out the spare room, actually,' said Drew, grinning self-consciously. 'As a nursery.'

They all called out at once, disbelief, congratulations, delight.

'When? When's it due?' asked Harry. 'Oh, please, please may I baptize it? Don't ask Isobel, she turns babies away, you know she does.'

'I do not!' cried Isobel.

'It's due in April,' said Natalie happily. 'We've only just started telling people.'

In the chatter that followed Isobel couldn't help noticing Johnny had fallen silent.

'What about you, then?' Jan rounded on him. 'Still no patter of tiny Doc Martens? Or should one not inquire?'

'Honestly, Jan,' broke in Isobel, 'that's really none of your business.'

'It's never stopped her before,' said Johnny. They all laughed again, but he didn't answer the question.

The evening wore on, but Isobel couldn't summon even the tiniest spot of self-discipline and tear herself away. On request Johnny treated them to impersonations of various parishioners. Kath Bollom, Jan, Drew giving the notices, Walter Goodwill. The latter was so accurate that Isobel was practically weeping with laughter, only to discover Johnny was able to hit off her helpless honk perfectly. She was just thinking it was as well he didn't have a cruel streak when he launched into a devastating impression of

Harry fending off the drunken attentions of Joan. The laughter was edged with discomfort. Natalie protested, but it took a raised eyebrow from Harry to check him.

'He used to phone me up pretending to be the Archbishop,' said Jan, wiping her eyes.

'He used to *answer* the phone pretending to be him,' said Drew.

'I got caught out once, though,' replied Johnny. 'I picked up the phone one day and said, "Bishop of Jarrow here," and a voice at the other end said, "No. Bishop of Jarrow *here*."'

In the end it was Drew who made the first move, concerned that Natalie was getting overtired. She yawned happily and agreed she was. Then Johnny stretched and got to his feet.

'What?' protested Jan, getting up as well. 'Are you off?'

'Why, aye.' Johnny put an arm round her. 'I'm gannin', flower. Workin' dee the morrer.'

'Ah,' sighed Jan. 'Never could resist that accent. Except in court, of course, where I am unimpeachable.'

Isobel peered in her bag and began rummaging, hanging back as the others made their way to the door.

'Want a lift, Isobel?' called Johnny.

'No, no!' she called back. 'It's not far. I'll walk.'

'Don't be daft. It's on my way.' He was waiting for her with the car door open and it seemed churlish to refuse.

Her heart pounded in a ridiculous manner throughout the short drive, even though he was chatting in a desultory way and there was clearly nothing to worry about.

He drew up outside her house. She foresaw an awkward patch – ought she to peck him on the cheek? A handshake was absurd, and to offer no gesture felt like an omission.

'I used to live there,' he remarked.

'I know.' She undid her seat-belt and braced herself. 'Well . . .'

'Funny, that. Has it changed much inside?'

'Oh, I doubt it.' Was he hinting? She hurried on. 'Well, it's been a lovely evening, thanks for the lift.' The peck? She groped instead for the door handle. 'Goodnight.'

He glanced at his watch. 'I've probably got time for a quick coffee.' He switched off the engine and undid his seat-belt.

'Oh, I mustn't keep you.'

In the silence that followed she heard the sound of his seat-belt slithering back. He was about to move.

'Goodbye.' She got the door open, but in climbing out, managed to hook her bag handle on something. The contents spilled out – pens, paper, purse, tampons, lipstick – and tumbled all over the car seat and floor.

'Oh, God.' Isobel bit her lip. She never blasphemed. Maybe it was a prayer. Johnny said nothing, just helped her scoop things up and shovel them back into the bag.

'Goodnight,' she said again, straightening up and hitting her head on the door frame before hurrying to the house.

Once inside she stood shaking in the hall. Had he gone? She crept into her dark study and peeped through the window. The car was still there. Why wasn't he going? She drew back in case he saw her. Please go. After an eternity she heard him start the engine. She stood listening until the car turned on to the main road and the sound faded away.

*I've probably got time for a quick coffee.*

*Oh, I mustn't keep you.*

She continued to stand in the dark, playing this fragment over and over, straining after some nuance, some clue that would tell her what had really been meant by those words. Was she just a complete fool, panicking like that? Or had she done the right thing?

## CHAPTER 17

Before Tatiana moved away she and Isobel gave each other presents. Isobel had saved up for ages and bought a tiny penknife for her friend, small enough to hide from the enemy (grown-ups) in the spine of a book. It had a pale blue pearlized handle but was difficult to open if you bit your fingernails. Isobel wrapped it in a piece of paper on which she'd written 'In memory's golden casket drop one pearl for me.' She had copied these beautiful words from a Laura Ingalls Wilder book they had both read.

Tatiana gave Isobel a notebook. But it was a really brilliant notebook. It was about six by five inches and had a blue polka-dot cover. Inside Tatiana had written, 'Isobel, your a great friend and I will never forget you. Love from Tatiana Anastasia George.' This was the fourth different middle name Tatiana had laid claim to.

'It's brilliant. I really really really love it,' she said.

'It's for you to write secret messages in. And stuff.'

'Thanks! I'll keep it for ever.'

'And I'll keep *this* for ever,' said Tatiana.

But the years passed and Tatiana faded from Isobel's life. At some point the book must have been lost or thrown out and Isobel forgot it had ever existed. Occasionally, though, when she saw little spiral-bound notebooks in stationery shops, a swift sensation would thrill through her. It vanished, leaving her momentarily puzzled as she reached for a ream of photocopier paper.

After a night of soul-searching, Isobel arrived at the conclusion she'd been ridiculous. Johnny had simply – and understandably – been seeking to defer the moment when he'd have to confront his dreadful wife. Last night had given her reason to speculate that Johnny longed for children but his wife, perhaps, did not. Whatever, Isobel had no patience with the kind of woman who called herself a feminist, yet indulged in face-slapping secure in the knowledge that the man couldn't retaliate. Small wonder Johnny had shown an inclination to linger. Isobel wished this had occurred to her at the time, so that she could have been a bit more understanding and hospitable. After all, nothing in his behaviour had ever given her reason to doubt his motives. It was humiliating to acknowledge she had shown herself up as the kind of deluded woman who imagines men are making passes at her all the time. She had the wit to see that there was nothing she could do about the situation now. Best to forget the whole thing.

Where on earth were her keys? She'd be late for morning prayer. And where had her favourite lipstick got to? She rooted through her bag. Annoying to have lost it. It was practically new and not exactly cheap. The minutes ticked by. She hunted for the spare keys and couldn't find them either. I'll have to leave the door on the latch. She paused to put in her collar and caught sight of her keys balanced on top of the mirror. How on earth had they got there? She snatched them and hurried out. Well, she'd been in such a flap last night she could have flushed them down the loo without registering.

The door slammed behind her as she rushed down her path. Kath Bollom was lurking on the other side of the road. She raised a hand and wheezed something.

Isobel called, 'Morning!' and sprinted for the corner, smirking at the memory of Johnny's impersonation. She slowed to a brisk walk when she was safely on the main road and arrived at church out of breath.

After saying the morning office, she and Harry went through to the vestry for their staff meeting. Isobel bade farewell to the floral displays. Mrs Porter would be in on the dot of nine to pack the produce into boxes for the needy, but not before she'd dismantled Jan's arrangements and stuffed the hogweed into bin liners with a satisfied 'There!' The gaping bags would be left by, not in, the church wheelie-bin for Jan to see on Sunday.

The air in the vestry seemed pale and flat after the tension of the previous evening. It might almost have been a different room.

'I think last night went very well,' said Isobel.

Harry let out a strangled, 'Aagh!'

'Seriously,' insisted Isobel. 'Once the service got under way.'

'I can't *believe* I survived him for three whole years!' He clutched his heart. 'I'm too old, these days, Isobel. I'm just too old.'

Isobel felt obscurely offended by this. Not that one wished to give one's colleagues coronaries, exactly.

'The saga didn't end when you left,' went on Harry. 'I had Mara on the phone at one-thirty asking where he'd got to.'

'Really?' Her heart bumped. 'Well, he just dropped me off and went.'

In the silence that followed she feared this sounded defensive, like a lie, almost.

Harry regarded her steadily. For an awful moment she thought he was going to press her. The scene in the car flashed across her mind, the slithering seat-belt, the scattered contents of her bag – that's where that lipstick is! She flushed.

'Well, I imagine he turned up,' said Harry at length. 'She didn't ring again.'

'Good.' She couldn't meet his eye. Dear God, said a shaky voice in her head. We'd have been caught! She opened her Filofax.

'OK. PCC standing committee tonight. Quite a lot to get through,' said Harry. 'I've got a meeting with the hospital chaplain and the volunteers, this afternoon. Deanery Synod on Wednesday, blah-de-blah. Session with the frustrated charismatics of Asleby to explain why I don't think the time's right for full-blown exorcisms during the Sunday Eucharist. Meeting at Gerry McGee's to prepare the Churches Together Advent service – I'll cover that, it's your day off.'

Isobel was staring at her diary unable to make sense of the page.

'So what does your week hold?' Harry was asking.

'Um . . .'

'Is everything all right, Isobel?'

'Yes, fine.'

Out of the corner of her eye she caught a movement. A glass fell with a smash from the table where it had been standing. They both leapt to their feet. Isobel clutched Harry's arm.

'It moved!' she gibbered. 'I saw it move!'

They stared at the fragments.

'Hmm,' said Harry. He waited, head cocked, analysing the atmosphere. 'I don't like this.'

She realized she was still clinging to his arm and let go in confusion. 'Sorry. How ridiculous. I must be seeing things.' But how had it happened? The glass must have been balanced on the edge. 'It was probably traffic vibrations.'

They listened. The road outside was quiet.

'Or subsidence,' she offered. 'Old mines, or something.'

'Don't say that!' exclaimed Harry. "We've only just had the roof done.'

They fell silent again. Isobel went over that split second – a movement, the crash. The back of her neck prickled.

'I'm scared.'

'Don't be,' said Harry. 'This is the house of God.'

She nodded, shuddering.

'Why don't I pray?' He did, a simple Celtic encircling prayer. She normally found these a bit twee, but as he spoke she experienced a vivid sense of darkness retreating before an expanding light. When she opened her eyes it was just the shabby old vestry again, still in need of a good tidy. She got out the dustpan and brush.

'I never liked that glass, anyway,' remarked Harry, watching her sweep up the pieces. 'Careful,' he warned, as she wrapped them in newspaper.

She tutted crossly. 'I know what I'm doing – ow!' A fragment punctured the paper and stabbed into her palm.

'Isobel! Are you all right?'

She dropped the bundle. Blood welled up. 'Ow!' It was surprisingly painful for such a small wound. It must have gone deep. Blood dropped on to the glass.

'Let's see.' He took her hand. 'Isobel! You poor thing.'

She found a wad of tissues and pressed them to her palm.

Harry hovered anxiously. 'Does it need stitches?'

'No, no.' Her knees were trembling. 'How stupid. I wasn't thinking.'

At Harry's suggestion they went to the vicarage for a plaster and to finish their staff meeting.

She sat in his study as he made coffee. She could hear him in the kitchen. Normally she would have taken the opportunity to snoop and see what new books he had on his shelves, but today she sank her head back and closed her eyes. It felt like a dream. Lack of sleep, no doubt.

*I've probably got time for a quick coffee.*

*Oh, I mustn't keep you.*

Now the exchange seemed loaded with unspoken desire again. She knew her manner had aroused Harry's suspicions, but she couldn't clarify things without either casting herself in a foolish light or Johnny in a bad one. There was nothing to say. Nothing had happened. She screwed up her face in despair. Why was she so inept in this area? It was like a form of social dyslexia. She couldn't read the signs. Her hand throbbed under the plaster. Perhaps she'd been assuming that a clerical collar, like a wedding ring, exempted one from the whole silly game. She resolved not to waste another single thought on the incident.

Harry came in and set down the tray. He pressed down the cafetière plunger thoughtfully. 'Isobel, there's clearly something going on.'

'Really, it's nothing!' she bleated.

'I'm afraid I've got to take it seriously.' He poured her some coffee. She moved unhappily in her chair. Best to get it over with. 'What did Gabriel say about it? When he came that time,' he clarified, seeing her confusion.

'Oh, *that*.'

Harry frowned. 'Why? What did you think I meant?'

'Nothing. Gabriel – well, he seemed to think it had something to do with *me*! Ha ha! Well, one hardly thinks of oneself as causing paranormal activity,' she added, when he didn't laugh.

'Did he say what he meant?'

'I assumed he told you.'

'Of course not! Anything you discussed was in confidence.'

'Well, he said there were things I'd lost and never grieved over, or something.'

He contemplated this. 'Did that ring any bells?'

'Oh, I don't know. Maybe.'

'Do you need to talk to him again?'

'Possibly.'

'Think it over.'

'All right.' She looked down at her diary.

Harry cleared his throat. 'I wonder . . .' Isobel tensed again. 'Next time, do you think you could smash that tacky statuette of the Sacred Heart?' She glared at him. 'Just a thought. Now, next week. What have you got lined up?'

She told him and they talked business for a while.

'Um, sorry I teased you about baptism last night,' he apologized. 'I realize that might still be something of a raw nerve.'

She winced. 'I'm afraid I'm having some difficulty forgiving that reporter.'

'Hmm,' he said gravely. 'Can I offer you a little tip I sometimes find helpful?'

'Please.'

'When someone's injured me in some way I occasionally find it cathartic to take a pen into the bathroom and draw their face on the loo paper.'

Her jaw dropped. 'Harry!'

'Just a thought.'

'You don't actually do that!'

He smiled angelically. 'Sometimes I have the entire senior diocesan staff lined up ready for use.'

'Well, I just hope my face doesn't feature!'

'No, no! Well, not so far,' he assured her, as he saw her to the door. She stepped out into the sunny garden.

'Oh, Isobel, I meant to say.' He turned his attention to a rose-bush by the path, nipping off a couple of dead heads. 'I dare say you picked up that Johnny's in a bit of a bad way at the moment.'

Her cheeks burned. 'I gathered.'

'Just to say that if, by any chance, he contacts you to unburden himself, or whatever, I'd like you to pass him on to me. No need for you to get involved in his problems.' He glanced up. 'Is that all right?'

'Of course.' She pretended to look at her watch, aware that she was receiving another little vicarly hint, and grateful, as ever, for his tact. She felt a surge of honesty welling up – she owed it to him – but what, exactly, could she be more frank about? Her feelings?

'He's an attractive man, naturally,' she said.

'Yes. I know.'

This admission left Isobel paralysed. 'Well,' she managed.

He smiled. 'Goodbye. Don't go near any china shops.'

'Oh, shut up!' she snapped, jolted out of her embarrassment.

Of course, she rebuked herself, walking home. Why hadn't it occurred to her before? It was nothing to be shocked about. God didn't condemn homosexual tendencies, *per se*. She had no reason to think less highly of Harry – indeed, rather the reverse. His behaviour was above reproach. He was an admirable model of celibacy, and she would do well to take a leaf out of his book. If he felt like that and had worked with Johnny for three years – oh! Was that what he'd been referring to in the vestry? Clutching his heart and saying he was 'too old'. Too old for that kind of emotional turmoil and renunciation, perhaps? And there I was, totally absorbed in my own misery, thought Isobel. Really, there were days when she didn't like herself one little bit.

Right, she said. Right! – as if to galvanize herself into action, though what particular action she couldn't decide. Everything felt diffuse, fragmented. She'd better make herself a list the moment she got in.

'Oh, Isobel!' It was Kath Bollom.

Damn, thought Isobel. I should have gone round the back way. 'Good morning!' Her tone was final, but Kath was not deterred.

'Saw you last night. Looked like that lad, curate he used to be, what do they call him? Johnny. Just giving you a lift, was he?'

'That's right. He'd been preaching at the harvest service.' Isobel smiled brightly, but inside experienced that frisson again: *Dear God, that was close!* Ridiculous!

Kath was wittering on: 'Canny lad, not like a vicar, used to be a builder, they have all sorts in the church these days, but I'm all for that, I can still see him now, up on the roof after the storm, you know the storm, back in 'eighty-seven it was, not as bad up here as it was down south. There he was, checking the chimney-pot. "Be careful," I says, "I'm all right, me," he shouts, "spent half me life doing this". His wife's a funny lass, mind. 'Course, they weren't married back then. She used to visit him. Not overnight. Stayed with his parents, she used to, up Ponteland way, done well for hisself, his dad has, big house, not that I'd've had anything against her staying here, you've got to move with the times, they're only human after all, vicars, I'm not one to judge. They say she never goes to church.'

'That's a matter for her,' said Isobel, aggravated into a perverse defence of Mrs Whitaker. Besides, you never go yourself! she almost added.

'It's not right,' said Kath, shaking her head, 'I'm old-fashioned, me, but for me the vicar's wife's got to be there, running things. Reverend Halliwell's wife, now . . .'

Escaping took a further ten minutes, but at last Isobel was safely on her doorstep.

'And another thing,' Kath's voice pursued her across the road, 'insisted on keeping her maiden name. Can't be doing with feminism, me . . .'

Isobel stomped into her study 'Bollom!' she exclaimed, trying out Harry's favourite swear word. It had a satisfying ring. The spare keys were lying on her desk. Odd. Perhaps she hadn't been able to see them for looking. Right. List. She sat and imposed some order on her life.

The weeks passed. October came and went. The confirmation service passed off satisfactorily. Johnny didn't phone. Isobel had never expected him to. She could have wished Harry hadn't sown that particular seed in her mind, though. It caused her to jump for a whole week each time the phone rang. The subject was not mentioned again between them, as if out of an unspoken mutual concern for one another's sensibilities. Isobel aspired to Harry's equanimity. She prayed, and eventually the strength of her feelings for Johnny wore off, as she'd always told herself they would. Starved by lack of new contact they became mundane. She could get on with things now that a calmer frame of mind prevailed. She replaced the missing lipstick and that was that. On the whole she'd acquitted herself adequately. Strange, then, that she caught herself feeling nostalgic for September's mad intensity.

But there was always Davy to stop her from brooding. By now he'd become a familiar feature in her life. After the first flurry of congregational speculation had died down he was accepted (in disappointment) as her 'friend'. Father McGee confronted her on Stockton high street and after teasing her about her baptism policy, threatened her with hellfire and the wrath of God for poaching.

'But he still goes to your church!' she protested.

'Ah, but it's the slippery slope, the slippery slope!' He shook his head. 'These young lads, they're so impressionable. They see a pretty face in the pulpit and one minute it's helping with the youth work, the next – bang! they're going over to Canterbury'

'How did you know about the youth work?'

'Aha, my spies are everywhere.'

It was true, Davy turned up now and then to the youth club. He was a great boon on outings. He'd gone with them to the bonfire-night display and to see the illuminations at Sunderland, although this was a city he appeared to nurse a prejudice against, for some reason. She wondered what she'd have done without him keeping control in the back of the minibus while she drove.

Advent drew near, the start of a new church year. Isobel looked forward to it, preparing afresh for the coming of the Saviour. Of course, being ordained meant she couldn't relish the major festivals with the innocent pleasure she'd previously enjoyed. These days there was too much to fret about. What if the Advent candles wouldn't light? What if a spat broke out between the choir and the music group? Supposing the lay-led intercessions were way off beam? And, above all, what if nobody came? The fact that people always did never fully banished this last fear.

It would be nice just to sit in the pew for once with no responsibilities; but that was ministry for you. She was called, like the Saviour himself, not to be served but to serve.

> *Almighty God,*
> *give us grace to cast away the works of darkness*
> *and put on the armour of light,*
> *now in the time of this mortal life,*
> *in which your Son Jesus Christ*
> *came to us in great humility . . .*

The great truth of the Incarnation had the power to move Isobel almost to tears. She was no sentimentalist, but she loved the season of Advent. So much more than tiny windows on glittery calendars and shopping-days-till-Christmas! If only she could instil something of its message into the hearts and minds of her congregation.

To this end she laboured harder than ever over her sermons and pastoral visiting. In particular she expended a great deal of effort on her 'Inquirers' Group'. Brenda and up to nine other women met each week in Isobel's study. They were cheerful to the point of raucousness, always keen to discuss anything except the subject in hand. Isobel spent all her time dragging them back to the worksheets in front of them. If red-herring-ing ever became an Olympic event, she'd have a gold medal team on her hands. We've got *nowhere*! she mourned, after they'd gone. If she tried to explore the cross, someone would have a nephew who'd once banged a nail through his hand. Sometimes in desperation she hogged the floor and just *told* them the crucial doctrines, but she always got the unpleasant sensation that she was squeezing the life out of the Gospel as she spoke. Where was she going wrong? Harry suggested that red herrings might be important. They might be symptoms of a different approach to learning. To Isobel it was sheer sloppiness. When she'd led student groups like this she'd never had any problems. She redoubled her prayerful efforts.

The local bookshop rang to let her know that the books she'd ordered had come in. She drove there as soon as she found a moment and collected her swag. There was nothing like books to cheer one up. Two Bible commentaries, one a Christmas present for Harry, one for herself. The rest were presents as well, *Where The Wild Things Are* for Teddy. She'd been quite shocked to discover Annie hadn't already bought it for him. *The Oxford Book of Nursery Rhymes* for Hannah. Isobel leafed through, enjoying the charming woodcuts before inscribing the front with a message and the date and wrapping it up in pretty paper. Isobel never economized on gift wrap. It was a little weakness of hers, but the cheap stuff was so flimsy. It diminished the present, somehow. The rest could wait till the day she'd set aside in her diary for sending cards and presents.

That afternoon the phone rang and the doorbell went simultaneously. Isobel dithered for a second and opted for the door. The answer-machine was on, after all.

She found a large, dishevelled man on her doorstep, not one of her regulars. Predictably, his Giro had been held up and he just needed the train fare to Glasgow where his granny was dying. He reeked of alcohol and, after explaining she never handed out money, Isobel beat him down to a bag of sandwiches. She shut the door, leaving him on the step, as she always did on these occasions, and went through to the kitchen.

'I can't eat cheese,' he bawled through her letterbox. 'It's the acid.'

She made him ham. Lucky she had anything in the house. The bread was past its best, but beggars ... Honestly, the number of grannies dying in Glasgow must add up to the population of China. It was like the fragments of the True Cross. You'd think they'd do us the courtesy of thinking up a new tale now and then. She went back to the door, reminding herself that it might one day be one of her brothers who'd slipped through the net and ended up homeless. She handed over the carrier-bag of food. He mumbled something and wandered unsteadily off.

Back in her study once more, Isobel played the message. It was Harry.

'Isobel, I've just had a man at the door wanting money, ex-con, big, half his ear missing. If he calls round, on no account let him in. He was extremely violent and abusive and I don't want you to take any risks. All right?'

She rang back immediately.

'Harry! Are you OK?'

'A bit shaken. I've got the police here. Listen, don't answer your door unless you can see who it is.'

'Too late. I've just given him sandwiches.' She explained what had happened.

'Well, thank God.' He put his hand over the receiver and she heard him telling someone – the police, presumably, where the man now was.

'What happened?' she asked.

'He got abusive when I wouldn't give him cash, so I shut him out. He smashed in the glass in my porch, but the inner door proved a bit more stubborn, fortunately.'

'Harry! What if – What would you have done if he'd got in?'

'Punched his bloody lights out. I've been helping him on and off for years. He knows I won't give money. I don't know what the problem was today.'

She heard the sound of sirens wailing past. Well, that'll keep Kath happy for a bit.

'Still,' he sighed, 'no real harm done. So long as you're safe.'

'So long as *you*'re safe, Harry. Poor old you.'

'Oh, well. That's ministry, sister.'

They hung up. Shock caught up with her. She sat, trembling at the thought of what might have happened.

That evening after the PCC standing committee, she got back to a message from Davy, who had heard about the incident. She rang him at work and got a lecture on self-defence and not answering the door to dodgy characters. 'You cannot afford to run risks, Isobel.'

It was a dilemma she'd never solve. Of course she mustn't be foolish, but it was hard to radiate trust and acceptance with your door on the safety chain. True, women priests were vulnerable, but on the other hand, it was possible that they were more likely to be treated with deference than their male colleagues. Harry had been abused and threatened today while she had not. She found the episode hard to shake from her mind. That night every tiny noise jolted her awake and for days afterwards the sound of the doorbell jangled in her head like a fire alarm.

There were no more unexplained breakages in the vestry, mercifully. With no way of checking what had really happened that morning, Isobel was inclined to believe she had imagined it all. Her mental state had hardly been at its most pacific. Harry was keeping a quiet eye on her, though. She bore this as graciously as she could. He would occasionally ask if everything was all right, and she was always quick to reassure him. After all, there was always some logical explanation for the little puzzles that continued to occur from time to time. Lost keys turning up in bizarre places, phone left off the hook: it was absentmindedness. Books shoved back from their proper position at the front of the shelf, pictures hanging askew: it was the Youth Group. Lights left on, washing-machine switched off in mid-cycle – these were not the kind of thing to pester Harry with. Everything was fine.

Yes, fine. Apart from that sense she occasionally had that some-one had just left the room she was entering. Each time it happened she froze, eyes hunting swiftly round for clues. Once a mug was swinging slightly back and forth on the rack in her kitchen. The others hung motionless. It was as if an unseen finger had poked one. She listened, terrified, to the tiny rocking sound until it dwindled into silence. Well, there must be some logical explanation, she heard her father's voice say. Think. Perhaps she'd hung it up crooked and it had only just slipped back into place. That would account for it. But in the silence she could feel someone watching. I'm here, it said. I'm waiting for you.

'What do you want?' she asked. Her voice broke the spell. I'm being ridiculous. She nerved herself, reached for the offending mug and set it down on the draining-board before filling the kettle and finding her cafetière. Suddenly she remembered reading *The Exorcist* under the desk during rained-off PE lessons, instead of drawing all the positions on a hockey pitch as they'd been told to do. She and Victoria had agreed that the book was complete rubbish, but at night for months afterwards it had taken all her father's calm rationality to see the spectres off. The memory was illuminating. The silly incident in the vestry must have triggered those adolescent fears. Not to mention the completely reasonable fear of violent alcoholics calling round.

The tension seeped into her dreams. She was forever running away from something and her legs wouldn't work properly. Her subconscious took to throwing up an exotic gallery of sexual partners for her to contemplate – even *Harry*, for goodness' sake, which made morning prayer a somewhat ticklish business for a couple of days. There were also the dreams in which she was given charge of a small child or a baby, and inexplicably she failed to care for it properly or, worse, lost it and spent hours in frenzied search. And then there was Tatiana.

*I keep dreaming about you*, Isobel would say, knowing that *this* time, at last, it wasn't a dream.

Perhaps she ought to go and see Gabriel? The thought nagged away at her. Sometimes she woke in the night and couldn't get back to sleep; then she promised herself she would contact him, but the next day things never seemed bad enough to warrant it.

And then one night she was woken by singing. She sat up and listened. There was nothing but the sound of the wind about the house. Yet she could still hear a remnant, the tail end of a song, four notes in falling cadence, then the echoes dying away.

The phrase returned at odd moments over the next weeks, until it began to drive her mad. It came without warning, always the same four notes and the trailing plangent echo. She mentioned it to Harry.

'You're lucky,' he said. 'At least you haven't got a bunch of morons singing the theme song from *Chitty Chitty Bang Bang* twenty-four hours a day.'

Of course, she ended up singing it for the week, but that was different. She heard it the way she could hear chunks of Mozart if she thought about it. The other music came suddenly in a burst, as if it was being broadcast in her brain. She *heard* it. Play a bit more of it, she pleaded, for she knew she knew the tune, the voices, and was always on the brink of placing it when it was gone.

It was time to organize herself for Christmas. Isobel had set aside her day off for card-writing and present-wrapping and accomplished the task far more quickly than she'd expected, which left her with an afternoon and evening to fill. She didn't dare show her face in the parish as Harry had been very stern with her earlier in the week for not taking enough time off. Quite frankly she couldn't face another bout of Thelma so soon after the *Uncle Vanya* episode. Resentment bubbled up at the memory and she asked herself yet again why she had ever agreed to go. Or, indeed, why she ever did anything with Thelma at all, given how much her friend grumbled and groused. She thought fleetingly of embellishing her loo roll with Thelma's face, but dismissed the idea. Honestly, Harry could be so naughty at times. But the thought, unworthy though it was, cheered her up. So, where to go? What to do? It was several months since she'd seen Annie. It wouldn't be long till Teddy's birthday, so perhaps she could call in with his present.

She was in the process of wrapping the wooden jigsaw puzzle when she heard Davy's motorbike pull up. What was he doing off work? She went to the door.

He pulled his helmet off with a grin and came into the hall. 'Hiya. Fancy a trip somewhere?'

'Lovely! Why aren't you at work?'

'Some nutter went for us with a Stanley knife. Got the rest of the week off.'

She gasped. 'No! Are you all right?'

'Why, aye! Few stitches. It's nowt. Where do you want to go?'

She looked at him sharply. He was looking a bit white round the gills.

'Shouldn't you be resting?'

He fended off all her solicitous questions, and before long they were heading north to Bishopside. He had suggested he took her to meet his family, but she had demurred, saying she had a gift to deliver.

Isobel couldn't help worrying about what Annie would make of Davy. He wasn't being presented as a boyfriend, but deep down she had to admit to some reluctance, some horrible unacceptable snobbery over his accent, his background. She winced at herself. Really, she was no better than the insufferable Jacks brothers. In her Oxford days she'd always swelled in indignation at their attitude to friendship. People were mere lifestyle accessories for Andrew and Alex. One would no more have boring friends than one would contemplate buying china figurines out of the back of the *Radio Times*. She knew she was neither interesting, louche, talented nor flamboyant enough to enter their precious coterie. Perhaps she feared that Will, first cousin of the Jackses and possessing such towering good taste himself, would disparage Davy. However, Will would be at work.

These tangled concerns kept at bay the thought that she would be within half a mile of Johnny's house ...

Annie answered the door. Rather to Isobel's satisfaction, the sight of her in a crash helmet and leathers seemed to disconcert

213

Annie totally. Isobel made some introductions and explained that they had just popped in to deliver Teddy's birthday present. This brought Teddy himself padding down the hall to investigate. He clung shyly to Annie, peering round her legs with his huge round brown eyes.

Davy squatted down. 'Hiya, bonny lad. What d' they call you, then?'

Teddy shrank back further with a grin.

'This is Teddy,' said Annie. 'Come and have coffee. Will's off work at the moment.'

Isobel's heart gave a nasty bump.

They followed Annie to the kitchen. 'Um, I'm not *entirely* sure how much sense you'll get out of him,' continued Annie nervously. 'Will, Isobel's here with a friend.'

Will was lounging at the table. Isobel's initial shock at seeing a doctor smoking gave way to horror. Pot. Davy. Help.

Will smiled up at her sunnily. She shot him an anguished look of warning but he only laughed.

'Um,' said Annie. 'This is Davy, a friend of Isobel's from Asleby.'

'Davy's a police officer,' said Isobel swiftly.

Will froze. Isobel saw fear cross Annie's face.

'I'm off duty,' said Davy. There was a tense silence. 'Do you grow your own, like?' he asked.

Will made no reply. Neither Annie nor Isobel knew how to intervene. Teddy, sensing the atmosphere, cowered closer to his mother's skirts. She picked him up and hugged him close.

'Because if you *are* cultivating cannabis on these premises,' went on Davy, 'my advice to you, sir, would be ...' He sounded so pompously like a policeman that Isobel's face burned. Will was scowling down at the ashtray, forced into a show of contrition. '... pinch the tops out now and then and you'll get more shoots.'

It was a moment before this sank in.

Isobel watched and saw a slow grin dawn on Will's face. 'You fucking bastard,' he said.

'Will!' protested Annie.

Then both men laughed. Will slumped down and wrapped his arms round his head, giggling, 'Oh, God, oh, God,' into the table.

Davy sat down opposite him and observed, 'He's out of it.'

'Shall I make coffee?' asked Annie, in desperation. But Teddy was clinging so tightly that she was helpless. 'It's all right, poppet,' Isobel heard her whisper.

'Let me,' offered Isobel.

'It's for medicinal purposes only,' Will was protesting.

' "I swear to God, Officer," ' supplied Davy, which reduced Will to further fits of laughter.

'I've got a bad back,' he said. 'Swear.'

'Got a dodgy knee meself, come to that,' remarked Davy. The joint was promptly offered. 'Oops,' he said, intercepting a fierce stare from Isobel. 'Got me orders, there.'

She saw the unspoken pact form: men against nagging women. She would have been grateful to witness Will's acceptance of Davy had she not been so angry with the pair of them. Davy was actually encouraging him! And did Will not care what he inflicted on his wife – the fear he'd be arrested, imprisoned, struck off? What kind of an example was he setting his child? Annie seemed to sense her disapproval.

'He genuinely only smokes it because of his back, these days,' she whispered as Isobel measured coffee into the cafetière. 'He's off work at the moment with it. The alternative is spending his time dosed up to the eyeballs with painkillers.'

It's still a banned substance, thought Isobel. But she remembered the circumstances of his injury and said nothing. The afternoon passed with Davy giving 'motorbike' rides to Teddy up and down the hall, with Teddy in a crash helmet squealing with mingled glee and terror.

'He seems nice,' remarked Annie, fishing delicately.

'Yes.' Isobel smiled, but didn't oblige.

'Hidden depths, young Isobel,' remarked Will. He stretched and winced. 'Well, I'd better get on. I'll be on the computer,' he said to Annie.

Isobel watched him leave. He was in pain. One could see it. Perhaps she ought cautiously to revise her view of cannabis? She made a mental note to do some serious reading on the subject.

*

On the way home Isobel was annoyed with herself for being so anxious. Davy was quite capable of looking after himself. It was her own screwed-up middle-class angst. Terrified of being unwittingly classist, she could no longer conduct herself naturally. It was like her fear of being found racist. It rendered her incapable of uttering the word black unselfconsciously. The race awareness course she'd been on at theological college had only underlined the extent to which she remained racist despite her best intentions. She knew all too well that, given the right circumstances, the coarsest prejudice would surface. Like that ghastly time when she'd been a student and someone had cut her up aggressively at a roundabout. She tooted her horn. The other car had braked, blocking the road, and a large angry black man had emerged. She'd had time to think as he approached, but when he thumped on the roof of her car and yelled, 'Are you honking at me, white trash?' she responded, 'Shut up, you black bastard.' The incident still troubled her profoundly years afterwards.

When they arrived back at Isobel's house she asked Davy in, but he declined, saying he needed an early night. Concern for him rushed back, but he shrugged off her questions as he had before. She let herself in and went to the study to check her answer-machine. One message from the part-time parish secretary reminding Isobel that the press date for the *Asleby Bulletin* was tomorrow, and had Isobel written her 'Letter from the Clergy' yet? Yes, yes, yes. Isobel had never entirely forgiven Linda for editing her first contribution to the parish magazine. The woman seemed to have a piddling, pettifogging obsession with avoiding repetitions. This is a parish magazine, for heaven's sake, not *Just a Minute*! Isobel wanted to shout. She refrained, however. Linda was one of those huffy women everyone tiptoed round. What was it, exactly, that knack of instilling guilt in others? Linda had it in spades. 'If it's a problem I'll type it myself,' Isobel had told her, on more than one occasion. To which Linda would sigh and say, 'No, I'll do it.' Don't force yourself, you old bag, Isobel never said.

Harry, predictably, had found it hilarious. Mottoes and quotations in his handwriting appeared on the vestry noticeboard among the rotas: 'Home sweet house', 'To be, or not to exist, that is the question.' His last year's Christmas card to her had read, 'We wish you a merry Christmas, we pray you'll experience a joyful Yuletide, we invoke for you a cheerful celebration of the Birth of Christ, and a Happy New Year.' Silly man.

That night the mysterious tune woke her again at four in the morning. She lay unable to get back to sleep. The events of the afternoon kept coming back to her. She felt bad, as if she'd done something wrong and not yet repented of it. Why did this vague guilt persistently cling to her over Davy? Was it because of her tendency to keep him away from her other friends? Why had she never made a real effort to introduce him to Harry? Or Jan and Natalie and Drew? Why wouldn't she meet his family? What, exactly, was her problem?

This proved to be the first of many bad nights. Waking became a habit, and as she tossed and turned in the dark all the day's worries crowded into her brain. Her mental lists grew to nightmare proportions and in the end it was better simply to get up and tackle her correspondence or sermon preparation. Things would settle down after Christmas. She could catch up on sleep then.

## CHAPTER 18

The Christmas when she was seventeen was utterly miserable for Isobel. She had just been rejected by Cambridge. This was the first time she'd ever failed anything academic and she felt it keenly – both her brothers had got in. The school had been expecting her to walk into a scholarship and, without ever being boastful, she had shared their confidence. Not even to be interviewed! And she couldn't console herself with the dubious comfort that she hadn't really been trying. She'd slogged her guts out and her best had not been good enough. However, Durham would be wonderful, marvellous, she was looking forward to it immensely. Everyone appeared sympathetic, yet it felt as though the very air was smirking at her. *Didn't get into Cambridge, eh? Ah, diddums!* It was as though she had FAILURE branded on her forehead. She faced down her imagined detractors with dignity, determined no one should suspect just how terrible it felt.

And Gary had broken up with her. After one last blizzard of pressies he vanished. It was for the best, he told her. His job had moved and he didn't know exactly where he'd be and all that stuff, anyway, she'd be better off without him, she wouldn't want someone like him hanging around when she was off to college. All good things come to an end, darling. But why? she'd demanded. That's life, he'd said. Got to move on and all that. He was tense and twitchy. But can't you give me an address? He shook his head. What you don't know can't hurt you. Love you.

And that had been it.

It might have been easier to bear if she'd had someone to talk to, but all through the whole mad affair she'd kept her own counsel. Her friends knew about him, but she never introduced them to each other. He was a bit of her life that never connected with the rest, a parallel existence where she could be a bad girl, not a good sensible girl who gave other girls a moral lead. She

218

had an uncomfortable sense that she'd betrayed Victoria and Annabel by her silence. Surely that's what one's girlfriends were for – to gossip with about men and sex. But they couldn't have matched her anecdote for anecdote. They would have listened in awe, or perhaps disgust, and never been able to shriek, 'I *know*! I know *exactly* what you mean!' Sometimes she caught herself despising their virginal swottiness.

Gary, in turn, had kept her away from his friends and 'business contacts'. Not her sort, they weren't. And now he'd gone there was nobody to chew it over with, to opine that he'd found another woman and wasn't worthy of her, or that it had been great while it lasted but there were plenty more fish in the sea. Was there a certain quiet satisfaction on the faces of Victoria and Annabel as they observed her misery? Had they prophesied to one another that it would end in tears?

Surely he'd ring or write, though, despite what he'd said. Surely. But each time the phone shrilled in the Wrecktory's echoing hall it was not him. Days. Weeks. A month.

'We don't seem to be seeing quite so much of Gary at the moment,' Mrs Knox ventured to observe.

'Oh, we've split up,' said Isobel airily.

'That's probably sensible,' said her father.

She affected not to care either about Gary or about Cambridge, but some kind of outburst soon became inevitable. She could sense it brewing, like a thunderstorm. The clouds finally burst on New Year's Eve. She was being driven back from babysitting by Mr Peacock, the children's father. He was still in jolly party spirits and freely admitted to being over the limit. He took the back route to avoid the police. Suddenly it was all too much for Isobel. Tears spilled over, then gave way to audible sobs until Mr Peacock was obliged to pull off the road into a secluded woody spot and comfort her.


'All set for Christmas?' Isobel was asked this several times a day as she went about her parish duties. Honesty forced her to give the unpopular answer 'Yes.' She was always well ahead of the final posting dates. She was not having to cook for herself on Christmas

Day – Natalie and Drew had invited her for lunch together with Harry and Jan. She didn't even have a turkey to fret over. Of course, people didn't ask because they wanted to know how Isobel's preparations were shaping up. All they really needed was an opportunity to exorcize their guilt by boasting about how much they still had to do. Isobel was compelled to listen with a polite smile as these sins of omission were paraded before her. If thought bubbles had been visible, hers would have read, 'Stop whingeing and get on with it, then.'

Another seasonal irritation was the round robin Christmas newsletters some people saw fit to send with their cards. If they couldn't be bothered to write to her personally, Isobel really didn't see why she should be bothered to read them, especially when they routinely contained such delights as 'And Toby has done his first poo on the potty!!!' She gritted her teeth as yet another photocopied sheet arrived, garlanded with computer-generated holly and infested with exclamation marks at a ratio of fifty per hundred words. Some wittily purported to be written by the eighteen-month-old baby, or even (arf arf!) by the family dog. Most annoying of all were the ones which took it upon themselves to remind her of the True Meaning of Christmas. I'm *ordained,* for heaven's sake! she wanted to yell. I *know* the true meaning of Christmas! Still, she ploughed through them dutifully and filed them away in her cabinet for future reference, in case she ever needed to know what so-and-so's eldest sprog was called, or precisely what mark young Bethany had attained in her Grade I piano.

A card arrived from Edward, the inside filled with his confident but illegible scrawl. After squinting at it over breakfast, Isobel discerned that he'd met 'a super Christian girl. No news yet, but watch this space.' There goes another one, she thought glumly.

Isobel knew she was overworking, but she was locked into it and helpless. There was nothing she could do but ride the ecclesiastical roller-coaster until she flopped off it, exhausted, on Christmas Day. She had only herself to blame, but saying no to speaking engagements, or the dozen other worthy causes that needed her skills, was something she was constitutionally unable to do. Managing without spare time, or eventually sleep, was the price she had to pay for her folly. Just as well she wasn't having to juggle family commitments too. Still, they were half-way through Advent. There wasn't long to go now.

Walter Goodwill summoned her to attend his quarterly grousing session. She faced the ordeal in better spirits than usual, knowing he had been well and truly trounced over the pews, two of which, even now, were being cut down and stripped ready for their new life in Natalie and Drew's breakfast room. Bad luck, Wal, me old darling. The goose saw her coming and charged. She booted it aside and rang the bell.

It was Walter's daughter who answered the door.

'He can't get up, he's got a bad toe,' she said. 'Silly old fool insists on cutting his own nails. He'll give himself gangrene. Diabetics can't be too careful, but will he listen?' This was addressed directly to Walter who was scowling in his armchair with his foot on a stool. 'It's the curate for you, Dad.'

'Hear you won't do baptisms,' was his opening gambit. 'I've been telling everyone it's the vicar's policy. You're just doing what you're told. But it gives you a bad name, you know.'

'Water off a duck's back,' lied Isobel. 'How are you, Mr Goodwill?'

He grumbled his way through a list of topics.

'You'll be round for your Christmas box, no doubt,' he sneered eventually.

'I'll be round to bring you home communion,' she countered.

'If I'm still here,' he muttered. 'The way they carry on you'd think I was in me grave already.' He jerked his head towards the kitchen.

'You! You're as tough as old boots,' said Isobel.

'Hmmph!' He looked pleased.

She said a prayer with him and left. She beat the goose to the gate. It stared impotently at her through the bars with its beady manic gaze. 'Christmas is coming,' she hissed at it.

She walked home, bone weary. There was a chattering and chur-ring in the hawthorn hedge. She glanced and saw a crowd, thirty, forty even, of crested birds perched there. She gasped. Waxwings! There was no one to tell. If only Dad was here, she thought. A waxwing winter. She paused for several minutes watching the exotic visitors with their redtipped plumage and flashes of yellow, then she turned and continued home.

Only one message on the machine. She pressed the button. Silence. At first she thought it was a nuisance caller, but then a voice said, 'Isobel, it's Mike here.' There was another silence. Oh, no! Something's wrong! 'Um, look, could you come round when you're back in? 'Bye.' She grabbed her Filofax and bag and hurried to the car. He's lost his job, she thought. Poor old Sue will have to go back to work after all. It would be a horrible wrench with Hannah still so tiny, but it wasn't the end of the world.

There was a police car outside the house. Her heart plunged in sick dread and she sprinted down the path. It was Davy who answered the door.

'Bad news, I'm afraid,' he said, in a low voice. 'The bairn's dead.'

'No!' She clamped a hand over her mouth to stifle her cry. 'How?'

'Cot death. We're just taking a statement. We're nearly through.' His hand was on her arm. 'Isobel, I'm truly sorry. I know she was special to you.'

She nodded. 'Where's – ?'

'At the hospital. They've got to do a post-mortem.'

A sob shook her. Mike appeared. 'Isobel!'

The sight of his grief made her thrust hers aside. She put her arms round him and let him weep. Davy withdrew. In the other room Isobel could hear Sue sobbing and a woman's voice, another police officer, probably, comforting her.

Isobel looked back on that day in disbelief. It was as if she'd vanished and her place had been taken by some model curate, programmed to cope and be compassionate. At every turn the delicate balance was in danger of being upset – the sight of the cradle still bearing the dent of a small head, the little socks drying on the radiator, the empty bottle on the draining-board – she must look away and be sensible, enduring until it was all behind her. What use would she be if she dissolved? All those tears to wipe away, all those bitter self-recriminations to listen to. If only we'd had her in bed with us, if only we'd checked her again. We were just going to congratulate her on sleeping through for the first time and now . . .

That little bundle – cold.

Isobel shut out the picture till later. Davy and the other officer left, having taken names of people to be contacted. Isobel watched Davy with detachment, seeing how good he was at his job, this awful task of dealing with the bereaved. Odd that their respective professions meant they should be sharing it. But his part was done now. Hers had hardly started.

Harry came in the early afternoon and she saw him crying and rocking Mike in his arms. She hurried away to make more tea. If she gave way even a little she'd be finished. And there was the school assembly to do. At half past two she excused herself and drove to the school. Dear God, please help me. Get me through this. She looked out across the hall full of bright young faces and her heart bled for them all sitting there, not knowing yet what life could be like. One of the teachers said to her, weeks later, that she'd never have guessed from Isobel's manner what had happened. It seemed like praise.

That night when she got home, she gave herself permission to collapse. Mike's message was still on her answer-machine, followed now by one from Davy, commiserating again and saying to ring if he could do anything. Then came a string of other parishioners' voices, all saying they'd just heard the terrible news and was there anything they could do? She erased them all wearily and went through to the dining room.

There on the table was the book of nursery rhymes wrapped up and ready to give. What could she do with it, now? She'd written in it, 'To Hannah, for your first Christmas, with love from Isobel'. There was no taking it back to the shop. Should she keep it, hoping, absurdly, that one day the description would fit some other little girl? Or should she send it to a charity shop? She'd have to cut the dedication out, or some stranger would read it, and the thought was unbearable. Would it be cruel or kind to give it to Sue and Mike? Would it bring home their loss, or help them to come to terms with it? 'I don't know what to do with you!' she cried at the book. It took on a symbolic status. If she could solve this conundrum, she could begin to explain others. How come *this* child had to die? Why was she lying in the mortuary, not her cot? Why had Sue such difficulty conceiving when other dim-witted, feckless women had four, five, six abortions?

My Hannah, my little Hannah. I'll always remember her baptism – that tiny hand reaching out to grab my surplice front as the water surprised her. I walked round the church with her, showing her off, thought Isobel. It amazed her that she couldn't cry. One tear seeped out of her right eye and slid down her cheek. That was all. Perhaps it hasn't sunk in yet, she told herself. I'm still at the stage of denying it. She knew this was common and that it would pass. She was protecting herself, aware that there was the funeral to get through. She didn't know yet whether Sue and Mike wanted her to officiate. Which would be worse? Having to preach, or having to listen to Harry?

She realized she was standing in the middle of the room hugging the parcel and rocking it as she would a child who needed soothing. She laid it gently on the table and went to make herself some dinner. The fridge was empty. She'd been intending to zoom to the supermarket, but she'd forgotten. She continued to squat staring into the empty fridge until the phone roused her. It was Harry.

'How are you?' he asked. 'How did the assembly go?'

'All right.'

'Have you eaten?'

'I'm not terribly hungry.'

'Are you sure? Would you like to pop round for some pasta?'

'Well . . .'

'I've made enough for two,' he said. 'It'll only get wasted. Fresh Parmesan, porcini all *wasted*. How can you bear the thought?'

She couldn't, of course. 'Harry, you're shameless.' And I'd be lost without you, she added privately, picking up her keys.

The funeral was a grim reprise of the baptism. The same cast was there, the parents and godparents, the grandmas and grandads, relatives and the congregation. Isobel hoped never to endure another day like it. Harry was weeping openly as Mike carried the tiny coffin down the aisle in his arms. His tears were still streaming as

224

he spoke the opening sentence: 'The Lamb who is at the throne will be their shepherd and will lead them to springs of living water; and God will wipe away all tears from their eyes.'

Isobel held herself in check, knowing that she was not like Harry. If she lost her grip she'd be unable to preach. She feared her sermon was totally inadequate. She'd been forced to go to Harry in desperation the night before.

'Just do what you always do,' he advised. 'Talk about the deceased, talk about the Christian hope. That's all that's required. You can't offer explanations, Isobel. Don't torment yourself with trying.'

'Well done,' said Harry.

They were walking back together from Sue and Mike's, leaving them to grieve with their parents. Isobel had been unable to eat and the glass of sherry she'd accepted had gone straight to her head.

'It doesn't feel real,' she said. Denial again. It was textbook stuff. 'I can't cry,' she confessed.

'Don't be hard on yourself,' replied Harry.

There was a painful lump in her throat. She attempted to swallow it away 'I bought her a Christmas present and now I don't know what to do with it.'

'Why not ask Sue and Mike nearer the time?'

'It was *The Oxford Book of Nursery Rhymes*.' She paused and bit her lips. 'The Opie one. With the woodcuts by Joan Hassall. Every child should be given one. It's part of our national heritage.'

Harry was weeping again. 'Isobel, Isobel.'

'Don't. Please. I'll be all right.'

Over the following weeks either she or Harry called in on Sue and Mike each day. Isobel had already been far too busy, and now this. She couldn't resent time spent with grieving parents, but the fact was there were only twenty-four hours in a day. Dimly she grasped that she'd made a subconscious decision to defer her grief and she knew this wasn't ideal, but what else could she do? She couldn't mope in the house leaving Harry to do all the work. It was all part of ministerial life, putting others before self.

Her patience with difficult parishioners wore thinner than ever. One evening when she'd just got back from Sue and Mike's, numb with exhaustion, Linda called round. Some footling query over my copy for the parish magazine, thought Isobel crossly. She'd planned to spend the evening doing her sermon preparation. On this occasion, however, Linda's burden was nothing to do with the *Asleby Bulletin,* important though that was. Linda had come as a Frustrated Charismatic, a representative of what Harry called the DTs, the Deep Teaching brigade. One or other of the group periodically presented themselves to the clergy to complain about the lack of Deep Teaching in the church. When analysed, this amounted to a rather lurid interest in spiritual warfare and demonology. Normally Isobel would have listened courteously and thanked Linda for her suggestions, but tonight she found her anger mounting with every passing minute.

She watched Linda's face. It looked like a mask, pasty, the lips twaddling on. Why doesn't she pluck her eyebrows? Why am I being forced to listen to this pathetic woman grizzling about Harry's and my failings? How nice for her if we said, 'Yes, you're right, it's demons, Linda. That's what's messing your life up. It's not you, it's not your responsibility to pull yourself together. You can blame it on the Evil One. Or on the clergy.'

'And, basically, we just don't feel that the church is taking the reality of Satan seriously enough,' Linda was saying. 'There's no real deep teaching about spiritual warfare.'

'Linda,' said Isobel, 'listen to me. I have just come from the house of a couple who have lost their baby. They're desperately hanging on to God because they have nowhere else to go in their grief. I'm not going to insult them by peddling demons from the pulpit.'

Linda's chin went up at that. 'This is exactly what I mean.' She folded her arms in satisfaction. 'This is what's wrong with the Church of England today.'

'No,' said Isobel. What are you doing? What are you *doing*? squeaked a voice in her head. 'This is what's right with it. What "deeper teaching" *is* there than the love of God for us in Christ, for crying out loud? We preach this faithfully week by week. It's enshrined in the liturgy. We celebrate it in the Eucharist. What *you*

226

want is called Gnosticism and, I'm sorry, you'll have to go elsewhere to find it.'

Linda snatched up her handbag and Bible, and left without another word.

Isobel sat in her study breathing hard. Oh, God. That's all hell unleashed. Well done, Isobel. She picked up the phone and rang Harry immediately to explain. He listened gravely. 'I'm sorry,' she said. 'I just lost my rag.'

'Hmm,' said Harry. 'Full metal jacket for Sunday. Well,' he sighed, 'don't worry. I'll back you up. Thanks for warning me.'

'I'm sorry,' she repeated helplessly.

'No, no. It probably needed saying at some point. And, hey, this way I get to feature as the good guy for once.'

'They may leave the church.'

'Perhaps a card saying you'd had a rough day and sorry if you seemed unsympathetic?' suggested Harry.

Isobel swallowed her gall. 'I'll think about it.'

He was right. She wrote an equivocally grovelling card to Linda and slipped it through her door that night. To her relief it did the trick. There was no march-out by frustrated charismatics, although Harry received a couple of delegations, more concerned than ever about the dire state of modern Anglicanism.

'I explained that you're being oppressed by a demon of stroppiness,' he whispered to her on Sunday, after the service. 'They're praying for your release.'

As Christmas approached Isobel found herself skating faster and faster over thinner and thinner ice. She would probably have got away with it, had it not been for the ghastly day when she double-booked herself and failed to turn up and take the Remembrance Service for stillborn infants. Of all the things to forget! It would haunt her for the rest of her ministerial life. Short of missing a funeral, it was hard to imagine a worse pastoral faux pas. Why couldn't she have forgotten the Mothers' Union, or some dreary fraternal? The possibility that at some level she was deliberately sabotaging her own cause occurred to her, but she dismissed it. Fortunately – fortunately for the hospital and the poor bereaved parents, though excruciating for Isobel – Harry happened to be in when the chaplain phoned, and he was able to whiz into Stockton and take the service instead.

He listened in silence to her anguished explanations and apologies at their next staff meeting. They were in his study, as they always had been for these meetings since that strange glass-breaking incident in the vestry.

'May I see your diary?' he asked eventually.

She clutched her Filofax. 'Now, Harry . . .'

But he put out his hand and waited till she handed it over. She watched as he turned to the present week. Her face burned. There was no disguising the fact that she'd left herself without an inch to manoeuvre.

'Isn't this your day off?' he asked, pointing.

'Well, yes, obviously, but . . .'

'How much of this can you realistically cancel?'

'Cancel?'

'Yes. I want you to clear the whole day, including the evening, and get right out of the parish.'

'Harry! I can't possibly! I've – it's –'

'Unless you'd rather I did it for you?'

There was an incredulous pause. 'Are you *threatening* me?' she demanded.

He met her gaze steadily. 'Here's the phone. Why don't you sort it out while I make us some coffee?'

He vanished before she could protest any further. That is *so* patronizing! she wanted to shout after him. You can't treat me like this! The memory of that forgotten memorial service flashed across her mind. She went hot then cold. He could have made things a lot more humiliating for her if he chose. She picked up the phone and began dialling. There was a nasty pinching sensation in her throat.

Eventually her day off began to look free again, but Harry was not finished with her yet. Together they went through the next fortnight ruthlessly pruning her engagements. On a couple of occasions Harry insisted on taking over commitments for her. It was so shaming. She felt like a frivolous wife who had gone around running up debts, which her long-suffering husband was now having to honour. He did it all so kindly that she was close to tears.

'So what will you do on your day off?' he asked, when they were done.

'Oh, I don't know. Go to Northumberland,' she suggested, forcing herself to make an effort.

'Good. Find a hotel and have a nice spoily lunch, then go and wander on the hills. Forget all this.'

She nodded unhappily.

'You haven't failed, Isobel,' he said.

'It feels like it.'

'No, no. That's the whole point of curacies. The same happened to me, as you know. Some things can only be learnt by trial and error.'

She nodded again, not trusting herself to speak.

'So don't worry,' he persisted. 'You're doing a good job. You've got a heart for the Gospel. You're polite, cheerful, conscientious – what more could a vicar ask of his curate? I haven't always been so lucky – let the reader understand,' he added significantly, in coded reference to her predecessor.

'Thanks,' she managed, gathering her things together. They stood up.

'Do you suppose God enjoys having you around?' he asked.

The idea dumbfounded her.

When she didn't reply he went on, 'You don't think He might quite like your company – even on your day off? When you're not actually trying to serve Him, I mean?'

Isobel turned the question over. There was a lump in her throat, which she couldn't swallow away. 'No,' she admitted. 'I suppose I don't really believe anyone *enjoys* my company.' The last words were scarcely audible.

'Well, I do.'

She grimaced.

'Oh, no – stop me, stop me!' he begged. 'I can feel a piece of serious professional misconduct coming on! I'm about to hug you.'

She half laughed. 'Don't be silly.'

He hugged her anyway. She breathed in his ravishing cologne and for a second almost broke down and sobbed on his shoulder. 'Now, you go away and take things easy,' he admonished her. 'Have a lovely time in Northumberland tomorrow.'

'I'll try.'

'Good. Do you want a lift tonight, by the way?'

'Tonight?'

'It's the deanery Christmas party at the corpse's house.'

'What corpse? What are you on about, Harry?'

'The local paper. It said "The Reverend Kenneth Stanley has recently been made Rural Dead of Stockton." Shall I pick you up at quarter to eight?'

Isobel groaned.

'You *know* you'll enjoy it!' cried Harry. 'We get to play funny games and have a seasonal quiz!'

'Exactly.'

'And this year we've been asked to wear amusing hats!'

Isobel ground her teeth. 'I don't *have* an amusing hat.'

'Tell you what, when we get there we'll pinch the nicest bottle of wine, hide under the table and get drunk.'

Well, thank God that was over for another year. The evening had passed like a nightmare cross between Barbara Pym and Kafka. Being the youngest and prettiest woman there, Isobel was repeatedly cornered by older colleagues in amusing berets who insisted on cantering their obscure hobby-horses up and down for her benefit. Harry, in his 'kiss me quick' mitre, was trapped on the other side of the room. Occasionally he caught her eye and vibrated his clockwork eyebrows at her in sympathy. Where on earth had he bought them? As she fell asleep that night voices kept bumbling, 'And the truly *fascinating* thing about lepidoptera . . . Bernard of Clairvaux, on the other hand . . .' Was it for this she had been ordained?

When her day off arrived its emptiness was unnerving. Obedient to Harry she drove out into the wilds, but was dogged all morning by a background dread, as though she were in the process of missing an important exam. No amount of mental expostulation shifted the sensation. She pottered around Hadrian's Wall trying to relax, but it was hopeless. A brief distraction came when she glimpsed a sparrow-hawk. She pulled out her binoculars. The bird was locked like a missile on the trail of a finch, twisting, turning in flight as it closed on its prey. Then, as if in mimicry, two fighter jets ripped overhead, one chasing the other. The landscape rocked.

Suddenly it occurred to her that she was within striking distance of the Friary. Perhaps she should go and see Brother Gabriel. All at once the thought seemed divinely prompted. Yes, the time was right. She would swallow her pride and pour out her heart to him. She got back into her car and set off.

Her nerves grew increasingly jittery the closer she got. Then on the Friary drive she encountered a cock pheasant that couldn't decide which way to run. She felt the nasty thunk as she hit it and, glancing in her rear-view mirror, saw it stagger broken to the verge. She winced, knowing her father would tell her she ought to put it out of its misery. How? Reverse over it, maybe? But she couldn't bring herself to. If it's still twitching when I leave, I'll deal with it, she promised, as she parked and got out.

When she reached the step she stood there and took a deep breath. This was going to be one of those profoundly significant encounters. Was she quite ready for it? She rang the doorbell before she had the chance to change her mind. A burly friar answered.

'Hello. I, er, was hoping to see Brother Gabriel,' she stammered.

'I'm afraid he's away on holiday.'

'On holiday! How lovely!' she added, with equal emphasis, hoping this would disguise her indignation. For a second she felt completely bereft; betrayed, even. But why shouldn't Franciscans go on holiday, for heaven's sake?

'Can I help at all?' inquired the other brother.

'Oh, no. Not really. I was just passing and thought I might pop in . . .' Why was she lying like this? She feared it was obvious.

'Well, he'll be sorry to have missed you. Who shall I tell him called?'

'Isobel. Isobel Knox.'

'I'll tell him when he's back, Isobel,' repeating her name to commit it to memory, the way one was supposed to.

'Thank you.' She hesitated, wondering whether to leave a message. The friar waited, his head tilted in a pastoral manner. 'I'm afraid I hit one of your pheasants,' she heard herself confess.

'Really? Where?' he asked, with interest.

'I'll show you.'

They set off up the drive. Well, at least some good had come out of the incident. Who better than a Franciscan to minister to wounded wildlife?

'There it is.' She pointed.

'Ah, yes. Come along, you poor darling.' She watched his big hands reach gently into the bracken.

'Is it dead?' she asked.

He turned his back. There was a swift movement.

'It is now,' he said cheerfully. 'Oh, goody, goody, goody. This'll liven up tonight's casserole.'

Isobel stared open-mouthed.

'Tricky business, clipping them without flattening them,' he remarked, stroking the burnished feathers. 'Gabriel's got it down to a fine art. He's been known to leave the road in pursuit of a nice phezzie. Are you on holiday up here?'

'Um . . .' She shook herself. 'No. Just on my day off. I'm a curate on Teesside. Place called Asleby.'

'Oh, yes. Father Harry's church?'

Father Harry! She smirked. 'That's right.'

They chatted for a little longer and then she returned to her car. She glanced back as she pulled out and he raised the pheasant aloft in a vaguely benedictory manner before disappearing into the house once more.

Isobel drove aimlessly through lanes populated with more suicidal wildlife, trying to deal with her unreasonable sense that Gabriel had let her down.

Eventually, she found a nice quiet place for lunch, but it was invaded a quarter of an hour later by an office Christmas party. Each whoop and cracker left her feeling more Scrooge-like, and in the end she left without having pudding.

232

The whole day turned out to be unsatisfactory, in fact. On impulse she made a detour through Bishopside to pop in on Annie, even though she'd called only weeks before. Her eyes scanned the streets nervously for Johnny, but she was safe.

She spent an hour with Annie and little Teddy. It was his teatime and, despite Annie's reassurances, she felt as though she was intruding. There was a postcard stuck to the fridge which said, 'Ask your milkman about potatoes.' Isobel recognized the handwriting as that of Ted, a former colleague. He and Annie had shared a great many impenetrable jokes of this kind at Coverdale, and Isobel didn't bother asking what it meant.

'Where's Davy?' asked Teddy.

'Well, he's at work, I'm afraid,' explained Isobel. 'He's a policeman. Did you know that? He drives a panda car.'

'What does a police car say?' prompted Annie.

'Nee naw, nee naw,' replied Teddy, engrossed in smearing yoghurt on his high-chair tray.

'Is Will any better?' asked Isobel.

'Much, thanks. Could you, um, say thank you to Davy, by the way, for not –' She glanced at Teddy. 'For not, um, apprehending one's spouse.'

'Do little pitchers have ears *that* big?' asked Isobel.

'This one does,' laughed Annie. Teddy looked up sharply. 'So where did you meet Davy?'

'Oh, he helps out with the youth club now and then.' Isobel listened to herself in alarm. What was wrong with the truth? 'Of course, the parish are dying to know if we're going out, but we're just friends.'

'Oh?' said Annie encouragingly.

Isobel felt a rushing impulse to confide, to explore her feelings for Davy and see if her friend could help her analyse it, to tease out the subtleties of platonic male/female friendship – was it ever possible? Was she kidding herself? What about the class thing? In the silence she could tell that Annie was hoping she'd say more.

'Are you going away for Christmas?' Isobel asked instead.

'Not this year. Will's on call. What about you?'

'I'm not sure. I usually go to my parents, but they're off to Turkey.' She heard how pathetic she sounded and tried to buck herself up. 'Still, some friends have asked me for lunch on Christmas Day, which will be great fun.'

'Is ... is everything OK?' ventured Annie.

'Oh, yes. I'm probably working too hard, but you know how it is.'

'If ever you want to use the cottage, just let us know,' said Annie. 'Nobody's there over Christmas and New Year. You look like you could use a break.'

'Oh, I'm fine,' breezed Isobel. 'It's the busy season, that's all.'

'Well ...' Annie was regarding her with concern. 'So long as ...' The sentence trailed off doubtfully as so many of her sentences did.

'I'd better be on my way,' said Isobel. 'Give my regards to Will.'

'He'll be sorry he missed you,' Annie remarked. 'Even without the leather trousers.'

Isobel gave her a hard stare before deciding that this was just a joke. 'Thanks for tea. 'Bye, Teddy.'

She got back into the car and started for home. Johnny was still nowhere to be seen. The chances of encountering him were slight. Bishopside was a big place. All the same, her heart pounded until she was safely back on the A19 heading for Teesside.

Her evening proved frustrating. Davy was working nights and Jan was out. She rang Natalie and Drew, but they were just setting out for the cinema. Natalie urged her to join them, but Isobel thought she had discerned the faintest pause before the invitation was issued. She imagined a nobly suppressed 'Oh, no! We wanted to be alone!' and it forced her to pretend she wasn't in a film mood.

There was nothing on TV. She sat slumped in front of the screen with the remote still dangling in her hand, trying to motivate herself. She could go out and get a video: there were a couple she really ought to watch. She could find the local rag and see if there were any concerts on. But she continued to sit dully, grousing uncharacteristically about the miseries of single life. You had to organize your leisure in advance if you wanted to avoid moping about the house. Couples took their built-in companionship for granted. It made them lazy. They always assumed – with the occasional rare exception – you'd go and visit them, as if somehow that were more logical. Annie had never once got herself down to Teesside. It was like people in the south thinking it was far easier for you to drive down the country than it was for them to struggle north against a kind of Londocentric national gravity. Being single in the north, she supposed, was a dual social handicap. Just occasionally she got fed up with doing all the legwork.

This reminded her that she still hadn't finalized her post-Christmas plans. Harry had begun to nag her gently about this. Why was she dithering? she asked herself. To be frank, she didn't particularly want to stay with either of her brothers; and she concluded from the fact that neither of them had bothered to follow up their initial invitation that they weren't falling over themselves to have her. Maybe she was still feeling let down by her parents' defection to Turkey. That would be silly and selfish. She sat up and reached for the phone. So, Alistair or Chris? It ought to be Alistair, probably, to repair any damage done by their earlier altercation.

No, I honestly can't. She flopped back. I don't feel up to a week of relatives, of being a bit of a spare part no matter how diligently everyone remembered to include her, and feeling obliged to offer to babysit so the parents could go out for the evening. I need a proper break, she thought. Much though I love them all, of course. If only there was a tactful alternative . . . Maybe this *was* a good moment to take up Annie and Will's offer of their cottage in Northumberland. Assuming Annie had really meant it. Yes, that's what she'd do. She picked up the phone and arranged it. Good. Then she rang each brother in turn, thanked him, and declined his invitation. This gave her a quiet satisfaction, for she knew that at some level she remained 'poor old Isobel' in her brothers' minds. *Thirty-three and not married.* Whereas in fact she was lucky old Isobel, who could zoom off to exotic places at the drop of a hat without having to worry about childcare. Admittedly, a cottage in Northumberland wasn't exactly exotic, but there was always her post-Easter break, when she could zip to Florence or wherever.

She peered in her fridge. As usual there wasn't much. A chunk of Parmesan, skimmed milk, eggs. Her vegetables were looking a little tired, but they weren't rotten so she'd better use them up. Ho hum. She cooked and ate them dutifully with an omelette, then wandered into her study and ended up doing a spot of sneaky sermon preparation after all.

Later she was inclined to look back on this day as pivotal. If only Gabriel had been there – if only she'd talked to the other brother, even – then things might have taken a different course. She knew this was fatalistic. The grace of God was infinitely ingenious and resourceful. His purposes were not thwarted by untoward circumstances. But blaming the circumstances was so much more palatable. It let one off the hook – like Linda's ever-obliging demons. It allowed her to believe that things had conspired against her, and not admit she'd been riding for a fall all along, Gabriel or no Gabriel.

## CHAPTER 19

Isobel never cried. Well, she did, but she tried desperately not to. Crying was cissy.

> Cry baby cry,
> Put your finger in your eye and tell your mother it wasn't I,
> Cry baby cry!

If you cried on your birthday you were a baby for seven weeks. Only *girls* cried. That's what Isobel's brothers said. Except *they* cried sometimes, she'd seen them. She pretended not to at the time, because it was embarrassing, actually. A couple of days later if they were teasing her she might jeer, 'Well, I saw you crying, so ha ha!' But then they thumped her so hard it wasn't really worth it.

There were two things you were allowed to cry about:

1 If your mum and dad died.
2 If you really, really hurt yourself, like breaking an arm or something.

Sometimes Isobel made herself cry in bed at night (which didn't count) by imagining she was an orphan and then both her brothers were tragically killed as well. She was an orphan and her step-mother and sisters hated her and made everyone at school pick on her, but that didn't stop her becoming a famous hurdler or ballet dancer, like in *Mandy* and *Bunty* comics.

It wasn't easy. There was so much that could make you cry: other children being spiteful; B.R.O.T.H.E.R.S.; grown-ups being sarcastic, or saying it served you right or, well, life isn't fair; animals getting killed; nicknames; little birds falling out of their nests; your best friend moving house. You had to be on your guard the whole time and use your secret weapons. These were: biting the inside of your bottom lip, sometimes till it bled; staring up at the ceiling so the tears drained back into your tear ducts; pretending this wasn't the real you, you had escaped and left a robot in your place. The robot was so lifelike it fooled everybody, but it didn't have feelings, so nothing that happened to it really hurt.

By the time she was a teenager Isobel had pretty much given up crying. 'She's a sensible girl,' her parents would say. At school they called her the iceberg.

Of course, now she was a minister she could appreciate that there was a healing aspect to tears. She had seen lives transformed through the release that weeping could bring. Admittedly, wild sobbing did strike her as a little unnecessary, but she managed to repress her distaste. No doubt she would cry more often herself if she were made that way, but she was genuinely not a crying sort of person, and that was all there was to it.

In the week before Christmas four funerals came in.

'Why do parishioners die in droves at the worst possible moment?' grumbled Harry. 'Do they lie there on their deathbed going "It's all right, Doctor, I can hold out till Holy Week . . ."?'

'Harry!' scolded Isobel, although the same thought had crossed her mind.

'There are twenty-five weeks after Trinity when nothing's happening. Why can't they die then?'

'What's got into you this morning?'

'I'll tell you. It's that − excuse me, colourful expression coming up − *bloody* undertaker. He said, "What are you grumbling about? Sixty quid for half an hour's work." I could've hit him.'

'That wouldn't be Leighton's, by any remote chance?' asked Isobel, knowing it was. She shared Harry's sentiments. True, a funeral service might only last half an hour, but that was on top of funeral visits and sermon preparation, as the undertaker well knew. To say nothing of the emotional cargo involved. It was like those wags who observed that vicars only worked one day a week.

'This is why you have to leave a bit of slack in your timetable,' ventured Harry. 'Crises are never predictable.'

'Yes, I realize that,' replied Isobel ungraciously.

He glanced at her, but didn't pursue the point. 'Are you OK with Leighton's, by the way? I know some women in the deanery have trouble with Terry.'

An image of the funeral director's leering face obtruded itself. 'Oh, it's fine. He just . . . makes childish remarks about the coffins.'

'The *coffins?*' repeated Harry.

'Oh, you know, lewd comments. About the size.' *My, that's a whopper. Bet you've never had one that big before. Ooh! d'you think it'll fit?*

'I just ignore him. And I always take my car, so I don't end up next to him in the hearse.'

She considered, with satisfaction, the other tactic she sometimes employed on men of Terry's stamp – the Masonic handshake. It was like administering a sharp little electric shock, judging by their flinch of horror.

'What's so funny?' asked Harry.

He guffawed when she told him.

'Show me. Oh, you wicked, wicked woman. Where on earth did you learn that?' he asked, as she obliged. 'I thought they were sworn to secrecy.'

'A short course on Freemansonry at Coverdale Hall.' She smirked, aglow at having made him laugh so hard.


'One down, one to go,' muttered Isobel, as she drove back from the crematorium a couple of days later.

It ought to have been a pretty straightforward affair – an old lady dying in a nursing home – but the bunch of relatives driving up from the south had been uncooperative. Aunt Nellie's death was little more than a nuisance to them, thought Isobel indignantly, forgetting her recent conversation with Harry. She'd dealt mainly with one of the nephews, an overbearing man in his fifties, and had tried to glean enough information about the deceased to compose an appropriate sermon. His response had been that he wasn't going to do her job for her, and by the way, he didn't want her bringing religion into it. Then perhaps he ought to have considered a humanist ceremony, Isobel had countered. 'I just want a traditional funeral. None of your Bible-bashing,' said Mr Bossyboots.

Honestly! What, precisely, did he imagine he'd have left if he eradicated all scriptural references from the service? 'Bye-bye,

Aunt Nellie, we commit your body to be burned. Anyway, she'd swallowed her outrage and done her best, resisting the urge to begin her sermon with the words 'Unloved and abandoned though Nellie undoubtedly was by her nearest and dearest, she was still a much loved child of God . . .'

For one moment, as she stood at the front of the crematory chapel watching the coffin come in, memories of Hannah's funeral surged up. Mike cradling the tiny box, Harry's tears . . . She wavered, then regained her professional poise. Her suppressed grief throbbed, a tight lump in her throat, but she managed to conduct the service properly.

And Terry! That bloody (good word, Harry!) undertaker had surpassed himself. She could still picture him stamping his feet like an old bull outside the crem, blowing plumes of steam into the cold air from his unsavoury hair-choked nostrils.

'See you're finding it a bit chilly too, your reverence.' His eyes groped the front of her cassock in search of an erect nipple.

Isobel stared back in wordless contempt.

'Why?' she demanded out loud in her car. 'Why can I never think of a crushing riposte?'

As if in reply her brain played that elusive fragment of music. Yet again she was a hair's breadth from identifying it when it vanished. Isobel let out a cry of frustration. A moment later she became aware that the car behind was flashing at her. She looked in her mirror. Oh, no! It was a police car. She pulled over, shaken, hoping it was only Davy.

It was not. Damn. She turned off the engine with trembling fingers. How fast was I going? she wondered.

This was, indeed, the first thing the policeman asked as she wound down her window.

'Um, I'm afraid I didn't notice, Officer.'

'And what's the limit along here?' he asked sternly.

'Forty?' She knew it wasn't.

'Tut tut.'

Isobel flushed. 'Thirty.'

Another officer called from the car, where he'd been talking on the radio, 'We've got a reverend here.'

'I know,' said the first. He jerked his head. The second man came across and peered in through Isobel's window.

'Ooh, a *lady* reverend.'

'A very naughty lady reverend,' confided the first. 'Doing fifty in a thirty zone.'

'You little devil!'

I don't believe this, thought Isobel. There was nothing she could do but grit her teeth while they chose to amuse themselves with their pathetic little finger-wagging power games. If she answered back they would promptly book her, which they might well do anyway, that was the whole fun of it. She cheated them out of some of their pleasure by producing her licence and documents on request. Eventually they wound up their comic double act and let her off with a caution.

She drove home at a steady 31 m.p.h. with the patrol car following her all the way. They gave a cheery wave as she turned into her road. Very droll. I bet they're Masons, too. For all she knew they'd be having a giggle with Terry at her expense at the Lodge tonight. Bunch of ridiculous overgrown schoolboys all in cahoots with one another. She prayed they didn't know she was a friend of Davy's. If he found out she'd never hear the last of it.

She parked and got out, slamming her car door.

Davy was on her doorstep. 'What did *I* dee?' he asked, bewildered.

'Are you a Mason?' she rapped out, letting herself into the house.

'What? No.' He followed her in.

'Well, you'd hardly admit it, I suppose,' she sneered.

'I've said I'm not! What's your problem?'

'*My* problem!' she cried, flinging her robes down. 'I'll tell you what my problem is – men.'

'Aye, well, I could've told you that.'

She glowered at him but didn't stoop to respond.

'Aw, don't be like that,' he said, sliding an arm round her. 'Come and have a cuddle.'

'Don't be ridiculous.' But she subsided grumpily on his chest. There were not, after all, many people she could safely hug. 'Sorry.' She sighed after a moment. 'Difficult morning. Funeral.'

'Tell us all about it, then.'

241

'Oh, obstreperous relatives and so on. And the undertaker was more than usually tiresome.'

'How d'you mean, like?'

'He was staring at my breasts, actually,' she said, with dignity.

'What? I'll have him!'

His territorial tone didn't please Isobel and she thrust him away. He amended his response. 'Can you not make a formal complaint?'

'To whom?' she scoffed. 'The Worshipful Guild of Gravediggers?'

'Well, to us. If it ever got really serious.'

'But that's the whole point – it never does get really serious. It's always borderline, to make you feel you'd just be making a fuss about nothing.'

'What if he turned nasty? How good's your self-defence? Apart from the judo, I mean.'

She ignored this quip. A few weeks before she'd seen him unloading a judo kit from his washing-machine and when challenged he'd admitted he was a black belt. 'I can look after myself, thank you, Davy.'

'Fair enough.' He shrugged. 'Have you got the time on you?'

'Yes.' She consulted her watch in surprise. 'It's –'

A second later her arm was twisted up behind her back and his hand was clamped over her mouth.

'That's a classic one, that,' Davy informed her, as she struggled. 'Asking for the time. Always say "no". Now what you ganna dee?' he asked as she was busy trying to drum her heels into his shins. Dimly through her rage she heard him suggesting various tactics.

'Not bad,' he said, letting her go. 'Try stamping on his instep. Now, what about if – *shit!*' He leapt away as she aimed a vicious kick at his groin. 'Isobel, man!'

The doorbell rang. Davy was poised, eyes wary, repeating, 'Calm down, calm down,' like a caricature of a policeman.

What on earth are you playing at? she asked herself. 'Sorry. I'd better, um . . .' She gestured to the door.

He collapsed on to the sofa. 'Bloody hell,' she heard him groan as she left the room.

It was Jan with a saucepan.

242

'Hello, hello, dearest heart. I thought you were looking a little wan on Sunday, so I've brought you some nourishing broth. There's some nice olive ciabatta to go with it.' She dumped the pan in Isobel's hands and came in.

'Thanks. You really don't need . . .' She tried to block the doorway. 'I'm afraid –'

'Everything all right?' asked Jan, sweeping past. 'You seem a trifle flushed. Do you have company? You do!' she cried, spotting Davy. 'And who's this? Not your gorgeous *gendarme*, by any chance? Aha, it is. I recognize you from the courts, don't I? Name?'

'Jan, Davy, Davy, Jan,' recited Isobel, furious at the timing of it all.

Davy got to his feet.

'My my, you *are* a tall youth,' remarked Jan, savouring every inch of him as she shook his hand. 'And is everything else in proportion, might one inquire?'

'*Jan!*' snapped Isobel.

'Nah,' replied Davy. 'Or I'd be nine foot six.'

Jan hooted. 'You'll do.' She patted his arm and turned to Isobel, who was standing with the soup catching up with what he meant. 'Does he remind you of anyone?'

'He's nothing like him!' snarled Isobel.

There was a pause in which she sensed both the others filing this little outburst away to contemplate later. She turned to hide her blush. 'Well, shall I put this on the stove? It smells delicious.'

Isobel was uncomfortable for the rest of the day. Jan and Davy had both stayed for lunch, bantering in that easy manner Isobel had never mastered. You see? she taxed herself. They all like him. What are you so het up about? It's not as if he was a prospective fiancé for your friends to vet.

There had been no chance to apologize for her near-assault on Davy's manhood. Her face burned at the memory as she hurried to the Christmas tea at the local rest home. When had she last felt incandescent rage like that? As a child, pinned down by older brothers? If she'd been asked that morning she would have asserted that she didn't have a violent temper, had no problem with anger at all, in fact. Irritation, yes.

What she really needed was a quiet hour in which to pray and sort herself out, but she simply didn't have a spare minute until the evening. She pulled crackers with the old dears and behaved as a curate should. Harry was on the other side of the lounge with a pink paper hat perched on his head, listening to some dotty monologue with his customary good grace.

'Have you remembered tonight?' asked Harry, as he drove her home.

'Tonight?'

' "Churches Together at Christmas",' he sang. 'It's down at St Paddywhack of the Holy Bones.'

'I'll tell Father McGee you call it that,' she threatened.

'No! Mercy! He won't give me my Christmas whiskey!'

Glancing at her watch, she decided there was just enough time left to nip to the supermarket and buy party fodder for the Youth Group. This turned out to be a mistake. The aisles were clogged and the tannoy was playing schmaltzy carols. *Pa-rupper-pum-pum!* How had it come to this? Was this why she'd been ordained – to stand in a queue to purchase cheap cola and carcinogenic snacks for a bunch of ungrateful teenagers? And there was no *way* the woman in front had got ten items or less! Isobel tapped her on the shoulder and mentioned this.

'Too bloody bad,' came the reply. The woman turned her back, leaving Isobel to boil impotently.

She drove home, caught in the worst of the traffic. Rain streamed down her windscreen, smearing the municipal festive lights. So much for that as a time-saving exercise. She let herself in, made a cup of coffee and went through to her study to pray.

The moment she sat down the phone rang. It was Davy, calling from work to pull her leg about her brush with the law. She retorted that one didn't relish being pulled over by Pinky and Perky. He repeated this and she heard shouts of laughter from his end.

'Ee! You cannot say that.' He chuckled.

It only occurred to her afterwards that Tom and Jerry might possibly have been a happier soubriquet for a couple of police officers. And she still hadn't apologized to Davy. However, he appeared to hold no grudge, so perhaps the less said the better.

She roused herself. The time had gone, frittered away. Off to St Patrick's for some ecumenical jollity. She'd have to sing dutifully about 'mercy mild, God and sinners reconciled' when her heart was distracted and God had seldom felt further away. She resolved to set her alarm and get up an hour early tomorrow and have a good pray before morning prayer.

She was woken at nine by the phone. It was Harry checking she was all right.

'Oh, no!' she cried, sitting bolt upright in bed, appalled. 'I'm so sorry! I must have slept through my alarm. Harry, I'm really, really —'

'Don't worry,' he laughed, 'you probably needed it.'

'But this never happens to me! I can't *tell* you how —'

'Forget it, darling.'

There was a pause.

'Did you just call me "darling"?' asked Isobel.

'Absolutely not. You must be imagining things.'

They both laughed and rang off. Terms of endearment from one's male colleagues were normally a red rag to a bull. Isobel was disconcerted by the rush of pleasure Harry's slip had provoked.

The extra sleep seemed, if anything, to make things worse. Isobel felt stunned and incompetent. She hurtled round the parish delivering Christmas cards and service invitations. Parishioners kept popping in with presents, and it was only polite to offer them coffee and biscuits. There were the sick communions to do. If she'd been high church she could have simply doled out the reserved sacrament ('And here's some I prepared earlier!'), but this never felt right, so she ended up doing a shortened communion service in each house she visited. On each occasion she was pressed to stay for sherry and mince-pies. She turned down the alcohol, and was obliged to drink tea instead, for fear of seeming churlish.

Walter Goodwill handed her 'her Christmas box' as threatened when she called at the farm. It turned out to be a goose. Not the one from the yard, unfortunately. Isobel brandished the carrier-bag at it by way of warning as she went out of the gate. A goose! What on earth was she supposed to do with it? It oozed on the back seat of the car. She couldn't give it away in case he asked how she'd liked it.

Aha, she'd hand it to Natalie. She was passing her road now.

'I've brought you a goose,' she told her. 'Walter gave it me and I've no idea what to do with it.'

'Ooh! I'll ask Harry. He'll know. We'll have it for Christmas, shall we? Are you coming in?'

'Can't stop. I'm in the middle of sick communions.'

By the end of the day she was awash with tea and never wanted to see a mince-pie again in her life.

That evening was the annual parish carol singing. She tramped the streets in the rain, avoiding Joan, who was reeking like a distillery and stumbling on the kerbs. Snatches of Johnny's wicked imper-sonation kept coming back to her. Isobel knew she ought to have been shielding Harry from Joan's amorous advances and atoned for her failure by making the effort to seem friendly to Linda and the DTs. They grumbled about the traditional carols they were singing. There were plenty of modern Christmas songs, which were so much more 'relevant'. Relevant to what? thought Isobel, crossly. How can they be relevant when nobody's ever heard of them? But she saved her breath for singing.

Afterwards it was mulled wine and – oh, no! – mince-pies at the vicarage. Harry made his own mincemeat and pastry so they'd be superior to the deep-filled luxury supermarket jobs that had been collapsing in her hand and drooling sludge on her all day. Everyone bundled into his sitting room. The pink lights on his tree twinkled. This year he'd bought a lot of (in Isobel's view) slightly vulgar rococo angels, but the overall effect was stunning. I must buy a tree tomorrow, she thought. Her father had always bought the family tree on Christmas Eve, and that was what still seemed right to Isobel. But it meant one more thing for a busy day. Harry was circulating with a tray of glasses. Plates of mince-pies were handed round. Natalie complimented him on his light touch with pastry and he curtsied. The sound of parish chatter thundered in Isobel's ears. All the smiling faces had a fever-tinged weirdness, looming, dwindling. She sat dazed in her chair, trying to summon the energy to help Harry with the serving.

He threaded his way through the crowded room to her side and whispered, 'Go home, Isobel.'

'I can't possibly!'

'Go home. Hot bath and off to bed. Them's me orders.' He handed the tray to Jan, took Isobel firmly by the arm and ushered her to the door.

'Harry,' she pleaded, 'I'm fine.'

But he was adamant. She walked home alone with the rain streaming down her face.

It was Christmas Eve. There was usually some distinct moment during the seasonal rush at which she felt truly 'Christmassy'; a little echo of the excitement of childhood, like the magic of falling snow, or the heft of a full stocking at the bed end. She went to buy a tree and found that only the wonky specimens were left, apart from one that was ten feet tall. She had three feet lopped off it, shoved it in her boot and tied the door closed with a bit of red ribbon left over from the World Aids Day service. Just her luck if those clowns pulled her over for driving with her load not tethered properly. She got it back safely, however, and hurriedly hung the branches with her tasteful plain glass baubles. It looked a bit sparsely decorated, given its size, but that was just too bad.

The enterprise had failed to conjure up the magic of Christmas. Oh, well. She resolved to turn on the radio at three o'clock for the service of nine lessons and carols from King's College chapel. Ah, that first limpid phrase of 'Once in Royal David's City'! But when the time came she was still out running errands about the parish and missed the broadcast. It didn't even cross her mind to turn on the car radio. The loss left her forlorn. She couldn't remember how many festivities she'd attended – Mothers' Union, Infants' School, Brownies, deanery, parish – they had all merged into one ugly blur. Perhaps if she'd been going to her parents' house . . . She caught herself back. It was the truth of the Incarnation that really mattered. Hankering after some special 'Christmas feeling' was sheer self-indulgent sentimentality.

What on earth had possessed her to invite the Youth Group round for a games evening before the midnight communion? Isobel was in her kitchen standing guard over the non-alcoholic punch to prevent the odd half-bottle of Southern Comfort finding its way into the mixture. Steam rose from the pan. The sound of mistletoe-related hilarity came from her study where the youngsters were packed in a sweating, snickering mass. They had already desecrated her tree with tinsel, saying it looked sad. There had been much nudging and snorting as the lads dared one another to manoeuvre the curate under the twig for a snog. She'd dealt with this by saying, 'Come on, then,' and indicating which portion of cheek they were permitted to peck. For the moment she was leaving them to it, although before long she would have to go and force them to play Pictionary. It was only nine-thirty, she thought despairingly. Almost another two hours to fill.

'Need a hand?'

She turned in surprise. Offers of help were almost unknown from Fitz.

'Well, you can stir this, if you like.' Her eyes frisked him for evidence of bottles stashed in pockets.

He took over with the wooden spoon. To be fair, he'd done a spot of growing up over the summer. He must be fifteen now, and it seemed to have dawned on him that there might be more interesting challenges in life than annoying one's parents.

His first conversational gambit was, admittedly, at odds with this impression: 'Are you shagging him, then?'

'I beg your pardon?'

'Him. The filth. The Bill. The pig.'

Isobel waited while he exhausted his store of synonyms. 'His name's Davy, as you well know, and no, I'm not. He's just a friend.'

Fitz resumed his stirring. She noted he was wearing aftershave; not as nice as Harry's, but pleasant. Something with a citrus tang, more sophisticated than the type usually favoured by teenage boys, which appeared to Isobel's sensitive nose to have been bought by the litre and applied with a hose.

'You smell nice,' she remarked, without thinking.

'Yeah. It's called Swive.'

'Thank you, Fitz. I do know my Chaucer,' she said.

He flashed her a grin. For a fleeting second she glimpsed the man inside the callow youth. She found herself observing the veins and hair on his forearm as he stirred the punch. He was tall, almost her own height, these days, and rapidly filling out his broad-shouldered frame; and yet for all that he was a boy.

'Is it because he's so much younger than you?' he asked.

'I'm sorry? Oh, Davy. Not really. Relationships with a large age gap can work very well. It depends on the individuals.'

'Yeah. Right.'

Something alerted her. This was more than an idle spot of curate-baiting. Expensive aftershave – a gift? Oh, Fitzy, she thought. What have you got yourself into? They both watched the orange slices and cloves swirling round the pan. Ought she to confront him? She guessed he had come with an impulse to confide. One whiff of being treated like a kid and he would clam up.

'Of course, if one partner was very young,' she ventured, 'particularly if he – or she – were under age, I might begin to wonder about the older partner's motives. Whether there was an unhealthy element of exploitation.' Had she gone too far?

'Mmm.' He handed her the spoon and a frown of intense concentration crossed his face. She waited. He broke wind rippingly. 'Aaah, that's better!'

'OK. Out!'

Instead he drew closer, and showed her the tip of his tongue, sly, yet blatantly sexual. His breath touched her face. She called his bluff and waited. Then the smell of ripe fart crept up on them and Fitz sniggered like a six-year-old.

'*Not* a particularly romantic ambience, I'm afraid, Fitzy,' she said, in damping tones.

\*

249

Well, it was over and done. Not honourably done, not even particularly well done, but at least she'd survived. She sat at her kitchen table too weary to get herself off to bed. Her sermon: feeble. She was aware of this. And how much more feeble it might have been had Davy not turned up and taken control of the rabble, allowing her to escape down to church for a quiet half-hour before the service. Go to bed, you silly woman. She continued to sit. She was wearing a Newcastle United shirt – Davy's Christmas present. He'd brought it round after ferrying some old ladies home from the midnight. Bless him. Was there no end to his thoughtfulness? She remembered the horrid fear that had clutched her as he thrust the package into her hands – Oh, no! Soft, squashy, something to wear? Nightie! ran her terrified thoughts. She'd laughed in near-hysterical relief when she opened it.

He was such a dear boy. She was eternally grateful to him. That was all it had been: gratitude. And bone weariness. It would have been heartless to deny him a kiss at Christmas. She simply hadn't had it in her to say no. He'd made her laugh by saying, 'Come on, then,' and pointing to his cheek as she'd done to the boys earlier. Instead she'd wrapped her arms round his neck and offered him her lips. No, no-oo, she winced. Silly. Very silly, after all the effort she'd put into not encouraging him. At some point she was going to have to unravel all this. It just wasn't on to raise his hopes like that. Oh, Lord! So much to worry about. Davy, Fitz . . .

Outside – surprisingly – a bird was singing. Wasn't that what they were supposed to do on Christmas night? And all the cattle in their stalls would be kneeling in homage – or so the old legend had it. The bird carolled on under the street-light in the pattering rain. Silent night, holy night. Probably a mistle thrush, she thought, hauling herself up to bed. A stormcock.

It was still singing as she plunged steeply into sleep.

# CHAPTER 20

Isobel went home after the Christmas morning service to pack for her holiday and change into something more festive. She knelt in front of her wardrobe, got out a box and lifted its lid, trying to suppress the absurd excitement she was feeling. Beneath the tissue paper lay a pair of knee-high black winter boots, the kind her mother would never buy her. At last! She pulled them out and breathed the leathery smell. Such soft, supple leather. They'd been shockingly expensive, but they'd last for years if she looked after them. She put on her new tailored skirt, above the knee, but opaque tights were always modest. And now for the twin-set. She studied herself in the mirror. I look like a sixties fashion plate, she thought. Just managing to catch the trend second time round. Her Youth Group would probably denounce her as sad.

She loaded the car and drove to Natalie and Drew's. The others were already several drinks ahead of her.

'Oh, I hate you!' cried Natalie, as Isobel took off her coat. 'You're so-o-oo skinny. I feel like a beached whale.'

'The word's "blooming", darling,' said Drew, putting an arm round his wife. 'After me: "ber-*loom*ing".'

'Bal-*loon*ing,' laughed Natalie. Her bulge was just beginning to show. They went through to the kitchen. 'It's the beginning of the end for my waistline. Iz – what are you drinking?'

'A tiny, tiny, minuscule, wee sherry, very dry?' suggested Drew.

'Well, I'm driving, so it had better be –'

'Give her some champagne, for God's sake!' butted in Jan. 'It's Christmas, Isobel. We have a special dispensation from His Holiness Pope Harry to get pissed.'

The pontiff beamed and raised his hand in squiffy blessing.

'But –' began Isobel.

'Oh, Isobel,' they all groaned. It reminded her of the girls at school when she was head girl, so she gave way.

'So I should bloody think. This is vintage fizz,' said Jan. 'And don't worry. I personally guarantee you'll be in a fit and legal state to drive by four o'clock. Trust me. I'm a JP.' She put an arm round Isobel's shoulders and gave her a squeeze. 'You look stunning. Very Jean Shrimpton.'

'I'm telling Father McGee on you,' said Harry. 'You'll be leading his flock astray.'

Isobel flushed hotly, remembering Davy and the mistletoe. 'Don't be ridiculous.'

'Right. Everything's under control food-wise,' said Drew. 'The goose is sizzling, the pudding is doing its thing. Let's open some pressies. Go on. Shoo, shoo!'

They went through to the sitting room, which was now dominated by a twelve-foot spruce lavishly betwiddled with Victoriana all in gold, dark green and burgundy to match the decor.

They sat and presents were handed round. 'In Dulce Jubilo' was playing on the stereo. Isobel unwrapped a gift from Natalie and Drew. Out of the corner of her eye she saw Harry pulling the paper off his present from her. Would he like it? She took out a beautiful velvet scarf.

'Oh, thank you!' she cried.

'And thank *you*,' said Harry, flipping through his Bible commentary.

'You don't already have it?' she asked anxiously.

'No, not this one.' He studied the blurb.

Up and down the country, thought Isobel, there would be millions of people going through this grim ritual. Honestly, it was so nerve-racking. All these presents and what they accidentally betrayed of one's innermost thoughts. She opened her gift from Jan. It was furry. For one hideous moment she thought her friend had bought her a cuddly toy, but it was a hat. She laughed in relief. 'I thought it was a bunny,' she confessed.

'It used to be,' said Jan, ghoulishly.

'Nonsense, it was a dear little lamb,' said Drew. 'Thanks for this.' He waved the book on scumbling and stencilling Isobel had bought them. One couldn't really go wrong with books.

Isobel put on the hat.

'You look like a Slavonic princess,' said Jan.

'If *only* I'd had it in time for the deanery party,' remarked Isobel.

Harry guffawed, but Jan was admiring the book on Burne-Jones Isobel had chosen for her. Just the present from Harry. It was small, too small to be a book. She undid the paper, intrigued. It would, of course, be something pleasant yet with that neutral book-equivalent status.

Scent.

Her eyes raced to meet his in shock. He smiled.

She looked back down at the bottle in its package, fearing it had cost a fortune.

'What've you got?' demanded Jan, peering. '*Vanille Tonka.* Ooh! Try some on, then.'

'Harry!' protested Isobel. 'You really shouldn't . . .'

'I know, I know,' he said, hiding behind a tasselled cushion. 'Totally self-indulgent, but I couldn't resist.'

Her anxiety took a new turn: what if she hated it? Vanilla, cloying, sickly sweet.

'Try it!' Jan was ordering her.

She obeyed. It was . . . 'Vanilla?' she ventured. 'And cinnamon?'

Jan sniffed. 'Ravishing. Good choice, that, Vicar.'

'Do you like it?' asked Harry.

'I love it.' She glanced at him reproachfully. 'But you're very naughty. I only got you a commentary on Romans!'

'But it's a *wonderful* commentary on Romans!' cried Harry, hugging it protectively. 'I'll sleep with it under my pillow.'

He crossed the room and sat beside Isobel on the sofa. Her pulse danced as he leant and breathed in the perfume on her throat.

'Mmm.' He slumped back and closed his eyes in bliss.

'The vestry'll pong like a bloody tart's bedroom with you two in it,' commented Jan.

'*Un boudoir d'une tarte, if* you please,' murmured Harry. He slid sideways till his head was resting on Isobel's shoulder. 'Save me, someone.'

'Ah!' said Natalie, looking at them as if they presented a happy ending to some heartrending saga.

If only, thought Isobel.

'*No* more alcohol for that man,' said Drew sternly.

'*Jauchzet, frohlocket!*'

Isobel was driving north, listening to Bach's *Weihnachtsoratorium*, which she adored. Each year she was strict and saved it up for Christmas Day itself, but there was little exultation in her soul that afternoon. She was navigating virgin realms of exhaustion. It seemed to be affecting her spatial awareness, making it difficult for her to judge distances. Perhaps she should, after all, have had a brief nap after lunch before setting off; but bad weather was threatening and it had seemed sensible to press on. In any case, there wasn't much traffic on the roads.

Not long to go, she reminded herself. Tomorrow she would be able to lift her eyes to the quiet hills and let the still waters and green pastures of Northumberland restore her soul. The ghastliness of the run-up to Christmas would be forgotten. There would be time to reflect on little Hannah's short life and grieve. The nursery-rhyme book still lay like an unsolved puzzle in Isobel's dining room. Thank goodness Sue and Mike had gone away for Christmas. She was relieved for them that they'd reached the point when they could leave the house without feeling they were abandoning Hannah.

Isobel stirred and caught a whiff of her new perfume. Its warm sensuality was alien, unsettling; not yet *her*, but it would become her signature, the scent that made people think 'Isobel'. She knew it would be forever associated in her mind with the ambiguity of the moment she'd received it. From another man she might have known how to interpret the gesture. But from Harry, what did it mean? He was always so careful not to overstep their professional boundaries. Short of buying her silk camiknickers, his choice couldn't have been more inappropriate. She was not offended; his manner precluded that possibility. It probably just tickled his naughty sense of humour – the impulse to buy sexy perfume for his prim curate. What would she have bought for him if she'd known they were playing by a different set of rules? A cashmere scarf? Some –

254

A horn blared behind her. Isobel came to with a lurch. She had crossed a lane without noticing. The other car sailed past with the driver gesturing furiously and mouthing at her. Same to you, fathead! she thought. You aren't exactly keeping your eyes on the road, either. Her heart thumped. Still, the adrenaline would keep her awake for the rest of the journey. She sat upright and increased the volume on her cassette player. *Bom BOM ba ba ba ba Bom Bom!* She hummed along determinedly.

It was a pity she hadn't felt able to turn down Annie's offer of dinner and a bed for the night. There were few things she fancied less than an evening of being sociable. She'd shot her bolt at lunchtime. Why had she not simply rung from Drew and Natalie's to explain how shattered she was? She could have enjoyed a few more drinks, a good night's sleep and set off tomorrow morning, refreshed.

At a distance the evening had seemed like a cheery prospect. Or so Isobel had told herself. If one were to turn over a few subconscious stones, all manner of creepy-crawly motives would probably be revealed. Was she hoping Johnny had been invited too? Or the famous film-star brother? Then there was Will, who still had the power to fascinate. He was notorious for his incivility and foul mouth, yet even when stoned he had never been anything other than scrupulously polite to Isobel. She was aware that this was no compliment. Tonight would be the longest she had ever been in his company ... The car was drifting again. She opened the window to let in a bracing draught and arrived at last in one piece in Bishopside.

It was getting dark. The wind was churning the branches of the civic Christmas tree, making the bulbs dance. Smaller trees spangled in some of the windows along Annie and Will's street. At others she glimpsed menorahs, for this was the Jewish part of town, the Oxbridge of the Ultra Orthodox world; though frankly she had difficulty imagining Bishopside as the Oxbridge of anywhere. Before getting out she checked her reflection in the driver's mirror. Did she have the panache to carry off the furry hat? Never mind; it was warm. She got out of the car and hurried into her coat, remembering she mustn't leave anything valuable in the boot overnight. A friend had nearly had his car stolen from this very spot a couple of years ago. Quite why Will insisted on living in such a run-down area was baffling. One would have thought that concern for his wife and child would have outweighed other considerations by now.

She hauled out her things, slammed the boot and locked it. A man was walking past. She bent down for her bags and heard him stop. She glanced up and let go of the handles in shock.

'Johnny!' Dear God – he looked so old!

'Anastasia!' He saluted her with a kiss on each cheek, accompanied by a stream of improvised gobbledegook in a thick Russian accent. She was too appalled at the change in him to laugh.

'You've lost weight!'

'Aye.' He slapped his midriff as he had all those months ago at the Friary. 'Not a fat oaf any more, eh?' His grin didn't disguise the gauntness of his face. What had happened to him?

'Are you – you're not . . . ill, are you?'

'Why, no. I'm fine. Just . . . Well, to be honest, I've felt better, pet. I've felt better.' He shuddered in the cold and got out his cigarettes. 'But that's life. How are you?'

'Well, thank you. Are you going to Annie's?'

'I've been there all afternoon.' He hesitated. 'Nah. I mustn't stop. My mam's expecting us.'

'Oh.' There was no sign of Mara. 'And your wife? Is she . . . ?'

'Who knows?' he said, through his cigarette as he lit up.

She's left him! She clutched her throat.

He blew out a cloud of smoke and watched her, waiting for her response. A first handful of rain scudded along the street.

'I'm so sorry.' She touched his arm briefly. 'I had no idea.'

'Aye, well. It's not common knowledge.'

'I'm sorry,' she repeated. His misery was almost unbearable to watch, but what comfort could she offer? Limp platitudes? Indignation? *She's mad. She didn't deserve you.* The cold was making her face ache.

'So,' he said, rousing himself, 'you're off up to the cottage, then?'

'That's right.'

'With friends, is that?' he asked casually.

She felt a thud of panic. 'No. I decided I could do with time to myself.' The rain was stinging down in good earnest now. 'Well, I'd better go.' She bent down to pick up her bags.

'Isobel –'

Don't, she begged inwardly, hearing the desperation in his voice. 'Goodbye, Johnny.'

'I need to talk.'

She set off. 'I'm afraid I'm already late.'

'Tomorrow, then? The day after? I'll drive up.'

'I'm, I'm not sure if . . . I don't know what I'm doing yet.' She reached for the gate. It squealed open and clanged. A curtain was pulled aside and Isobel glimpsed Christmas-tree lights and Teddy's face pressed against the window.

The thought of Harry came like an answered prayer. She remembered what he'd said back in the autumn. 'Why don't you ring Harry? Go and see him.'

The front door opened. Teddy was hopping up and down.

'Izzer Bell! Have you dot me a twesent, Izzer Bell?'

'Hello! Come in,' laughed Annie. She caught sight of Johnny. 'I thought you'd gone.'

'I'm away.' He leant and kissed Isobel's cheek. 'See you.'

''Bye.' She escaped up the path.

'*I said, did you dwing me a twesent?*' shouted Teddy.

'Ssh!' said Annie.

Isobel blundered into the warm hall. Annie was admiring her hat as she hung it up and shushing Teddy. 'Yes. Well,' said Isobel, struggling out of her coat. 'Presents. Right.' She rummaged in her carrier-bag and found the book she had wrapped earlier and handed it to Teddy.

Will was approaching. Isobel straightened up hastily, gift in hand, trying to recall whether they were on cheek-kissing terms.

They evidently were. He left an arm draped across her shoulders, then remarked conversationally, 'Well, fuck me.'

Finding this unanswerable, Isobel handed him a bottle of wine.

'God, the legs. The perfume.' He buried his face in her throat. 'Mmm.'

Isobel attempted delicately to peel him off.

'Oops!' giggled Annie. 'Are we a tiny bit drunk, darling?'

257

'No, darling,' he drawled. 'We are completely fucking rat-arsed.'

'He's never quite recovered from seeing you all in leather,' explained Annie.

Will curled his lip and snarled softly at Isobel, then bent down to Teddy who was tugging on his trouser leg. 'What is it, sweetheart? *Where The Wild Things Are.* Yeah! I'll read it.'

'Um, shall I make some coffee?' wondered Annie.

Isobel followed her to the kitchen to escape the dubious honour of Will's appreciation. Her face was still burning. How on earth did Annie put up with him? She sat down and watched her friend dithering about, peering in jars as if she still hadn't learnt her way about the kitchen. In her own timid style, Isobel reflected, Annie could be as trying as her husband.

'So how is everything?' Annie ventured.

But at that point Will reappeared and caught her in the act of making instant coffee. He ejected her. Isobel retreated speedily to the sitting room, where Annie was starting to read to Teddy.

The room was warm. In the distance Isobel heard the clatter of coffee beans being ground. Would Annie be able to shed any light on Johnny's situation?

'How many monsters can you see?' Annie was asking.

'Ninety-eleven,' asserted Teddy.

Isobel was going to have to be patient. Her eyes wandered round to see how much had changed since she'd first sat there. On that occasion – another snowy evening some three years earlier – the room had represented the epitome of her own particular taste in interior design. No fuss, no clutter, just the best of everything. Today the oatmeal carpet and ivory sofas bore the battle scars of life with small children. It was depressing that even the best taste in the world seemed powerless to repel the tide of primary-coloured plastic that swept in with parenthood. Surely a little imagination would enable children to see the merits of traditional wooden toys? And a little firmness would ensure that they put them away after they'd finished with them.

Will came in with the coffee, kicking a path clear across the room. He sat beside Isobel. She turned herself to face him in a friendly manner, while drawing back a prudent eighteen inches.

258

'So how's Izzer Bell?'

Before she could answer Teddy leapt on him, slopping his coffee. Another stain on the sofa.

Isobel sprang to her feet. 'Do you have any upholstery cleaner?' she asked. 'If you're quick it won't stain.'

'Forget it,' replied Will. 'It's buggered, anyway.'

Annie mopped vaguely with a handful of tissues.

Isobel winced. She waited for Will to repeat his inquiry about her well-being, but he did not. Eventually it dawned on her that there would be no adult conversation until Teddy was tucked up for the night. She sat longing for silence and bed, her mind janglingly awake from a combination of caffeine, Will's lechery and her encounter with Johnny.

The meal was nearly over. How soon could one decently excuse oneself? The other two were yawning, but making no bedward moves.

'More wine?' asked Isobel, moving the bottle nearer to Annie.

'Um, I'd better not.' Annie glanced at Will and they shared a smile. 'I'm, actually, I'm, um, pregnant again.'

'Congratulations!' cried Isobel, her enthusiasm masking an unpleasant pang. 'That's *wonderful* news. When's it due?'

'Oh, June-ish. Another accident, I'm afraid,' sighed Annie.

'We think we've worked out what's doing it,' added Will, droolingly.

Oh, honestly, thought Isobel. Some doctor you are.

He read her expression and gave her a shameless grin, at which she coloured. She sometimes feared they were aware of her attraction to him. Poor old Isobel, she imagined Annie giggling. But this was paranoia.

Upstairs a little voice began wailing.

Annie got wearily to her feet. 'I'll go.'

Isobel was left alone with Will, hoping he wouldn't misbehave without his wife's chaperonage and force her to make an issue of it.

'How's the parish?' he asked politely.

'Busy,' she replied.

He was watching her intently. 'Been overdoing it?'

'Yes. Probably.'

'God, this is turning into a rest home for shagged-out clergy,' he said. 'We've had the vicar asleep on our floor half the afternoon.'

Isobel smiled, but to her dismay felt her eyes filling. 'We had a rush of funerals last week,' she explained, trying to keep the tears at bay. 'Plus all the home communions.'

'Bad funerals?'

'Not . . . it was an earlier one that . . . it was a baby.'

'Christ. I'm sorry.' He put a hand on her arm.

A lump swelled in her throat. 'It's just so hard, explaining. Trying to explain . . . explain why . . . It's just that they'd had so much trouble conceiving. And –' She bit her lips. Not now. Don't let it all come out now. She sniffed and tried to get a grip. 'Anyway, I'll be glad of the break. Thanks again for being so generous.'

'It's nothing. You don't have to have all the answers, surely,' he said gently. 'You just need to know where they can take their questions.'

She remembered he was a vicar's son himself, and nodded dumbly. His kindness was harder to bear than his earlier harassment.

'You're probably doing more for them than you realize just by being there.' She nodded and sniffed again. His hand tightened on her arm for a moment, then he let go. 'Hang on in there, Izzer Bell.'

Annie reappeared and had just sat down when the wailing began again overhead.

'Oh, fucking hell,' groaned Will. 'I'll go and read the Riot Act.' He dragged himself upstairs.

Annie yawned. 'Oh, excuse me. I'm completely . . . I expect you are too. We've had Johnny asleep on our sitting-room floor this afternoon.'

'Mmm. Will said.' Isobel's heart pounded. Now was her chance. 'He looked dreadful.'

'I know. Poor Johnny He's in a bad way.'

'Yes. He told me his wife's left him.'

'What?' exclaimed Annie, startled in mid-yawn.

'Oh! I thought – oh no! Perhaps I shouldn't have –'

'Well, I knew she was spending Christmas with her family, a long-lost cousin who's turned up or something, but —'

'Maybe I misunderstood.'

'Goodness. Um.'

'I just assumed ... I've obviously spoken out of turn.'

'No, no.'

'You'd better forget I —'

'Oh, yes, of course.'

They both knew it was impossible. Isobel cursed herself. Hadn't he said it wasn't common knowledge? What had possessed her to blurt it out like that? Surely it was obvious he didn't want anyone in the parish to know.

'Goodness,' said Annie again. 'Well, I knew things were a bit ... I mean, with them not, um ...'

Not what? Isobel wanted to scream. For heaven's sake, fill in the gaps! But Will was coming back downstairs, and they fell silent.

Sleep, oh, let me sleep. Seldom had the sleeve of care felt so ravelled. Isobel twisted in bed. Guilt over her *faux pas* bit with fresh savagery each time she thought about it. There was nothing she could do except emphasize once again to Annie tomorrow that she had inadvertently betrayed a confidence, and rely on her friend's discretion. Then she began to worry that she had failed to make herself sufficiently clear to Johnny and that he would turn up at the cottage 'to talk'. She went over the encounter repeatedly. It was like that absurd episode after the Harvest Supper. She was imagining things. She was *not* imagining things. Well, she would just have to phone him. Better still, drop him a line. A postcard of Northumberland. Sealed in an envelope. 'Dear Johnny, I hope I didn't seem rude [unkind?] when we met. I am concerned for you, but I'm sure you agree with me that I am not the right person for you to discuss [personal matters? your marriage?] with.' The misplaced preposition rankled, but she didn't want it to sound like a business letter. 'I do hope you'll take up my suggestion and get in touch with Harry. Yours in Christ, Isobel.'

Or was that too placating? What about 'Dear Johnny, under no circumstances are you to attempt to contact me.' This was some

261

way short of compassionate, admittedly. She thrashed this way and that in Will's Egyptian cotton sheets. At least, she assumed they were his. Annie had been addicted to stripy winceyette at theological college. 'Dear Johnny, keep away, I'm too much in love with you.' Wasn't that the truth of it? She stifled a wild impulse to giggle. 'Dear Johnny, by all means come up. We'll sit in front of the fire, open a bottle of wine and discuss anything you like . . .' She saw instantly that this would have been better left unarticulated, even as a joke. It was dismissed, but it was not fully dismantled. It lay ticking softly at the back of her mind as she tried to sleep.

Well, it was very kind of them to lend her the cottage, Isobel reminded herself, as she set off. But what a ghastly morning! She had been the first one down and consequently had to disarm the house alarm, horrid thing. Teddy had followed her, dressed in a yellow plastic fireman's helmet, a pair of wellies and nothing else. He was using what looked like a dressing-gown cord as a hose. It would have felt rude to help herself to breakfast, so Isobel had ended up reading *Fireman Sam* stories to Teddy for what felt like hours until Will appeared, bad-tempered and alarmingly louche in a cordless dressing-gown. Sitting opposite him, clad thus, at the breakfast table was not an experience she was keen to repeat. She attempted some polite small-talk, then gave up. He had a habit of maintaining eye-contact several seconds longer than was conventional, then making a slight moue, as if deciding against speaking his mind. He appeared to be making a private diagnosis of her condition, and the outlook was not optimistic.

Then there was the cottage keys fiasco, with Annie rummaging feebly in drawers while Will swore at her and Teddy 'helped'. Isobel had sat in agony, the innocent cause of this mounting domestic tension. The keys turned up, of course, but not before Will had flung on some clothes to drive to his surgery for the spare set. Isobel braced herself for the final explosion, but he had only laughed.

They had assembled on the doorstep to wave her off. Yes – they'd been very generous. Why did she picture them dancing in the hall – *she's gone, she's gone, she's gone*?

That night as she settled down by the cottage fire with a good book it all felt worthwhile. She had the best part of a week left in which to unwind. There was no sound apart from the occasional spitting or shifting of coal in the hearth. Outside there was nothing, no wind, no traffic. Yet the silence didn't seem peaceful; more alert, watchful. As though something were about to happen ... Hah! She was listening for the sound of Johnny's car, his footsteps approaching the door, his knock. You great fool. One, he was not going to come; two, she would send him packing if he did.

Then, unmistakably, came the sound of approaching wheels. They drew to a halt outside the cottage. Isobel sat, scarcely breathing. A slam. Footsteps.

They dwindled away down the lane and she heard the sound of a door opening, then shutting in the neighbouring house. She flopped back in her chair sneering at herself.

The following morning she looked out of her window and saw she was safe. A good foot of snow had fallen in the night. The village would be cut off. Well, a day of snuggling by the fire and reading. She had plenty of coal and food and nothing else to do.

By the evening she was fretful and bogged down by guilt. It was ridiculous, but at some level she evidently equated relaxation with sloth and self-indulgence. She reminded herself of Harry's wise words that she was no use to anyone if she was exhausted. By lounging about she was genuinely doing her duty. If only it felt as though she was. She'd been expecting a great rush of sorrow about Hannah, now she had the leisure for grieving, but there was nothing. It was as if she'd snuffed all the warmth out of her feelings. All that was left was a cold, ashy numbness, and, if she was honest, a relief that she was being blessed with a break from Sue and Mike's grief and her powerlessness in the face of it. If only Will was right, and she was helping just by being there. Maybe she ought to put the parish completely out of her mind. She'd probably got a mild dose of cabin fever. Tomorrow she must get out, if humanly possible. The neighbours had been up and down the lane a couple of times in their four-wheel drive, so she'd probably manage unless it snowed again. By now the larger roads would have been cleared by ploughs.

Which meant –

She squashed the thought and went to bed. That night she dreamt she was standing in a kitchen. She didn't recognize it, but she knew it belonged to Will. She was at the sink washing up. For some reason she was dressed only in her new knee-length leather boots and a short T-shirt. Then Fitz was there. He knelt behind her. She bent over and felt his hands on her buttocks, parting them, then the tip of his tongue. Instead of pushing him away, she shifted her feet, spreading herself wider –

No! Isobel woke with a start. That's it! You're not getting away with this! She wasn't sure whom she was addressing. The panel of jokers in her subconscious, she supposed, the ones who cooked up these diverting little interludes while her self-control was out of action. But Fitz! No, no, *no*. And yet, on reflection, one could account for it, identify the dream's separate influences – that troubling incident with Fitz over the mulled wine, Teddy wandering about naked in his wellies, the sex-charged atmosphere of Will's kitchen. Yes, very droll, ho ho. But sex with teenagers? I think not.

With these brisk thoughts Isobel hoped to brush the dream aside. But it continued to trouble her. She'd never been quite sure whether such nocturnal concupiscence was something of which one ought to repent. Was it negligence or weakness? It wasn't deliberate fault, but she felt somehow in need of forgiveness all the same. It was later, as she attempted to pray the matter through, that an unwelcome illumination occurred. Was the dream not, in fact, about Davy? She squirmed at the idea. Davy. Not so many years since he was a teenager, was it? Why had she not pushed him away on Christmas Eve under the mistletoe? He'd expected to be rebuffed, so why had she let him kiss her, part her lips and slip his tongue, not just the tip, either, deep in her mouth?

Oh, but this wasn't fair. She'd admitted at once that she'd been wrong, hadn't she? She felt quite silly enough already without hauling the whole thing out all over again. She'd apologized to Davy on the spot, made him leave before things got out of hand, she'd repented, rebuked herself and put it all behind her. She was hardly going to let it happen again. What more could she do? Let's get things into perspective. It was only a kiss, for heaven's sake!

This was what came of having too much leisure. One ended up refining on trivialities. What she needed was a bit of structure to her day. She went at once to the drawer full of brochures and made a list of things to do.

She spent a contented day tootling through snowy lanes. She visited her favourite secondhand bookshop, had a nice bowl of homemade soup in a restaurant, wandered round a ruined castle, did a spot of food shopping and had an indulgent cream tea before making her way back to the cottage. The sun was setting in fiery splendour, dyeing the snow orange and casting long purple shadows. There. That was better!

She parked the car and, clutching her shopping, made her way across the slippery lane to the door. She was just reaching for the keys when she noticed a footprint on the doorstep. Large, with deep treads. A man's boot. He'd been! She glanced fearfully up and down the lane. By now it was considerably churned up by cars and feet. She looked back at the print. Impossible to conclude anything from it. It might belong to anyone. A neighbour. The coal merchant, even, who had clearly called, judging by the scattered lumps on the snow. She let herself in, unable to believe she was being this feeble.

Over the next few days she kept herself busy. Teashops, bracing walks, birdspotting, forays to Craster to buy kippers. And, anyway, life members of the National Trust were never at a loss for things to do while on holiday. She was turning into a maiden aunt! Perhaps that was how her fellow holiday-makers saw her. But they were not privy to the attacks of lust that ambushed her as she went about her maidenly pursuits. The triggers were random – a workman shovelling snow, Will's brother's face on a magazine cover, an untimely memory of Will himself at the breakfast table. Really, one was almost inclined to laugh. It was as though her body had been requisitioned by a Martian nymphomaniac.

But she'd encountered this before. Her experience last autumn was a case in point, when a little bit too much leisure had resulted in a silly fixation with Johnny. Meeting him like that in the street must have provoked a replay of feelings. It didn't *mean* anything. Or did it? She questioned herself sharply and became aware of a certain inner evasiveness. In her heart of hearts she knew her dread that Johnny might appear had long since given way to a hope that he would and, more recently, to disappointment that he had not.

She sat down and gave herself permission to indulge in uncensored thought. There was no other way of smoking out her true feelings. What, exactly, was she hoping for? That Johnny would come and – let's not mince matters – they would have sex? She found to her relief that this was not what she wanted. Of course, Johnny was incredibly attractive and she experienced a very human longing for intimacy and affection. Yes, one found sex enjoyable, but without the security of a solid relationship it could bring nothing but misery and guilt. The sense of having failed God and violated the integrity of her calling would far outweigh any short-term gratification, which was why she had instinctively repulsed any advances Johnny had (or possibly hadn't) made.

So, she asked herself again, what do I really want?

You might as well admit it: you want him to divorce Mara and marry you, don't you? That's what you're hoping will happen. You hope he'll drive up and pour out his heart to you and realize in the process that you are his ideal partner after all – someone who shares his love of the Gospel, who could minister alongside him, accept him for what he is without trying to separate the man from his calling. And certainly not punch his face in!

So.

Isobel took a deep breath and tried to laugh. Better out than in. Her duty was clear. What God had joined together it was not for Isobel Knox to put asunder. All her prayers and efforts ought, instead, to go into helping Johnny and Mara achieve reconciliation. Not even in thought must she do otherwise. If, at some distant future point, Johnny were a free agent, well, that might be a different matter. Remarriage of divorcees was something Isobel had always been quite clear about. Christ's teaching was unambiguous. She would have some serious thinking to do –

Castles in the air, Isobel. The truth of the matter was that there was nothing she could do except watch and pray. She set about the task at once, repenting of her own unworthy motives, holding up both Johnny and Mara before God in prayer. She went to bed that night feeling much more wholesome and at peace with God and herself.

Strange, then, that she should wake the following morning in a foul temper. Her holiday was almost over. *And he hasn't come!* She stomped over the snow-clogged Cheviots, trying to get away from the happy tobogganing families. He's completely ruined my week! she cried, knowing she was being irrational. Tomorrow was New Year's Day and she'd be driving back to Asleby. And tonight she'd be sitting pathetically in front of the television while others were out partying. Well, why didn't she go home a day early and see if either Harry or Jan fancied some kind of celebration?

No. She'd see it through. It was not like Isobel to give up. She was too cross to ask herself if this was because she hadn't quite abandoned hope of seeing Johnny.

And so she found herself that night watching humorous round-ups of the passing year as the clock ticked round towards midnight. In her hand was a seasonal glass of malt whisky that she was shuddering her way through and trying to like.

He was not coming. He was *not coming.*

She'd been a fool even to wish it. Better to go to bed now without watching the maudlin crowds in Trafalgar Square bawling about Auld Lang Syne with a bunch of strangers they would probably never meet again.

Oh, it was all so unfair! She got to her feet and then –

Ah.

She stood, heart sledge-hammering, listening to the car pull up and the footsteps . . . going past! No, coming back, coming to the door. There was one last minute to remember her resolutions before the soft knock-knock-knock.

She went to the door to let him in.

## CHAPTER 21

No. *No.*

The fire spat.

Oh, no!

What do you mean, oh, no? You knew this was going to happen.

She shoved him off her in loathing, almost treading on him in her desperation to escape upstairs.

She brushed her teeth viciously and spat blood into the bathroom basin. She washed, then washed again.

There's no point, Isobel. No undoing it now.

She went through to the dark bedroom and sat on the bed edge not bothering to bleat, *I couldn't help myself.* Of course she could. It was the fact she hadn't that was so dumbfounding. Why? When she knew that guilt would so far outweigh pleasure – *why?* Moonlight was shining through the open curtains. It was a bitter night, picked out in diamond-hard stars.

Isobel gnawed her knuckles, trying to force her sick disgust with herself into remorse.

Jesus, forgive me! I don't understand myself.

He was coming up the stairs. *Get out!* She could feel the words rising in her throat. But he went into the bathroom. She heard him urinate assertively, on and on.

I hate him. The lavatory flushed.

'Isobel?' He came in. 'Isobel? Can I put the light on?'

'No.'

He fumbled blindly towards her and sat on the bed. His fingers groped for her hand, but she snatched it away

'Aw, Isobel, man. I'm so-o-oo sorry. Why didn't you stop me?'

'Why didn't you stop yourself?' she cried. 'Why did you come here at all? You must have got the message by now!'

'But I love you!'

'Get out.'

'Isobel! Please –'

'I mean it. Get out!' Her voice rose to a screech.

He left silently.

You're so cruel. Why are you punishing him like this? She bit her knuckles again. God forgive me. I'm sorry, Lord. *I'm sorry!*

But her prayers clattered back down again as useless as toy arrows. She sat for a long time, hearing the distant chapel clock chime the quarters. If only she could cry. If only she'd been drunk. If only she had some tiny fig-leaf scrap of an excuse she could cover herself with.

If only it had been Johnny, not Davy.

What have I done? This isn't me. I'm not like this. I don't do this kind of thing! She hugged her arms round herself. Somewhere, in some dimly imagined future, there would be a point when she'd be able to look back on it all. A day when it would be confessed and forgiven and tidied away. But, oh, the work that lay between now and then.

Well, she must start now. Pray, though prayer felt like hypocrisy. Put things right with Davy. She could hear him moving around. It sounded as if he was getting dressed. Supposing he just left? She must not let him go before trying to explain and ask his forgiveness. There must be no blaming him, no squirming out of her own responsibility in all this. When she got home tomorrow – today! oh, God, today! – she must confess to Harry. She was in no doubt as to her duty. It would mean shame like none she'd experienced before, but she was not a coward.

How, *how* to repent? She felt like a child who has smashed something precious. Why? Because she had not valued it. Even if she were granted the chance to go back and try again, she knew she'd probably repeat her folly. This knowledge made a mockery of repentance. Yet repent she must. The futility of it overwhelmed her. I've failed. I made my vows and I haven't kept them. I'm an adulterer before God. Oh, yes, she knew adultery could be forgiven, but the marriage would never be perfect again. The cracks would show. Anyone who looked closely would see where it had been patched up. One might as well just throw it away. She made her lips move to the words of the general confession: 'Almighty

God, our heavenly Father, we have sinned against you and against our fellows, in thought and word –'

She broke off, hearing the sound of Davy thundering up the stairs. He flung the door open and snapped the light on. Isobel clutched the duvet to herself.

'I will not be tret like this!' he announced.

Repentance vanished. 'Don't take that tone with me!'

'I bloody will! I've got feelings and I deserve a bit respect.'

'A bit *of* respect, you mean,' she shouted. 'Why can't you speak English?'

'*What?*' She watched him wrestling with his fury. 'Y'kna something, Isobel? Sometimes I think you hate me.'

She bit her lips. 'I'm sorry. I just feel so –' Tears – they were the way out of this impasse. Why couldn't she cry like other women? 'I'm truly sorry I said that. It was hateful. I just need time to think.'

'Do you want me to go?' he asked.

'I don't know. *I don't know!*' Her voice rose again. Why does it always have to be *my* choice, *my* responsibility?

'Well, do you want me to *stay*?'

'Oh, for goodness' sake, Davy!'

'Just say what you want, woman!'

She remained obdurately silent.

He sat down beside her and waited. There was something like contempt on his face.

'What?' she cried.

'I'm not stupid. You want another fuck, but you're too proud to ask.'

Isobel slapped his face so hard her hand stung.

'Bitch.'

She went to hit him again.

'Well, that's one way of asking for it,' he said, gripping her wrists.

A single word from her would have stopped him. She knew it. But instead she fought him, forcing him to overpower her, to *fuck* her, while she closed her eyes and pretended it was Johnny. Why not? The damage was done now.

They lay in silence. She knew he'd be the first to speak.

'Y'aal reet? Ee, you must think I'm a bloody caveman.' He tried to stroke her face, but she cringed from his tenderness. 'Now I feel really bad.'

'Well, you can always go to confession, can't you?'

'Don't be like that. Mebbes I will.'

'No!' She sat up in alarm. 'Not to Father McGee! You can't!'

'Why not? He's my parish priest.'

'I see him at fraternals! You'll have to find someone else, Davy. Promise me.'

'OK, OK. Calm down.'

She lay back again, panic twittering in her mind. Supposing everyone found out? She pushed his face away as he tried to kiss her breasts. How would she live with the shame?

'What happened here?' he asked, cupping her and stroking the scar with his thumb.

'I had surgery.'

'Never in this world! To make them bigger, like?'

'Smaller, actually.'

'You're kidding! Why? How big were they?'

She showed him. 'Out here.'

His eyes widened in awe, but he had the wisdom not to say what he was visibly thinking. 'D'you not think we should just accept worselves as we are?'

'It was surgery to correct an *abnormality*!'

'I'm not judging you.' He bent his head and sucked her nipple into his mouth. Lust tugged on her, aching like hunger.

'Don't, Davy.'

'Will they still, y'kna, work, like? Will you be able to feed your bairns?'

'I doubt I'll have any.'

'I'll give you some.'

'Don't be ridiculous!' A dry sob shook her, but still no tears came.

'Why not? Because I'm too young for you? If we love each other, where's the problem?'

He thinks we'll get married. Her conscience writhed. 'It's not that simple, Davy.'

271

He studied her face. She saw dread cross his own. 'There's not someone else, is there?'

'Of course not!' He didn't grace the lie with contradiction. In the silence that followed she tried to think of a way of mitigating the truth.

'But I don't understand,' he said at last. 'Why would you sleep with me if you're in love with someone else?'

Why indeed? She wrung her hands. 'Davy . . .'

'I saw you with him, didn't I? Back in the summer.'

Andrew, she thought. 'No. That was someone else.'

'I bet he's married.'

'Yes. Look, Davy, I'm just using you,' she blurted.

'Because I remind you of him?'

She started in shock. 'What makes you think that?'

'Something Jan said that time.'

*Does he remind you of anyone?* Why had she not admitted it to herself? Perhaps then she'd have seen all this coming.

There was another terrible pause. Don't let him cry. She couldn't bear to see men weep. 'Aye, well, to be fair, you did warn us,' he managed. 'That's what you meant, isn't it? Saying there was no chance of us getting together.'

Guilt burst out into resentment. 'Why didn't you listen?'

'Because I was getting plenty other messages as well!'

'Well, don't blame me!' she snapped. 'It's a problem with your reception, not my transmission!' What's the matter with you? What's the *matter*? Why are you treating him like this?

He got up and began putting his clothes on again. 'If you think you're giving off unavailable vibes, then someone's wired you up backwards, pet.'

'That is *so* typical!' she exploded. 'Always the woman asking for it!'

He paused in the act of pulling on his shirt and stared at her in scorn. 'Well, I'm just a simple Geordie copper, me; but I tend to count a tongue down the throat as encouragement.'

'You started it!'

'Christmas Eve, I'm talking about. Under the mistletoe. Aye, that's right!' He wagged a finger in her burning face.

272

'Well, you –' she began furiously.

'Yes? Well, I what? You cannot take being in the wrong, can you, Isobel?'

He finished getting dressed and left without another word.

Isobel walked up and down the same stretch of beach, heedless of the salt water on her new boots. It was bitterly cold. Snow lay on the sand above the high-tide mark. Repentance was easy now she was drowning. God, save me, save me! What had she unleashed? Some other Isobel, bursting like an evil genie from its bottle prison. As she walked in the raw, aching morning, she was herself again; able to admit how deeply in the wrong she was. Perhaps she was going mad. At any rate, she could sense the holes the marbles would disappear down if her world tilted just a fraction more. Steady, hold everything steady.

She turned and walked back the way she had just come, treading down her own footprints. To have identified the danger, yet to have underestimated its power so disastrously! *Fool!* How could she have been caught out looking in the wrong direction like that, outmanoeuvred by such a simple decoy tactic? The humiliation wrung her cruelly. Johnny she could have explained. But Davy, *Davy*! The signs had been there all along, but she had been unable – or unwilling – to read them. It was as if she'd been possessed last night. It would be nice to think that, wouldn't it, to weasel out of the responsibility. Possessed by a demon of fornication.

She turned again. She knew she was deferring the moment when she'd have to admit it all to Harry. Sheer foolishness. What was she hoping for – some form of words that would save her face? The tide was coming in. As she approached the estuary she saw sea meet river and clash in cold turmoil. That's it! she thought. She almost pointed. That's how I feel. She watched the waters battling. And yet it would be all right. The river would race out. The tide would come in. Somehow the two were reconciled.

There was something bobbing in the waves. She drew closer to see what it was, but it disappeared. The water was a mass of seaweed. She waited. The waves churned. Just as she was about to give up the thing revealed itself: a dead baby. Isobel cried out soundlessly.

The child rolled and vanished. Isobel dashed in up to her knees. When the wave receded she would rescue it. Her eyes hunted among the roiling fronds. There was nothing there. Another wave drove her back up the beach. Dear God! What was she to do? The police. She must call them. No, she couldn't abandon it – another wave might fling it up on the shore. But the longer she waited the less sure she became. Maybe she'd been seeing things. Corded heaps lay all around. Her feet squelched and slithered. Here and there the knuckled ends protruded, pallid, like tiny fists or half-formed limbs. She strained for another glimpse. Unless – Why, of course. A dead seal pup. Yes, that would explain it. There was nothing she could do anyway. It was long gone by now. Sucked out to sea. There was no point wasting police time. There was nothing I could do. Nothing, nothing. Best forget it. It was gone. Over and done with.

She turned. No! The sea had sped up behind her. She was cut off on a sandy island. On one side the river rushing, on the other the racing tide. There was nothing to do but run for the shore. She set off, staggering, at times wading up to her thighs in the icy water until she reached dry land and hurried to her car.

Ridiculous! How ridiculous! Thank heavens there had been nobody there to witness her idiocy. Why, they'd have had her carted away. Isobel went to laugh, but no sound came. Surprised, she tried clearing her throat. Still nothing. How odd. There was something stuck in her throat. She could feel it. A fishbone, perhaps. She stood by the boot of the car, keys in hand, trying to dislodge whatever it was with a variety of coughs that never materialized, until it struck her that she must look like a madwoman. She opened the car and dug in her case for some dry clothes. Well, that was her beautiful boots wrecked. By the time she was in the back seat struggling out of her wet things it had become clear that she'd landed herself with a thorough dose of laryngitis. Her teeth were chattering, but that was the loudest noise she could make. She peered at the back of her throat in the driver's mirror but could see nothing.

The whole thing struck her as faintly hilarious as she drove to Bishopside to drop off the key. She'd had throat infections before which had left her hoarse, but nothing like this. Strange that it could have come on so suddenly. Ironic, too, losing her voice when she was on the brink of having to confess to Harry. Well, if the worst came to the worst, she'd have to write it down. She banished the unworthy thought that Harry would be more likely to take pity on her if she was poorly. The roads were almost empty and she reached the house quickly. She had just rung the doorbell when she remembered in searing horror that she hadn't bought any condoms to replace the one Davy had pinched from the bathroom cabinet. No chance to go back now. Could she invent some excuse to hang on to the keys? Or explain privately to Annie? She squirmed. Someone was coming to the door.

It was Will.

Isobel opened her mouth, forgetting she couldn't speak. Then she pointed at her throat and mouthed, *I've lost my voice.*

Will regarded her strangely. 'Come in. Have some coffee. I've just made some.'

She found herself following him to the kitchen.

'Annie's taken Teddy to the park. They shouldn't be long.'

*Keys.* She jingled them and put them on the table, miming her thanks. *How much do I owe you?*

'Nothing. Had a good time?'

She nodded vigorously, still shivering from her unplanned dip.

'Are you ill?' he asked, handing her a mug.

She shook her head. *I got wet. The tide came in behind me when I wasn't noticing.* It came out in a rasping whisper.

'How long has your voice been like that?'

*Since this morning.*

'Sore throat? Too much preaching over Christmas?'

She shook her head. *It feels like there's something stuck.*

'Want me to take a look?' He vanished and reappeared with his doctor's torch. She opened her mouth obediently. 'Hmm,' was his verdict.

*What?*

'Can't see anything. It was OK yesterday?'

She nodded. *There's something there, I can feel it.* Why was he looking at her like that?

275

She heard the sound of the front door. Annie reappeared with Teddy.

'Darling,' called Will, 'Izzer Bell's here.' There was something in his tone that seemed to betray a private joke and she blushed.

Annie came in with Teddy. 'How lovely! Did you have a nice time? We saw Davy in the supermarket the other day. He'd lost the address for the cottage. Did he turn up?'

Isobel nodded and bent to admire Teddy's new toy fire engine, face redder than ever. *So that's how he found out where I was.*

'She's lost her voice,' said Will.

'Poor old Isobel! Are you all right?'

Isobel straightened up and nodded again.

'No, poppet,' Annie told Teddy, who had found the dreaded *Fireman Sam* book. 'I'm afraid Isobel can't read to you. She's got a poorly voice.'

They sat round the kitchen table. It felt distinctly odd being unable to contribute to the conversation. She kept forgetting, and was surprised afresh each time no sound came. Will's eyes were on her more often than she liked. Her involuntary muteness gave her the opportunity to worry over what she would say to Harry. In the end she couldn't bear it and finished her coffee, turning down their invitations to stay for lunch.

Will accompanied her to the door. No chance of a private word with Annie. Surely nobody counted their condoms, anyway. Isobel always found parting a faintly awkward business, more so now it was impossible to gloss over it with polite nothings. Silence felt too intimate as he kissed her cheek, so she tackled him again over the matter of rent.

*Can I write you a cheque?*

'You can,' he said. 'But I won't cash it.'

*Well, thanks.*

'My pleasure. Get yourself to the doctor, Isobel.'

His serious tone frightened her. *Why?*

'Well, you need a voice in your profession, don't you? And to be brutally frank,' he went on, 'you look in a worse state now than before you went away.'

*Oh, it's just . . .* She couldn't think of a glib explanation.

276

He hugged her close for a moment. 'Take care of yourself. I'm worried about you.'

She was on Harry's doorstep. *God grant me the right words. If only she could speak properly.* She rang the bell.

His face lit up when he saw her, then immediately clouded.

'Isobel! Is something wrong? Come in.'

He led her to his study as if sensing his kitchen would be too informal a setting. They sat.

'What's wrong?'

She tried clearing her throat, knowing it was pointless, but hoping all the same. *I've lost my voice*, she whispered.

'So you have, you poor thing.'

His compassion was unendurable. She looked away. *I'm sorry. I've let you down. I've done something stupid, Harry.*

He let out a sigh, like someone hearing a piece of long-anticipated bad news. 'OK,' he said carefully. 'Can you tell me what, exactly?'

*I slept with someone.*

'Oh, Isobel.' His disappointment wounded her deeply. There was nothing to say that might lessen the offence. 'Has this been going on for long?'

She shook her head. *Just last night.*

'OK. Well, thank you for being so quick to tell me. Is it going to happen again?'

She shook her head again, violently.

'Um, sorry to press you, but how can you be so sure?'

*I won't let it.*

'But you let it happen last night,' he pointed out gently.

*I've repented. I give my word it won't happen again. It was just a stupid mistake, Harry!* She tried in vain to swallow the lump in her throat.

'Forgive me, but as I think I've said before, there are people in this world it's impossible to be sensible about.' There was a pause. 'I'm assuming we're talking about Johnny, here?'

She bowed her head in shame. *Davy.*

'Ah.' Harry sat back, blinking slightly. At length he asked, 'Do you . . . love him?'

277

Her cheeks burned and she shook her head. *I like him. He's been a good friend, but –*

'So this isn't a relationship, um, with a future?'

*No. That's why –*

'Then let me say, unequivocally, that you are not to sleep with him again. I've been known to cut engaged couples a bit of slack, but I won't countenance this. No, Isobel. No, no, no.'

*OK, OK. I've given you my word!* She was quivering with humiliation.

'And, believe me, I'll hold you to it,' he said. 'I absolutely will not turn a blind eye to immorality in my curate.'

Why was he lecturing her like this?

'And I expect you to make your position crystal clear to Davy.'

*I will.* She'd come expecting disappointment and sorrow. It hadn't occurred to her he'd be angry, though of course he had every right.

'Listen, Isobel,' he said, his voice kinder again, 'I'll help you in any way I can. I know it's hell. I want you to ask yourself why you did it. If you don't understand yourself, you're not going to find will-power easy.'

She nodded. Davy was right. She couldn't take being in the wrong. Not graciously, anyhow. She was swelling with resentment at Harry's treatment of her. He'd been *fine* as long as he thought it was Johnny.

'Oh, Lord.' He ran his hands through his hair. 'I think we need some coffee,' he said. He touched her arm. She turned her face away. Rebuffed, he went out to the kitchen.

I don't deserve him, she thought, conscience-stricken. She followed to apologize and entered the kitchen in time to witness him pounding his forehead on a cupboard door. He heard her and whipped round.

She gawped at him.

'Um, I was just . . .' He coloured and laughed helplessly. 'Er, yes. Coffee, wasn't it?'

Well, it was done. Thank God for Harry. He'd been wonderful. There was still Davy to face. She'd phone him now, except she couldn't talk. What a fool she'd been to make such a huge mountain out of this rather mundane molehill. It was, after all, a fairly dull, predictable sin. From now on she'd be quicker to show compassion to those similarly caught out. Oh, what a blessed relief it was to have it all sorted out. She hadn't taken into consideration how much her sense of accountability to Harry would help. Well worth the anguish of admitting her failure to him, grim though that had been.

It was about seven o'clock. She made herself a spot of dinner with the odds and ends she found in the freezer. Tomorrow was a fresh day. Isobel tried and failed to hum. Everything would be all right.

The doorbell rang as she was drying the dishes. She went to the door, plate in hand. It was Davy. She blushed violently. Oh, well. Better to get it over with. They stood awkwardly in the hall as she sought in her pained whisper to explain. It had the effect of making him whisper too.

'I'm sorry,' he said. 'I was wrong to blame you.'

*I was very much to blame.* She clutched the plate. *I only hope you aren't too hurt?*

He clearly was. 'Aye, well. That's life.'

*Have you got someone you can talk to?*

'I went to confession – don't worry, not to Father McGee.'

*Thanks.*

'He was dead canny.' He bowed his head. She could see how embarrassed he was, unversed in speaking about religious experience. 'It was, like, *meant*, y'kna? I wasn't going to, only I saw him on the street in his collar, like. Turns out he was C of E, but I guess it still counts.'

Horror surged through Isobel. *Where was this?*

'Oh, don't worry. Nowhere round here. Up my parents' way. Bishopside.'

*Johnny Whitaker?* A veil of red slid across her vision.

'Aye. D'you –'

Isobel smashed the plate down on his head. He cried out and crumpled up against the wall. She watched in terror as the blood welled up between his laced fingers.

*Davy! Oh, God, Davy!*

He groaned. She raced to the kitchen and ran a clean tea-towel under the tap. Her fingers were too weak to wring it out properly. She stumbled back and gave it to him. So much blood!

*I'm sorry, I'm sorry,* she whispered over and over.

'Yer fuckin' mad, ye.' He winced. 'Does it want stitching?'

He peeled the cloth away. She flinched at the sight.

*Yes. Shall I drive you to Casualty?*

'Aye.' He struggled to his feet. His legs buckled, but he steadied himself, leaving a bloody handprint on the wall. 'Ee, sorry.'

*Don't apologise!* she half sobbed.


She waited with him at the hospital. He sat with his head in his hands, bloody cloth still clamped in place, saying nothing. She'd listened in mute shock as he told the nurse what had happened: he'd straightened up and hit his head on a cupboard door, which had been left open.

*You don't have to lie for me,* she said afterwards.

'I'm not,' he said curtly. 'I'm deein' it for me. You think I want "Some lass broke a plate ower his heed," on my notes?'

They waited, marooned in their separate silences. Isobel was trembling. I could have killed him. I'm losing it. Davy hadn't asked yet what had provoked her, but he would. How on earth could she explain? A fresh surge of rage swelled at the memory, terrifying her. It doesn't matter! So Johnny knows? Who cares? But she did care. Davy had wrecked her chances. Destroyed the one thing she hoped for.

At last he was seen to and they were able to leave.

*Forgive me,* she pleaded.

'I'm workin' on it.'

He insisted he was fit to drive himself home from her house. She let him go with misgivings. He paused before getting into his car.

'Just for the record, are there any other priests you're in love with that I'm not to talk to?'

He drove off, leaving her on the pavement. In the house opposite a segment of light vanished as Kath's curtain slid back into place.

That night Isobel experienced something close to a panic attack. Being able to name it was not enough to ward it off. She became convinced that Davy had collapsed with a brain haemorrhage and lay dying in his house. This fear laid hold of her and shook her till her teeth rattled and her brain gibbered. Common sense was powerless against the assault. It was one in the morning. She couldn't phone because she couldn't speak. In the end she got dressed, drove to his house and rang the doorbell. There was no reply. She rang again, then again, finger slipping from the button. Eventually a light came on upstairs. She leant against the door frame, trembling.

He opened the door in his dressing-gown and stared in amazement. 'Isobel!'

*Are you all right?*

'Well, my bloody heed hurts and some bugger's just woke us up at two in the morning, but apart from that, aye, I'm *fine.*'

*I thought you were dead*, she whimpered.

'What? Don't be daft, man. You'll have to try harder than that!' And seeing her distress he relented and drew her inside.

Kath Bollom, stationed behind her nets, noted Isobel's return with interest. Seven in the morning was a bit early for madam to be up and about her parish duties.

## CHAPTER 22

She got out of her shower and reached for a towel. Well, this little episode was going to take a bit of explaining to herself. And, worse, to Harry. She had till eight p.m. to think up an excuse. He had invited her round for drinks, perhaps to reassure her that, fundamentally, nothing had changed, he still trusted and respected her. Last night was going to put paid to that, though, wasn't it? On the glass shelf stood the bottle of scent he'd given her. She couldn't bring herself to wear it. Not now, now that she'd betrayed him. She didn't deserve it or him.

All through her adult life Isobel had coped with things by seeking to explain them to herself, but today her powers of analysis deserted her. She no longer had any grip on what was driving her. The only possible course of action was to repent and throw herself on God's and Harry's mercy once more. Why did the prospect fill her with such rage?

Maybe the truth was that she had fallen in love with Davy but couldn't acknowledge it because he was too young and there was such a disparity in their backgrounds. *Was* she in love with him? It would solve everything if she were. They could marry and – No. *No!* Every instinct recoiled. But what if this were just denial? After all, she was hardly the kind of person who hopped into bed with a man for whom she felt nothing. She must be fond of him, at least. She was, she *was*. He was fun, and while not academic he was not unintelligent. It appeared one found him attractive sexually. Maybe all this would amount to love if she weren't too proud to admit it. On the whole, she decided it might be wiser to say nothing to Harry until she had got things a little clearer in her own mind. No, there was nothing to be gained by telling Harry about last night.

\*

This eminently sensible resolve proved impossible to carry out. Harry asked her bluntly if she'd kept her word, and honesty obliged her to admit she had not.

He paused in the act of opening the wine. 'What? You *what?*' He thumped the bottle down on the kitchen table. 'How *could* you be so stupid?'

His anger ignited her own. *It's a private matter between him and me,* and hissed, *and no concern of yours!*

'It damn well *is* my concern!'

*What right have you got to judge?*

'What right?' Suddenly he erupted. 'What *right?*' he yelled. 'I'm the fucking vicar!' His words vibrated in the air. He seemed as shocked as she was. 'I'm sorry. I'm just not handling this!' He raised his hands in a gesture which was half placating, half despair. 'Sorry. Sorry. Five minutes. Give me five minutes to calm down, OK?'

He was not Harry, he was just some fool of a man telling her what to do. She ground her teeth, felt her face twisting.

Suddenly he ducked. A glass smashed on the cupboard door behind his head. She whirled round to see where it had come from, then sank to her knees in terror.

'Jesus!' He was crossing himself like a superstitious peasant. 'Isobel, how did you – ? Oh, dear God. "Look, no hands!"' He half laughed. 'Get a grip, Preece.'

*I'm choking!* She tore at her throat. All the cups and tumblers in the kitchen began to buzz, waiting to hurl themselves. *Harry, help me!*

He raised a hand. 'Stop it.' The silence roared. Dimly she heard him speak the blessing. She groped towards him. He reached down and helped her to her feet. The roaring ebbed away. On his dresser a single cup swung back and forth, back and forth, until it rocked itself into stillness. Harry let out a long breath.

'Um, would you mind using the cheap glasses in future?'

She was looking at her reflection in a mirror. Where on earth am I? The obvious answer was 'in someone's bathroom'. She was standing at a basin apparently in the act of washing her hands. The tap was still running. She turned it off. Was she dreaming? It was certainly the oddest bathroom she'd ever seen. The ceiling was deep blue and sprinkled with gilt stars like a medieval cathedral. The dark red walls had frescoed panels of angels and saints. Brass candelabra glittered overhead. The lavatory cistern had just finished filling. Perhaps she was having a strange dream about peeing in a private chapel.

The thought was somehow reassuring. She looked up at the ceiling once more and a childhood story came back to her – *The Princess and the Goblin*. The princess had a bath in her grandmother's tub and it was full of stars like the night sky Grandmother gave her a magical thread, which she must follow, but she could only go forwards, never retrace her steps, for then the thread vanished. No, she must trust it and follow it, even if it led her down into the heart of the mountain where the goblins lived.

Well, for a dream it was pretty slow-moving. She dried her hands on the white towel. Ah, perhaps this was Will and Annie's house, only everything was curiously different in that way dreams had.

She ventured on to the unfamiliar landing and called, 'Hello?' only no sound came. This had happened before when she was dreaming. She glanced in through a door and saw a four-poster bed with dark blue velvet hangings. On the landing there was a bust on a plinth. Charles Haddon Spurgeon. He had a joke mitre on his head. She made her way to the top of the stairs and the house promptly turned into the vicarage. Indeed, there was Harry at the foot looking up at her. She smiled at him and tried to speak, but again, no sound came.

'Better?' he asked. 'Look, I'm really sorry.'

She approached, puzzled. It felt less and less like a dream; yet what was going on? Wasn't she supposed to be on holiday in Northumberland?

*I seem to have lost my voice*, she whispered.

'Well, yes,' he agreed in surprise.

She stared at him, hunting for clues. Why was he watching her like that?

*What am I doing here?*

'I asked you to come.'

*When? How did I get here?*

'Um, in your car, about half an hour ago. Don't you remember?'
*No.* Her bewilderment turned to panic.

'Ah.' He bit his lips and frowned. 'What's the last thing you can remember?'

*I was in the cottage. Watching TV. It was New Year's Eve.*

'Isobel,' he said gently, 'that was two days ago.'

*What?* Horror surged through her. Two days! What had happened in the meantime? She could have been doing anything! *How did I get here?*

'In your car.'

*When?*

'Half an hour ago,' he repeated patiently. 'I think we'd better get you to hospital.'

*What's happening to me?*

'You seem to be suffering from amnesia.'

She felt her head for bumps. *Concussion, you mean?*

'No.'

Questions crowded into her brain. Why? What had she done in all that lost time? What if she'd disgraced herself in some way?

How *did I get here?*

'In your car. Come along. I'll take you to Casualty.'

She began to fear that something deeply compromising had taken place between them. Yet his manner didn't suggest this.

*What happened?*

'Um, Isobel, I'm a bit at a loss.' His hesitancy alarmed her further. She'd done something awful! 'It might be better if you remembered for yourself. Let's see what the doctors advise.'

Supposing she'd propositioned him, undressed herself?

*Why was I in your bathroom?*

'The downstairs loo's broken.'

They left the house and got into his car. All the way to the hospital she cudgelled her brains. Where had she been? What had she done? She'd been sitting in the cottage watching some satirical news thing, then she'd found herself in Harry's bathroom.

*Did something awful happen?* she whispered.

'Listen,' he said, after a moment. 'If you find, after a while, that nothing comes back, I promise I'll try and fill in the gaps. OK?'

*How did I get to your house?*

'You drove there, Isobel.' Something in his tone made her wonder if she'd already asked this.

It was midnight before she was in bed in Jan's spare room.

'Of course I'll look after her. You poor, poor lamb!' Jan had cried.

So here she was, tucked up in nice cuddly winceyette sheets with a mug of cocoa. She wasn't to worry. It was a case of temporary short-term memory loss, probably brought on by stress. Apparently it was not uncommon. She was signed off work for a fortnight. There was a tablet for her to take if she found she couldn't sleep. Tomorrow her GP would call and talk things over. He would also take a look at her throat and find out what was wrong with her voice. It felt like something was stuck, a lump of something, but she couldn't see it in the mirror. She may or may not recover the missing memories. Rest was the key.

She pulled the sheets up to her chin. The hot-water bottle clucked as she moved her feet. There was even a teddy bear for her. She looked at his battered face on the pillow beside her. He had been fiercely loved. One amber glass eye was hanging off. She could see the thread attached to the hook. It had belonged to Jan's son Hugo, and he was long dead. She felt a tear ooze. Poor bear with nobody to cherish it except Isobel, who was incapable of love.

She was walking down the long steep road that led to the village where Tatiana had lived. Sheer chalky banks rose up on either side. That was the place where they'd had a secret den. They used to escape from Perpetua – Tatiana's little sister who always wanted to tag along – and play for hours, hidden from the occasional passing car by the curtain of old man's beard that hung from the trees overhead. Today she hurried on because she needed to find Tatiana's house. When she arrived it was lying vacant, as she'd known it would be. The door was open. She went in and climbed the stairs to the empty blue-walled room that had belonged to her friend. She checked. Everything was as it should be. She could leave now.

Then she was outside in the open air. It was a sunny morning. The hill rose impossibly steep in front of her, but she began climbing up the road. Soon she discovered that if she bunched every muscle and willed herself to do it, she could fly. Before long she was level with the treetops. Ornate golden birds with filigree tails were flying alongside. Higher and higher she flew into the blue morning, laughing at how easy it all was.

When Isobel woke she knew instantly where she was and what had happened. Her mind raced to greet the memory of her missing days. There was nothing there. She tried again, still confident, but was confounded once more. It was like running a finger along the shelf for a familiar volume and encountering the empty space where it should be. She clenched her fists in frustration. What had happened? Why couldn't she remember? But anger would get her nowhere.

Calmly, she summoned the last few hours in the cottage. There she was in front of the TV. How was she feeling? The emotions crept back. She was feeling angry and disappointed because Johnny hadn't come. Isobel lay pondering. Some flicker of recognition told her this was the key. Supposing something so awful had happened that blocking it out was her only way of coping with it? Dear God! I never did, did I? The question swelled into conviction: Johnny had come and they'd spent the night together! In horror she flung back the covers and searched her body for proof. There was a small bruise inside her left thigh. How had it got there? What have I done? What have I let him do? She curled up under the covers, trembling. Her flesh felt violated. Had it just been a kiss, then she'd thrown him out? Had he seduced her, forced her? Or had she thrown herself at him? Until she remembered she was powerless to cope. What kind of sin was it? How big, how heavy to bear?

She ground her knuckles into her temples as if to gouge out the truth. Think! Think! She tried to steady herself. Well, what was the worst that could happen? That she never remembered and was obliged to seek information from Johnny. Would the humiliation be preferable to ignorance? Could she see her way to explaining about her amnesia and simply asking if she'd seen him at all after their conversation in the street outside Will and Annie's house? And if nothing *had* happened, he would presumably say, 'No,' in a puzzled voice and that would be that. Her pulse slowed again. Patience, she must have patience. It might yet all come back to her. There was no urgency.

Unless she'd had unprotected sex, of course.

She snatched up the alarm clock. Eight-thirty. For a full minute her mind was too terrified to make the simple calculation that less than seventy-two hours had elapsed and emergency contraception was still a possibility. A voice in her head protested that the morning-after pill wasn't ethical, it prevented implantation, not fertilization. Surely as a Christian she wasn't contemplating it? But it was the only sensible thing. It's a grey area, she told herself. Better that than an illegitimate child. Almost sick with panic she stumbled to Jan's bathroom, showered and pulled on yesterday's clothes.

Jan looked up from her *Guardian* crossword as Isobel entered the kitchen.

'Hello, darling girl. Sleep well? What can I get you for breakfast?'

Isobel tried to speak. Her throat and jaw were locked in some kind of rigor and she couldn't even whisper. After a moment Jan handed her the paper and biro.

'I've got to see a doctor,' wrote Isobel.

'You are doing,' pointed out Jan. 'He's calling at eleven.'

Isobel thought swiftly. Yes, that would still be soon enough. She nodded and tried to smile. 'I'd forgotten,' she scribbled.

'Sit down. Croissants? Cup of coffee?'

Time passed with agonizing slowness. Isobel flipped through the magazines and paper Jan had given her, trying to hold down the panic that surged every few minutes. She told herself that there was nothing she could do, but her mind still hammered itself against the blank wall in her memory. What, *what* had happened? Then it occurred to her that Harry had promised to fill in any gaps. He would not have said this if he knew nothing. And if he had any information, it could only mean she had confided in him. Of course! Of course she'd have confessed. Moments later she heard his car pull up.

There was some murmured conversation between him and Jan in the hallway before he came into the room where she was sitting.

'How are you?'

Jan tactfully retreated to the kitchen.

Harry sat beside Isobel on the sofa. 'Remembered anything?'

*Half*, she tried to say, but her throat seized up again and she only managed a choking sound. She mimed scribbling and he handed her his Filofax. She found an empty page and hesitated before selecting the words and forcing herself to write: 'What if I've done something foolish and need emergency contraception?'

He read it and flushed. 'Ah. Good point. Right. Um, well . . .'

It was true! She scrawled: 'I told you?'

'Yes. But, er, not in that kind of detail. I didn't inquire.'

She made another choking sound, then bit her lips hard. So I failed. After all that hard work, all that struggling with temptation, I failed. Johnny. Johnny. What had it been like?

He put a hand over hers. 'But you still can't actually remember?'

She shook her head.

'Look, wouldn't the simplest thing be to get him over here so you can talk?' He saw her flinch. 'I know it's horrible, but at least you'd know. Shall I give him a ring for you?'

Seeing the good sense of this she nodded. He took his Filofax and went across to the phone.

Deep breaths, deep breaths. He'd probably be out. It might be days before he'd be able to find the time to drive down. Well, she'd have to ask the doctor for the pill anyway to be on the safe side. 'Unprotected intercourse with casual male partner', they'd put on her notes. How could she bear it? Better that than – Her heart lurched as she heard the phone being answered.

'Hello, Davy?' said Harry. 'It's Harry Preece here.'

Isobel shot across to him gesturing wildly. He fended her off. 'Have you got a moment?'

Isobel listened in impotent horror as Harry explained she'd lost her memory and arranged for Davy to call round. By the time she'd prised the Filofax from his grip and written in desperate capitals '<u>JOHNNY</u>, NOT DAVY!' Harry had hung up.

'No, Isobel. You told me it was Davy. Sorry.'

'Never!' She thrust the word under his nose.

'Isobel, I can't believe you'd have lied to me about something like that.'

She pressed her hands to her cheeks. He was right. Unless she'd been trying to protect Johnny? There had to be some explanation.

'When you came back from holiday you confessed to me that you'd slept with someone. I admit I assumed it was Johnny, but you said it was Davy.'

She was shaking her head.

'We talked. You assured me it wouldn't happen again. However,' he frowned at the page she had scrawled on, colouring slightly, 'when I spoke to you yesterday evening you confessed you'd, er, spent the previous night with him. Davy, that is.'

Impossible! She reached for the Filofax again. 'Did you believe me?'

'Yes. Yes, absolutely. To the point of losing my rag and swearing at you, I'm afraid.'

Tears stung her eyes. It had to be false! And yet here was the man she trusted most in the world insisting it was true. Her fingers trembled as she wrote, 'But why would I do it?'

'I can't answer that for you,' he said.

She tilted her head back and looked up at the ceiling so that her tears wouldn't spill over.

'Isobel, I've mishandled this whole thing disastrously,' said Harry. His distress was evident. 'I've – Look, I'm afraid I've had to contact the Archdeacon. I'm sorry. I'm completely out of my depth. If it was me yelling at you that triggered this amnesia, then I'm deeply, deeply sorry. I was – Um, and, er, on top of everything else we appear to have triggered another bout of – of paranormal, um, between us.'

*What?*

'Nothing to worry about, apparently. Gabriel has been round. Just a spot of poltergeist activity, he says. Not uncommon when tension's running high. Unlikely to recur, in his view.'

Something icy was clutching at her throat. *What happened?*

'Um, a glass sort of whizzed across the room at me.'

*What – on its own?*

He nodded.

*Are you sure?*

'Yes. And, to be honest, it was completely, utterly, bloody terrifying.'

If anyone else had been telling her this she'd have dismissed him as a madman. *So . . . what does Gabriel think?*

'That the whole thing's totally understandable.' She saw a glimmer of a smile. 'Most sane people want to throw things at me.'

Before she could respond the doorbell rang. It was Davy.

He came in seeming the same as ever. She wouldn't have known from looking at him that they were supposed to have shared two nights of passion. Nothing but concern showed on his face.

'Y'aal reet?' he asked, sitting down. His eyes sped between her and Harry. 'He says you've lost your memory.'

She nodded and began to speak, but her throat closed up again. She gestured to Harry to speak for her.

'Um,' said Harry, who had been about to leave them alone together. 'Right. Well, Isobel's lost her voice, so . . . Er, am I right in thinking you went to see her in Northumberland?'

'Aye,' agreed Davy. 'New Year's Eve, it was.'

'And you spent the night with her?'

There was a pause. Davy's eyes caught Isobel's fleetingly. 'Well, aye. Oh! You think – ?' He laughed. 'I wish! Nah, I was downstairs on the settee, me.'

Thank God! Oh, thank God! thought Isobel. She turned to Harry. *You see?*

'Aaargh,' said Harry. 'Um, so you're saying you didn't have sex?'

'Of course not!' He turned in shock from one to the other. 'Isobel's always made it quite clear that's out of the question.'

There was a long silence. Tears of relief slid down Isobel's cheeks.

Harry cleared his throat. 'Right. And supposing I told you that Isobel confessed to me, before she lost her memory, that you'd slept together?'

Davy was motionless.

'And that she spent the night before last at your house?' Getting no reply he pressed on, 'Oh, come on, Davy, this isn't helping. Isobel needs to know quite urgently if there's any possibility she might be pregnant.'

The word seemed to fill the room.

'Not by me she's not!' insisted Davy. 'Like I said, I was on the settee. Look, let me talk to her in private.'

Harry slipped out and closed the door.

*Are you telling the truth?* whispered Isobel.

''Course I'm bloody not!' hissed Davy. 'I'm trying not to land you in it. You really, really cannot remember?'

*No.*

'Why not? You weren't drunk.'

*So we – ?*

'Aw, ha'away! I'll admit I was surprised you didn't hoy w' oot, like, but I wasn't about to argue.'

Isobel sat numb with shock. Here were the missing pieces. She tried to make sense of them, but they felt as if they'd come from a different puzzle. Surely at any moment someone would point this out and they could all laugh at their stupidity.

*What . . . happened?*

He was covered in confusion. 'Isobel, man.'

*What?*

'What d'you mean, "what"? You're embarrassing me. It was . . . I div'n' kna, the usual stuff. Incredible, like,' he amended, 'but – Well, you were there.'

*Did we . . . take precautions?*

'Aye, of course! I had one condom in my wallet and I nicked the other from the bathroom cupboard, remember?'

Twice!

Davy was clutching her hands. 'How come you've forgotten? Isobel, what's happened to you?'

*It's stress*, she tried to say.

'Because of what we did? Isobel, if I thought for one minute –' He broke off.

She could see something black in his hair, like spider's legs. Had he got stitches?

*Have you cut yourself?* she whispered.

He stared. 'Can you not remember running us to Casualty?'

*No. What happened?*

'Oh, split ma heed on the kitchen-cupboard door.' He watched for a reaction.

*Poor old you.*

'Will it all come back to you?'

*They don't know. Maybe.*

'Isobel, if this is my fault, I'll never forgive myself.'

She was overcome by pity for both of them and began to weep; dry choking sobs with no tears to soothe the pain.

'Isobel! Isobel, don't, man,' begged Davy. He tried to take her in his arms. 'Please. I'm sorry, I'm sorry. I should never have done it.'

She wanted to say she didn't blame him, but something was happening to her. She couldn't move her hands. They were bending inwards, turning into claws. The room was growing black. She tried to scream for help, but every muscle was locked rigid.

Davy sprang to his feet. 'Harry! Quick!'

Harry and Jan came running. Panic swirled overhead. I must be dying.

'I'll call an ambulance,' came Jan's voice.

'Wait,' she heard Harry say. 'The doctor's here.'

She was aware of the GP standing over her and saying, 'It's just a panic attack. Do you have a paper bag?'

The snow had mostly gone, eaten away by the rain that had fallen all day. Isobel watched the runlets wandering down Jan's french windows. She was sitting in a reclining chair with a blanket over her legs like an old lady in a nursing home. Here and there drops hung and shuddered in the wind. The darkening garden was suspended upside down in each one, tiny, until the bead collapsed and trailed away.

She ought to be thinking it all through, trying to come to terms with the fact that she was the sort of woman who fornicated and was subject to panic attacks and bouts of amnesia. Instead she was watching the rain and remembering how, as a child, she used to go round with her mother delivering newsletters for the local history society. She would sit watching raindrops on the windscreen while her mother chatted on doorsteps. What if the car drove away with her in it? Mum explained that this was impossible. Cars needed someone to drive them. At worst the car might begin to roll slowly if it was parked on a hill, but only if the brake wasn't on. She showed Isobel the handbrake and how to pull it up. Try. There, you see? You're perfectly safe. But Isobel sat in dread, freezing at each tiny tick or creak. Hurry up, hurry up! Sometimes she had nightmares about the car careering off down a steep hill with no grown-up there to stop it.

She ought to be praying. Her intercessions notebook was at home, but Jan would be able to lend her a Bible. She ought to be repenting. Forgive me, Lord. Davy, everything, I didn't mean – And there were the thank-you letters to be written. Credit-card bill. Sue and Mike, they'd be back from holiday and she must visit them, or they'd think people had stopped caring about Hannah. What about her parents? She must contact them when they got back from holiday. What day was it? Grant us true repentance, forgive us our sins of negligence and weakness and our deliberate sins. Things rotting in her fridge from before Christmas. Key to the cottage – she must find it and post it to Annie. Harry was taking over her preaching commitments until her voice got better. Ear, nose and throat specialist when the appointment came through. Forgive me.

She clamped the limp paper bag to her mouth and breathed in and out. Why was she being so pathetic? How long was she going to lie like an invalid, allowing herself to become infantilized by Jan and Harry's mollycoddling? It was pure self-indulgence. Surely she could pull herself together, make a list?

Her attention was caught by a movement in the dusk. A rag of white plastic was snagged fluttering on the hedge. It made her think of ghosts, of Agnes fleeing from her cell. A new thought struck her: in all her careful research Isobel had been so concerned to establish what Agnes was escaping from that she had never stopped to wonder where she was heading.

The problem absorbed her until the garden had melted in darkness and all she could see was her own reflection brooding in the glass.

## CHAPTER 23

Harry and Jan protected her, defending her from the well-meaning and curious. Harry had informed the parish that she was suffering from nervous exhaustion and laryngitis. He emphasized that what she needed most was rest, and discouraged people from calling or phoning. Dozens of cards came through her letterbox and bunches of early daffodils were left on her doorstep. The phone fell eerily silent for long periods at a time. Those who did ring were greeted by a message in Harry's voice, briefly explaining that Isobel was on sick leave and asking them to ring him at the vicarage if it was urgent.

He phoned Isobel's parents to put them in the picture. The following day a big bunch of flowers was delivered. It was a blaze of sunny colour and she knew Mrs Knox had instructed the florist to send 'something cheerful'. It was followed by a letter saying, 'if there's anything we can do ...' What Mr Knox made of it all Isobel didn't know. He probably thought she was daft to burn herself out for something that was basically a load of pious clap-trap. Maybe she'd been driven partly by a desire to impress him. Do your best, stick to your guns, slog on with it – these were the things he respected. And where had they landed her?

Over the following days Isobel felt increasingly helpless. There was a boundary of anxiety round each activity: fear of being unable to communicate, fear of another panic attack, fear of losing her memory again when she was miles from home. Driving was impossible. Even leaving the house became an ordeal. Each day the net tightened and her life shrank a little more. Jan drove her to the supermarket or to the doctor's. Drew and Natalie also offered their chauffeuring services and sent her a box of goodies and a bottle of tonic wine 'to buck her up'. She knew this was a joke, but it made her want to cry.

Davy defied Harry's injunction and called round repeatedly, but she hid from him. Occasionally she glimpsed him from an upstairs window, and saw, guiltily, how miserable he looked. In the end he weighed so heavily on her conscience that one evening she did open her door to him. Outwardly he appeared as breezy as ever and she was surprised by a momentary pleasure. She remembered that he was, or had been, one of her best friends.

'Buggers at work giving me a hard time,' he told her, as they sat in her study. 'We were called out to this woman's house. The neighbours reckoned she was dead. They'd knocked and when she didn't answer they looked through the letterbox and they could see her lying on the hall floor. A couple of us broke the door down, but it was tricky, like, because of how she was lying. Anyway, me mate was first in, gans, "Aye, she's dead." I'd just got hold of her to move her away from the door, when her arm grabbed me roond the neck. Jesus! Sorry – I tell you, though, I yelled. Bloody hell.'

*So she wasn't dead?*

'No. Died later in hospital, mind,' he said. 'I'm never going to hear the last of it. The bastards rigged up this fake arm in my locker which fell out when I opened the door.'

She laughed hoarsely.

'So how are you?' he asked.

The tension hidden behind his garrulousness became visible. The thought of what they'd done broke in on her again. It was as if he had pornographic films of her stored in his memory banks.

*Surviving.*

'Back at work yet?'

She shook her head.

He looked surprised. 'And they've still not got your voice sorted? Do they not know what's wrong?'

*No.*

'And there's nowt you can be getting on with in the meantime?'

Did he think she was skiving? Her throat cramped tightly. She felt her fragile composure start to crumble.

Instantly he was all contrition. 'Ee, I'm sorry. I was just asking, like. I didn't mean you should be working, only, well, it's been a while now. I thought you were over it.'

He needs me to be over it, she thought. And for his sake, she ought to get a grip. But it was impossible. She was trembling, pressing a hand to her mouth, blinking the tears away.

*Could you please go?* she choked.

She saw the raw pain on his face. 'Isobel, man! I've only just got here. I won't say another word. There's nowt I can dee?'

Just go, she thought. Go.

But he stayed, trying to care for her, insisting on getting her tea, wanting to run errands for her, making her lie on the sofa so that he could stroke her forehead. In the end she feigned sleep, hiding her face from him, until at last he tiptoed out, shutting the door softly behind him.

I can't take it, she screamed inside. I can't stand him near me.

Harry called round later that evening and saw the state she was in.

'Isobel, this won't do. I'll tell him you need a bit more time to recover.'

*But he'll be hurt.*

'I know, but he's doing more harm than good. He won't want that.'

She felt heartless, but agreed to let Harry speak to him.

But the following evening Davy called round again. Harry had let her down. He promised he'd talk to him, she thought, and now I'll have to do it myself.

She tried to swallow. *Davy, I –*

'Did you send the vicar round to tell me to back off?' he demanded.

She gestured in despair. *I'm just not coping.*

'You did!' he said. 'I cannot believe you did that. Why can't you say it to my face?'

*Because –* She turned away.

'Isobel, you know I'd do anything for you. Anything. Even not see you, if that's what you really want.'

*I'm sorry.*

'Just tell me yourself. Don't send *him* round. He's never liked me.'

*Harry? Oh, no, I'm sure you're wrong.*

'He blames me for all this. I can tell.'

She sobbed in despair. *No. He blames me.*

297

'What? Has he been upsetting you?' he exclaimed. 'He wants bloody sorting out.'

*Please, just listen. I meant it's my fault. He's right to* –

'No. It's my fault. If I hadn't led you astray ... All I want is the chance to make it up to you.'

*There's nothing you can do.*

'Except leave you alone?'

She nodded, hating to do this to him.

'Oh, well.' He made a heartbreaking attempt at resuming his jaunty manner. 'I'll be on my way, then.'

After a swift inner struggle she managed to say, *Couldn't you talk to Father McGee?*

She heard a sharp breath. For a second he looked as though he wanted to hit her.

'You told me not to.'

*When?*

'When do you think?' he snapped. 'I'd've been by now if you hadn't made me promise.'

*I'm sorry. I had no right.*

'Oh, well,' he said again. 'No harm done.'

She waited for him to say he was on his way, but he lingered.

'Can you ... put some kind of timescale on this?' he asked. 'I mean, when can I see you again?'

*I don't know.*

'Rough guess?'

*I said, I don't know*, she cried desperately.

'Well, you know where I am. Keep me posted.'

Oh, please let him leave me alone now, she prayed as she watched him walk away. Don't let me be any crueller to him. He doesn't deserve it.

The phone was ringing. It was her mother. Isobel listened as she left a message. 'Hello, hello! It's Mum here. I know you can't talk to me, but we just wanted to keep in touch. Um, so, here I am, keeping in touch, ha ha. Darling, you do know that if you need a bolt-hole, you can always come here for a bit. That's not supposed to put pressure on you. Just a thought. And we missed you at Christmas. Oh, here's Dad. He wants a word.'

Isobel started. Mr Knox was not a great one for the phone.

'Hello, Isobel.' She felt tears welling up at the sound of his voice. 'Are they looking after you properly? That vicar of yours sounds a sensible chap. I gather you're off to see the specialist. Hope that goes well.' There was a silence. 'Well, here's your mother again.'

'You look after yourself. I wish there was more I could do. But remember – any time! 'Bye.'

Isobel listened to the tape rewinding itself. I want to go home. But running home to Mum was admitting defeat. I'm a grown-up now. I'll pop back at Easter, like I planned. But Easter was so distant. Oh, why am I being so pathetic? she raged at herself. If only I could speak, everything would be OK.

Her voice loss had long since ceased to be an amusing inconvenience. All she could manage was a hoarse whisper, which sounded so painful, although it wasn't, that her friends winced and begged her to rest.

The following day, without warning, her condition worsened. She made herself venture to the corner shop to buy a paper and was caught in the street by Kath Bollom. Kath's greedy eyes feasted on her as she delivered her New Year monologue on the iniquities of dustmen and the lack of decent films on the telly.

'So I hear you've not been so good, then? What's wrong?'

Isobel began to answer, but suddenly her throat and jaw clenched so tight that not even a single word could pass her lips. Kath waited encouragingly. Isobel began to panic. She knew the signs by now. This was what had happened that awful time at Jan's. Oh, God! Not now! I can't have a full-blown attack out here in the street in front of her. She pointed desperately at her throat and fled back into the house.

Half an hour later she was still curled in a heap on the floor rocking herself when the door opened and Harry came in.

He knelt beside her. She felt his hand on her shoulder.

'Come along. Let's get you on to the sofa.'

Gradually, with his arm round her and his voice reassuring her, she began to unclench.

'Sorry to let myself in like that,' he said. 'Kath rang me and said you were "acting funny".'

*I couldn't open my mouth.*

'Yes, Kath's a bit like that when she gets started.'

*No, literally. My jaw locked. Then I panicked.*

'Five minutes of Kath Bollom is enough to give James Bond a panic attack.' He gave her hand a squeeze. 'Try not to worry. It might be a one-off. You've got an appointment to see the specialist. You can mention this to him.'

*Or her.*

'Or her.'

She saw he was winding her up on purpose and tried to smile for him.

But the attacks continued. She never knew when it would happen, and this made her more and more reluctant to risk speaking. Sometimes the tension in her throat was so bad she couldn't swallow and began to choke on her saliva. This triggered another humiliating panic attack. Eventually she only dared speak to Jan and Harry. Even Natalie and Drew were too overpowering; she prayed that they would understand, but it was impossible to believe they didn't feel hurt by her rejection of them. It was simpler to resort to writing for anything other than the most routine exchanges. Jan took her to the stationer's and she bought a notebook that fitted neatly in her handbag. Something about the size and shape of it was pleasing and the feel of its spiral binding reassured her when she groped in her bag to check it was there.

It became clear that this was not just a case of a fortnight's rest to sort her out. She went back to the doctor and was signed off indefinitely. Every public aspect of her ministry was disrupted. She couldn't preach, lead worship, advise, go visiting or even pick up the phone. Her sense of who she was eroded away. All her life she'd fought to hold her own in conversation and insist, by the way she spoke, on being taken seriously. As a teenager words had been her only way of counteracting the impact of her bust. She had refused to be treated as a dumb blonde. But now she was one. People began addressing her loudly and slowly, or they dropped their voices too, and communicated in conspiratorial whispers. They tried to spare her feelings by answering for her or speaking over the top of her head, demoting her to the status of a child.

Where was God in all this? Was He not the same God, slow to anger and abounding in steadfast love? She knew He was, but she didn't feel it. Perhaps she never truly had. Her faith had been so bound up in her profession that there was nothing left now that her powers had deserted her. Had Christ been nothing more than her superior in the workplace? She felt as though she'd been sacked without warning. She dared not seek an explanation. Gross professional misconduct? Spiritual fraud? Going to church was impossible. The pews were full of the people she had been called to serve but had failed. Sue and Mike – she'd simply dropped them, abandoned them to their grief. And there was her Inquirers' Group, left struggling without her to lead them. The Youth Group were forced to meet at another venue, and Harry was running the sessions for her.

She sat at home with her service book trying each morning and evening to read the office. It felt like wading through a manual in a foreign language. How could she have been reduced from full and active Christian ministry to this desperate point in so short a time? The speed of her collapse terrified her.

One morning as she sat with her open Bible, a tap on the study window startled her. It was Father McGee. Isobel would have screamed if she could. There was no escape: he'd seen her. She had to go to the door and let him in. His large outline loomed through the coloured glass. Oh, please, don't let him be too angry, she whimpered, as she opened the door.

'Hello,' he said. 'I've brought you these from the presbytery garden.'

It was a little bunch of snowdrops. Isobel crumpled.

'Now, now,' he said, coming in and ushering her to her study chair. 'I'm not cross with you, darling. I've just come to assure you of my prayers. You're not to worry about young Davy. I'll take care of him. Now then. Now, now. Will I make you a cup of tea?' He clucked around her.

*I'm so sorry*, she choked.

'Ah, your poor voice!' he cried. 'I'll make you a toddy. I've got me flask, like the drunken Paddy I am.'

*I can't possibly.*

'Sure you can.'

*No, really* —

'You bloody will. Don't you "no, really" *me*! Is this what Harry has to put up with? Do as Father says, you wicked girl. Jesus, Mary and Joseph!' He swept out to the kitchen. She could hear him muttering, 'Bloody Anglicans. They think the Church is a democracy.' He came back a few minutes later with a steaming mug. 'Drink that, now.'

She sipped obediently.

He sat and dropped his mad-Irish-priest act. 'Seriously, now, are you all right?' he asked. 'Harry's looking after you properly?'

She nodded.

'Ah, you'll be all right. He's a good man,' said Father McGee. 'A good man. For a Prod.' He sighed and got to his feet. 'Shall I say a prayer? Will you accept a blessing off an old papist?'

She crumpled again and nodded. He laid his hands on her head and prayed for her, then slipped away. She sat clutching the mug and trembling. The little bunch of snowdrops lay on her desk, their stalks wrapped in tin foil. She imagined him gathering them from along the presbytery hedge, his big face getting redder from stooping. Oh, I can't bear this kindness. If he'd cut her dead at fraternals, she'd have understood, but to come round like this without a word of condemnation ... At least she knew Davy was in a safe pair of hands. When she was better she'd go round and thank Father McGee properly. Surely a few more weeks' rest would do it?

All her hopes were pinned on the ENT specialist. It could all still turn out to be something ridiculously simple, like a fragment of fishbone lodged in her throat. Jan drove her to the hospital and waited for her. But the specialist found nothing, no physical cause for her voice loss. She suggested, given Isobel's profession, that it might be a case of strain brought on by overuse. She was referred back to her GP, who in turn referred her to a speech therapist, and hinted that at some stage she might find it helpful to see a psychiatrist.

This brought out into the open what Isobel had dreaded all along – that her condition was psychosomatic. She nursed this fear secretly for days. It made her more determined than ever to turn her life round and pull herself together, but the harder she tried the worse things grew. It seemed that she had only to focus upon something as a target for the task to become impossible. She tried to sort out her correspondence one evening and ended frozen in indecision. I can't even put them into piles, she thought. I'll make a list. But she found she couldn't get past the first item: *Archdeacon*. The day of her visit drew relentlessly nearer. She had to cope. It was vital to present a rational front to him, to convince him that this was nothing to worry about. Oh, don't let him say I must resign!

The day came. Jan had offered to take her, but it was Harry's car that pulled up outside her house.

'Change of plan,' he said, a little self-consciously. 'I think it's important I speak to Bazza-boy as well. He needs to know the, um, full picture.'

Isobel flushed crimson. *You think I'd try to cover it up?*

'What? Oh, no, no. Of course not. I meant, he probably ought to know what I'm – my version. Of things. How it all strikes me, that is.' He seemed to be getting tangled. 'All I mean is, there's stuff I ought in all honesty to tell him.'

There was a long silence. Suddenly it dawned on her what he was driving at, the cause of his embarrassment. *Do you think – What if – What if it's all in my mind?* she blurted.

'Well, I don't think that would be too incredible, would it?' he said reasonably. 'Physical and mental well-being are all bound up in each other.'

She went cold. He's thought it all along. Now he was going to tell the Archdeacon. He was right. In all honesty it had to be said. And the Archdeacon was no fool. He could work it out for himself. For all she knew it was the conclusion everyone had come to ages ago. Perhaps they even suspected that at some level she was controlling her symptoms, malingering. Was everyone's sympathy

303

and patience wearing thin? Even Harry's, though he never once grumbled?

'Isobel, there's nothing shameful about it.'

There is, there is, she thought. I can't be one of those weak, hysterical women. It has to be voice strain. It has to be. She glanced at Harry's profile. Was he hoping she'd resign so he could get a proper curate? Was that what he was going to tell Bazza-boy? They might agree that she was using up a much-needed place that an abler man or woman could fill. Her job was on the line.

It was with this thought that she entered the Archdeacon's study.

She passed out cold and collapsed on his carpet.

When she came round she was lying on a sofa. His wife was setting a cup of tea on a little table beside her.

'Are you any better, my dear?'

She sat up. Her head swam. *Goodness. I've never done that before.*

'Not to worry. You just rest a little. I'll tell my husband you're alive and well.' She smiled reassuringly and crept out.

Through the open door Isobel glimpsed Harry sitting tense, head in hands, like a husband outside the labour ward. *Dear God! What have I done? This is the end.* In a strange way she couldn't care. She waited, detached, for the Archdeacon to appear and announce her fate. What was his name? She didn't want to end up calling him Bazza-boy. What was he called?

After a while he came in and perched on the edge of a chair nearby. Barrington. That was it. Barrington Lindop. He had his fingers laced tightly together – perhaps he feared she'd swoon off again – but he was looking at her kindly enough.

'Are you feeling a little recovered?'

*Yes, thank you.*

'Well, I won't tax you with any questions now. But perhaps if you could contact my secretary and rearrange . . . ?'

The thought of postponing it was too much. *Do you want me to resign?* she whispered.

'Gracious me, no! It's not come to that. But we can discuss all this later.'

*Please, I need to talk now. All this waiting. Waiting for specialists, waiting –*

'I take your point. Well,' he paused, 'it was on my mind to sug-gest you might find it helpful to talk things over with someone outside the situation. There's a retired bishop we sometimes use . . .'

'Use'. His voice continued talking, but she couldn't take it in. 'A retired bishop we sometimes use'. She was being fed into the diocesan mechanism for dealing with naughty priests. This wasn't a helpful suggestion. It was the polite Anglican equivalent of an order. If she didn't comply, she'd find her curacy at an end with no guarantee of further employment.

'. . . and after we've heard his feedback,' the Archdeacon was saying, 'we'll be in a better position to make an informed decision. We'd normally ask you to meet him four times. How does that sound?'

She nodded. *Fine.*

'Good, good.' He beamed at her. Perhaps he would have been a little brusquer – more like a manager and less like a kindly uncle – had it not been for her invalidish posture on his sofa. 'How about a top-up? I'll ask my wife to bring the pot.'

She was left to rest. Outside someone was snipping a hedge or pruning roses. She could hear the snick-snick of the secateurs. From the Archdeacon's study came the murmur of voices. Well, after her performance earlier there was no point fearing what Harry might say. She'd amply demonstrated her fragile mental state. There was no longer any hiding from the truth.

Her first session with the speech therapist was the following morn-ing. She would have postponed it, had it not been for the thought of waiting weeks for another appointment. She arrived in the waiting room feeling wobbly and fully aware of her pitiful situation. She, who had always refused to be intimidated, was now a pathetic wreck, reliant on Jan's services as chauffeur and interpreter and barely able to leave the house for fear of being spoken to by some well-meaning parishioner. She was sure the therapist would take one look at her and pack her off to the loony-bin.

Mercifully it was not like that. The therapist, a woman not much older than Isobel, began by taking a careful case history. The sim-ple fact of seeing someone nod in recognition as she described her

305

symptoms filled Isobel with relief. She poured out all her foolish fears, her panic, her sense of disintegrating and the therapist pointed out that this was entirely natural. It became clear that her approach was to concentrate on the physiological aspect of Isobel's condition, not delve into the psychological causes. Thank God, thought Isobel. 'Muscular constriction' sounded so much more manageable than the 'hysterical aphonia' her GP had mentioned.

Over the following weeks the relaxation techniques and breathing exercises the therapist gave her began to take effect. Little by little they helped her regain her confidence and control over her throat muscles. Most days, if she remembered to stay calm, she was able to manage her scratchy whisper. She learnt to recognize the onset of a choking attack and try to prevent it developing.

Jan drove Isobel to the address the Archdeacon had given her. On the journey she tried to compose an account of her breakdown which she would be able to repeat without too much difficulty. 1. She had been overworking. 2. She had fallen in love with a married man. 3. She had underestimated the degree of sexual frustration she had been experiencing, which had led her to seek relief with a man she didn't love.

'Well, this looks like it,' said Jan, pulling up outside a large house. 'Ooh, la–di–*dah*. Very grahnd.'

*It's divided into flats*, said Isobel. *He doesn't own it.* She wondered why she was defending this retired bishop she'd never met. Perhaps because it was so vital that she should like and trust him, that he shouldn't turn out to be a pompous old nincompoop.

'I'll tootle into the town and come back in an hour,' said Jan. 'Will that give you long enough?'

*I jolly well hope so*, muttered Isobel. *Thanks.* She waved Jan off and went up the drive to the big door and knocked.

Her first impression of Bishop Theodore was of his immense kindness. He welcomed her in and shook her hand. When she met his eye she saw with relief that he was also shrewd and intelligent. If her problems were to be laid out under anybody's scrutiny, then let it be his.

They went to his study and while he made some coffee she took the opportunity to snoop at his bookshelves. It was a fine collection. He was clearly as much a Bible scholar as a systematic theologian, if his books reflected his life's work. And he had not stopped thinking upon retirement. There were many recent publications on his shelves and half a dozen periodicals on his coffee table.

'So, Isobel,' he began, when they'd got the preliminaries out of the way, 'it sounds like you've been having a rotten time.'

*I've been very weak and stupid*, she said.

'Perhaps you can tell me what's happened?'

She took a deep breath, remembering all the techniques she'd been taught, and gave him the account she had prepared.

He sat back reflecting. Eventually he said, 'Why do you regard that as weak and stupid?'

*Because it is.*

'Why was it weak and stupid to sleep with Davy? Why not rebellious, for instance? Or unfortunate? Or natural and understandable?'

She tried to think.

'Why those words?' he prompted. When she didn't answer he said, 'Perhaps you might like to ponder that.'

She nodded.

They were silent for some time.

'Did you tell me the name of the other man, the one you say you're in love with?'

*No. It's not import* – Her throat was closing up. Relax, she told herself. It was too late. Her jaw was locked rigid. She struck her fist on her knee in frustration and reached in her bag for her notebook.

'This happens sometimes,' she wrote.

'When does it happen? Randomly?'

She was about to nod. Was it random, though? 'I hadn't stopped to ask,' she wrote.

'Worth asking, I'd've thought,' he commented.

His perspicacity was beginning to make her feel hounded.

'Is this too much?' he asked. 'Let's just sit for a bit.' He leant his head back in his leather armchair and closed his eyes.

She watched him. He had mad tufty eyebrows, white, like what remained of his hair. In repose he might have been any sweet old man having forty winks, but she knew his brain was alert on her behalf, slicing through the thicket of her problems to let in the light. He was frowning, nodding occasionally. Eventually he opened his eyes and smiled at her.

'Which of the following would best describe you: child of God, servant of God, friend of God?'

*Servant*, she replied without hesitation. Then Harry's voice came back to her: *Do you think God might quite like your company, even when you're not trying to serve Him?* She found she was battling with tears.

'Another thing to think about,' said the bishop gently.

Over the course of her four visits to him she began to feel she was making some kind of sense of what had happened. Bishop Theodore told her she might have to restrain her librarian's skills, her impulse to solve problems by classifying and shelving them. The accuracy of this description made her wince and smile. He asked her to reflect on the significance of her amnesia and voice loss. He put it to her that she might be exercising a kind of subconscious censorship. Why might that be? Seeing her frustrated struggles, he counselled patience.

But patience, hard thing! Perhaps she was making progress, but it was unbearably slow. There was a limit to how long she would be able to sit in Asleby waiting for things to get better. She felt like a ghost trapped between two worlds until its unfinished tasks were completed. There had to be something that would jolt her out of this limbo state.

Her mind still returned repeatedly to the gap in her memory. Despite the Bishop's caution she couldn't help thinking that if she could recover those lost days, then everything else would fall into place. She had slept with Davy. This much she had to accept as fact. And yet those few seconds in which she'd been sure it had been Johnny remained far more real. It was as if the imagined event were true and the truth an obscene fabrication.

308

When she woke in the small hours and heard the familiar night-time sounds it was to Johnny that her thoughts crept. He had lain in the same room and heard the same noises: swish of wind in branches, a distant goods train rumbling by. How was he faring? Her mind conjured up his gaunt image standing in the snow, shivering and pleading with her: *Isobel, I need to talk.* Could things have turned out any worse if she had agreed? Was there any purpose in all this? Were their courses linked? Was he lying awake thinking of her, now his wife had gone?

It was early spring. Lent had begun. Some seasonal impulse set Isobel to the task of tidying and purging her files. She was still not well, but her confidence had returned in some measure. It was time to get a grip, to move her life on. Throwing things out was an activity she always found quietly restorative. She couldn't face tackling her recent correspondence yet, but old minutes and letters, out-of-date catalogues – into the bin-liner with them.

She came across the notes she'd taken while researching Agnes. There were photocopies of old maps of the parish. She was about to sling them when she remembered her query. Where had Agnes been fleeing to? Isobel spread out the oldest map. It didn't tell her what the parish would have looked like in the thirteenth century, but she studied it anyway. There was the church. Whenever people claimed to have seen the ghost it was always in the same spot. A white figure running from the cell through the churchyard. Isobel traced the path with her finger. Westwards. In the eighteenth century there had been a scattering of cottages, then farmland. No clues. Then her eye fell on a name, and she knew the answer. 'Windmill Hill Farm.' Agnes the miller's daughter had been heading for home.

## CHAPTER 24

Tatiana and Isobel invented their own language one morning. They worked on it instead of doing their maths. By the end of lunch they could hold simple conversations with each other and pass notes, that nobody else in the whole wide world could understand. There were only two dictionaries, one each, which they swore to guard with their lives and not reveal on pain of being walloped to death by a non-stop spanking machine known in their new language as *arg chargum*.

Mr Woodford intercepted one of their notes and his competitive instincts were roused. He asked them to write him a page-long letter before afternoon break. They obeyed, adding swathes of new vocabulary until they had enough obscenities to do the job properly. *Lob tod arg podwattle, Gar Thotwolb!* they scrawled, laughing till they were almost sick. He bore the page off to the staffroom with a smirk.

Break was over. They sat at their desks waiting. Mr Woodford appeared and flung the paper down.

'Your *code*,' he sneered, 'has no logic to it.'

'That's because it's not a code. It's a language,' they crowed in unison.

'I see.' His face was red. 'Well, I'd like you to write a description of the people who speak this language. Where do they live? What do they look like? Two sides each.'

Huh! They jolly well weren't going to. He'd only told them to in the first place because he knew they'd got him well and truly this time.

That night at Tatiana's house they wrote a national anthem. Roughly translated it went:

> *Down with teachers, down with grown-ups.*
> *Girls for ever and ever and ever!*
> *Never divided, always triumphant,*
> *Girls for ever and ever and ever!*

Isobel sat huddled and tense as the train headed for London. Familiar towns went by. She saw York Minster, Doncaster Minster and Peterborough Cathedral. She was moving on at last, galvanized by the example of the anchorite into going home. It felt like failure. She tried to raise her spirits by regarding this as the beginning of a quest. *A quest for my lost things,* she thought. At this an image of Gabriel flashed across her mind. Poor man. She'd slapped him down rather that time. *You've lost things and never grieved over them.* He'd been right all along, only she'd been too arrogant to believe him.

Isobel sat up with a jolt. Zechariah – struck dumb for rejecting the archangel's message! She got to her feet and hastily pulled down her bag from the overhead rack. The woman opposite was pretending not to watch. Isobel had a sudden vision of herself as a twitchy, erratic madwoman, eyed by fellow travellers who were poised to move to another seat if she accosted them. She unzipped the pocket of her bag and pulled out her Bible, fumbling for Luke's Gospel:

*And the angel answered him, 'I am Gabriel, who stand in the presence of God; and I was sent to speak to you; and bring you this good news. And behold, you will be silent and unable to speak until the day that these things come to pass, because you did not believe my words, which will be fulfilled in their time.'*

Isobel closed the Bible and sat trembling. Her arms and face were tingling, and though her breathing was exaggerated, it was steady. It didn't feel like panic. 'Unable to speak until these things come to pass'. The lost things must be found. They must be grieved over. And then, like Zechariah, would her mouth be opened, her tongue loosed and would she at last speak and praise God again? It was most unlike Isobel to treat Scripture in this whimsical manner. It smacked of fanaticism. But what had she left to lose? A kind of feverish calm possessed her. Let the treasure hunt commence. In the back of her mind was an image of Bishop Theodore, warning her to restrain her librarian's impulses. She caught the woman opposite staring and met her gaze aggressively.

Isobel's mother was waiting at the station. Mrs Knox was a nervous driver who had embraced an anti-car lifestyle with relief, but today the battered old 2CV was there on the forecourt. She must be really worried about me, thought Isobel, who had been expecting to make the last part of the journey in two different buses and then on foot.

'Oh, darling,' cried her mother, hugging her fiercely. Isobel felt the familiar pulse of mother love. Mrs Knox might have spent half their childhood apparently ignoring her offspring, but once roused from her book she would readily kill anyone who hurt them, if that would gain anything in the long run.

*Thanks for coming*, said Isobel.

'Your voice! I thought you said it was getting better!'

*It is.*

'Have you tried cider vinegar and honey?' Mrs Knox put Isobel's bag in the boot and slammed the door. The whole car rocked. 'What do they think the problem is?'

*They don't know. Either it's voice strain, or it's psychosomatic. The doctor called it 'hysterical aphonia'.*

'Oh, charming! Did they prescribe a smack round the chops?' They got in. 'That's the standard treatment for hysterical women, isn't it? Honestly!'

The silence that fell was full of speculation. By the time they reached the house Mrs Knox would have come up with several robust theories about Isobel's condition; most, if not all of them, reflecting badly on her own role as mother. She knew better than to air them, but Isobel found even silent analysis of her psyche intensely annoying.

*I go to see a speech therapist*, said Isobel pre-emptively. *She uses relaxation tapes. It's all about regaining control.*

'Control!' exclaimed her mother. 'That's a recurring motif in my life at the moment. You know, so many women –' She broke off, apparently reminding herself that it was Isobel and her needs that were the focus of this conversation. 'Is it proving valuable?'

*Yes.*

They arrived at the Old Wrecktory and went in. The interior was pleasant and welcoming these days, but there was always a split second in which Isobel smelt damp and dry rot, heard the wind through broken panes and felt hollow inside.

Her father saw them arrive and came to meet Isobel in the hall.

'Hello, hello!' he said, pecking her on the cheek. They weren't a terribly kissy family, but they always made the effort.

*Hello, Dad.*

'That sounds bad,' he commented. 'Used to happen to me when I was still teaching.'

'They've told her it might be "hysterical aphonia"!' said her mother indignantly

'Hysterical, eh? You look pretty calm to me. Never had much time for Freud, myself.'

'You can't just lump all therapy under the Freudian label and dismiss it,' said Mrs Knox, rising to the bait. 'Jung's an entirely different kettle of fish.'

They walked down the tiled passageway to the kitchen.

'It comes from the Greek for womb, you know,' went on Mr Knox. '*Husterikos.* They used to think mental illness was caused by disorders of the uterus. A roaming womb, which would rise up and strangle the patient. Come to think of it, you could probably find some New Age practitioner who's resurrected the idea if you tried hard enough.'

'Of course! *King Lear,*' said Mrs Knox, ignoring his last quip. ' "O, how this mother swells up toward my heart!/Hysterica passio – down, thou climbing sorrow,/Thy element's below!" '

Isobel saw more clearly than ever before how much her parents' daughter she was. That irrepressible urge to inform, explain things and set people right. She'd been more aware of the tendency since it had become impossible. Perhaps by default her listening skills were coming along in leaps and bounds. While she would never have interrupted in pastoral situations, she had generally treated the slightest pause as a chance to deliver her opinion. It was her response that counted, not the other person's problem. The arrogance of this had not struck her at the time.

'Right. Time for a cuppa,' said her father. 'Leaded or unleaded?'

That night Isobel lay awake. Why had she come here? It was a waste of time. A wild-goose chase. What kind of answers was she expecting to find? She felt panic creeping up on her. What if there were no answers and she never regained her voice? But it was too

313

early to be saying that. She must wait patiently and things would emerge. If her parents didn't drive her bonkers first, of course.

They knew she was supposed to be resting. She hadn't mentioned the treasure-hunt aspect of her visit for fear of activating her mother's conquistadorial zeal. There was a nagging in her conscience. She listened until she located its source. Perhaps it was egocentric to imagine that this was a solitary quest. There were others on the road, too. Her history and destination might be bound up in theirs. She would have confided by now if it hadn't been for the pleasure she knew her mother would feel. Why was she reluctant to make her happy? Because it would mean Mrs Knox was right and Isobel was wrong.

You can't take being in the wrong, can you?

This accusation shot like a missile out of nowhere. With it came a claustrophobic sense of *déjà vu*, so intense it was almost a memory. Her mind clutched at it, but it eluded her like that irritating fragment of song that had plagued her before Christmas. She was sure someone had said it to her. Who? When?

Whoever it was had hit the nail on the head. She hated being wrong. It was linked with being a bad loser. Well, she would address this unattractive trait. When she found the right moment she would explain the true situation to her mother.

I do love them, she thought. It was impossible to say this to their faces, but she truly did. They were odd, but that no longer caused her cold sweats of embarrassment as it had in her teens. Since retiring, her father had been free to indulge his lifelong passion for birdwatching. He enjoyed nothing quite so much as lying for hours in the mud in some remote marsh hoping for a glimpse of a 'lifer' – a species he had not yet seen in the flesh. His other hobby, as far as Isobel could make out, was being resident pain in the backside to the local planning department. He was currently organizing opposition to the building of a windfarm at the top end of the village on the grounds that (a) it would be an eyesore and (b) if you did the sums you'd pretty soon see it was an inefficient way of generating electricity, given the prevailing winds. The campaign was basically an outlet for all his innate Yorkshire cussedness, but Isobel knew that if anyone put this to him he'd deny it. It

314

wasn't a question of him being awkward. The project was daft. It didn't add up. As an engineer he had an obligation to point this out. As she slid into sleep Isobel could picture the mills twiddling madly on the hilltop. Perhaps he was right. Not the same as a proper windmill, like the one we could see from the old house. The old house. She jolted awake. Of course. She had come back to the wrong home. She needed to go to the village where she'd grown up.

It was all there in her memory. The mile-long walk to school. The cement works dominating everything with its clashing and grinding, the red lorries, the white dust. She could walk every step of the way, see the houses, the hedges, the roads, the walls she'd walked on, the big ash tree, the brook beside the school . . .

Yes. Tomorrow she'd go back.

It will all have changed. Everything will look smaller, she reminded herself. The bus trundled through the countryside stopping like a dog at every lamp-post. She'd ducked the issue when her mother asked what her plans were for the day. It was important that she did this one thing alone. She didn't want her mother tagging along, telling her what had happened in the village or suggesting that she contact old friends. No, the experience must be unmediated.

Look, there were the hills! She'd have known their outline even after a hundred years' absence. Five tall chimneys rose out of the landscape. The cement works. And there was the turning that led down to the hamlet where Tatiana had lived. Not long now. The bus whined down the long hill and into the village. Branches clonked on the bus roof as they pulled up.

Isobel got out. It was raining. She stood for a moment at a loss. I'm here. It's exactly as it was. She was standing outside the library. It was closed. She peered in through the windows and could see all the shelves, the librarian's desk in the gloom as if everything had stood still in an enchanted sleep all these years.

She crossed the road to the village green. No, it didn't seem smaller, because the trees had all grown and kept pace with her. The gigantic copper beech still dwarfed the bus shelter. Those old iron railings were the same ones she'd climbed over as a child. She went through the gap and on to the play area. The huge old metal slide and swings had gone, replaced by smaller wooden versions. Gone, too, was the rock-hard tarmac. Isobel's shoes sank in the soft bark chippings. The wind stirred and the empty swings swayed. Rain pattered from the trees. She turned and carried on down the hill.

There was the alley that led to the short-cut home across the fields. There was the lamp-post she'd run into, knocking herself out. There was the old Wesleyan chapel where she'd gone to Girls' Brigade. It still had blue railings. The little Co-op was gone. That was Linda Puddefoot's house. And there, there was the school entrance. Her pace quickened. What if it had been closed down and demolished?

It was still there. She felt no rush of feeling. It seemed so ordinary. What would an outsider see? A woman in her early thirties outside a primary school, perhaps going to collect her child?

Isobel stood in the rain. That was her very first classroom. She'd been there when the brand new school was opened in the sixties. The playground was deserted. Was there a square inch she hadn't played on? She was glad to see the two beautiful lime trees still standing on the field.

*I draw a snake upon your back. Who will put in the eye?*

Glen Austin, Steven Darvil, Neil Forbes. Julie Halsey, Cindy, Linda, Angela. The empty playground teemed with vanished children. Isobel remembered Gabriel's idea about place memories. Were the shrieks and laughs and tears of her childhood games recorded here? Was she inhabiting a living palimpsest? It was fanciful, but the thought comforted her. What she had once been was not lost without trace.

She set out for home. The garage, the police station. She ticked them off mentally. The big ash tree and the low wall to walk on. The street names reeled off like a skipping rhyme: Glebe Close, Albion Road, Queen Street. The cement works loomed across the fields. She listened for the familiar clankings but heard nothing. All the way she was keeping as sharp an eye on her responses as her mother would have done. She felt as though she was failing to experience it all as intensely as she ought. There was the old

316

village shop where you could buy freshly baked bread wrapped in tissue paper and burning your arm on the way home. Friday was pocket-money day. We always asked to look in the sixpence box. Or bought sweets from the big jars. Cola cubes, toffee bonbons, winter mixture. Variegated sherbet, like a coloured sand souvenir from Alum Bay.

She reached the crossroads. The rec. That's where we played on the way home from school. She began to walk down her own road. They've mowed the grass right up to the pavement, she thought. It looked neater. The saplings were sturdy young trees now. Time had been kind to the place, had softened its contours and made it prettier. Tears filled her eyes. I'm the same me, she thought. I'm still the same me as I was then. I'm still me.

She rounded the corner. In a few more paces she'd be able to see the house. To her surprise she couldn't. The trees had grown and blocked the view. Young wheat was green in the field. The first hawthorn buds were breaking on the hedge. Snails crept on the pavement as they always had and she walked carefully, remembering the sickening crunch of innocent creature under shoe. And the slugs. Monsters six inches long, liquorice black or sultana brown.

Where was the house? Surely it should be just there? There! No. Yes. Yes! Painted cream. Isobel gasped. How could they? If someone had shown her a picture she would not have recognized it. She hurried closer. All the old sash windows had been replaced. That was my bedroom! The garden! No! They'd built a bungalow on it. And there was a little road lined with houses where the old track to the man's land had been. Spring flowers nodded in hanging baskets. I should never have come!

She stared at the pretty scene. Her memories were obliterated. They'd chopped down all the old trees, the ancient apples, the yew, the horse-chestnut. No, wait – the conker tree was still there. It had been pollarded to fit the smaller-scale garden, but it was the same tree. Rain dripped from the sticky buds. I bet I could still climb it. She could imagine the bark under her hands. Her feet would know where to plant themselves, her arms where to reach, easy as a ladder, almost.

A face appeared at a window and Isobel turned, walked back down the lane and continued along the road past her old front door. Well, she could hardly knock and ask to climb their conker tree.

As the bus carried her back to her parents', she wondered why she hadn't knocked anyway, or gone into the school and asked to look round. The whole visit had been bungled through lack of preparation. All she could think of were the things she'd failed to notice or explore. Why hadn't she gone to Tatiana's house as she had in her dream? And if only she'd popped into the school! She could have stood on the very spot where their shared desk had been.

But maybe she'd done all she needed to do. There was no knowing. The scope of this quest was endless. Was she supposed to blunder about on a picaresque journey round all the battle scenes of her past life? Go back to library college? Visit her secondary school, ghastly thought? One was grateful for one's education but, really, had anything of life-forming significance truly happened at that place?

Well, in a sense, yes. She supposed by any reckoning the termination of an unwanted pregnancy loomed pretty large in a teenage girl's life. It was not something one dwelt on afterwards but, yes, it was significant. She was fortunate not to have been dogged by guilt as many women were, even later on when she'd come to view abortion as wrong. It was part of her sinful past and, as such, dealt with.

That evening when her father was out at a local council meeting Isobel decided to venture on to Jungian terrain with her mother. She began by telling her that she'd been back to their old home.

'Why didn't you say?' said Mrs Knox, as Isobel had known she would. 'I could've come too. Did you call in on anyone?'

Isobel shook her head. *I needed to be alone.*

Mrs Knox respected this. They talked for a while about the village, the fact that the cement works was about to be pulled down, about the new houses on the man's land, about everything except why Isobel had gone there. Her mother was valiantly

318

fighting the temptation to ask, while Isobel was battling with her irritation at knowing this.

*I'm trying to* find *myself,* she managed grudgingly, hating the cliché.

Mrs Knox nodded, still resisting. 'Well, that's good.'

After a long pause Isobel opened her mouth. At once her throat seized up. Dammit, she'd not wanted her mother to see this happen.

'Darling! What's wrong?'

Isobel waved her away.

'Can I do anything? Would a drink help?'

After trying her breathing exercises in vain, Isobel resorted to her notebook: 'Don't worry. It'll pass.'

She consented to a cup of camomile tea. The constriction in her neck and jaw eased and eventually she was able to whisper, *Just think, I could have a fifteen-year-old by now.*

'Sixteen,' corrected her mother.

The swiftness of her response appalled Isobel. Had her mother been keeping track all these years?

'You made the right decision, however,' said Mrs Knox. 'Oh, no question. I know you've probably come to view it differently, but I honestly think you've nothing to reproach yourself with. It was the sensible course of action and you dealt with it very maturely.' But there were tears running down her mother's cheeks. She was repeating the words Mr Knox had uttered all those years ago, perhaps still trying to believe them. The sensible course of action, he said, implying that this atoned for his daughter's earlier stupidity and weakness. I've been weak and stupid, she heard her voice whisper to Bishop Theodore. The two sins her father least tolerated.

'I'm sorry.' Mrs Knox blew her nose loudly. 'Getting maudlin in my old age.'

What lay behind this sorrow? The ghostly grandchild in every family photograph. No name, no gender, just a question mark. For the first time Isobel allowed herself to wonder how it might have been. A little more courage and her whole life would have flowed down a different course. Her parents would have supported her. Well, it's your decision, they would have said, but she'd known

319

what they wanted and seen their secret relief. But a child, an adult, almost, by now. Boy or girl? Standing as high as her shoulder. Or taller.

*Perhaps I should have gone through with it.*

'Don't be silly.' Her mother sniffed. 'You were about to go up to university. An early termination doesn't amount to infanticide, for heaven's sake. Yes, it was unfortunate, but there we are. If the father had been . . . I know it sounds snobby, but – *suitable*, or *around* even . . . No, you did the right thing. You do know he ended up in prison, don't you?'

*What, Johnny?* she asked in surprise.

'I thought his name was Gary.'

*I meant Gary*, Isobel blushed. For once a Freudian slip passed Mrs Knox by.

'Oh, yes. He was done for handling stolen goods. Some big scam involving high-performance cars, I think. It was in all the local papers. You were up at Durham and we didn't see any point bothering you with it by then.'

So that's what happened to him, thought Isobel.

'You did absolutely the right thing,' repeated Mrs Knox once more.

Isobel bit her knuckles. Oh, God, please help me tell her. Her stomach plunged as if she were lining up for a race.

'You mustn't be too hard on yourself!' cried her mother.

She reached for her notebook again and forced herself to write. 'It wasn't Gary. It was Mr Peacock.'

Her mother read the words, then sprang back. 'What!' she shouted. 'Mr Peacock! He – why! That – that – that corpulent *bastard*! When?'

To her dismay Isobel found she was quivering with laughter.

'Is this a joke?' demanded Mrs Knox.

Isobel shook her head. *It was New Year's Eve. I'd been babysitting and he was running me home*, she whispered.

'No! Darling, this is terrible! You should have told me! Did he force you?'

She shook her head again. *I was upset because, um, Gary had dumped me. Mr Peacock was comforting me. He was drunk. Things got out of hand.* Oh, the relief of telling it after so long! She could hear his whisky-thickened voice as he kneaded her breasts – 'Oh, my God, ooh, oh, my *God*! They're magnificent!'

Her poor mother was struggling to take this in, possibly trying to reconstruct the ghostly grandchild in the likeness of Denis Peacock.

*He had to take his glasses off,* said Isobel. *They kept steaming up.*

'Don't!' shrieked her mother. 'So that's why you stopped baby-sitting for them!'

Isobel nodded, still taut with hysterical laughter.

They looked at each other. She knew what was going through her mother's mind: Gary I could understand, but *Denis*?

Suddenly the pattern sprang out at her. Its symmetry shocked her. New Year's Eve. The beloved not there. Sex with the wrong man.

'What is it?' asked her mother, seeing Isobel freeze.

*Nothing.*

She lay awake again that night. In her mind's eye she saw her emotional baggage going round and round on an airport carousel. Maybe this same conjunction would go past every sixteen years, waiting for her to claim it. This is me. This is what I'm like. I was lonely, I was desperate, he was there.

At breakfast Isobel could sense that her mother had informed her father. Mr Knox said nothing as he ate his bacon and eggs. Perhaps there was nothing to say. He couldn't now, so long after the event, turn up on the seducer's doorstep and threaten to knock him down. Maybe Mr Peacock had long since forgotten that drunken roll with a teenage girl, told himself it hadn't happened. He was the same age as Dad. It was the first time the thought had struck her. Old enough to be my father and he should have known better. All this time I've been blaming myself, while in fact I was the vulnerable one. Not much more than a child.

She poured herself another cup of tea and reflected that the balance of power had shifted. It had never occurred to her before, but she could appear like a bad fairy one day, some chosen happy day – perhaps the baptism of a Peacock grandchild – and deal out a long-overdue justice.

Mrs Knox was stirring her coffee very fast. Her agitation gave Isobel a couple of seconds' warning of what was to come.

'I told your father about Mr Peacock,' she announced.

There was silence. Mr Knox continued mopping up egg yolk with his fried bread. He was as strong as an ox and had no truck with cholesterol anxieties. The intended bout of family sharing and openness withered in the face of his implacability. In another moment Mrs Knox would charge from the room and cry in secret. Isobel intervened out of pity: *Maybe I should've said something at the time.*

'What for?' asked Mr Knox. 'No harm in keeping your own counsel.'

'Oh, but there can be!' said her mother in a rush. 'These things can come back and haunt you! For all we know Isobel's current problems could stem from –'

'Don't be daft,' cut in Mr Knox. 'Think about it, she uses her voice all the time. Ask any ENT specialist and they'll tell you it's actors, clergy, lecturers and the like that end up with voice strain.' He pushed his plate away and smiled. 'Thanks, love. Set me up nicely for a morning in the garden, that will.'

They heard him in the back porch putting his boots on. The door opened then shut and his footsteps trudged away up the path.

'Your father's not very comfortable with inwardness,' said Mrs Knox.

*I must go and listen to my relaxation tapes*, replied Isobel.

An hour later Isobel was lying on the bed staring up at the ceiling. This was where she'd slept until she left home, but it was only in recent years that her mother had redecorated it and turned it into a guest room. She had been careful to consult Isobel over this, not wishing to convey the message that her daughter was no longer welcome. The contents of the cupboards and wardrobes had been transferred to the loft in boxes and were awaiting Isobel's attention. 'What's in them? A-level notes? Sling them out, for goodness' sake!' Isobel had said on more than one occasion, but Mrs Knox refused.

Isobel, who had lived happily for years without the contents of these boxes, couldn't understand what the fuss was about. To tackle the job now felt loaded with symbolism. But there was nothing else to do. She went down to the kitchen and found a couple of bin-liners before heading up the narrow stairs to the attic.

The moment she opened the little door she was greeted with the smell that said dens, secrets, adventure. Grandma's attic with the old doll's house. The loft at the old house where she wasn't supposed to go because it wasn't properly boarded out and Chris had once put his foot through the ceiling. For a moment she simply stood breathing in the smell of hardboard and dust, and listening to the hissing chuckle of the cold-water tank. The wind blew, sucking in and out the polythene that lined the roof, as if this were the lungs of the house.

Her stuff was at the far end near the little window that looked out over the garden. She negotiated her way through the vast store of oddments that might one day come in handy. Honestly, no wonder she was such an inveterate chucker-out of things with such squirrels for parents. When she reached the window she looked out and saw her father digging in the vegetable patch. He had his back to her. She saw him pause and she knew he would be watching a bird, a robin, probably, which had ventured close in the hope of worms.

Well, she might as well get on with it. It would probably only take half an hour. The first boxes contained school notes and essays, as she'd supposed. 'Radical Sects in the Interregnum Period.' ' "Character is fate." Discuss with reference to Hardy's *Tess of the D'Urbervilles*.' All in neat handwriting, titles prissily underlined with a ruler. She dumped them in the bin-bag. Next came the exercise books. Flicking through, she glimpsed a kaleidoscopic impression of coffee in Brazil, electrical circuits, sines and cosines, *der gute Mann, des guten Mannes*, zinc, iron, copper, lead and M. Bertillon, *le douanier*. The books joined the files in the rubbish.

Isobel moved on to the next section: clothes. The reason they'd survived was obvious. They were too ghastly to have been taken up to college. Had she really worn that smock? Clogs! And here was her school Aertex shirt with her nametape stitched on the left breast. Hockey boots, clumsy wooden tennis racket – oh, surely you can see I don't want all this, Mother? At the bottom she found a couple of ugly clay forms, the making of which had convinced Isobel that O-level art was not the subject for her. It was the one area of school life where diligence was not properly rewarded. If you were hopeless at drawing, no amount of swotting would help. Isobel prickled briefly at the unfairness of it as she tossed the glazed lumps in with the rest. Well, that hadn't taken long.

The last box, unlike the others, had been sealed. She dragged it closer. The brown parcel tape, once robust, was now frail and transparent and split open as she tugged. Why had her mother taped it up? Or had Isobel done it herself? What? Red knickers! Where on earth – It was never the presents from Gary! It was. Here they all were – the perfume she'd hated, gold charm bracelet, padded card 'For Someone Special'. She pulled them out one after another and each caused her a remembered pang. And he'd gone to prison, poor Gary. For how long? she wondered. And where was he now, what was he doing? She held up the nylon leopard-print negligee. Something fluttered out. It was a photograph, colours fading now, but still clear enough. She stared for a long time at her sixteen-year-old self. A skimpy white vest, one bra strap showing. Tan. Yes, it had been a hot, hot summer that year. The grass she was lying on looked parched. Funny that all she could remember of being a teenager was how much she'd hated her body. And yet to look at this snap you wouldn't have known. You'd have thought, What a happy, sexy girl.

## CHAPTER 25

Mrs Peck wouldn't let girls wear trousers to school. The Head said it was OK, but Mrs Peck took no notice of him. It was a stupid rule, so Isobel broke it now and then, knowing the teacher couldn't send her home to get changed. When she asked why she wasn't allowed to wear trousers, all Mrs Peck could say was, 'It isn't appropriate.' What kind of an answer was that supposed to be?

In the end she defied the rule once too often and got punished. Mrs Peck made her stay in all lunchtime and write a two-page argument, one for, one against girls being allowed to wear trousers to school. Isobel rattled off the first page in next to no time. The second had her stumped. There *were* no reasons. It was stupid, stupid, stupid and not fair. In the end she filled the page with the words 'because it's not apropriate, because it's not apropriate' over and over again, adding at the bottom, 'even if the Head says we can'. It would get her into more trouble, but she didn't care.

Mrs Peck skimmed the pages and tossed them in the bin. 'Appropriate has three Ps, actually, Isobel.'

Well, the pieces were beginning to look as though they might all belong to one puzzle after all. She studied the faded photograph repeatedly as if it were a message from her former self. There had been a time, just that one summer, when she'd tried another approach to being Isobel Knox with the big bust and discovered she loved sex and could rejoice in her body. The results of the brief experiment had been disastrous, but had her drastic action of opting for surgery been the right response? She knew she could rummage in the bureau and find a dozen snapshots showing her round-shouldered and miserable, folding her arms to disguise her breasts. She could cite her sense of post-operation freedom, the relief at being able to run without inciting lewd comments, the lack of ogling in the street. She could reiterate her argument about it being corrective, not cosmetic surgery. But she was forced to admit that the real problem had been in her mind, not her figure. It would have been possible to be happy as she was. If things had turned out better. Or if she'd responded differently to the crisis. Oh, if only she'd had someone to talk to. Someone like Bishop Theodore. Perhaps she could arrange to see him again when she returned to Asleby.

At the thought of his kindness and wisdom she could have burst into tears. What would he say to all this? He would inquire about the symbolic power of her breast reduction. Could it, for instance, be viewed as a cutting off of her womanhood, a token reversal of a much-hated puberty? Or was it to be placed in the same category as her amnesia and voice loss – an act of self-censorship? He might also press her to ponder the unfortunate pregnancy and its termination. Why was she content with a bowdlerized version of her life?

Her mother was keeping a respectful distance, interpreting Isobel's silent wrestlings as mourning for an unborn child. For all her protestations that Isobel had done the right thing, Mrs Knox seemed to feel the loss keenly. One hoped her grief was now tempered by relief at not having to witness Denis Peacock growing up in their midst. Isobel knew her mother was still shrieking his name mentally several times a day.

Did all this represent progress of a kind? Isobel wasn't sure. Certainly her voice was no better and she still found prayer impossible. Her inability to speak had seeped into her silent articulations to God as well. Words were the problem. Words. She couldn't summon any, and without them there was no communicating with him, no praise, no intercession for herself or others. She tried to recite prayers from anthologies or read through her daily office, but with each well-turned phrase her distress mounted until she would have screamed if she could. Just pour out your heart, she told herself. Sometimes it felt as though her heart were frozen solid. At others she could picture it already poured out on the ground, spilled, wasted. It would sink into the earth and be gone.

*

'How about a stroll?' said her father one afternoon.

Isobel took this as a hint that moping about the house never did anyone any good. *OK.*

'I'll stay here with my book,' said Mrs Knox. 'I struggled round the shops this morning, so I've had my fresh air.'

Her mother's slightly laboured response made Isobel fear this was a set-up. They had decided it was high time she had a heart-to-heart with her dad. On reflection she decided it was probably just her mother spotting an opportunity and improvising.

They put on their coats and set off along the road towards the woods, her father with binoculars round his neck. It was mild. Dog's mercury and celandines were beginning to appear in the undergrowth.

'Heard the first chiff-chaff this morning,' said her father.

*No willow warblers?*

'Not yet.'

They trudged on in silence. Was he just quietly enjoying the spring air, or was he wondering how to broach some tricky subject? If so, this would be a new development. Mr Knox was not a great one for pussyfooting around. They climbed the stile and followed the path into the wood.

'So how was the parish when you left?' he inquired.

She made no reply.

After a moment he observed, 'Well, can't have been easy for you, I suppose.'

She swallowed. *Mum's probably right about my voice, actually.*

'She may well be, but you don't want it discussed over breakfast.'

This rare concession to sensitivity brought tears to her eyes. *That's neither here nor there*, she said bravely. *If it's true I should be prepared to accept it.*

'You can't live your whole life as if your feelings were irrelevant, love,' he replied.

It was a moment before this heresy sunk in. *But that's exactly what you brought me up to think!* she protested.

He absorbed this and chuckled. 'Well, you can't go through your life believing your old dad is right all the time, either.'

*Why do you always have to have a good answer for everything?* she burst out.

He was silent for so long she began to fear she'd wounded him. *Sorry. I didn't mean that.*

'It's a fair point, though.'

The beech boles were as grey and solemn as cathedral piers as they passed between them.

'I'm getting annoying in my old age,' he said.

You've always been like it, she thought. You never once admitted you were wrong unless faced with sound evidence. You bowed to the truth, not to other people. Occasionally mistaken, but never in the wrong.

'Funnily enough,' he remarked, 'I once said a similar thing to my father. "Why do you have to be right the whole time?" He was right because he submitted to the Word of God, of course. There was no arguing with him. The earth was four thousand years old and God put the dinosaur fossils there to confound arrogant men who thought they knew better than the Book of Genesis.'

His eyes followed a wood-pigeon in the treetops. 'Looking back, I can see he was basically a kind man. He was at odds with himself. Part of him was proud of me for what I achieved, but his beliefs prevented him from admitting it. His faith turned him into a harsher man than he was. I'll always find that difficult to forgive. I doubt you'll remember him,' he said.

*He always gave me butterscotch from his cardigan pocket.*

'Yes, that'd be right. Did he make you goblets out of the gold wrapper?'

*Yes! I'd forgotten that. I wonder what he'd make of me being ordained?*

'Oh, he had no time for the C of E. Bishops and infant baptism – slippery slope to Rome. He used to cross the street to avoid Catholics.'

And what do you make of it? she wanted to ask. Do you approve? Are you proud of me?

They walked side by side, each isolated from the other until from deep among the trees came a woodpecker's thrum. They turned to each other in shared joy.

'Now, *that's* a lesser spotted!' exclaimed Mr Knox, whisking out his binoculars. 'There it is again! More prolonged drumming than the greater spotted. Come along, let's see if we can get a look at him.'

And they set off with Isobel following her father through the undergrowth in excited quest as she had since her childhood.

That evening after dinner Isobel looked through her parents' CD collection, trying to decide what kind of mood she was in. Her mother's latest interest appeared to be the kind of polyphonic music Andrew Jacks had so industriously helped bring to 'the masses'. His snootiness still rankled. She liked to think she knew her Palestrina and Tallis; but aware of her basic ignorance she put on a CD offering 'the hauntingly beautiful music of the high Middle Ages'.

Isobel's Latin was not as good as it might have been. Half-understood phrases rose and melted as the voices wove in and out of one another. *Et stella maris.* It must be an Ave Maria. Were these pieces performed publicly, or had they been private, part of the daily routine in the monastery where they were written? she wondered. Poured out into the air and then vanishing with no audience to applaud. A group of celibate monks singing love songs to the Virgin. It was strangely unlike a modern hymn with one tune supported by harmonies. She'd never stopped to articulate this thought. Impossible to say who was carrying the melody. It moved from part to part; or wait – each part was a different melody. She lay on the sofa thinking what a good image of corporate worship this was, the synthesizing of individuality, not the suppression of it in favour of one dominant strand. How many times had she insisted from the pulpit that conversion was not some kind of sausage machine that churned out identical Christians? And yet hadn't she been diligently feeding herself through a process of this kind, with her rules and regulations and notions of the right way to serve God? This was why she'd been so affronted by the idea that God might call someone like Andrew Jacks.

She remembered, suddenly, the time when the choir of her Oxford college had put on Stainer's *Crucifixion*. The two solo parts were taken by the Jacks brothers. It had upset Isobel that one of her favourite pieces of religious music should fall into their clutches, however gifted they were, musically. She'd overheard them rehearsing, periods of singing – 'For my sake forgive' – followed by some profanity or other. They were capable of flipping between the two without turning a hair. On one occasion Alex's sneering voice had reached her: 'The whole thing reeks of masochistic Victorian piety.' This is a travesty, she thought. No doubt they would produce a brilliant show, but it would be hollow. Better for it to be done by believers, even if the end result was less accomplished.

But she'd been wrong. Something had happened that Good Friday in the chapel when the piece was performed. It was the most powerful rendering of the passion narrative she'd ever experienced. It should have taught her once and for all that the wind blows where it wills, that Christians had no monopoly on God.

But why did it have to be like this? Why had she been passed over, she who had served God so faithfully all these years? All fine and well being one of the ninety-nine righteous when the angels threw a party over the likes of Andrew Jacks when he bothered to stroll up and repent. Yes, yes, she knew that the righteous had all been that 'one sinner who repents' at some point, but she'd never felt rejoiced over. It seemed to her that God actually preferred riff-raff to people who tried to be good. Was *that* the kind of God she wanted to serve? She knew the right answer was 'Yes.'

Isobel stirred angrily. Mrs Knox looked up from her book inquiringly. Isobel smiled.

'Can I get you anything? Cup of tea?'

*I'm fine, thanks.*

There was always a danger of acting like the older brother in the parable of the Prodigal Son. But the man had a point, for heaven's sake! His bitter outburst might have been her own: 'Lo, these many years I have served you, and I never disobeyed your command; yet you never gave me a kid, that I might make merry with my friends. But when this son of yours came, who has devoured your living with harlots, you killed for him the fatted calf!'

But she'd swapped roles now, hadn't she? She was like the younger son – in a far country, prostrated by sin, cut off from her Father, starving, with no one to care for her. God's disreputable largesse could be poured out upon *her* for once. Except she still felt like the older brother, whose response to the father's plea was not recorded. He might have said, 'Oh, well, if he can get away with it, so can I!' and flounced off in some petty rebellion fuelled by self-righteous indignation.

The following morning she woke and discovered she could speak. Her mother shrieked with joy. Mr Knox pulled her leg that there'd be no getting a word in edgeways now. Isobel sang hallelujah at the top of her lungs and was warned by both parents not to overdo it. They stood in the kitchen laughing together with relief.

'Odd that it should just come back,' said her father.

'The speech therapist said it might. The old patterns are still stored in the brain, or something, and normal speech can be triggered again.'

'So it's a neurological thing. Hmm. That's fascinating.' Her father loved this kind of problem. 'So what triggered it?'

'I've no idea,' said Isobel. 'The chance to unwind, maybe? Quite frankly, I don't care, so long as I can get on with my life again. It's such a relief.'

'I'm sure it is, darling,' said her mother. 'It's been so ghastly for you and you've coped really well. Does this mean we'll be losing you?'

Isobel smiled at this tactful query. 'Yes. I can't get out of work any longer, I'm afraid,' she joked. Thank the Lord, she added belatedly. A glorious instance of the unmerited grace of God. What a fool she'd been to think she could *earn* her voice back.

Later that day she phoned Harry. Her feet were tapping, eager for the return journey. He picked up the phone, but as she heard his beloved voice saying, 'Asleby Vicarage,' she felt her throat close.

No! No, please, no! She tried to override it, but it was impossible. She uttered one desperate choking sound, then replaced the receiver with a crash.

*You can't do this to me! I was better!* she screamed at God in a hoarse whisper, cursing Him for playing games, for His cruelty, His unfair treatment of her.

The phone rang. It would be Harry. She didn't answer. It rang on and on. Her parents were out. She pictured him standing in his study waiting, waiting. Shut up! she screamed silently. Go away and leave me alone. Ring ring. Ring ring.

In the end she snatched her handbag and left the house. As she walked down the lane she could still hear it ringing in the distance behind her.

It occurred to her on the bus that she should have left a note for her parents. Oh, well, she'd be home before the end of the day. Her anger was spent. Nobody had ever promised her that recovery would be a smooth progression. Ups and downs were perhaps inevitable. She'd jumped the gun a bit, that was all. It was lovely to know that she could still speak. What worried her was that she'd been fine until she'd made contact with Harry. It wouldn't do for Asleby to become the focus of the problem, or she'd never be able to go back to work there.

However, some good had come out of it. The experience had jolted her into action again. It was years since she'd been to Oxford. Misty-eyed nostalgia had never been an indulgence of hers. She wasn't one for looking back. 'Would you describe yourself as a rower or a canoeist?' Bishop Theodore had asked her in one of their counselling sessions. 'Do you travel through life facing the direction you're going, or with your back to it?' She was definitely a canoeist, she told him. 'Whichever you are,' he'd gone on, 'you will always find yourself vulnerable to what lies behind your back. In your case, the past.'

Returning to Oxford went against the grain. It was a closed chapter and Isobel seldom reread books. She viewed it as self-indulgent when there were so many other important works waiting to be read. But here she was on the city's outskirts. She was going to tackle head-on the thing she dreaded most by knocking on the door of Dr Alex Jacks, looking him steadily in the eye and laying his unwholesome ghost to rest.

The plan was a simple one, but as she drew close to the college her heart began to pound. It was lunchtime and he might well be out. His working patterns had never been predictable. He might even be off somewhere on sabbatical. For all she knew he could even have left Oxford for good, although Andrew hadn't mentioned it last summer. Her mouth was dry. She could tell from the tightness in her throat that she wasn't going to be able to speak to him, but she was determined to force an encounter of some kind.

She passed through the porter's lodge. Nobody recognized her. Supposing he had his oak up? Would she dare breach Oxford etiquette and knock anyway? He'd been known to emerge screaming like a rabid werewolf if disturbed in mid-thought by someone not realizing the significance of the closed outer door.

His rooms were on the far side of the quad. How many times had she tried not to look up at his window on her way to the library? She set off briskly. An elderly don in a wheelchair was trundling his way slowly towards her. Their paths crossed.

'Isobel?'

She glanced politely, then stopped dead. It was Alex. Her hand clutched her throat in shock.

*Alex!*

'Were you coming to find me?' His voice was a stroke-victim's drawl.

She nodded. What could have happened? Some terrible wasting disease. He looked like a dying man.

He gave a twisted smile. 'Speechless?'

*I've lost my voice.*

'Christ. Don't come near me.'

*It's not catching,* she assured him. *It's* – She tapped her temple and shrugged.

'Hah.' His head rolled slightly. He looked drugged. 'So fucking . . .' She waited as he summoned the words. '. . . insulting. Psycho . . .'

*Somatic?* she offered.

Anger flickered. 'Piss off,' he mumbled. 'Finishing my sentences.'

*Sorry.*

He made a slight beckoning gesture. She squatted. They looked into one another's eyes.

*What happened? I mean, you're ill. What* – ?

333

'ME,' he said. 'Chronic fatigue thing.'

*What?* She stared in disbelief. *This is what it does?*

'Yeah.'

Some students came towards them. Pretty young women. They cast him kindly smiles. One called, 'Hi, Dr Jacks.' The group parted to walk round him, then continued up the path, chatting. Isobel had an absurd impulse to shout after them, He used to shag the likes of you on his desktop! To see him reduced to this – an object of pity, a recipient of kindly smiles!

He was watching her indignation wryly. 'I'm going home. Coming?'

She nodded. So he wasn't living in his college rooms any more. They set off. She matched her pace to his in a snail-like progression across the quad, unsure whether an offer of help would seem patronizing.

He left the wheelchair in the porter's lodge. A taxi took them from there to north Oxford. Alex's flat proved, unexpectedly, to be part of an old vicarage. She wondered if his invitation implied that she'd shifted category from ex-colleague to friend, but decided he simply craved the company of someone whose every glance reminded him that this frail relic was not the real Alex Jacks.

'I'll need a hand with the stairs,' he said, after unlocking the door. He took the rail in one hand and her arm in the other. She had an image of the old Alex leaping down four steps at a time, hair and coat-tails flying, some snatch of song trailing after him. How could he bear it? They paused three-quarters of the way up and she realized that without her support he would have sagged to his knees. He was trembling with exhaustion, but he dragged himself up the last steps and sank on to the nearby sofa.

His eyes were shut. She sat on the footstool watching him. All his long curls were shorn off, revealing the delicate shape of his head. His lips moved.

*Sorry?* She leant closer.

' "He has broken my strength in mid-course." '

*Who? God?* she asked uncertainly.

'I always despised Christians who said, "Why me?" What kind of faith is ... eroded ... by hardship?'

Isobel waited, but he seemed to have finished. *I'm afraid I'm not sure what you're trying to say.*

'My atheism. Undermined.' He was almost asleep.

She couldn't come up with an adequate response. In the end she said, *Can I do anything?*

'Painkillers. In the bathroom.' She found the large bottle of paracetamol on the shelf and took them to him with a glass of water. He struggled with the childproof lid and in the end she had to open it for him. She watched as he swallowed the tablets and slumped back again.

*Can I get you anything else?*

'Tea. Please.'

She went downstairs to where she'd glimpsed the kitchen in passing. It was a high-ceilinged Victorian room, which still had its original built-in dresser. She filled the kettle and located cups and teapot. Her mind couldn't take in the change in him. Tears kept gathering in her eyes. She was just wondering whether he managed by himself or if he had a housekeeper when she heard footsteps approaching. The front door opened.

It was Andrew. His face lit up with a pleasure that completely floored her.

'Isobel! What are you doing here?' He kissed her warmly.

*I came to see Alex.*

He dropped his voice. 'Where is he? Upstairs?'

*Yes.*

'Why are we whispering?'

*I've lost my voice.*

'Don't breathe on him, for God's sake.'

*I'm not infectious. It's brought on by stress.*

'Stress, hmm?'

*I really only popped in to say hello,* she said, mistrusting the gleam in his eye.

He picked up the loaded tray with a smile. She followed, vowing to escape as soon as politely possible. Alex was asleep.

'Come on,' said Andrew. 'We won't disturb him.' He led her through to a large bedroom and set the tray down. 'Have a seat.' There was only a double bed. She perched on the edge and

335

glanced round. On a chest of drawers stood a photograph of a man laughing and she guessed it must be Raphael. The thought that he and Andrew had once shared the bed on which she was sitting unnerved her.

'I *lurve* this place,' he announced. He stood for a moment at the window looking out. Isobel craned round. The church formed the left-hand boundary of the old vicarage garden. The dull backs of stained-glass saints lined the lawn. Andrew lay down beside her, stretching himself out.

'We moved in the day before Advent. I woke the next morning to the strains of *Wachet Auf.* The tune from the bank advert,' he whispered.

*I know!* she snapped. *So you live with Alex now?*

He inclined his head and gestured to the window behind their heads. 'Annexed to the church, as you see. That's the vestry down there.' He pointed to the floor under the mantelpiece. 'The sound of choir practice wafts up the chimney and gets broadcast through the fireplace. I hear Duruflé and weep for my lost innocence. Tea, Vicar?' He poured her some.

*Alex seems to think God's punishing him,* said Isobel, after a while.

'Hubris,' he remarked. 'Alex would rather believe anything than that he's an ordinary man with an ordinary illness.'

*What do you believe?*

'I don't know. ME's a funny thing. He's deeply, deeply pissed off by the thought that it may be psychological. He woke up on his fortieth birthday and couldn't move, you see. Personally I think that's just coincidence, but who knows?'

His fortieth birthday. She'd been dreaming about him that very night. And he'd always threatened to kill himself when he hit forty. *Will he get better?*

'Hmm. Maybe. About half make a full recovery. He'll certainly improve to some extent. We're looking at years not months, though.'

*And you're taking care of him?*

'For my many, many sins. It took him two months to admit he couldn't cope. Then he employed an Aussie nurse for a month who treated him like "an elderly moron", which I confess I enjoyed. In the end he sacked her and here we both are.'

*But he still manages to work?*

He grimaced. 'We fight over that one. All the stuff I've read suggests that he'll recover faster if he doesn't push himself. But he still struggles into college most days.'

*Surely he can read, though? And think?*

'Isobel, he can't even remember why he used to want to.'

*It's terrible!* she choked.

'Oh, just focus on all those times you wished someone would take him down a peg or two,' he said airily. She sensed the mood change. 'Now, then. Let's hear about this stress of yours.'

She snorted. *You're the last person I'd tell!*

'Why's that?'

*Because, quite frankly, you've always been a complete pig to me.*

'Not a *complete* pig, surely. I don't remember taking that much trouble.'

*Well, I don't trust you*, she said.

'What? Not even in my redeemed state? I hope you kept your promise to pray for me, by the way.'

She blushed. *I did to start with. But recently I haven't found prayer easy.*

'Prayer is never easy,' he chided.

This needled her into asking, *How's the big vocation coming along?*

He gave her a withering look. 'I'll tell you one thing: if they won't let me wear Birkenstocks, I'm not doing it.'

A thought struck her and she sniggered. *Surely you should become a Franciscan if you want to be trendy? Brown is supposed to be the new black.*

'Black is the only black,' he said blightingly.

*Seriously, though.*

'Seriously? Well, after I spoke to you I went to see someone. To talk.'

*Who?*

'Just *someone*, Isobel.' He drank his tea. She could tell he was toying with the idea of confiding.

*What did this someone say?* she prompted.

'After a while he said, "Andrew, why don't you go out and come back in and we'll start all over again?"'

*What? Why?*

'Because I was being a prick. My last-ditch attempt at outsmarting God. The theory was, if I behaved really badly I'd get thrown out and that would be the end of it.'

*Honestly, Andrew.*

'I said, "If I walk out now, I'm never coming back." He didn't reply, so I went.' He laughed. 'I lasted about ten days. During that time I learnt that the door to the kingdom is *this* high,' he stretched an idle hand over the side of the bed, palm eighteen inches off the ground, 'and the only way in for the likes of me is on my hands and knees in the dirt. You can use that in a sermon if you like,' he offered generously.

*So you went back?*

'I did. I had my story worked out. Bloody waste of time *that* was. I didn't get past the first word. He sat and waited while I sobbed my heart out. Then he said –' There were tears on his face again now. 'He just said, "Welcome home." '

## CHAPTER 26

This is almost certainly a mistake, she thought, sitting down on the bed in Andrew's spare room. But the phone call to her parents had been made, the toothbrush bought, the pyjamas lent. It would be discourteous to change her mind now; not to mention the fact that the last bus home had left hours before.

'*That's* what we've been needing,' Andrew had said to Alex over dinner. 'Company to cheer us up.'

This was generous, considering she'd managed, quite by accident, to do the reverse earlier while helping him set the table. At his request she'd reached down the box of best wine glasses from the cupboard and smiled when she saw a little note inside reading, 'Andrew, these are Bohemian crystal. If you put them in the dishwasher, I'll kill you.' Without stopping to think, she handed it over to him. He flinched, then turned abruptly away.

Raphael. You great tactless fool, she castigated herself. *I'm sorry.*

He said nothing. She listened to the sound of blade on board as he continued chopping mushrooms. Gently she lifted the glasses from their tissue and set them on the table. He was crying. She went and touched his shoulder. He flung down the knife, covered his face and wept. She had put her arm round him and waited.

It was half past nine now. She listened. He was playing the piano. It was the Chopin nocturne Alex had played all those years before; this time at a more leisurely tempo. Alex had already gone to sleep, exhausted after the meal.

I spend so much of my time consoling people, she thought. Not that she resented it. Never. How could she, being so fortunate, her life basically intact, her loved ones still alive and well? But the grief of others seeped into the comforter until they needed comforting, too. Perhaps she had not been tender enough with herself in Asleby.

Andrew had dried his eyes at last. 'I can't believe it was two years last month.'

*Do you think you're beginning to get over it?* she asked.

'You never do. It's always there. The absence. But gradually it becomes part of the landscape.' He picked up the note and looked at it again. 'I never even *thought* of putting them in the dishwasher, you bastard.'

There was a gentle tap on her door.

*Yes?*

It was Andrew. He hesitated, uncharacteristically. 'I'm . . . going to say compline. Do you want to come?'

*OK*, she said, in surprise.

The church was dark. He switched on the lights in the chancel and they sat together there. The reredos was covered and a Lenten austerity overlaid everything.

'I normally sing the office,' whispered Andrew.

*Carry on. I'll listen.* She looked at the plainsong booklet in her hands, relieved that she wouldn't have to muddle her way through the squiggles aloud. She could barely sightread ordinary music.

'Will you say the responses?'

*You do it.*

The silence was a little tense. She feared that her presence would unnerve him and he'd be tempted to camp it up. He began self-consciously, but as the service progressed they both managed to relax. She listened to his voice, as beautiful as ever, and their history melted away, all the cruelty and resentment they'd ever dealt one another, until they were no more than two servants standing by night in the house of the Lord.

> *Keep me as the apple of an eye.*
> *Hide me under the shadow of thy wings.*

Rain pattered briefly on the roof, like the footsteps of vanishing ghosts. She thought of the poltergeist activity and realized it had stopped. No strange breakages and misplaced items. No swinging mugs on her parents' dresser. Or flying glassware. Would it all start up again when she got back to Asleby? She froze, then realized, No. It's over, whatever it was. The child waiting to be noticed, that she'd described to Gabriel:

340

*Be present, O merciful God, and protect us through the silent hours of this night, so that we, who are wearied by the changes and chances of this fleeting world, may repose upon thy eternal changelessness; through Jesus Christ our Lord. Amen.*

He was made for this, she thought. When the office was over she told him.

'Yes, I think so.'

*You believe that God has a plan, a purpose, for your life, then?* This was partly mischievous, and she knew it: to see how he'd handle that old chestnut of God's omnipotence and human free will.

'A plan? Not a rigidly scripted one, no,' he answered. 'Strict Calvinists would disagree with me, of course, but only because they're predestined to.'

She smiled. *What do you really think?*

'There is a script, but it's improvised.'

*Controlled by the actors, not the playwright, you mean?*

'Apparently. But supposing, in spite of everything, the playwright can hold it all in his mind – all the characters, the plots and endless chaotic sub-plots, the red herrings, the cock-ups, the disastrous death of the hero – and weave all the strands together? I picture the action as being brooded over by a keen, but infinitely kind, intelligence and he will bring it all to its fitting conclusion.'

She was moved. So he was capable of laying aside his endless clever games and being sincere. Did it feel like intellectual naked-ness to him, after all this time?

*If the conclusion is inevitable, why bother?* she asked. *What does our puny contribution mean?*

'Everything and nothing. God doesn't need us, but He's chosen to work with amateurs.' He replaced the compline book on the pew shelf and got to his feet. 'You should go away and mug up your Barth, my girl.'

This was more what she was used to. *So you're not a lightning conductor for the wrath of God any more?*

He looked at her as though she were some tiresome student of his. 'There's never an easy correlation between sin and disaster. Nor

341

between virtue and blessing, for that matter,' he said. 'Or we'd run into trouble with the crucifixion, wouldn't we?'

*Yes, Father Andrew.*

'Oh, piss off.'

He linked his arm through hers and they walked together out of the church.


She ended up spending a week with them in Oxford. It was like going AWOL, knowing Harry was growing increasingly frustrated by her refusal to get in touch. But it was over now. She was on the train north. Although she'd enjoyed the last few days, nothing had really worked out as she'd imagined on the train down. It hadn't been a jolly treasure hunt, solving one clue after another until she claimed the prize: her voice.

The narcissi would be out in her garden by now. It was Holy Week and she was going back to help Harry as best she could. He was up to his ears running a children's holiday club. She felt her old friend the invisible hand fingering her throat, waiting to grab and choke her. So much to face when she got back! She had talked at length to Andrew and, while not agreeing all the time with his unsettling insights, they had at least provided her with a new perspective.

I can't believe I told him all that stuff, she thought. The train slid to a halt north of Doncaster. She stared at the patch of field outside the window, wondering how much of a risk she'd taken confiding in Andrew. When she'd told him about Davy, instead of looking suitably grave he'd said, 'God, men in uniform! Did he use his handcuffs?' She rebuked him for not taking her sin seriously and he'd said, 'Well, how serious is it, for God's sake?' Was that what Bishop Theodore had been driving at, she wondered, when he picked her up on her use of the words 'weak and stupid'? Why not rebellious, unfortunate, he'd asked, or natural and understandable? Andrew clearly found it the latter. It was only in confessing to him that she recovered a sense of how much she liked Davy, the fun they'd had and the fact that it had only been in his company that she could put her feet up and stop being a professional. He had preyed on her mind a lot over the past weeks. Once, to her alarm, she thought she'd glimpsed him on St Giles, but she'd been seeing things. It must be guilt at the way she'd treated him. When she got back she would try to salvage something of their old friendship.

But *what* had possessed her to confess her feelings for Johnny, as well? She frowned at the memory. If she'd stopped to think she'd have remembered that Andrew knew him. But she'd blurted out his name and there had been no going back.

'You too?' sighed Andrew. 'I wasted years on him.'

*His wife's left him.*

'So one gathers. He rang me to see if she was here.'

It *was* true, then! *Have you spoken to her?*

'Not recently. I'm in the doghouse.'

*Why? For taking his part?*

'For speaking the truth in love, as St Paul commends. Please, I'd no more discuss Mara with you than you with her.' His eyes glinted.

Isobel wasn't entirely sure she found this reassuring. *But if she doesn't come back . . .*

'She will. I know it can be hell for them when they're together, but believe me, it's even worse hell when they're apart. Izzie,' he said, 'don't let yourself hope. Find someone else. What about Harry?'

*Harry!* she snorted. *I think you'll find he has, er, other fish to fry.*

'Speaking as a *cordon bleu* fryer of other fish, let me assure you you're wrong.'

You don't know everything, mate, she thought.

The train lurched, then began to glide forward again at last. Some problem with signals, explained the announcement. Isobel wondered if she could trust Andrew not to talk. He was quite capable of taking it upon himself to sort out her life for her and inform Mara or Johnny of her feelings. Or was she being unfair? She pondered that equivocal assurance about confidentiality he'd made.

He was right about Johnny, though. She must abandon hope. And as to his notions about Harry's orientation – that was irrelevant at this precise moment. Given that the train would soon be approaching

343

York, a much more pressing question was how on earth she was going to face him. She couldn't even offer proof that she'd been doing anything valuable in her absence. She was returning empty-handed with her problems still unsolved. Why couldn't she admit that there was not going to be an easy solution? She thought about her parents, who, in their different ways, were convinced that answers could be had if only one persisted. She was the same. All she had done was substitute Christianity for psychotherapy and science.

She closed her eyes and leant her head back. So what have I gained, then? She listed the unpleasant memories she had now confronted. Mr Peacock, the abortion, her breast surgery, her sometimes ungovernable appetite for casual sex. They were like ugly bits of furniture, expensive mistakes she would now have to live with. Shoving them in the attic hadn't worked.

And she had gained a friend. It made her smile to think how intensely she'd loathed Andrew when she'd lived in Oxford. In an absurd way, this was the closest she'd come to recovering the kind of passionate friendship she'd shared with Tatiana. Some of the same feelings were there – the intensity, the silliness, but also the sense of being less funny and clever than the beloved and fearing she'd be abandoned. While he couldn't bend spoons like Uri Geller, he had worked another piece of magic by locating that tricky snatch of music which had teased her for months. She'd described it as best she could and he picked out the notes on the piano.

'Is this it?' he asked, putting on a CD of medieval church music. '*Alma redemptoris mater.* It's a piece I dug out of some French monastery archives in eighty-nine.'

As the music started the memory rushed back: a summer afternoon. The sound of singing had drawn Isobel to the library door. The Jacks brothers. Music filled the stairwell, strange, haunting, yet with an edge of wild joy. The two parts twined in and out, chasing one another, until the song ended with the falling cadence of four notes, which was to torment her so many years later.

The echo died. Ironic applause came from the library. The brothers laughed.

'My God,' said Andrew. 'Better than sex!'

She had the CD in her bag now. Although she'd listened to the piece a couple of times, it didn't reproduce that first fleeting rapture. Maybe the recording was technically better, but when the Jacks brothers sang together some intuition flowing between them meant that the sound was greater than the sum of the parts.

They used to stride like demons or demigods across my Oxford, she thought. What were they now? Ordinary men? To Andrew's relief her presence as a guest had excused Alex from the routine of going to 'work'. Most mornings she took him in his wheelchair to the University parks. They passed young mothers pushing babies in buggies and she hoped that the irony didn't strike him. He never said much, although once, to her surprise, he remarked that he was glad she had come because she made Andrew happy.

She was at a loss. As far as she could see she had nothing to offer either man. In a flash Theodore's question came back: which are you – friend, child or servant of God? Was her silent companionship worth something in its own right, both to God and to others?

Alex would sit with her and watch the river and the waterbirds and the wind riffling the poplars. Sometimes he took her hand. Six years ago she would have given anything for this calm intimacy, but now – what? It puzzled her to know what she felt for him. Sorrow, affection, compassion. Before, it was as if he'd existed for her only in a blur of motion and now that he lay still before her gaze, like a juggler's spent firebrands, the essence of him had vanished. What did he think about? Where had he gone? What would the new man be like when he emerged from this debilitating illness?

At present he was trapped in his proud invalid's tyranny, demanding pity yet slapping down any expression of it. It's all right to be weak, she wanted to tell him. We're allowed to be mere humans. But she didn't say it. Perhaps they were ideal for one another. She could barely speak and he had barely the energy to listen. They continued to sit as the clouds chased across the bright sky and the poplars rushed like waterfalls.

Darlington. Isobel got off the train and went to consult the timetable for Asleby. There was a tap on her shoulder. She turned. It was Harry. She dropped her bag and flung herself into his arms.

'I've missed you!' they both exclaimed.

'Whoar! Get stuck in, Vicar!' yelled a group of passing lads.

'Ahem!' said Harry, releasing her with a laugh. 'Should've come in mufti.' He took her bag and they walked to where he'd parked the car.

'So, how are you?' he asked as they set off. 'You're looking very well.'

*I've still not got my voice back.*

'No. Poor you. But are you feeling any happier in yourself?'

*I suppose I am,* she admitted. *Harry, I feel dreadful about leaving you in the lurch all this time.*

'Don't be silly, Isobel,' he said sternly.

*I've tried to stop saying that.*

'But I love it!'

There was a pause. Was he flirting with her? She cursed Andrew Jacks.

*How's life in the parish?*

'Walter Goodwill died last week.'

*Oh, I'm sorry.* Isobel was surprised by affection for the cantankerous old man. *Who took the funeral?*

'Me. We were reconciled at the end. He was rushed into hospital with gangrene in his foot − not uncommon with diabetics, apparently − and the family summoned a priest. He wanted you, of course, but it was an emergency. When I arrived there was uproar on the ward. He'd just heard he'd got to have his leg amputated. The family were shouting, "Shut up, you daft old bugger, it's for your own good, do you want to die, or something?" and he was beside himself. I stood there and yelled, "Would it help if I said a prayer, Mr Goodwill?" Silence fell. Oh, Isobel!'

*What?*

'It was just awful!' He was laughing. 'I took out my Bible to read a nice soothing psalm. "I lift up my eyes unto the hills. From whence cometh my help?" We were doing all right till I hit verse three.'

*Oh, no!*

'Exactly. "He will not suffer thy foot to be moved". How I made it to the end of the psalm, I'll never know.' He wiped his eyes. As it happened, he died of a heart attack that night.'

*Perhaps it was a blessing,* she murmured.

'That's not the end of it,' quavered Harry. 'The family wanted a church funeral. Our organist was away, so I arranged cover. Unfortunately, Jim had forgotten to hand over the keys to the organ loft and I must have left mine at home somewhere. Ten minutes before the service I was frantically trying all the spare sets knocking about the vestry. The congregation were all gathered. "There's nothing for it," I hissed. "We'll have to shoulder-barge the door." I don't know what the mourners made of the running feet and crashes, but we couldn't budge it. Where's Johnny Whitaker when I need him? I thought. He'd have got it open in three seconds.'

Isobel laughed self-consciously. *Oh, Harry! What did you do?*

'I got the ladder. The organist shot up and dived over the balcony into the loft. I saw his legs kicking. The verger and I carried the ladder back down the aisle just as the coffin was coming in. It was like the Marx Brothers.'

*Maybe old Walter would have enjoyed it?*

'I bet he was crowing. I could hear his voice in my ear the whole time "Ee, you useless bugger. Couldn't organize a piss-up in a brewery, you couldn't." '

*How's the holiday club going?*

'Very well. We've had between sixty and eighty kids along most days.'

*You've had enough helpers?*

'Yes. Natalie's off on maternity leave now, so she's been there. So has Brenda.'

*Brenda!*

'Yep. She's excellent with the naughty boys. Keeps them in order. I'm scared of her myself. She gets a bit worried she won't know the "right" answers, but as she herself says, "We'll burn that bridge when we get to it." '

They both laughed.

'She now runs that Inquirers' Group you set up, by the way. Without any help from the vicar, I might add.'

Isobel received this with mixed feelings. Of course, she was delighted they were still meeting together, but it left her feeling redundant. She was a little surprised Harry hadn't insisted on sitting in on the sessions. There was no knowing what heresies they were unwittingly straying into. But he always took a laid-back approach.

She was relieved to hear she'd missed Fitz giving everyone a scare by running away from home.

'He was missing for two days then turned up in France, of all places. He'd hitched out there in hot pursuit of the French *assistante*. You knew she'd been lodging with the Fitzgeralds?'

Isobel nodded.

'Poor old Fitzy seems to have convinced himself they were destined for each other. Oh, to be fifteen! Dr Fitzgerald had to drive over and bring him back in disgrace.'

*Was there anything going on between them?* asked Isobel, recalling Fitz's behaviour before Christmas.

'No. She denies it.'

*She would, though.*

'Well, Dr Fitzgerald is pretty sure it's a case of wishful thinking.'

*Hmm.*

She told him about her time with her parents and in Oxford. She'd forgotten, momentarily, that he knew the Jacks brothers, and he surprised her by admitting he'd already heard about Alex's illness. She wondered if he knew about Andrew's vocation as well, but he didn't mention it. During the rest of the journey he continued to chat about parish matters. She was grateful to him for giving her a chance to rest her voice and for not pestering her with searching questions.

When they pulled up outside her house she said, *You've been busy. I wish I could be of more use to you. I'll do whatever I can. Shift chairs. Whatever.* A deep sense of uselessness assailed her.

Harry laid a hand on her arm. 'You're back. That's the main thing.'

She let herself into her house. The door closed behind her and she stood in the hall. The air was a little stale. She looked around at the woodchip-papered walls and the carpet she would never have chosen. *I'm here. I'm back.* There was a smear of what looked like dried blood on the wall. How had that got there?

She went into her study and caught sight of the pile of unopened post on her desk and her heart almost failed her. How would she ever catch up? Everything was there – her computer, books, files, robes hanging on the back of the door, all waiting for her to resume her life. It felt like a trap closing round her. She thought of Agnes thrust back into her cell. Had she gone quietly, or had she kicked and screamed? Had her sobs echoed round the church each night until at last she sat and stared at her wall, a broken woman?

If only one knew what had happened to her. But after her return Agnes had slipped from the records. Isobel had found no trace of her and the most likely explanation was that she had continued in uneventful piety till her dying day. Maybe she'd gone back humbled, resigned to the knowledge that she would never be a saint, or even a famous holy woman pilgrims would travel miles to consult. There would be no visions, no signs and wonders emanating from her cell; except the unspectacular miracle of a life schooled by long obedience.

'Assist us with Thy grace, that we may do all such good works as Thou hast prepared for us to walk in.' Isobel had always vaguely pictured a path strewn with acts of charity for her to undertake as she happened upon them. But supposing one day as she strode along, ticking off her worthy deeds as she completed them, the road was blocked with one towering Good Work that would cost her everything? She had always paid lip-service to the notion that without God she could do nothing, but her abilities and education were there as a safety-net. While acknowledging that it was only God who could move hearts and change lives, her every action proclaimed that it all depended on Isobel Knox. And now Isobel Knox could do nothing. What was the point of her?

Was this how she ought to perceive her present situation – God stripping away everything in which she took refuge until at last she threw herself wholly on His mercy? Except Andrew was right yet again: there was no easy link between sin and disaster. He thought her dumbness was self-inflicted. At some level, as he put it, she found her public self – epitomized by speech – so unacceptable, so much at odds with her inner life, that in the

349

end she had silenced it. Certainly this fitted with the Bishop's image of censorship.

She sorted her post automatically into three piles – bills, anything in a manila envelope, personal letters – then went to put a load in the washing-machine. In an hour or two she'd be at the vicarage trying to tell Harry 'where she'd got to in her thinking'. What could she say?

She was still asking herself this as she walked the familiar route from her house to his. It was drizzling. All the local blackbirds were whistling in the March evening. *You know the answer, Isobel*, a voice whispered. Tears welled up. She blinked them away as she walked down the vicarage drive and rang the bell.

They sat at Harry's kitchen table and he made some coffee. She hadn't been there for months, not since before Christmas. Or wait – she'd been there during those missing days and propelled a wine glass at his head. He'd confessed the incident had been terrifying, but without any memory of that night, it struck Isobel as comical. Poor old Harry, she thought guiltily. He was chatting happily about this and that. Once the coffee was poured he sat opposite her, smiled and said, 'Well?'

*Harry, I've come to the conclusion* – She broke off and pressed a hand to her mouth. *I've decided that the sensible thing would be for me to resign.*

He registered this with a tiny flinch. Then he nodded. 'OK. If that's what you want.'

*It's not exactly . . . what I want, but I can't see any other way out.*

There was a long silence. 'How are we, er, going to handle this?' he wondered out loud. 'Supposing you stayed until the end of June? That would mean you'd done two years here. That's a perfectly respectable length of time for a curacy.'

*That wouldn't leave you with any time to fix up a new curate*, she pointed out.

'Well, I mustn't assume the Bishop's going to give me one. They're still cutting back. And, to be honest, they're unlikely to make any new appointments until this team ministry mess is sorted out.'

350

Isobel could scarcely remember why she'd been so bothered by the St Margaret's episode. They both sipped their coffee.

'So, when might we think about making an announcement?' he asked.

They discussed it and fixed on Pentecost. Then they pondered what Isobel might do after leaving. She agreed to talk things over with the Archdeacon after he and the Bishop had reviewed her case. In the meantime she was to carry out whatever duties still lay within her power. Everything was so painfully courteous, so civilized, like an amicable marriage break-up. It shouldn't be this easy, she wanted to cry. But Harry's manner left no room for raw emotion.

He walked her home and they said goodbye outside her gate. He turned and left, already seeming distant. As she went into her study she tried to banish the feeling that he'd let her down tonight by his calm, professional response to her decision. What had she been hoping for? They were, after all, work colleagues. He was only treating her with the respect she had always demanded.

She sat at her desk. Surely she ought to feel relieved, now the decision was taken. There were just over seven weeks until the formal announcement was made. It was a manageable chunk of time. She could soldier on till then. After that there would be a fortnight until she left. This would provide a chance to tie up loose ends, make arrangements about her future – oh, God! She would never cope. What on earth could she do? She was virtually unemployable. Some kindly bishop somewhere might carve out a half-role for her. Failing that she would have to fall back on librarianship. I can still go ssh! she thought bitterly. Was this it – that overwhelming Good Work – to give up the calling she'd cherished for so long?

Her hands began leafing through her post, some of which, shamefully, had been untouched for months. There were some get-well cards from fellow clergy, Christmas thank-you letters from relatives, a little Celtic notelet from her mother wishing her a happy return. The last envelope bore unfamiliar handwriting, bold, semi-literate. She opened it and froze in shock.

*Dear Isobel,*
*You're not answering your phone. Have I upset you? I called at the cottage,*
*but you were out. I'd still like to meet up, if that's OK with you. Give me*
*a ring some time.*
*Johnny.*

It was dated 6 January.

## CHAPTER 27

During the next few days Isobel turned the letter over and over in her mind. So he *had* called at the cottage. It had been his footprint on the step. All she could see in her mind's eye was images of Johnny. Johnny shivering in the wind, Johnny making the whole room laugh, Johnny telling her to fuck off, baiting her, hugging her, wanting to come in for coffee, to see her again ... What on earth should she do? Or had she already 'done' something, by inadvertently not replying? If he had any sense he would have interpreted her silence as rejection, in which case the episode was closed. There wasn't even any point mentioning it to Harry. It would only diminish Johnny in his eyes. Then it struck her that all along she'd found valid reasons for not telling Harry. Perhaps if she'd been more honest she'd never have got into this sorry mess. But she was leaving now, and Harry was becoming increasingly remote. There was nothing to be gained from souring his relationship with Johnny. He was as courteous as ever, but they were just coexisting, marking time until she went. He no longer told her silly anecdotes or teased her. Did he feel betrayed by her decision to go? Maybe he was relieved. She began to fear he saw her as a quitter, or that he'd never really liked her.

Natalie, now spending her days at home, was one of the first people Isobel nerved herself to call on.

They hugged. It was an awkward affair, only in part because of Natalie's swollen belly.

*Are you sure it's not twins?* Isobel joked.

'Nope. "One highly active singleton", is what they said at the first scan.'

They went to the kitchen, which had become blue and yellow since Isobel had last been in it. Natalie filled the marigold kettle, then stood with her hands pressed into the small of her back.

'Not so active now. Three weeks to go. Except first babies are usually late. Not enough room to dance about any more. You just play football with Mummy's bladder, don't you?' she asked the bump fondly.

Isobel cringed at Natalie referring to herself as Mummy, although, to be fair, she practically was.

*But everything's all right?*

'Fine. Blood pressure up a bit, but nothing to worry about.'

They both fell silent. Isobel could tell that Natalie wasn't sure how to proceed; whether to inquire about Isobel's health. Stuck on the fridge was an ultrasound scan image of the foetus, a black square with blurred traces of white, like a night sky with a crescent moon, which Isobel imagined must be the skull.

'It's good to have you back,' ventured Natalie.

*Thanks.* Isobel was guilt-stricken. She'd be gone for good shortly after the child was born. The friendship needed a surge of con-fiding honesty to revive it – I've had a breakdown, I had it off with that policeman, I'm resigning.

*Things have been a bit tough, but I think I'm on the mend*, she said unhappily.

'And your voice ...?'

She shrugged. *Have you decorated the baby's room?*

They took their tea upstairs. Natalie paused at the top of the first flight and caught her breath. 'No room for my lungs, either.' She laughed.

They entered the little nursery and Isobel duly admired the wallpaper and cot. The baby was a safe topic. They discussed names and nappies with apparent cheerfulness, but by the time Isobel left, she was filled with unexplained misery, weeping inside and unable to remember why.

She went home for dinner to discover the second post had brought a rare letter from Thelma. It had been franked by the library where she worked, Thelma not being a woman to squander her stamps lightly. Isobel opened it and read:

354

*I conclude, from the fact that you have made no effort to contact me for the last three months, that you no longer wish to pursue our friendship. No doubt you are busy and fulfilled in parish life, in which case I quite understand that your old friends are more of an encumbrance than a pleasure. I had been hoping that the two of us might go out and celebrate my promotion, with its albeit modest remuneration, but you clearly have better things to do with your time. Please don't trouble to acknowledge this if it's a nuisance.*

She was still open-mouthed in indignation when the doorbell rang. It was Jan.

'Hello, hello! Welcome back, dear one! How's things? Here.' She shoved an icy bottle of something into Isobel's hands and hugged her.

*Thank you. What's this?*

'The label says, "Best drunk *immediately*",' hinted Jan.

Isobel carried it through to the kitchen and found her corkscrew.

'And what have we here?' Jan rummaged in her bag. 'Smoked salmon! Have you got any bread? I knew you wouldn't have.' A crusty brown loaf was thumped on to the table, followed by a lemon.

Isobel opened the cupboard to find two dinner plates. She stared at the pile, puzzled. There were only eleven.

'What's wrong?' asked Jan.

*I've lost a plate.*

'Well, did you break one?'

*No.*

'Did you bear it to church laden with mince-pies, or something? It'll turn up.'

Isobel shrugged.

'So, how are you?' asked Jan.

*Fine.*

'Don't give me "fine". How are you?'

*Well, I'm back.*

'Able to resume duties?'

*To a limited extent.*

'Not resigning your orders or anything drastic – I didn't just ask that,' she added scrupulously. 'Harry ordered me not to give you the third degree.'

It was an invitation to confide. *I'm just . . . Things aren't* – she floundered.

'Well, are you going to open that wine or am I?' demanded Jan.

Isobel picked up the bottle.

'Right,' said Jan. 'Breadknife?'

Isobel pointed to the drawer. This is awful, she thought. I feel like I'm betraying her trust. She wondered if she should ask Harry's permission to tell Jan she'd be leaving in June.

'Well, of all the bloody cheek!'

Isobel turned and saw Jan reading the letter from Thelma, which she'd left on the work surface. *You read other people's correspondence?* she asked in shock.

'Only if it's lying about. Who is this Thelma person?'

*I can't* believe *you did that!*

'Oh, come on, we all do it. I hope you rattled off a snorter in reply,' said Jan.

*It's only just come*, replied Isobel, still outraged.

'"Albeit with its modest remuneration",' chortled Jan, impervious to Isobel's indignation. They sat down to eat. '"My dear Thelma, I've been ill, so piss off, you neurotic self-absorbed bag. Sincerely."'

*I couldn't*, giggled Isobel, against her will.

'"PS Please find enclosed five pounds in modest remuneration of the phone calls you doubtless made to establish I hadn't passed away."'

*Stop it*, she begged. Small wonder she's as thick as thieves with Andrew Jacks, she thought.

'So how will you answer it?'

It occurred all at once to Isobel that she'd had enough of Thelma for one lifetime. *I won't.*

'Good for you.' Jan chuckled. 'After all, she specifically says not to, if it's a nuisance.'

They spent the rest of the evening discussing Alex and Andrew, and though the conversation bore all the hallmarks of intimacy, Isobel could sense restraint. She had not confided in Jan, and though this omission was not resented, it had been noted.

\*

356

With each subsequent meeting Isobel's feeling of duplicity grew. *Still holding out on your friend*, niggled her conscience. An unaccustomed awkwardness began to mark their encounters, and in the end Isobel stopped calling round. The thought that she was hurting Jan's feelings only made things worse.

'How are things going, do you think?' asked Harry, in their weekly staff meeting.

*I feel like I'm deceiving everyone*, she told him. *Jan in particular. Knowing I'm going, but letting her think I'm not.*

'Well, bear up,' he said, with what struck her as heartless briskness. 'Not long now. Tell me what you've been up to this week.'

*Visiting, mainly.* She could think of nothing to add. His brusque response had made soul-baring unattractive.

'Could I suggest you try and catch a word with Fitz? I know he respects you, and nobody else has made any headway with him.'

She nodded. *I must also . . . um, have a chat with Davy, I think. See how he's getting on.*

Harry pursed his lips. 'If you think that's wise.'

Her face blazed. *What do you mean?*

'No, no!' He coloured too. 'I wouldn't dream – it's just that he upset you so much by his – Well, as you wish. You're the best judge.'

*I feel I owe it to him.*

'Well, I'm sure you'll be careful not to raise his hopes.'

Something prompted her to blurt, *He thinks you don't like him.*

'Me?' Harry laughed and coloured again. 'I hope I've never given him any cause.'

Harry's ambivalence made her consider carefully. She'd come back determined to see if she could rescue her earlier friendship with Davy from the wreckage of their fling. Perhaps she was kidding herself. Harry was right to remind her how intolerable she'd found Davy's presence a month or two ago. Was she stronger now? On the whole she thought she was. She assumed he'd call round before long. He must have heard she was back. Once or twice when she was returning home she thought she'd glimpsed his car disappearing round the corner of her street and concluded she'd just missed him. It was frustrating. In the end she popped a note through his door asking him to call round for coffee.

On her way home she visited Sue. Mike was at work, but Sue asked her in, showing nothing but pleasure at seeing her once more.

*I'm sorry not to have been around*, said Isobel.

'You've been ill,' pointed out Sue. 'We totally understand. And in any case,' her eyes brimmed with tears, 'you'd already done so much. At the beginning, especially.'

Isobel swallowed painfully and nodded. They hadn't been blaming her, then, or feeling let down.

*Um, I'm not sure how to put this. I'd already bought Hannah a book for Christmas. Then I didn't know what to do with it. Would you – ?*

Sue gulped and nodded.

Isobel reached into the carrier-bag she'd brought and handed the gift over. Sue unwrapped it. Isobel looked away so she wouldn't see her reading the inscription. They both sat.

'Thanks,' whispered Sue at last.

*That's OK*. Her eyes were glassy with tears. Perhaps Sue had seen them, and would come across and comfort her instead for once.

'It's nice to think ...' began Sue. 'It's just that people aren't talking about her any more.'

Everyone's starting to move on, thought Isobel, leaving Sue and Mike alone in their grief, willing them to get over it, covering Hannah in a shroud of silence and tact. You never get over it, Andrew had said. There must be no end to her patient listening.

That evening she heard Davy's car pull up and his footsteps on the path. The doorbell rang and she felt sick with dread. Harry was right. I shouldn't have tried this.

*Davy!*

'Hiya.'

Isobel recovered first. *Well, come in! Coffee?*

'Nah, I'm fine, thanks.'

After a moment's awkward dithering they went into her study and sat down.

'So,' they both began together.

She gestured for him to carry on.

'So, you're home, then?'

*Yes.*

'Voice still not back?'

*No.*

This is terrible, she thought. She'd never seen him this subdued. After a moment she asked, *How's work? No more corpses grabbing you?*

This provoked a brief grin. 'Forgot I'd told you that.'

*Are you doing all right?*

He shrugged. 'Not so bad.'

*What about Newcastle?*

This, at last, was the right button to press. She got a detailed account of the club's fortunes over the previous three months.

*Well, I've been to see my parents*, she said, when the next silence yawned. *Then I went to Oxford.*

'Aye, I know.'

She frowned. *How did you know that?*

He barely skipped a beat. 'Well, you told me.'

*When?* At the time she had been conscious of the callousness of slipping away without informing him.

'Or mebbes it was someone else. I cannot remember.'

Could it have been Harry? she puzzled.

'Listen, now you're back, like,' he began.

Oh, no, she thought.

'Am I allowed to call round and that?'

*Well . . .*

His foot was jiggling, betraying his tension, despite his attempted nonchalance.

*Look, Davy, I just don't know what to say*, she admitted. *I feel mean if I say no and mean if I'm letting you hope.*

'I've got to see you,' he blurted.

*Mightn't a clean break be better in the long run?* she asked gently.

'No!' He no longer tried to conceal his desperation.

*But, Davy! Come on – you managed while I was away.*

'Why didn't you tell me where you were going?'

*Well, I'm afraid it didn't occur to me*, she replied defensively. *I didn't really tell anyone. The point is, you didn't see me for ages, and even if you weren't happy, you managed –* Something in his expression alarmed her. A memory burst in. *It was you! I saw you in Oxford, didn't I? You followed me!*

He didn't attempt to deny it. Her blood ran cold.

'If you'd only bloody told me where you were I wouldn't have had to!' he snapped. 'I'm sorry.' His eyes pleaded with her. 'I just needed to know if you were all right. I couldn't ring and hear your voice, even. Just the bloody vicar on the answer-machine.'

*You're still doing it, aren't you?* she heard herself ask.

'I'll stop. I swear.'

*How did you find out where I was?*

'Ha'away, it wasn't difficult. I'll stop,' he promised again.

But what if he didn't? Wasn't this how these dangerous obsessions started? He'd been tracking her every move, spying on her as she walked about the streets of Oxford. She'd have to call the — He *was* the police! Dear God, she'd never be able to escape him! He'd always be able to trace her. He had all the expertise, access to computers, records ...

'Isobel, man, I didn't mean to scare you!' He reached out a hand, then drew it back when she recoiled. 'Listen, aal I dee is drive past your house on a night sometimes. Just to see if there's a light on. I just, just have to be near you.'

What have I reduced him to? she thought.

*I'm sorry*, she said helplessly. *I know this sounds trite, but it will pass.*

'Aye. Logic tells me it will. That's just not how it feels at the minute. Still.' He shrugged. 'Life goes on.'

Her heart went out to him. *I've treated you so badly*, she said. *You deserve better.*

He shifted uncomfortably.

*I should have told you from the outset I'm in love with someone else*, she whispered.

'You did.'

*What? When?*

'After we'd, y'kna ...' He cleared his throat. 'The first time, like.'

*Oh!* They were both scarlet. Well, she'd behaved with slightly more integrity than she'd supposed, then, if she'd told him the truth. It was a while since she'd contemplated the gap in her memory. She'd almost grown reconciled to it, like a blank space of wall where a picture once hung.

*But . . .* She searched for the words. *Oughtn't that to help you, um, to get over me? I mean, to know you were just – forgive me – being used?*

'Better that than nowt,' he muttered.

*But that's sheer masochism!* she protested.

'Pathetic,' he agreed. They were silent for a while, then he said, 'We've got a couple of real stalkers on our files at the moment. Nuisance calls, letters, threats, the works. Sad bastards who can't take no for an answer. Never understood it, me.'

But now he can, she thought. And maybe she could, too. Hadn't she spent last autumn stalking Johnny's memory round the streets of Asleby, just to walk where he'd once walked?

'I just cannot take being lied to,' he burst out suddenly.

*I beg your pardon?*

'It was him all along, but you denied it.'

*What are you on about?*

'Don't give me that. You spent a week with him in his house. You went out for meals with him, helped look after his brother –'

*Him? He's gay, you fool!* she interrupted.

He broke off his tirade and stared. 'You're kidding.'

*Some detective you are!* She was shaking with rage. *How dare you spy on me like that?*

'You're sure he's gay?'

*Yes, and don't you ever, ever do that to me again.*

'An' div'n't you caal us a fool!'

There were angry tears in his eyes. He looked like a little boy. She softened. *Honestly, Davy, why didn't you just ask me?*

'Because you wouldn't let me talk to you!' he exclaimed. 'All this could've been avoided if you hadn't cut yourself off like that.'

'Cut yourself off'. It felt like being punched. Her mind made one of those symbolic connections Bishop Theodore had so patiently urged. This was always her response to danger – to cut herself off, to close off the option of sin; even, God help her, to the extent of literally excising bits of her flesh. Like a lizard sacrificing its tail.

'What've I said?' asked Davy in alarm.

*I think . . . Actually, I think you're right.*

The idea occupied her thoughts long after he had gone. It was still with some misgivings, but she had agreed to meet him again. A second attempt at just being friends. What if she fell again? It no longer felt as though this would be the end of the world, and strangely, a new kind of confidence crept through her.

She called at Brenda's and was welcomed back loudly by her Inquirers' Group. Brenda had 'organized them' and they had ploughed on through Isobel's worksheets without the benefit of her expertise, and three of them, including Brenda herself, had decided they wanted to get baptized and confirmed.

*I'm afraid you can't be baptized again, if you were christened*, explained Isobel.

But Harry had already told them this, and they assured her that they hadn't been 'done' as babies.

'I want a proper job, mind,' said Brenda. 'Full submersion.'

Isobel bit her lips. *It would have to be at the local baths, then.*

'Whatever,' said Brenda. 'We're quite happy to fall in.'

The others hooted.

Well, I must have done something right, thought Isobel, as she walked home. Quite what, she had no idea. The sessions had felt disastrous when she'd been leading them.

The following evening she joined them for the quiz night at the local working men's club. It would involve underplaying her intelligence a little, but she had felt it was important to accept their invitation.

The experience was eye-opening. Entering the unfamiliar smoky room gave her a sharp insight into how it felt to be an outsider in church. Was everyone staring? What if I make a fool of myself? Supposing I'm in someone else's seat? And it might be nice, she thought, after half a dozen questions, to be able to answer *one*. Her only useful contribution was providing the name of Moses' sister.

The group meandered home at eleven o'clock, chatting and laughing in the dark. They called goodbye at the end of Isobel's road.

'Same time next week, then?'

She raised a hand in reply. In another month or so she'd be abandoning them. Harry will look after them, she told herself. They've already shown they don't need me. But she still felt she was letting them down.

I'm not indispensable, she reminded herself each day. In her absence Harry had appointed a young couple from the congregation to take over the youth work. Isobel attended a meeting and was satisfied that they were making a good fist of it. The youngsters seemed pleased to see her. Her voice fascinated them.

'Does this mean we can do what we like and you can't bollock us?' asked Fitz.

He spent the rest of the evening baiting her, pretending to find her hoarse whisper sexy, until at last he was shouted down by the rest of the group for being mean. From then on he sat slumped in sullen silence, rousing himself only to snarl, 'Fuck off!' whenever someone dropped France into the conversation.

To her surprise he called round the following afternoon to apologize for his behaviour.

*That's all right, Fitz*, she said. *I assumed you were . . . unhappy for some reason.*

'Oh, yeah, like you don't *know* why,' he sneered. 'Like everyone's not talking about Fitzy's little escapade.' He rucked up his dangling sweater cuffs, got out a packet of cigarettes and defiantly lit one. Her heart went out to him at this clumsy attempt at sophistication.

*Come in*, she said.

'But we're not allowed to smoke in your house,' he pointed out.

*I'll make an exception.*

He hesitated. 'Nah, I'll put it out.' He dropped the cigarette and followed her into her study where they both sat.

Fitz slouched until he was nearly horizontal, chin on chest. He was not going to allow his spiritual freedom to be violated by adult constructs like the armchair.

*You've had a horrible time*, ventured Isobel.

'Like you care.'

*I do.*

363

'Everyone thinks I'm really sad. Having it off with a French *assistante* – in your dreams, Fitz. Nobody believes me.'

*I do,* she repeated.

He tried to sneer again, but his chin trembled.

Isobel waited. Tears smarted in her own eyes. She reached out and laid a hand on his arm. He broke down and wept.

*Fitzy,* she whispered. She wanted to cradle him while he sobbed, but she knew it wouldn't be appropriate. All she could do was hand over the box of tissues she kept for bereavement visits. He grabbed a fistful.

*Look, shall I make us some coffee?*

'Cheers,' he choked.

When she returned with the mugs he was blotchy but more or less composed. They drank for a while without speaking.

*What do your parents think?* she asked.

'Mum thinks I should concentrate on my GCSEs and not bother with girls for another few years. I'm nearly *sixteen!*' he burst out. 'And Dad gives me his doctor spiel about hormones and sperm production and male sexual arousal and I'm like, no! you're kidding – it *stands up*? I mean, what planet is he on?'

*Have you told him the truth?*

'What's the point? He believes *her.* I heard him telling Harry it's just "a spot of adolescent projection". She denied everything.'

*I bet she did.*

'Huh?'

*Well, she knew she'd be in big trouble for seducing a minor.*

'Wha'?'

*You're under age.*

He stared blankly. 'Oh, *minor.* I thought –' A grin flickered. Then the implications of what she had just said seemed to sink in and he sat up. 'You mean she could be, like, arrested?'

Isobel nodded. *I'm assuming she made the first move?*

'Of *course.* She's *twenty-three,* Isobel!'

Isobel failed to hide a smile.

'Well, that's old to me,' he muttered.

*I honestly think you should tell your dad everything.*

'He'd fucking kill me! Sorry, but he would.'

364

*He's more likely to kill her*, replied Isobel. Or call you a lucky dog, she added privately.

'I dunno.' He slumped again. 'He asked her when he came to fetch me. She acted half insulted and half laughing – "You think I sleep with schoolboys? Feetsy? Pff. He's a silly boy wiz a crush."' He mimicked her accent savagely. 'I thought she loved me. I didn't think girls did all that stuff unless they really, really loved you.'

*I'm afraid they sometimes do.*

His face trembled, but he held back the tears. 'So you reckon I should tell him?'

*Yes.*

'What if he doesn't believe me?'

*Show him the aftershave she bought you for Christmas.*

His mouth fell open. 'How did you know about that?'

*Intuition.*

'Cool,' he marvelled.

She went with him to the door.

'Thanks, Isobel.' He gave her a sort of punch on the arm and blundered past. He wheeled round on the doorstep and gestured desperately. 'The other problem is, how am I going to manage without it?'

*You tell me*, she heard herself reply.

'What?' He gawped in shock. She watched it dawn on him that for all her advanced years she might still be a sexual being. He blushed deeply, before rallying. 'Wanna quickie?'

She smiled. *Go away, you bad boy.*

He showed her the tip of his tongue as he had on Christmas Eve and she pushed him out of the door and shut it firmly. His trainers scuffled away down the road. Supposing she'd called his bluff – how would he have reacted? With alacrity, she feared.

She went back into her study and tried to pray for him. Dear Lord, please comfort Fitz. Help him to – Let him – She sighed in despair. Why could she no longer translate her compassion into words? Then the absurdity of it struck her. As if God relied upon her ability to articulate things. Instead she sat and thought about Fitz. She pictured the cheeky boy on a bike when she'd first arrived in the parish; the precociously smouldering fifteen-year-old. He would forget his present misery. She imagined him five years from now in a college bar, swapping stories of first sexual encounters. Looking back, he wouldn't believe his luck. But now, now was an endless hell of humiliation and ridicule and heartbreak. He'd thought she loved him. That little *assistante* had no idea what she was doing.

'I adjure you, O daughters of Jerusalem, that you stir not up nor awaken love until it please,' she quoted to herself. She'd last heard those words in the Friary chapel with Harry and Johnny sitting in the pew beside her. So much ill-timed love stirred up. Johnny. That letter. What she needed was a sense of resolution. Even the death of hope would be preferable to this long-drawn-out suffering. Was that too much to ask? A meeting with Johnny to decide things, once and for all. If they were meant to be together, then it would presumably happen, despite accidents of timing and unanswered letters.

She lingered mentally in the Friary chapel. Harry beside her, Johnny beside him. Sunshine on polished wood. The strange, tormented crucifix above the altar, Christ racked in victory. Then somehow Fitz was there as well. She could picture him slumped in the pew. As she waited, others appeared. Brenda and her friends. Jan, Davy, her parents and brothers, until the chapel was full of those she loved and worried over, Sue and Mike. Alex. Andrew.

For a moment they were all held there in the stillness of the imagined September day under the figure of the suffering Christ and there was nothing she needed to say.

Later that week she met with the Bishop and the Archdeacon. On the strength of Bishop Theodore's report they seemed satisfied that she was fit to continue in the ordained ministry. Harry had already informed them of her decision to leave Asleby, and on the whole they felt this was wise. The Bishop offered to find her another post, or to release her to another diocese, but there remained the problem of her voice. After much thought and prayer (he leant forward reassuringly in a way that made her dread what was coming next) he suggested she might consider an extended retreat.

*I'll pray it over*, she said cautiously.

'Excellent. If you were to decide that this is the way forward, I'm sure Barrington can make some recommendations.'

The Archdeacon smiled jauntily. He still appeared a little nervous of her and what she might do. Honestly. She was tempted briefly to slump back in her chair with her eyes rolled up in her head and give him something real to worry about.

She contacted him a week later and agreed to the episcopal suggestion. The speed with which everything was then arranged left her bewildered. She was to spend six months helping out at the Friary. An elderly academic clergyman had bequeathed the house his library, and part of Isobel's task was to sort through the volumes and catalogue them. It was not what she wanted – in fact, librarianship felt like a retrograde step – but she couldn't see another Way Forward.

Harry insisted she robed Sunday by Sunday. To Isobel it was all a sham. She knew she was contributing next to nothing to the running of the parish. Harry dealt with the situation by remaining unflinchingly professional, treating her like fellow clergy till the bitter end, anxious that her leaving should be accomplished smoothly.

'Right. One or two loose ends for us to think about,' he said, one morning in his study. 'It's only a week till you make your announcement. I think we should tell the churchwardens at this stage. It's only fair they should have advance warning.'

She clasped her hands together hard. *Ought I . . . ? Or –*

'Why don't you tell Jan and I'll tell Drew?' he suggested.

*All right.* Her heart pounded unpleasantly at the prospect.

'Um, and it might, er, be a good idea if –' He appeared to be studying his Filofax. 'You might like to consider telling Davy as well. I'm sure you won't want him to find out on the grapevine. And I, er, gather you're seeing him again.'

*Now and then.* She coloured, feeling his disapproval. *I'll have a word with him.*

'Have you made plans for your furniture to be put into storage?'

367

The bluntness of his question distressed her. It was as if he couldn't wait to be rid of her.

*I'll sort it out*, she promised.

'It's just that – if this is an awful cheek, please say – it's just that a couple of Coverdale students will be here on placement over the summer, and I wondered how you'd feel if they stayed in your house?'

She recoiled from the idea of strangers making free with her things. Yet it would save on storage costs. And it made her departure seem less irrevocable.

*If it would help*, she said.

'Thanks, Isobel. If you're sure, that is.'

She nodded.

'Single students are easier to place,' explained Harry. 'But these are newly-weds, so giving them a bit of privacy seems appropriate.'

Isobel recoiled again – my bed! – but managed a generous smile.

'Good. I'll give them a ring. Oliver and Perpetua,' he said, relishing each syllable. 'Oliver Colefax and Perpetua George – she's kept her maiden name,' he added, seeing Isobel's stunned expression.

This is one of those wretched dreams, she thought. Blood rushed hotly in her ears. I'll wake up and find it never happened.

*Does she have a sister called Tatiana?*

'I've no idea,' said Harry. 'Why?'

*I was at school with her. Tatiana George. She was my best friend. She had a little sister called Perpetua.* Isobel began to tremble.

'Well, I'll ask for you.'

*Find out where she is. What she's doing. Would you? Please?*

'Certainly.' He picked up the phone and dialled.

Then it's not a dream. She began to laugh inside. Tatiana. After all these years she was only a phone call away. She tried to govern her erratic breathing. I knew I'd find her one day. I knew.

Harry grimaced 'Answerphone.' He left a brief message.

Isobel thumped her fists on the arms of her chair, then drooped back and closed her eyes.

'Well, I'm sure they'll ring back,' he ventured, baffled by the evident strength of her feelings.

Tatiana. Where was she? What was she doing? I could find out at any moment! Tomorrow I could be writing to her; next week we could be meeting again. The thought cheered her as she contemplated the task of telling Jan and Davy she was leaving. Should she do the easiest first, or get the hardest over and done with? And which was which?

In the end she went to Jan.

'What ho, stranger!' Jan greeted her. 'Well, come on in, m'dear.'

Derek appeared and threaded himself round her ankles.

'A gin for old times' sake?' suggested Jan.

The offer sounded valedictory to Isobel's guilty ears.

*Lovely.* She sat on the sofa. Derek deposited himself in her lap, purring in anticipation.

Jan came in and handed her a glass.

'OK, break it to me,' she ordered, plonking herself beside Isobel.

*I – Trust you.* Isobel took a good swig. *I'm leaving Asleby. It'll be announced next Sunday.* She said it in a rush, fearing she wouldn't make it to the end of the sentence otherwise. A sob escaped. *I'm sorry. I would've told you before, but –*

'It's all right, my love. It's hardly come out of the blue, has it?'

*How do you mean?*

'Well, it's pretty clear that, for some reason, Asleby has become a walking nightmare for you.'

*Oh, Jan, I –*

'So,' continued Jan brightly, 'what are your plans, then?'

*Well, I'll be here till the end of June. Then I'm going to the Friary for six months. To let the dust settle. After that, who knows?*

Jan nodded. 'Sounds like a good wheeze.'

*I've been avoiding you*, blurted Isobel.

'Don't worry. It's pretty grim when your world collapses.'

And yet you'd hoped I might come to you, thought Isobel.

'I trust I'll be allowed to descend on you and take you out for dinner now and then?' said Jan after a moment.

*Yes, please.*

Derek purred and purred in the silence. At least someone was happy.

369

'So what was it all about?' asked Jan. 'If you feel inclined to tell me, that is.'

It was an opportunity to make amends. Her response would set the tone for the future of their relationship. *I'm still not sure what went wrong*, she began. *Basically, I – I fell in love with the wrong man.*

'Oh, God. Shall I get that gin bottle?' inquired Jan.

*Oh, shut up!*

'What was wrong with him? Married? Gay? Tory voter?'

*Married.* She noticed that Jan hadn't assumed it was Davy.

'Happily married?'

*His wife's left him.*

'Is he aware of your feelings? I'll back off whenever you say.'

*It's OK. Um, I think he knows.*

'Is it mutual?'

*Possibly. He – I don't know.*

'You think you've got grounds for hoping, though?'

*I'm probably imagining it.*

'Darling, if he weren't interested, you'd know.' Jan laughed softly. 'Rejection is pretty unmistakable when it comes along, I find.'

Isobel thought of the letter, the encounter on Christmas Day, the snowy footprint, the night of the Harvest Supper.

*I don't know what to do.*

'For your own sake, I think you should find out where you stand.'

They chatted for the rest of the evening about mutual acquaintances – Harry, Andrew, Alex and his illness, various parishioners. Isobel was aware that there was one person whose name neither of them were mentioning. Both seemed to be waiting for the other to introduce him into the conversation.

Jan's words goaded her all of the following day. Up till then she'd regarded the idea of contacting Johnny as weakness – that word again. Now it began to appear in the light of duty. Back and forth went the argument in her mind. She called round to talk to Davy, but he was at work. She'd lost track of his shifts. Back at home she paced her study floor, awash with nervous energy, unable to concentrate on anything.

Well, why not simply drive up to Bishopside and have it out with Johnny? A stream of objections flooded her mind. She dismissed them one by one. If she left now she'd be there by six – with a good chance of catching him in. If he was out she'd put a note through the door, or try to track him down at church. Something, anything, rather than this frenzy of inactivity.

She got in the car and set out. Her hands were tingling so much they were numb on the steering wheel. Allegri's *Miserere* filled the car. Psalm 51. 'Lord, have mercy, have mercy. Fill me with joy and gladness; let the bones which thou hast broken rejoice.'

The house was hard to find. She drove round and round the streets of Bishopside until she was close to tears. It was Friday evening and the orthodox Jews were preparing for Shabbat. Where, oh, where was he? It could have been another country. Why hadn't she looked up the address? Just as she was about to turn back in despair she came upon what was unmistakably a vicarage. She pulled up. I'm here. Her heart thumped and her face was burning. A downstairs light was on. A movement behind the curtains. He was there!

She got out of the car and went up the path to the door. The bell sounded. Have mercy, have mercy.

The door opened.

It was his wife, Mara, heavily pregnant, and a look of naked hatred on her face. 'What do *you* want?'

## CHAPTER 28

Isobel turned and fled back down the path.

'Wait!' commanded the other woman.

Isobel ignored her. Tears flooded over. She could barely see to unlock the car door. All the time that woman was watching. *I could have had your stupid husband, you witch!* Isobel wanted to yell. She wrenched the door open and hurled herself into the car. Tears splashed down. She smeared them away, but up they welled again. Her hand was shaking so much that she couldn't get the key in the ignition. All she wanted was to escape. Her throat ached as if something were dislocated. Still the tears streamed like blood welling from a gash. The keys slipped from her fingers. This was how she'd wept as a child, so violently that her lips were sucked in with each sob. *Stop it!* she raged at herself. *I never cry!* At any moment Johnny himself might appear to find out what all the fuss was about. Why ever had she come? Tissues were useless. She wiped her face on her sleeves and retrieved the keys. They slid from her grasp once more as she fumbled at the ignition. Her sobbing redoubled.

Suddenly the passenger's door opened. *Her!*

*Go away!* screeched Isobel hoarsely. *Just go away!*

But the other woman climbed in.

Isobel flailed at her impotently. *Please! L-l-l-* She was locked in a stuttering sob. *L-l-leave me!*

'Why did you come here?' demanded Mrs Whitaker. 'Why? Why can't you give us a chance to be happy?'

Isobel shook her head wildly. *I-I n-noth-noth-*

'Why do you have to wreck everything?'

*She's mad!* In desperation Isobel grabbed her handbag and rummaged for a scrap of paper and a biro. Nothing but last week's pew sheet and no space to write.

The bag was snatched from her.

*No!* she cried, as the other woman tipped out the contents. They were both grabbing, fighting almost.

'Well?' She brandished a lipstick in Isobel's face. 'I found one just like this in my husband's car!'

Isobel recoiled. She tried to sob out that she could explain, but the other woman was staring at her with contempt.

*Please go!* choked Isobel. Her throat was clenched rigid.

'Not till I get some answers.'

They sat side by side with Isobel weeping bitterly, powerless to stop herself.

'Look,' said the other woman jerkily, 'you'd better come into the house. He's not here,' she added.

This was the last thing Isobel wanted, but it was clear there would be no getting rid of her otherwise. She nodded and began to collect her scattered possessions and shove them back into the bag. After a moment the other woman helped, as if in tacit apology.

They went in. For a moment they stood in the sitting room, unsure how to proceed now they were indoors, whether in hostility or politeness. Mara made an abrupt gesture towards the sofa and Isobel sat. Her hostess lowered herself into an armchair. Isobel looked away from the swollen belly and struggled to control her tears. The other woman waited. The tension only mounted and Isobel felt coherent speech slide further from her control. She dropped her head into her hands and sobbed in despair. After a while she felt a tentative touch on her shoulder. A telephone pad and pen were being offered. Isobel blew her nose on a scrap of tissue and, no longer caring how it would appear, wrote: 'I was, and probably still am, desperately in love with your husband, but nothing has ever happened between us.'

Mara read it. Isobel heard her angry breathing.

'Did you agree this together?'

Isobel shook her head.

'You weren't having an affair?'

She shook her head more vehemently than ever. Their gaze locked. Then Mara looked away. 'I'm going mad,' she whispered to herself. Isobel watched in horror as Mara twisted her dark hair in her fingers, jerking it as if she was about to pull it out in clumps. 'They say it does this. Pregnancy. You get obsessed. Jealous. I try to believe him. He wouldn't lie to me. I know that. Then you turn up, just as I was – Why are you here?'

Stop crying like this! Isobel berated herself.

'Why did you come?' Mara repeated in a softer tone. 'Look, would you like a drink?'

Isobel nodded.

Mara hauled herself to her feet. She paused at the door, half inviting Isobel to come with her to the kitchen. After a moment Isobel followed.

'Tea?'

Isobel nodded again. She could tell the other woman's hatred was being overlaid by awe at these terrible gulping sobs. The kettle began to boil. Isobel helped herself to a length of kitchen roll and blew her nose.

*I j-just wanted to see how he was*, she blurted. *He seemed so down at Christmas when I saw him.*

Mara stared with her cold grey eyes. 'Why leave it nearly six months?'

*I've been away. Sick-sick leave. With my voice.*

Mara opened a cupboard and found two mugs. She set them down on a tray with care.

'You've got a crush on him? That's all it was?'

*It was stupid of me. I won't come again. Now I know you, you're . . . back.*

'Earl Grey?'

Isobel nodded.

'I came back when I discovered I was pregnant,' Mara bit out. 'I still love him, you know.' She made the tea and they went back through to the sitting room with the tray.

'Milk and sugar?'

Isobel shook her head. They waited while the tea brewed. Etiquette prompted Isobel to fill the void with small-talk, but what could she say without turning it into a parody-a vicarage tea party?

Mara poured the tea and handed Isobel a mug.

They sipped in silence.

374

'Was it your lipstick, then?' She seemed to hate herself for asking.

*Yes. He was giving me a lift after the Harvest Supper. I tipped my bag over somehow.*

The other woman had a curious twisted smile on her lips. Then Isobel saw with a rush of shock that she was fighting against tears.

'He got home at two in the *morning*!' She gave a laugh that came out like a wounded cry.

*He wasn't with me. I swear.*

They stared at each other. Then a thought ran between them like a cold wind. What if he'd been with someone else? In that instant Isobel glimpsed the anguish his wife must have been feeling all those months. Another woman! Who?

'I don't know what to think any more,' said Mara. Tears rolled down her cheeks. 'His attitude was, if I don't fucking believe him, it's my problem. I *know* I'm not imagining things. Unless I'm off my head. He didn't . . . say anything before he left? Not where he was going, or anything?'

*No.* Isobel cast her mind back. She heard again the silence after he'd turned the car engine off, the sound of the slithering seat-belt. *He just . . . said he had time for a quick coffee, and I said I mustn't keep him.*

A flush stained Mara's cheeks.

Ah, God, thought Isobel. She knows him. She knows what he must have meant by that. I was right. I could have had him.

*I expect he just wanted to talk*, bleated Isobel, aware she was only making things worse.

In the pause that followed, Isobel saw the other woman's face working in misery.

*I'm sorry.*

'No.' Mara swallowed. 'It adds up. I bet he was out sulking on the moors. He's *such* a wanker. Just tell me,' the humiliation of having to ask showed on every feature, 'did he try again?'

*No*, Isobel assured her, too swiftly.

They chose not to make eye-contact. Neither could bear any more honesty. It was enough. Isobel felt sick at her betrayal of Johnny and the pain she'd just inflicted. But surely it was better for his wife to know the pathetic truth than to torment herself by

375

imagining the worst? Or was there nothing worse than learning that she owed her marriage's survival not to her husband's faithfulness, but to another woman's integrity? All this time she's been hating me and now she must be grateful. More tears squeezed from Isobel's bloated lids.

*When's the baby due?* she snuffled.

'Two weeks.' Mara wiped her eyes. 'I'm booked in for a section. It's lying breech.'

*Oh dear. I hope it all goes well.*

'Thanks.'

Isobel rose to her feet. *I'd better be on my way.*

Mara struggled up and went with her to the door.

*I'm sorry if –*

Without warning the other woman hugged her. For a moment they clung together like strangers who had somehow survived the same wreck, then they broke away in embarrassment. Isobel went to her car. When she glanced back Mara was still on the step watching her.

Isobel drove home in a daze. Her tears had ceased, but her head throbbed viciously and her whole face felt swollen. The other vehicles seemed meaningless, but from long habit she drove safely. She was about half-way home when she remembered the note she'd written. No! Her horrified mind zoomed in on the image of the phone pad, a square of white on the dark red sofa where Mara had left it lying. For a second Isobel almost panicked and turned back, but a moment's reflection showed her the foolishness of the impulse. It might already be too late. She pictured Johnny coming in, his reflex glance to see if there were any phone messages, then his hand reaching out in disbelief as he read … *desperately in love with your husband.* Her face burned.

Let her have thought to destroy it! she begged. Unless Mara decided to use the note to confront him. How the scene would play itself out Isobel couldn't guess. Perhaps she would say nothing. So her husband was weak. He'd made a half-hearted pass at another woman and been turned down. A wife might learn to pity and forgive, once the humiliation passed. It could have been so much worse.

Yes, for Mara it must feel like a *dénouement*. Perhaps she and Johnny would thrash it all out, weep together and put the whole thing behind them. A fresh start. 'We've got the baby to think of,' they would say to each other. The door had shut on their happy ending, with Isobel on the outside.

In the distance ahead of her she saw the Teesside skyline, the chimneys and rising smoke, the flare stacks, a scene which, in just over a week, would no longer spell home.

When she got in the answerphone was blinking. It was Drew: 'Isobel! It's a girl! Henrietta Louise. Born at eleven-thirty this morning. Ten pounds two ounces, ye-ouch! Mother and baby both well, father completely knackered. Nat would love you to call round when she's back home.'

Isobel's tears dropped on to her desk. A little girl. I'm pleased for them. I'll send flowers tomorrow. I can't do anything now.

That night she went to bed early, hoping to sleep off her headache. She began to weep again, tears trickling down each temple as she lay on her back. They soaked into her hair and pillow. Outside, the wind was picking up. Rain rattled against her bedroom window. I didn't realize, she thought. I didn't know how much I'd let myself hope. Andrew had warned her that Mara would come back, but she'd chosen not to listen to him. It's better to know, she kept telling herself. I'll get over it. And perhaps she'd never really wanted him anyway. After all, each time Johnny had made the slightest approach she'd backed off in panic. Despite her daydreams, his actual physical presence had always dismayed her. The same was true of the other men she'd loved. She remembered the disgust she'd felt the one time she'd been kissed by Alex; her distress over the breakfast table at Will's *déshabille*. But I'm not frigid! she sobbed. I enjoy sex! It was just an accident that she'd never slept with a man she really cared for.

No. It was fear that had kept love and lust so rigidly separate. Fear of losing control of herself; of being subjugated, submerged. I don't want to be Mr Someone's wife. Someone's girl. I'm me. She had never met the man who was worth that sacrifice. No

377

man she trusted enough, respected enough. They were all weak and flawed, even the best of them.

It made her wonder why she was still crying. Was she weeping over the other woman's fortune, at the taut bulge pressed against her own body as they hugged? If things had been otherwise that might all have been mine, she thought; the man, the baby, the joy. Yet she did not wish it otherwise. Or was she was weeping for her own unborn child? At the time a disaster averted, later a sin repented. Not something to shed absurd tears over so late in the day. She thought again of little Henrietta Louise and tried to cheer herself up.

It was just that she had never dreamt back then that it might be her only chance.

It had rained hard overnight, and the wind remained wild. The morning was bright with water and sunshine as Isobel walked to church. A new world, rinsed clean by the rain. The last of the blossom was whirling in the air or driven scudding across the puddles. Isobel couldn't remember a day like it. She might have been waking from a long illness. The sense of a burden having been lifted was so vivid that once or twice she caught herself thinking she'd come out without something, her bag, her Bible, perhaps.

*This is the sun's birthday.* The phrase flashed across her mind. A fragment of a poem she'd once learnt, probably. The sun's birthday. The lime branches above her were tossing, the new heart-shaped leaves run ragged in the wind. Isobel felt a pulse of glee as if she were a child again and had just remembered that school was nearly over for the summer.

Tatiana! That was it. She'd forgotten. Perhaps Harry had heard from Perpetua. She quickened her pace. I might find out in minutes. She laughed out loud, then stopped.

'My voice!'

It was back. She laughed again, stock-still on the pavement under the dancing trees. She steadied herself with the reminder that this had happened once before, she couldn't count on it lasting, but the laughter kept brimming over. The lump in her throat had gone.

I must have wept it away, she thought. She set off at a trot for the church.

Harry's going to be so surprised! She went in through the south door. He was not alone. A handful of parishioners had joined them for morning prayer. This wasn't unusual for a Saturday, but Isobel was taken aback. Somehow it felt inappropriate to blurt out her news and distract everyone from worship. She decided to wait till afterwards.

Harry began with a sentence from the Psalms: ' "My soul waits in silence for God: for from him comes my salvation." '

Isobel followed the liturgy without opening her lips as she'd been doing for months. Concentration was impossible. She wanted to respond with a loud 'Amen' and startle them all. A giggle spurted up. Somehow she held in her excitement until the service was over.

Afterwards Harry caught Isobel's eye and indicated that he wanted a word. She went with him to the vestry. He seemed stern. She began to doubt the miracle. How could she find the courage to speak, knowing that nothing might come out?

'I wonder if we might meet tonight?' he said. 'To pray together and decide on a form of words to announce your departure.'

She took a deep breath. 'Fine.' I can still do it! She was tingling. 'What sort of time?' Her voice sounded odd in her ears after all this time.

'Eight-ish?'

He hadn't noticed! 'At the vicarage?'

'Ye – You spoke!' he shouted. 'Isobel!'

They both laughed and glanced towards the vestry door, wondering if the lingering parishioners could hear them. He looked as if he wanted to hug her.

'Isobel! This is wonderful! When, when, when? How? Why?'

'I don't know.' She shrugged. 'It just came back this morning.'

'I'd forgotten what you sounded like. Talk to me!' he begged.

She smiled. 'Don't be silly, Harry.'

'Ah!' He closed his eyes in bliss.

For a moment it was as if the last six months hadn't happened. If only I wasn't leaving, she thought.

'Um, does this,' he ventured, 'er, affect your decision to leave? At all?'

Did it? She hesitated. There was still time to reverse it all and stay the full three years as she'd originally planned. But even as she wondered she felt the first tell-tale tightening in her throat.

'I think it may be a result of my decision to leave,' she managed. 'I'm sorry.'

'No, no. I totally understand.' She saw him retreat into his shell of politeness. 'Still. I'm so pleased for you. Shall I spread it around?'

'By all means.'

'You've heard Natalie's had the baby?'

'Yes. Wonderful news! You get to do the baptism now,' she joked.

He gave a curious half-smile.

My voice, my voice! she sang to herself. It'll be all over the parish by lunchtime, she thought, on her way home. The phone would start ringing again after months of silence and she'd have to natter to all and sundry. The realization prompted her to take a detour into the park. Harry's reaction had unsettled her. The timing of her recovery was admittedly awkward. She ought to brace herself for a lot of people asking why she was leaving now that she was better. How was she going to explain? What 'form of words' would be adequate?

The wind had been busy in the park. Twigs and branches lay strewn underfoot. She cut across the field that led down to the river, but had only gone a few paces before she stopped in dismay. Half-way along the hedge a tree had been brought down in the storm. A great dish of earth stood perpendicular to the ground, raised aloft by the torn-up roots. She hurried to the scene. It was a horse-chestnut. Sap was still fresh in the leaves, and the splintered wood showed white like the inside of newly cracked conker shells. The twigs waved blithely as if they didn't yet know the truth. It seemed so untimely. To have survived the winter only to fall in May. Perhaps the weight of the leaves had done the damage. Her heart mourned. The gap would blur over, but it would take a hundred years to replace what was lost.

This made her think of Andrew.

It's always there. The absence. But gradually it becomes part of the landscape.

All you can do is endure. It was the thing she'd always found hardest. She hated to be delayed and thwarted of her purpose. Against all her expectations she'd come to admire Andrew. He was waiting till Alex recovered before he took up his vocation. In their different ways both brothers were locked into passivity. As I am, she thought. Then it came to her that this wasn't an interruption of the process. It was the process itself.

As long as she could remember she'd been straining impatiently ahead. It'll be all right when I go up to university, when I've got my degree, when I've finished library college, when I'm ordained, when I've got a parish of my own. I'll be content then. And now she'd been thinking, It will be fine when I've got myself sorted out at the Friary . . . Everything was makeshift and temporary. The real business was deferred to some infinitely receding future, and she would get to the end of her life without reaching her goal, whatever it was.

What is my goal?

It was supposed to be God; and of course it *was* God. Then why all the frantic activity? Isobel looked at the fallen tree and for the first time in her life thought: I'm going to die. I could die today, and what will become of me and all the things I was going to achieve? There is only eternity and the present moment. Nothing else.

She raised her eyes and looked out across the river to the distant hills. The wind was at her back, nudging. So it might not all be a waste of time, then, if her endurance became intent, focused, all-consuming. Some words from the Psalms came into her head:

*My soul waits for the LORD more than watchmen for the morning, more than watchmen for the morning.*

She turned and walked slowly home.

She was still some way off when she saw the car pull up outside her house and Johnny get out.

## CHAPTER 29

She slowed her pace, irresolute. There was a choice. She could turn and flee back to the park, or she could confront him. Her feet carried her on as if they knew what they were about, even if she didn't.

He was on the doorstep in the act of scribbling a note.

'Hello, Johnny.'

He jerked round, hastily crumpling the page. 'Shit! Isobel, I was just, um –' He was crimson. 'I was sent with these.' He stooped and swept up a large bunch of white lilies from the step and offered them to her.

She took them. Were they intended as an unambiguous symbol of purity? 'Well, thank you. They're beautiful.' Voluptuous scent filled her nostrils.

They stood.

'Have you time for coffee?' The words were out before she could stop them. She flushed.

'Aye, just a quick one.'

This sounded equally unfortunate and neither of them knew where to look.

Isobel found her keys. Her hand trembled, but she got the door open.

'Come on in, then.'

'Thanks.' He waved at Kath Bollom across the road. 'Ee, she's still at it. Bloody one-woman neighbourhood watch, she is.'

Isobel went to put the kettle on.

'New units,' he said, looking round the kitchen. 'And they've replaced the windows. Instant's fine,' he added, as she produced the cafetière.

'Sure? I'm having proper coffee.'

'Whichever, then.'

She trimmed the lilies and put them in her best vase. 'How's Mara?'

'Canny.'

'I expect you're looking forward to being a father.'

'Aye.'

He was leaving doing the donkey work. 'Another two weeks, isn't it?'

'That's right.'

'You've heard about Natalie and Drew?'

'Aye. Thought I'd pop in on my way back.'

'She's still in hospital,' pointed out Isobel. 'And visiting hours –'

'Nee worries. What's a dog-collar for?'

But Drew asked me to wait till she was home! Isobel didn't say it. Johnny had a habit of assuming the rules didn't apply to him.

'Listen, Isobel,' he said. 'About that time. Times,' he amended scrupulously. 'Thanks for . . .'

She tried to twitch the lilies into a better arrangement, but they rolled back. 'That's OK.'

'I'm a fool.'

She shrugged. 'You're a man.'

He looked at her as if trying to decide whether this was intended as mitigation or an insult. She didn't know either.

'Anyway,' he continued, 'thank you for sending me packing.'

'You're welcome. Any time.'

He gave her another look.

'Milk and sugar?' she asked, aware she was being mean, but not quite able to resist.

'Please.'

She fetched a little jug and put some sugar in the bowl.

'Do you use a butter-knife in private?' he asked.

It was her turn to glare.

He grinned, charm blazing as shamelessly as ever. She coloured and turned away to make the coffee, refraining for once from using her egg-timer to know when to press the plunger. The smell mingled with the scent of the lilies. When she turned back he appeared to have recollected himself and switched his appeal to a dimmer wattage.

'Mara said you'd lost your voice.'

'It seems to have come back.'

'That's good.'

There was a silence.

'How's the Bishopside team ministry coming along?' she inquired.

'Still at the planning stage.'

'You heard what happened here?'

'Yes. Bad news.'

They managed a few more ecclesiastical exchanges before she pressed the plunger down. The coffee had scarcely had a chance to brew, but she poured it anyway. Johnny put two spoonfuls of sugar in his cup and stirred. And now, she thought, I have totally run out of conversation. He tapped the teaspoon on the rim and set it down on the saucer she'd provided. They both drank.

'Nice coffee.'

'Thank you,' she said.

There was a pause.

'Decaffeinated?'

'No. Would you prefer – ?'

'No. This is fine.'

Another pause.

I'm going to start giggling, she thought in desperation. Unless I'm going to cry. She gazed out of the window, sipping her coffee.

'Is it fairly traded?'

She glanced then looked away. He was struggling, too.

'Of course.' Her voice quavered.

They both collapsed.

'I don't know why I'm laughing,' she wailed.

'Because it's all so bloody genteel. More tea, Vicar? Just call me a bastard and punch me, woman.'

'I'm not like that.' She wiped her eyes.

'Are you not? But seriously, I'm grateful. I cannot *believe* how close I came to blowing it. All right, I can,' he admitted. 'But thank you for not letting that happen. And, er, thanks for . . . setting Mara's mind at rest. She'd reached the stage where she couldn't believe anything I said.'

'Because you didn't tell her the truth.'

He appeared to bite back a retort. 'No,' he said carefully. 'I decided, on balance, there was no point upsetting her over nothing.'

'Which left her thinking she was going mad.'

'I'm fully aware I've made her very unhappy.'

He didn't add that he'd been unhappy himself. She could see his dilemma. He was a man who was used to getting away with things, but was trying hard for once not to trade on his advantage.

'Well, I'm glad if you've sorted things out,' she said.

'You're a good person, Isobel.'

'Not very, I'm afraid.'

He disconcerted her by inclining his head as if conceding a point. 'Aye, well. But a righteous man falls seven times and rises again.'

She flushed violently. Some gossip must have got out. 'What's that rubbish?' she snorted. '"The Prophet"?'

'Proverbs twenty-four verse sixteen,' he said, grinning again, before recalling that his animal magnetism was supposed to be under a bushel. He finished his coffee and got to his feet. 'Well, I'll be on my way.'

She went with him to the door. He kissed her on the cheek and said, 'It's the rising again that counts, sweetheart.'

'Give my love to Mara.'

'I will.'

She waved him off. Kath was stationed at an upstairs window, but was engrossed by something at the other end of the street. Isobel glanced and saw a police car in the road.

Johnny drove away and she managed to get back into the house before breaking down. At least she still had him as a friend. She'd still be able to see him now and then. He'd gone away thinking it would all be all right. He had no idea she loved him, that he'd been any more than a disgraceful nuisance to an understanding colleague. You made *both* of us very unhappy, you bastard, she sobbed.

Drying her eyes, she went through to the kitchen to wash up the coffee things. The scent of lilies had gradually been filling the kitchen. She paused and breathed in their perfume, studying the sharp leaves and snake-headed buds. She'd never know whether Johnny or Mara had chosen them. Several blooms were open, pouring incense from aching wide throats. A pale yellow stripe

385

ran along the centre of each petal and here and there they were smirched and shabby with pollen rust. At the end of the pistil three purple-black beads glistened, oozing some fluid. She brushed the tip with the back of a finger. It was cold. The smell began to overwhelm her and she drew back from the blooms, no longer finding them unambiguously pure.

Her last week in Asleby was filled with weeping. Twenty years' worth of unshed tears had now found their outlet. Despite her epiphanic moment beside the fallen tree, Isobel had wrongly assumed that she'd feel better once the announcement had been made. She'd been forced to give up protesting that this wasn't her, she never cried like this. This is me, she thought. Weeping into packing cases as she cleared her study, folding tears away with her clothes. She called round to Drew and Natalie's and had a cuddle with baby Henrietta. She wept into her little bonnet when Natalie invited her to be godmother. The service would probably be in August and Harry would be taking it.

One by one she ticked off the goodbyes. Last quiz night at the club, last Youth Group meeting, last mid-week communion, last game of pool in the pub with Davy. She'd snuffled at every one. Everyone wanted to have her round for dinner, or to take her out for treats. With each farewell it felt as though every dear, familiar thing she'd ever lost or left behind was being resurrected for her to wave off all over again. So many tears. She felt wrung out like a wet hanky.

Her visible distress was a great talking-point in the parish. A certain amount of anti-Harry feeling was abroad, instigated, Isobel suspected, by Kath Bollom. It wasn't right for the vicar to shunt her off when she so clearly didn't want to go! This was something she would have to tackle in her farewell sermon. Harry had offered her the opportunity to preach now she had her voice back. What was she going to say?

She looked back through her previous sermons and their assurance made her cringe. The Rev. Isobel Knox, with the benefit of her training and experience, will now preach down to the congregation. A new approach was long overdue. In the end

she decided to keep it short and honest. She'd talk about the prodigal son and his older brother. Over the last year the parable had
taken on a depth and texture she'd missed before. She'd tell the
congregation about Andrew – after all, he'd given her permission
to use him as a sermon illustration – and share something of her
own wrestlings with the grace of God in recent months.

As she prepared her thoughts she tried to picture the service.
It would be evensong, and afterwards there was going to be a
bunfight and a presentation, which Isobel wasn't supposed to
know about. Harry and the churchwardens had planned the
service and seen to all the other arrangements. All she needed
to do was preach. She imagined herself mounting the pulpit steps
and looking out over the sea of faces. Her throat tightened. What
if I can't do it? Panic fluttered. She forced herself to breathe
slowly.

Well, I must face that possibility. What is the worst that can
happen? That I seize up on this and on every subsequent occasion
when I'm due to preach. It seemed unthinkable. Public speaking
had never fazed her. She sat for a long time looking squarely at
this bleak prospect. Was there something about the act of climbing
up into a pulpit that encapsulated the problem? Perhaps there
was. In doing so she was quite literally setting herself above others.
There might be ways round this. After all, she could speak, and
perhaps she might deliver a 'talk' from the chancel steps, on an
equal footing with the congregation, as it were . . . Like Johnny did.
He hadn't really preached at that harvest service. He'd just wandered
about chatting and telling anecdotes. Was this a better model? She'd
disapproved of it at the time, of course. Then there was Harry, who
did use the pulpit unless the congregation was small. But Harry
was Harry. I'm just too bossy, she thought.

So what was she to do? Talk from the floor. She tried to picture
this. Still that sea of faces, that last deep breath before opening her
mouth – No. No good. It was still going to happen. She could
feel the constriction just thinking about it. It was turning into a
self-fulfilling prophecy. She began to cry. All I can do is prepare
something to say and warn Harry that I mightn't be able to say it.
The occasion was going to be too emotional. She probably needed

387

a small, low-key gathering for her first attempt. Thank goodness she'd anticipated the problem.

She sat at her desk and attempted to write. Her mind crowded with people she knew she had failed. Her sense of letting Harry down was hardest to bear. If only he'd unbend and reassure her. He kept forgetting to find out about Tatiana for her, and even her mildest reminders felt like nagging. She even found herself wondering whether he was doing it to punish her. He'd never be that petty, of course. He was just distracted by all the preparations for her leaving do.

Then there was Johnny. How much more needless torment was she going to put herself through? He was back together with his wife, they were about to have their first child. That was that. The day would come when she would no longer be able to hear the echo of his laugh or conjure up his face and gestures. It might be years before they chanced to meet again. What if she'd already seen him for the last time, waving goodbye outside her house the other day? What if that was it? Although the Friary wasn't that far from Bishopside. He might visit it regularly, for all she knew. One of the brothers could be his spiritual director, even. She might run into him in a corridor, or by the yew hedge again. And she might have cause to whiz across to Tyneside. To see Annie and Will, for instance. It would be natural to pop in with a small gift and see how Mara was getting on with the baby . . .

It will pass. It's like the tide, she told herself. It will go out.

He must have had a farewell service, too. This thought occurred to Isobel as she walked back from morning prayer. How did it feel for him? He was the first curate the parish had ever had. The tears that must have flowed that night! She was treading in his footsteps still, never as well loved or mourned over. Harry wouldn't miss her the way he'd missed Johnny.

There was a car pulling up alongside her. It was Davy.

'I'll give you a lift.'

'Davy, it's three hundred yards,' she protested. 'And you're on duty.'

'I want a word.'

She got into his patrol car and he drove her home. Kath will enjoy *this*, she thought.

'Well?' she asked brightly. Don't let this be a fresh declaration of undying love, she begged silently.

'Look, I've not been spying on you,' he began. 'It's just that I was called out the other day to a house up the road and I saw Johnny Whitaker and you going into –'

'I didn't know you knew him!' she exclaimed.

'Well, not really, like.'

'What's the problem, then?'

'Did he say anything?' he asked desperately.

'About what?'

He was searching her face for clues of some kind. 'I went to him for confession once.'

'Well, of course he wouldn't mention that.' She laughed. 'Honestly, Davy, we Anglicans are capable of maintaining confidentiality, you know.'

'Aye.' He laughed too.

'Was that it?' she asked.

He nodded.

She was about to get out of the car when a thought occurred to her. '*When* did you go to him for confession?'

He winced. 'Don't play war with us. It was after, y'kna . . . New Year's Day.'

Oh, no! She felt the tide of blood rush up neck and face. 'Shit.'

'That's the first time I've ever heard you swear,' he marvelled.

'It's the first time I've ever sworn.' Of all the excruciatingly perverse coincidences! For Johnny to know about that little episode. That's why he'd talked of falling and rising again. He'd known all along. Since January.

'What did you tell him?' she whispered.

'About us. What happened. I didn't tell him your name.'

'But you mentioned Asleby?'

'Ee, I'm sorry, Isobel. I didn't realize.'

'No. You weren't to know.' She swallowed, feeling tears rising. 'You weren't to know I'm, um, in love with him.'

389

'We-ell, that Oxford business threw me off the scent, but you told us at the time, like. That there was someone. A married man. When I told you before I'd been to confession, I kind of worked out from your reaction it must be him.'

'I see. You didn't – I hope you didn't tell him the bit about my being in love? Davy!'

He grimaced. 'Sorry.'

'No!' She shut her eyes and sank her head back, waiting for the pieces to form a picture. So, Johnny had worked it out. That's why he wrote to me. He knew that despite my protests, despite Davy, even, I'd been desperate for him all along. She had a sudden image of an alternative ending: Mara standing outside on the vicarage step and finding Isobel there opening the door. If. If. If. Was this the will of God? Selecting this action, discarding that; ensuring one way or another that His purpose prevailed? She sat for a long time surveying it. Then she let out a long, long sigh.

'Oh, well.'

Davy laughed. 'Well, you took it better second time roond.'

'Was I cross?'

He considered. 'I think psychotic's the word.'

Shit, she reiterated to herself, when she was safely in her house. Johnny knew. He knew. He *knows*. She paced about. He'd conducted himself well the other day, then, casting himself as the penitent wrong-doer and letting her save face. She laughed again at that polite conversation over the coffee-cups. Fellow clergy and fellow sinners. But it tilted into sobs.

I've worked so hard at serving God and being good, she reflected. Strange to find relief in failure. She'd been like a tightrope artist terrified of falling; but she had fallen, and found that there was a safety-net after all. Here was an idea for her sermon. She reached for her Bible. 'A righteous man [or woman] falls seven times, and rises again; but the wicked are overthrown by calamity.' Yes, it was the rising again that counted.

It was only me that had such exacting standards. Nobody else was expecting me to be perfect. Not God, not Harry, not the parish. She riffled through her Bible hunting for another verse.

'The steps of a man are from the Lord, and he establishes him in whose way he delights; though he fall, he shall not be cast headlong, for the Lord is the stay of his hand.'

Why this terror of making mistakes? Why do I find the idea of being helped along and supported so difficult? She knew the answer. *Stand on your own two feet. Don't be so soft. The child's got to learn.* True, there had been a hand on the bike saddle while she learnt, but after that she'd been on her own. Her father had taught her doggedness to overcome setbacks, but there had been no advice about living with outright failure. All he could offer was an ejector button: if you can't do it properly, don't do it at all.

It was not enough. She was in new territory now. The old maps no longer helped. She was not just a bad servant to be punished. She was a child to be forgiven, and a friend to be helped along by the hand.

She jotted these ideas down and sat for a long time in the silence, wondering if she would ever trust others to like her, or even truly like herself. It was probably true that she'd projected a squeaky-clean image of herself in an attempt at living a life above reproach. She could see now that this had had the effect of keeping people at arm's length. It would have been wiser to be more honest about her struggles and weaknesses.

Achieving greater openness was not straightforward. It required a willingness on the part of the recipient to welcome the attempt, as she learnt the following lunchtime with Jan.

'Will you keep an eye on Davy for me?' she asked.

Jan was busy tying fresh asparagus into bundles. 'I hope you're hungry. Garden-fresh. Organic. Makes you piss like a horse, mind you, but it's worth it.' She plunged the bundles into boiling water and sat down at the kitchen table. 'Yes, I'll look after your *gendarme*.'

'Thank you.' Isobel wrestled for a moment, then said, 'I'm afraid I've hurt him rather badly.'

'Get *down*, Derek!' Jan shouted at the Siamese, who had sprung on to the bench. 'Away to me, cat!' Derek stalked off. 'Dog talk,' she confided. 'He hates it.'

Isobel persevered. 'In a moment of weakness I stupidly had a fling with him.'

'Stupidly,' agreed Jan, showing no signs of surprise, 'but understandably. He's a damn fine specimen, if men are what tickle your pheromones.'

'It wrecked everything!' she confessed.

'It usually does, m'dear,' said Jan briskly. 'But we pick ourselves up and carry on.'

'You sound like a hockey mistress,' snapped Isobel.

Jan laughed. 'Well, life's a game. You know what?' she began meditatively. Isobel braced herself for some lacerating insight. 'I'm not going to bugger about with Hollandaise sauce. I'm just going to melt some butter.'

'Fine,' said Isobel, finding her friend's attitude faintly mortifying.

'Ah, food, food, food! When you get to my age that's pretty much all there is left to get worked up about.' She heaved herself up and crossed to the fridge. 'And wine, of course.' She pulled out a bottle of Chablis. 'Are you going to relax your iron rule and join me?'

'Why not?'

'Good girl!' She poured a couple of glasses and sat again. 'One's spies tell one that Johnny Whitaker is about to become a proud father.'

'Mmm. Yes.' Isobel marvelled at her own composure. 'I happened to see his wife the other day.'

'And how's she?'

'Oh, blooming.' She sneaked a hand to the corner of her eye and whisked away a tear.

Jan appeared not to notice. After a while the kitchen timer pinged and she got up to drain the asparagus.

Isobel looked down at the tender spears lined up on her plate. She breathed in the fragrant steam. 'Ah!'

'Exactly!' crowed Jan. 'Who needs men, eh?' She passed the melted butter. 'Although, having said that, there's something pretty phallic about these little chappies.'

'You do realize I was trying to bare my soul to you just then?' said Isobel.

'Some such thought did cross my mind,' admitted Jan. 'Are you sure you want to proceed down that particular path?'

'Considering you spend half your time prying into everyone's private lives, I just thought a greater honesty . . .'

'Ah, but I might feel inclined to do it back, though.'

'Would that be a bad thing?'

There was a pause. 'I think we've always understood one another fairly well by oblique communication. Some things are better off not put into words, m' dear.'

'It clarifies things.'

'It solidifies them. And then there's no going back, no unsaying of what's been said.'

'Yes, but however unwelcome it might *feel*, it could be progress.'

'Or termination.'

'How?'

'What if someone were to tell you something that you knew already, deep down, but hearing it said out loud obliged you to react, out of Evangelical integrity, in a way you've been seeking to avoid?'

Isobel saw that they were a hair's breadth from a confession of what she did, indeed, know deep down and had always feared hearing. Her eyes smarted. 'I don't think you could tell me anything that would make me love you less.'

There was a long silence. 'You're braver than I am.'

'I'm going to miss you,' said Isobel.

'Aha, I'll beetle up and rescue you from your grim monastic existence,' promised Jan. 'Can't be doing with monks, quite frankly. Give me the willies.'

Isobel walked home in a haze of good wine. Against all the odds she was feeling content. Although she and Jan had drawn back from the brink, they had both managed – obliquely – to utter truths they had balked at before. She began to hope she'd be able to leave Asleby well, after all. It struck her that a year ago she would secretly have applauded Jan's crass anti-monastic sentiment. What was Jan going to make of Andrew's vocation when he told her of it? He'd probably just turn up on her doorstep one day in his habit, knowing him. She smiled at the idea. I'll phone him when I get in, she thought, and tell him I've got my voice back. And thank him.

She reached her house and went straight to the study. She was looking for his number when the phone rang.

'Isobel,' said a voice, 'it's Andrew.'

'Andrew!' She laughed. 'It must be telepathy! I was just going to ring you. I've got my voice back.'

Silence.

'Andrew?'

'Christ, Isobel. Oh, Christ. Alex is dead.'

# CHAPTER 30

'No!' she cried. 'Andrew! How?'

There was another silence.

'He can't be dead,' she heard herself protesting. 'ME isn't terminal.' Questions thudded against her mind and fell incredulously away. How? How? But he was going to get better! He can't be dead. He can't be.

'Andrew?'

'Yeah, I'm here.' He swallowed. 'It was just hearing your voice. I'd steeled myself to leave a message.'

'But what happened?' she sobbed.

'Overdose. I meant to warn you before you saw the obits, but it slipped my mind.'

'I've not seen them.' Her eye fixed on *The Times* lying unopened on the chair out of reach. 'You mean it was suicide?'

'Yes. Paracetamol.'

'Oh, but why? Why?' All she could see in her mind's eye was Alex running down the library stairs, off somewhere, cutting it fine; living life faster than anyone she'd ever known.

'He'd just had enough.'

'But he would have got better!' she cried.

'Patience was never his strong point.'

'How are you coping?'

'It hasn't sunk in yet, mercifully. I've been arranging the funeral. When it's all over, and you turn to tell them how it all went and they're not there – that's when it hits you.'

'I don't know how you can be so – so *calm*, so rational!'

'I'm not. I've got the rest of my life to curse him. It can wait.' Suddenly his composure disintegrated. 'Oh, Christ, what am I going to do without him, Izzie? I hear him in the next room, then I remember, God, he's dead, I'm imagining it.' He regained control.

'Anyway. The funeral's on Monday, in the college chapel at twelve, if you want to come.'

'I thought he didn't want a funeral,' she burst out. 'Just shove him in a bin-bag, he said. Oh, I'm sorry, it's just —'

'I know.'

'I'm sorry,' she repeated.

There was a silence. 'He gave his permission, actually.'

'I didn't mean to criticize you.' She was swamped by anger that had no place to go. 'Did he leave a note, then?'

'No. He came and woke me on Tuesday night to tell me what he'd done.'

'But didn't you call an ambulance?'

'He'd deliberately left it too late.'

'But shouldn't you have at least tried?'

There was another silence. She could have bitten her tongue, but in the end he answered evenly, 'I've asked myself a thousand times. But I think I did the right thing. He took the tablets, I don't know, Sunday night? Basically after a couple of days your liver packs up and there's nothing anyone can do. He just came into my room and woke me to say —' She heard him gulp and whisper, 'Oh, Jesus.'

To say goodbye.

'What an appalling thing to do to someone!' she cried.

'That's Alex for you.'

'But at least you didn't just find him,' she said helplessly. 'You had a chance to talk.'

'He wasn't very lucid. I think he mistimed it, to be honest. His body was already run-down from ME and it all happened faster than he'd anticipated.'

'Was he scared?'

'I don't think so. He said, "If I'm right, then tomorrow there will be nothing. If you're right, then I'm a few hours from meeting my Maker." I asked him what he'd say, and he said, "I was wrong." Supposing He flings you into hell? I asked, and he just shrugged. When I asked him how he'd try to dissuade the Almighty, he said, "Judgement Day isn't a fucking balloon debate, Andrew."'

To her horror, Isobel almost laughed.

'So, there we are. He didn't console us with deathbed repentance, I'm afraid,' said Andrew.

His flippancy sliced through her like a blade. 'Don't joke about it,' she begged. 'You should have ...' She tailed off. Should have what? Urged him to repent, to trust in the blood of Christ? But what could you tell a theologian about atonement? 'What was the last thing he said?'

'I couldn't tell you. He was drifting in and out of sleep, muttering. Then one time while I was waiting for him to surface again he just didn't. And that was it. He slipped into a coma and died around dawn. I can remember hearing the birds.'

'Oh, Andrew!' All too clearly she could imagine the bed where they must have been lying and the first light grey at the window, the quiet garden, the church alongside.

'I've tormented myself since with all the things I should have said and done. But, then, you always do. You always do.'

Suddenly she remembered Raphael. And Jan's son, Andrew's best friend at school. 'It seems so unfair,' she lamented. 'Why should this keep happening to you?'

'Unfair! Aren't you supposed to tell me it's the will of God?' he jeered.

'But it's not! It was an act of free will by Alex.'

'Yeah, which God permitted.'

'Because He chooses to work with amateurs.'

'Don't do that!' His voice rose. 'Don't fucking quote me, you cow.'

She flinched. 'I'm sorry.'

'Go on – tell me I'm wrong. You're a priest. Tell me God isn't just smashing everything that's dear to me.'

She heard his fear, the wreck of new-found faith, and tried desperately to think.

'You can't, you see?' he said. 'He's the potter, we're the clay. He can do what he likes and sometimes, in His infinite wisdom, He likes to break people, yes? So that they submit to His will.'

'No!' she cried. 'He's not like that.'

'It's there in the Scriptures.'

'But that's a prophecy about the fate of Israel or something, not Andrew Jacks.' He was silent, so she ventured on. 'If you look at Christ you'll see the opposite is true; he won't break a bruised reed.'

'Fuck you and your loving God.' He hung up.

She cursed her clumsiness. The bereaved were often angry with God, but this was the first time someone had turned on her like that. Then her own grief rushed up on her again. Alex. Oh, God, Alex.

She picked up *The Times* and found the obituaries page. Alex's face leapt out, quizzical, on the brink of mocking laughter, and she called his name involuntarily. Her eye skimmed through his academic achievements, his talents and successes. For a second she feared the real man would disappear in mealy-mouthed eulogy, but the piece went on to state baldly that Dr Jacks had not been a popular man. His abrasiveness, his restless ambition were catalogued as unflinchingly as his triumphs.

> For all his erudition, religious experience remained a puzzle to him. It confronted him like a locked door to which neither his formidable acumen nor his philosophical training offered the key. His one glimpse of understanding came during a Good Friday performance of Stainer's *Crucifixion*, in which he took the part of the tenor soloist. Afterwards he admitted, 'For one moment it was as if it were all true and I believed it.'

I was there, she thought in shock. On that very same day. Her glance flicked to the end of the piece. It was by Andrew. No, oh, no -he shouldn't have had to write this. Yet who better? She went back and, weeping, read the whole thing again. How could you do it? she demanded of Alex's face. A month ago she'd seen this same photograph pinned to Andrew's noticeboard and commented on how well it captured the old Alex before he'd fallen ill. Now it had been plucked from the clutter of postcards to bear the weight of this new significance. Up and down the country strangers would be happening upon it as they leafed through their papers, and, arrested by the face, they would pause a moment before turning the page. She would keep it till it was old and yellowed, and years from now when she, too, was dead, someone going through her things would wonder who he was and what he'd meant to her before dropping the page on the pile with the other rubbish to be burnt.

Alex is dead. She repeated the words to herself at intervals through the evening as she tried to finish her sermon. Each time they astonished her afresh. At what point would the idea convince? That afternoon – impossibly, just that afternoon – as she'd walked back from Jan's, she'd been happy, only she hadn't known it. There was no telling when your last ten minutes of happiness was over, she thought. And who could say whether worse lay in store; new sorrows so awful they would dwarf this one and make her look back on today and say, If only I'd known how happy I was.

Alex is dead. She needed to talk. Harry – but their easy companionship had been destroyed. Or Jan? No, not now. She would have rung Andrew, but for the fear of making things worse for him.

She turned for comfort to her faith and found herself looking out over a black gulf. If only Alex had found Christ, even at the last, like the thief on the cross. And yet ... And yet, in a strange way, she half felt she'd have thought less of him if the approach of death had shaken his rigorous atheism. She oughtn't even to think these things. *Will not the judge of all the earth do right?* If Alex was mistaken in his belief that there was no God, then it was surely an honest mistake? She had heard him admit that Christianity had its own inherent logic once you were inside its belief system; but Andrew was right – Alex had found no way in. If he'd thought it was true, he would have believed. Might not God honour that? But what, if in his arrogant self-sufficiency, he'd put himself beyond the scope of mercy? Standing before the door with all his clever keys, it had never once crossed his mind that all he had to do was knock.

I'd let myself think he was changing, she thought. Perhaps in a mean, secret part of her she'd felt smug about his illness and his admission that it was undermining his conviction there was no God. In all that time she'd spent with him walking in the park she'd been too preoccupied with her own problems to grasp the extent of his depression. If she'd been less self-absorbed she might have seen and been able to help. She'd been so sure that a new and wiser Alex would emerge from the cocoon of illness. Somehow she'd been counting on walking with him in the park after he'd recovered and talking about faith. Now there would be nothing.

\*

At nine o'clock the doorbell rang. It was Harry.

'Isobel, may I come in?'

She nodded. He would know from her blotchy face that something was wrong.

'Have you seen the papers?' he asked gently.

She nodded again and hid her eyes. His hand touched her arm.

'I'm so sorry,' he said. 'I know he was a close friend.'

'How could he do it?' she burst out.

'Depression can be a killer, I'm afraid.'

She sobbed bitterly.

'Ah, Isobel, I'm so sorry,' repeated Harry. 'Do you still want to preach tomorrow?'

'I want to try,' she managed. 'But I'm scared I'll seize up.'

'Well, see how it seems when the time comes. Don't worry. I'll step in if necessary.'

'Thanks,' she choked.

'See if you can get some rest. Phone me if you need to.'

'OK.'

He gave her arm a squeeze and left.

It was a long night. Grief came in waves. At times she felt detached from it, watching it pass by her like a funeral procession. She heard her own wails and wondered where they were coming from. At others it was savage, racking, then dull, like rain on a ruined house.

She lay in the dark, drifting. Then the phone rang, wrenching her into horrible wakefulness.

'Hello?'

'It's Andrew.'

'Andrew, I'm sorry –'

'I've been thinking. You're right. It's Jahweh *vis-à-vis* the nations, not Christ and the individual.'

'I'm sorry?' She groped for her alarm clock.

'The potter. Oh, Christ – it's three-fifteen. I'm sorry. I'm in free-fall.'

'Don't worry.'

'I've been reading Job. "Curse God and die." Nice succinct piece of advice from his wife. I can't even do that.' He was weeping again. 'How can you curse a god who's already dying on a cross? I've got nothing left, nowhere left to go, no escape. I feel like St Peter – to whom can we go?'

He's been drinking, she thought. 'Oh, Andrew.'

She listened for more than an hour as he rambled, talking of his childhood and that volatile mix of love and hate he'd shared with Alex.

In the end he said, 'God, I'd better let you go. You'll have church in the morning. Are you preaching?'

'Yes.' My farewell sermon. She'd tell him another time.

'Don't worry about me. This isn't the end.' He hung up without explaining.

She could still hear his voice, his despair mingling with raw faith. Her tears began again. On Monday we'll be in the chapel and they'll bring the coffin in and the priest will say those glorious words: 'Jesus said, I am the resurrection and I am the life: he who believes in me, though he die, yet he shall live.'

But Alex had not believed. If she could, if it would have served any purpose, she would have pleaded with God to bend the rules, for no other reason than here was a man she had loved. What could she argue in his defence? Just that one Good Friday when he had stood in the same chapel and sung 'Thou Art The King', and for one moment it had all seemed true?

Just before dawn she dreamt she was in his rooms. The task of sorting out his books had somehow fallen to her. But there were so many of them. She opened drawers and they were full of his papers. She tried to read them, but the print turned illegible as her eye fell on it. In desperation she began to pull volumes from the shelves and try to arrange them in ordered piles, but when she opened them she found she couldn't read the title page. In the end she sank to her knees and sobbed hopelessly. The task was too great. She'd never do it.

Then she heard the sound of rapid feet. It was Alex, Alex as he'd been before his illness. He looked down in surprise at her grief.

'I thought you were dead,' she sobbed.

'Haven't you heard of the Resurrection?' he asked impatiently. He laughed and took a volume from the shelf and handed it to her. 'Here.'

She woke. A blackbird was whistling on the garage roof. Leaf patterns danced on her ceiling. Almost imperceptibly, the load had eased.


Isobel's last Sunday in Asleby was a perfect June day. She found there was a dulling mercy in bereavement. It allowed her to go through the ordeal like a sleepwalker, as if none of it mattered, or she would be back next week, or had never cared for the place or the people at all.

At the end of the morning service Harry gave out the notices, reminding everyone that tonight was Isobel's farewell. She listened dispassionately as if it referred to someone else. The same numbness shielded her as Harry announced that Johnny and Mara had had a boy, Alexander John, six pounds three ounces, mother and baby both doing well. He came early, was her only thought. It only struck her later that the child must have been named for Alex.

She had lunch with Jan and the two talked about him. His death unleashed things Isobel had carried secretly for years. She wondered afterwards if she'd betrayed him by speaking so freely of his faults, but she was still too stunned to know. They arranged that Jan would drive them down to Oxford and they would attend the funeral together. She supposed Annie and Will would be travelling down, too. Oh, how could she face it? Isobel shut out the thought. There was tonight to get through.

Back at her own house she moved restlessly from room to room. She was trying to say goodbye to her home, but found instead she was making nervous inventories and searching for undone tasks. Her bags were packed. Everything was springcleaned ready for the Coverdale students. She registered dimly that Harry still hadn't found out Tatiana's address.

Well, that was it. Time to set off. She applied her lipstick and, after a moment's thought, went upstairs and put on some of the scent Harry had given her. She'd not worn it for months. It evoked a swift pang of Christmas joy, followed by the dullness of failure.

She went back downstairs and picked up her Filofax and handbag. The smell of fresh emulsion lingered in the hallway where she had painted over the mysterious bloody smear. She left the house. Out on the street she almost crumpled. I can't do it. But it was important for others to mark the end of her time in the parish properly. She must go through with it for their sakes. The sky was a flawless blue. She saw the glassy new leaves and the red-brick terraces in the sunshine. The scent of lilac lingered at the street corner from an overhanging bush. This time tomorrow it will all be over.

I will never do this again, she thought, as she entered the churchyard. She went round the side of the church so as not to stumble upon any preparations for the surprise party, passing under the dark shadow of the yew, by Agnes's cell and in through the vestry door.

There was Harry. How had this happened, that she should feel relieved she wouldn't be seeing him again?

'Everything all right?' he asked.

'Yes, thank you.' She put down her bag and crossed to the robes cupboard, trying to silence the commentary within her, which was running the whole time: *This is the last time you'll fetch your robes from here, the last time* . . . 'Um, I've prepared a few words for after the service. The party I don't know about. Should the need arise, I mean.'

'Good.'

'Can I hand them to you if I choke up?'

'Of course,' he said politely. 'Ought I to cast an eye over them?'

She handed him a slip of paper and watched his eyes skim the simple words of thanks to him and the congregation.

'Fine.' He handed it back and turned away, busying himself with some papers on the table.

Wounded, she took out her cassock and pretended to brush at some dust. If she started crying now, she'd never stop in time for the service. To distract herself she reached for her sermon and tried to read it. Just one word of genuine kindness, she begged. Not this distancing politeness. She cursed herself as a tear crept out of her eye. She wiped it stealthily away and glanced at Harry.

He was weeping silently with his back to her.

'Harry!' she cried in alarm. 'What is it?' She crossed to him and caught his arm. 'Whatever is it?'

'Sorry,' he choked.

'Harry!' Unable to bear it, she took him in her arms and let him sob on her shoulder.

'Oh, no, oh dear, I'm so sorry,' he wept. 'I wasn't going to do this to you. I just can't bear losing you like this. I'm sorry.'

'It's all right.' For a long time they held each other and cried. Through her own tears Isobel could see the vestry clock ticking round to twenty-five past six. They were going to have to snap out of it.

'I just feel such a failure,' she heard him whisper.

'What? Don't be silly.' She gave him a shake. 'You're not a failure.'

He wiped his eyes. 'You came here happy and confident.'

'But I wasn't. Not really.'

'I've just mishandled everything.'

'No. I'd hate to think how much worse things would have been without you.'

'Well, it's very kind of you to say so,' he said.

'But I truly mean it.'

He hugged her close. 'You're wearing your perfume,' he said, after a moment.

'I love it,' she whispered shyly.

They both coloured.

'What time is it?' he asked, in sudden alarm. 'Bugger! Sorry.'

They pulled away from one another awkwardly. He hurried through to the little room where the ladies did the flower arranging. Isobel heard the tap running and the sound of him splashing water on his face. Why had it never occurred to her that the past few months had been a nightmare for him, too? He came back in, looking a little damp, but calmer.

'Sorry,' he repeated once again. They both turned to look at the clock. It was half past. 'Are we ready?'

'As we'll ever be,' she said.

'Shall I pray?'

She nodded and closed her eyes. Through the vestry door came the muffled sounds of the congregation, hushed murmurs, a dropped hymn book, the tones of the organ playing 'Jesu, Joy of Man's Desiring'. Then came Harry's voice:

> ' "God be in my head, and in my understanding;
> God be in mine eyes, and in my looking;
> God be in my mouth, and in my speaking;
> God be in my heart, and in my thinking;
> God be at mine end, and at my departing." '

'Amen,' she whispered.

He opened the door and the sounds rushed upon them. The church was packed. She scarcely heard Harry's words of welcome. During the first hymn she allowed herself to look out across the congregation. People whose babies she'd baptized, whose grandmas she'd buried. Mike and Sue. There were Brenda and her mates, who were still new enough to church to wave yoo-hoo when she caught their eye. And Fitzy and the rest of the Youth Group. And Davy. Davy had come. And Father McGee. He must have cancelled his evening service. She bent her head over the hymn book.

> Ponder anew
> What the Almighty can do,
> If to the end he befriend thee.

Wave after wave of goodwill seemed to surge forward and break over her. It was a losing battle. There was no possibility of making it through without bursting into tears. Did it matter, even? She pulled out her hanky and blotted her eyes.

Throughout the early part of the service she kept spotting people she knew. Kath Bollom had shown up, even. Walter Goodwill's family. Jenny the Methodist minister. We never did find time to go out for a drink. Drew and Natalie were at the back with baby Henrietta in her pram.

The Youth Group performed a sketch, the Mothers' Union presented a dramatized reading, and the choir and the music group each sang a couple of items. Then Jan came forward and read the New Testament lesson. The prodigal son. Isobel breathed in and

405

out as evenly as she could, willing her throat muscles to stay unclenched. Jan finished reading and sat down. Isobel rose to her feet and walked to the centre of the chancel steps and looked out across all the faces. They waited. For a second she felt like a high diver, poised on the brink. They were all willing her on.

Her nerve failed her. She turned to stumble away, but Harry was there at her side. A murmur of anguished pity ran through the congregation. She felt Harry's arm supporting her and his voice saying, 'It's all right, it's all right, Isobel.' Jan came and led her to the front pew where they sat together. Tears streamed down Isobel's cheeks. Jan held her hand tight as Harry stepped to the centre of the chancel.

He raised his hands and the murmurs died away.

'Sorry. You'll have to make do with me instead.' A ripple of laughter broke the tension. 'Let's pray.' He bowed his head. In the moments that followed a deep hush fell, a stillness which seemed to echo with eternity. At last Harry lifted his eyes.

'What can I say to you tonight, except that life's a bitch?' Shock lapped the walls. No one knew whether they should laugh.

Afterwards Isobel tried to remember all that he'd said. Only fragments came back to her. Someone had videoed the entire service, but she knew she'd never be able to watch it. He talked about her time in Asleby, of the good things, and touched on the problems she'd faced.

'Why does it have to be this way? Why does a young woman priest have to lose her voice, of all things?' Jan's hand gripped hers reassuringly. 'Why does illness strike a man down in the prime of life, driving him to such despair that suicide feels like the only way out? What am I to say to the young parents whose baby has just died? What am I supposed to think when a man takes a gun into a primary school and mows the children down? There are times when the only answer is silence and tears. Anything else is an insult, an outrage. I'd feel worse if our founder had died in comfort at a grand age surrounded by loyal followers and not at thirty-three in extreme violence and utterly abandoned. At that point there were no answers, just a question: "My God, my God, why have you forsaken me?"

406

' "The night is dark and I am far from home, lead thou me on."
We'll be singing that later. Once when I was at theological college
a group of us were away on retreat in the depths of the country.
We decided to go for a walk one evening. It was a moonless
night and the stars! You could see the Milky Way from horizon
to horizon, which you never can on Teesside. It was pitch black
and nobody had a torch. We started out across the grounds and
everyone was stumbling and laughing. In the end I said, "Oh, come
on, you great soft townies, who needs a torch? Follow me." I took
a couple of confident steps forward and promptly plunged down
into the ha-ha.'

Everyone laughed.

'Which is presumably how it got its name,' went on Harry,
as the mirth subsided. 'My friends still mention it now and then.
A torch would have been helpful. Floodlights more so. "Your word
is a lamp to my feet and a light to my path." We're not promised
daylight, or even a row of lamp-posts, just enough light to see the
path before our feet – thank God. Thank God we can't see all that
lies ahead, or how would we have the courage to go on? Just
enough light for the next step and the promise that darkness will
not have the final word.'

It was over. One by one people were drifting away, giving Isobel
hugs and crushing handshakes and wishing her all the very, very
best. A few remained to tidy up the church hall. Harry and Isobel
were left putting chairs away. She could hear fragments of conversation from the kitchen as the ladies washed up; just ordinary
conversation, the kind that had gone on in that kitchen before her
arrival in the parish and would continue for many years to come.
Jan was pushing a large brush up and down the floor, sweeping
up the fragments of crisp and quiche.

I was dispensable, thought Isobel. It felt like a kind of freedom.
Her throat ached from all the tears and smiles and the effort of
speaking. She'd managed to say a few words of thanks, though
what they'd been she couldn't now recall. The church's kindness
overwhelmed her. There was a stack of presents to stow in her car,
as well as a very generous cheque.

'Did you make that nice bread, Harry?' called someone through the hatch.

'Yes,' he replied. 'The secret's in the olive oil. Lots and lots of extra-virgin olive oil and a really hot oven. And I always bruise the rosemary first.'

Jan guffawed. 'Harry, you do say the nanciest things.' She paused and leant on her broom. 'No wonder everyone thinks you're gay.'

Isobel paused in the act of stacking the last chair. She glanced round to see how Harry would take this. Jan was looking at her as if to say, Well? Harry seemed amused.

'I think we're done,' he said. 'Let me help you with those.'

They carried the gifts out to Isobel's car. Her heart was thumping in anticipation of the worst goodbye. They stood.

'I'll just get my robes,' she said.

They went back into the vestry and she lifted her cassock and surplice from their peg and folded them into her robes case.

'Aagh!' exclaimed Harry. 'I should have given you this ages ago! I'm so sorry. Your friend's address.'

'Oh!' she cried in joy, snatching the slip of paper. Geneva? Why? Oh, oh, oh! 'Thank you, Harry!' She kissed him impulsively. He was covered in confusion. 'She was a very special friend,' explained Isobel self-consciously. 'I don't suppose you asked what she's doing now?'

'Erm . . . Doing now?' He rumpled his hair. 'Um . . . Oh, yes. She's um, a revolutionary Communist.'

'What? Come on, seriously, what is she?'

'Seriously. A revolutionary Communist,' he insisted.

She began to laugh. The curate and the Commie. It was glorious. For a second she forgot her circumstances. Harry's next words brought them flooding back.

'You will be strict with people, won't you? Don't let them keep pestering you while you're on retreat. And don't keep popping back to the parish.'

She flinched.

'I don't mean you're not wanted,' he said, in alarm. 'Just give yourself space.'

'I hope *you* might pop in,' she said in stilted tones. 'If you want to, of course. I know you'll be busy.'

He hesitated. 'I'd ... assumed I was one of the things you'd be glad to escape from.'

'Harry! No! How could you think that?'

'You've seemed so distant.'

'That's because you were!'

'Oh!' He looked at her in surprise. 'Well. Yes. I'd love to come and see you.'

She found she was blushing.

For a moment neither spoke. Then Harry roused himself. 'Um, this is just a little something for you, which I thought you might like.' He handed her a CD. Stainer's *Crucifixion*. Oh dear. She had a copy. 'I hope you haven't already got it.'

'Well, not this version,' she said, turning it over. 'Thank you. I'm sure –' She let out a sudden wail, and clamped her hand over her mouth. It was a recording of her Oxford college choir, the soloists Alex and Andrew Jacks. 'Thanks,' she whispered.

He hugged her. 'Go well.'

She nodded.

Neither could manage more. She picked up her case and left.

Tears splashed down on the closed boot of the car. Well, I've done it. It's over. She took one last look around the churchyard. Her eye touched the sun-warmed stones of the graves and walls. Goodbye, Agnes. Goodbye to the ancient yew she had never climbed.

Why hadn't she?

She remembered her argument with Johnny: *You're not allowed to climb it. It's very ancient. Great view from the top, mind.* I'm going to do it, she thought.

After a quick glance to see if anyone was coming she darted across, laid her hand on the scaly trunk and began to climb. It all came back. Never trust a branch thinner than your arm. Always keep two hands and a foot or two feet and a hand on the tree, then you can't fall. Up she went with mounting glee. Easy-peasy lemon-squeezy. She thought of Tatiana, whose address was now rustling in her breast pocket. Dust and dead leaves were gathering in her hair as she thrust her head past the twigs. Her linen suit would need dry-cleaning. She was near the top. The branches were swaying under her weight.

There! She wanted to call out in triumph, Yes! Asleby lay spread out around her. Off out over field and factory and river to the distant hills fled her eye. Down below she heard the vestry door shut. It would be Harry. She held her breath as his footsteps passed beneath the tree. After a moment she saw him go out of the gate and cross the road to the vicarage. He vanished from her sight behind his garden hedge. A car passed along the road. Silence. All over the parish blackbirds sang from the rooftops and trees. The swallows were flying high. It would be fine tomorrow.

In a minute or two she would climb down and get on with her life. Drive up to the Friary, then drive back down the next day and go to Alex's funeral. It was a mess. And afterwards, what? Enough light for the step ahead? She began to weep.

A movement caught her eye and she gasped. There on the church roof level with her was a peacock. Isobel watched, lost for a moment in the sunshine playing on the burnished feathers of the bird.

# THE CRYSTAL MAN

GRANT JOLLY

WITH LOVE x

Copyright © 2015 Grant Jolly

Edited by Moira MacDonald

Cover art and design by Grant Jolly